KU-540-580

Please return/renew this item by the last date shown.
Items may also be renewed by the internet*

https://library.eastriding.gov.uk

* Please note a PIN will be required to access this service
- this can be obtained from your library

The Penny Bangle

The Penny Bangle

Margaret James

First published in hardback by Robert Hale in 2007

Published 2012 by Choc Lit Limited
Penrose House, Crawley Drive, Camberley, Surrey GU15 2AB, UK
www.choclitpublishing.com

A CIP catalogue record for this book is available
from the British Library

ISBN-978-1-906931-77-3

Printed and bound by CPI Group (UK) Ltd, Croydon, CR0 4YY

*This story is for my mother
Florence Mary Neathway Laughton*

Acknowledgements

I'd like to say a big thank you to everyone at Choc Lit for all their hard work on this novel.

Chapter One

January 1942

'Miss, you've dropped your knickers!'

'He means you, love,' said a middle-aged woman, tapping Cassie Taylor on the shoulder and glancing back towards the ticket office.

Cassie turned to see an army corporal in crumpled, grubby khaki grinning and pointing at the station platform. She realised her granny's ancient shopping bag had split, all her bits of underwear were poking out of it, and her most disreputable pair of lock-knit drawers were lying on the dirty paving slabs of Birmingham's New Street station.

Red-faced, she scooped her knickers up, shoved them in the pocket of her coat, and trudged off down the platform to her train. She wished she had a proper suitcase, even a second-hand cardboard one would do, even if she'd had to tie it together with bits of string.

But of course there was a war on, and so you couldn't get anything you needed, unless you were a tart or knew a spiv. If being hard up and looking like a rag bag were both virtues, like Father Riley reckoned, when the bomb that had her name on knocked her on the head, she would be going straight to heaven.

Or maybe not. She'd have sold her soul for a decent pair of fully-fashioned stockings. These cheap cotton horrors, which were all she could afford, sagged and bagged around her knees and ankles, and made her look grotesque.

'Come on, you lot, make your mind up, are you getting on or not?' the guard demanded, as Cassie pushed her way past married couples frantically embracing, soldiers kissing girls goodbye, and fat old mothers saying fond farewells to lanky sons.

'You just hang on a moment!' She gave the guard a cheeky grin, and then she glanced behind to make quite sure she hadn't left any more underwear lying around on Platform 4. After all, she thought, I can't afford to lose my winter vests.

Jerking open a compartment door, she climbed into the carriage.

The train was full. She couldn't get a seat. They'd all been nabbed by servicemen, and nobody stood up for women these days, unless they wore fur coats and looked like film stars, and Cassie knew she didn't look like a film star – that's if you weren't counting Jackie Coogan in *The Kid*.

The journey took all day, stopping and starting, hanging around in sidings to let the troop trains through, and there was no heating and no refreshment carriage, not that she had any money to buy refreshments, anyway. She'd eaten her packed lunch of brawn and mustard sandwiches and drunk her bottle of Tizer soon after they'd left Cheltenham, and now she was starving.

'Do you fancy a cheese and pickle sandwich, love?' A woman who'd been standing next to Cassie since Devizes offered her a greasy paper bag. 'Go on, my darling, take one,' she said kindly. 'Take a couple, eh? You look like you could do with building up.'

'Thank you.' Cassie smiled and took a sandwich, biting into it with hungry relish.

'Where are you going, then?' the woman asked.

'Dorset,' Cassie told her though a mouthful of hard cheese.

'Ooh, it's pretty, Dorset. I've got relatives in Bridport, and my mother came from Portland. There's a lovely beach at Weymouth, too.' The woman glanced at Cassie's well-stuffed shopping bag, and grinned. 'But most folks don't choose January to take a little holiday at the seaside.'

'I don't suppose they do.' Cassie leaned against the

2

window, chewing her cheese sandwich and gazing at the frozen winter landscape flashing by.

This might be her first trip to the seaside, she thought grimly, but it wouldn't be a holiday. It wasn't as if she'd wanted to leave Birmingham at all, and if certain people hadn't carried on, then carried on some more, she'd still be there.

By the time she got to Charton Minster, a tiny station in the wilds of Dorset, she was so chilled she couldn't feel her feet, and both her hands were purple-blue with cold.

She knew she shouldn't have listened to her granny, who'd blethered on about Cassie being her only flesh and blood, about how if she stayed in Birmingham and working in that factory, cycling home at night after her shift and getting caught in air raids, she was going to be killed.

'I should have joined the ATS,' she muttered crossly to herself, as she got off the train. 'Then, I could have learned to type or cook, or I might have even driven a lorry.'

But her granny didn't approve of women being in the army, of women wearing uniforms, of women helping shoot down German planes. Of women doing anything that God made men – and only men, apparently – to do.

So, worn down by Lily Taylor's tears, Cassie had joined the Land Girls, even though she didn't know a turnip from a parsnip, even though she was terrified of horses, even though she'd never seen a cow. She'd never been out of Birmingham, so she had never seen a wood or field.

At the local Labour Exchange, where they'd been holding interviews, she had fibbed her socks off. She'd told the WVS lady she was good with horses, didn't mind getting up at crack of dawn or several hours before it, and she fancied living the healthy, outdoor life. Yes, she knew she'd earn a pittance, half what she was getting at the munitions factory.

3

But she thought she'd like a change, she'd said. She needed some fresh air.

So now she was in the middle of nowhere, wishing she had a warmer coat – a full-length mink or sable would do nicely – and feeling sick and scared.

'I need to get to Melbury,' she told the elderly man who came out of a sort of wooden hut to take her ticket, and peered at her in the gathering gloom.

'Why would you want to go to Melbury, then?'

'I'm g-going to work there,' Cassie told him, teeth a-chatter.

'I don't think so, miss.' The ticket collector gave her a just-escaped-from-somewhere-have-you look. 'Yes, there was a house there once, and that I'll not deny. But it's a ruin now. They had a fire about ten years ago. The place is falling down, and ferns grow out of it.'

'I'm going to work for Mr and Mrs Denham,' insisted Cassie, fighting down her panic. She rummaged in her bag. 'I've got the forms they sent me from the Ministry of Labour, and a letter from Mrs Denham. Look, the address is Melbury, Charton, Dorset.'

'Ah, then you'll want the bailiff's cottage, maid! Mr and Mrs Denham, they used to live in the big house at Melbury. But after it burned down, the family moved into the cottage.'

The station man grinned broadly, and then he began to pat the pockets of his jacket.

'Let's find a bit of paper and a pencil, and I'll draw a map for you – show you the shortest way. There's a road, but it's the long way round, so you'd be best off in the lanes. But first, you come and have a cup of something nice and hot. I've got my can of cocoa on the stove, and there must be a couple of biscuits somewhere.'

As she sat in the ticket collector's hut, drinking bitter cocoa and eating home-made oatmeal biscuits, Cassie thawed a little. Ten minutes later, she thanked the ticket collector for his kindness, and set off through the silent, snow-bound village.

She walked along a gravelled road which soon lost all interest in being a proper road and became a narrow country lane, muddy and full of ruts. Luckily the mud had frozen hard, so she didn't keep sinking into it. Although it was only five o'clock, the moon had risen already, and was shining on the snow piled up in pillowed drifts against the banks.

As she made her way along the lane, Cassie saw the looming, shadowy outline of what looked like a castle from a book of fairy tales. It was built of pale golden stone, it had tall, twisted chimneys, fancy turrets, and its small, dark windows all glittered in the moonlight.

But afterwards, there was nothing – just hedges, trees and fields. Or anyway, she thought they must be fields. They didn't look like the parks she'd seen when she had gone on outings with her granny, with swings and ducks and flowerbeds and ponds, even though there were trees.

Later, she passed the ruins of a house, its fire-stained walls and rotting timbers pointing drearily at the winter sky, but softened by a muffling of snow. Someone should come and level it, she thought, and make use of the bricks.

She went on down the lane, following the map and hoping she was nearly there, afraid she was going to freeze to death in this white, empty wilderness.

The cottage loomed up suddenly as she came around a bend. This too looked like something from a children's picture book, one she'd had when she was five or six. Long and low, with tiny latticed windows and a mossy, gabled roof, it was the sort of place where naughty children got made into pies.

She dumped her shopping bag in the front porch, flexed her frozen fingers and, after looking in vain for any sort of bell or knocker, banged a bit too loudly on the door, which could have used a lick or two of paint.

As she was despairing of anybody being in, a tall, middle-aged woman came from round the back, carrying two white enamel buckets. Cassie took in her muddy rubber boots, her hessian apron underneath a man's old army trench-coat, and her long dark hair escaping from a tartan scarf which had worked loose.

'Mrs Denham?' Cassie asked, and wondered if this woman had a mirror.

'Yes, I'm Rose Denham.' The woman put down one bucket, and then held out her hand and smiled. 'You must be Miss Taylor,' she continued. 'Miss Sefton from the WVS said we should expect you about five o'clock today. I hope you had a pleasant journey?'

'It was all right, thanks,' said Cassie, shaking Mrs Denham's hand and wondering why she lived in such a tiny little cottage and dressed in army trench-coats when she talked so posh?

'Come in, why don't you?' Mrs Denham added, kicking off her Wellingtons in the porch. 'I'll put the kettle on.'

The place was better once you got inside. It smelled of wood smoke, baking bread and Mansion polish.

The kitchen was very warm and welcoming, with a scrubbed pine table in the middle of the room and a dresser full of pretty china taking up one wall. There was a smell of something cooking, too – something with a bit of meat in it – and Cassie's mouth began to water.

Mrs Denham put a big black kettle on the hob. 'Sit down by the range,' she said. 'I'll make us both some tea. There might be a bit of seed cake, too. Or there was this morning, anyway.' She took down a cake tin, opened it and looked inside. 'Yes, there's still some left.'

Cassie sat, and soon she had her hands curled round her

cup, warming them blissfully. She sipped her tea and ate her cake. Eventually, her toes and all her other frozen bits began to thaw.

She glanced at Mrs Denham, who was standing at the sink and peeling something – vegetables for supper, she supposed. Now she'd taken off her awful coat and tartan scarf, Cassie could see her new employer was a pretty woman with a slim, attractive figure and a handsome profile, too.

Cassie had never liked her own snub nose and, if she'd had a choice, she'd have had a nose like Mrs Denham's, straight and elegant above a generous, well-shaped mouth.

If she had her hair cut, Cassie thought, if she wore some lipstick, she'd be beautiful. Some pale silk stockings and some nice high heels would set her off a treat.

'I'm sorry, I'm neglecting you,' said Mrs Denham suddenly, making Cassie jump. She smiled, and Cassie noticed she had near-perfect teeth. 'Do have another piece of cake, and pour yourself more tea.'

'Thanks,' said Cassie, wondering if she was dreaming this, and if she was going to wake up at her workbench in the factory any minute now.

'This will be your room,' said Mrs Denham.

She had shown Cassie all around the ground floor of the cottage, which consisted of the homely kitchen, a small, stone-flagged scullery full of pickles and preserves, and a cosy sitting room, in which there were comfortable armchairs, a well-polished modern sideboard on which there were lots of photographs in silver frames, mostly of some glamorous blonde, and a glowing grate. There were also shelves of books and piles of magazines. The place looked like a library.

Then she'd taken Cassie up the stairs, where it was absolutely freezing, and shown her to her room.

'It's rather small, I know,' she added, as she edged round Cassie's little bed. 'But it's the warmest in the house. It's right over the kitchen and the heat collects up here.'

I bet, thought Cassie sceptically, looking round.

The room was tiny, containing just a chest of drawers and a small iron bedstead, thankfully piled high with quilts and blankets and topped off with a fat, pink eiderdown. The ceiling sloped down at an angle almost to the floor and there was a little dormer window.

I'll have to be careful I don't brain myself when I get out of bed, she thought, looking up to see if this room had electric light. She hadn't noticed what was in the kitchen, and wondered if they had just oil lamps, out here in the wilds?

She put her bag down on the bed and looked at Mrs Denham. 'What shall I do now?' she asked.

'I beg your pardon?' said Mrs Denham, frowning.

'Work, I mean,' said Cassie.

'Oh, we'll talk about your work this evening, when we all have supper together, shall we?' Then Mrs Denham smiled again, and Cassie saw that her grey eyes were kind. 'So which part of Birmingham do you come from?'

'Smethwick,' said Cassie shortly. 'Do you know it?'

'I'm afraid I've never been there.'

'You ain't – I mean, you haven't missed much,' said Cassie. 'It's mostly factories and houses, and lots of them's been bombed to bits by Jerry.'

'You people from the cities are so brave,' said Mrs Denham, looking as if she meant it. 'Does your whole family live in Smethwick?'

'Just my granny, and she's all the family I've got.' Cassie shrugged her shoulders. 'She's getting on for eighty, and she says she's had her life, so she doesn't care if Hitler and his merry men go flattening all of Brum. But she wanted me to get away.'

'Mm, that's understandable, poor lady.' Mrs Denham sighed, then shook her head and flicked her long, dark hair out of her eyes. 'Well, I expect you're hungry. My husband and the boys should be in soon, and then we'll have our supper.'

'Boys?' repeated Cassie nervously, hoping Mrs Denham hadn't got half a dozen teenaged kids. Young ones she could manage, just about. All you had to do with them was cuff them round the head if they got out of line. But fourteen-year-old hooligans …

'Robert and Stephen, they're both in the army, in the Royal Dorset Regiment. At the moment, though, they're both on leave,' said Mrs Denham. 'I think I just heard someone coming in. Let's go back downstairs.'

The man downstairs was in his early twenties, Cassie guessed. Dark haired and six feet tall at least, he had to duck under the beams to walk across the kitchen.

He looked a mess, she thought. His trousers had great tears across the knees. His old tweed jacket was all frayed along the cuffs and seams. 'Mum,' he said, 'I'm starving. When will supper be?'

'In half an hour or so,' said Mrs Denham, and then she turned to Cassie. 'Robert, this is Miss Taylor. She's kindly going to help us on the farm.'

'Really?' said the man.

He looked her up and down. Quite rudely, Cassie thought, although now she noticed that his eyes were the most striking she had ever seen. They were large and dark, with long black lashes, rather like Clark Gable's, she decided – you could drown yourself in eyes like these.

'Good evening, Miss Taylor,' he managed to grunt at last.

'Hello,' said Cassie, still staring back at him.

He was quite good-looking, she supposed. Well-made, broad-shouldered, with a head of black or dark brown hair to match his equally dark eyes. Yes, he was very attractive – if you liked that sort of thing.

But, Holy Mother of God, the face on him – as long as from Castle Bromwich to Halesowen! He must have lost a quid and found a farthing.

He grumbled off upstairs to change his clothes. Or that was what she thought he'd said. Just like his mother, he talked as if he was a member of the Royal Family.

But what they had to swank and be so posh about, when they lived in this tiny little house, Cassie couldn't imagine.

They heard him clunking round above them. But then he stuck his head back round the door.

Cassie glanced up. The clunking was still going on, together with a bit of cursing now.

She frowned at him, perplexed.

He came into the room and smiled in welcome, holding out his hand. 'Hello, I'm Stephen Denham,' he began. 'You must be Miss Taylor, our new land girl?'

'Yes, that's right,' said Cassie. She looked up at the ceiling once again.

'Oh, didn't Mum say?' asked Stephen, and he grinned. 'I'm sorry, there are two of us. We're twins.'

Chapter Two

Mrs Denham sent Cassie to her room to get unpacked and, as she emptied out her shopping bag, she heard the twins discussing her in the hallway at the bottom of the stairs.

'She's very skinny,' muttered one of them – she thought it was the grumpy twin. 'I reckon she's a slum kid. She looks pasty-faced and feeble. I'll bet you she'll be useless, and she'll be bone idle, too.'

'Mum will fatten her up and crack the whip,' his brother told him, making Cassie shudder. Then they went into the kitchen. After she had put away her things, tidied her dark blonde hair a bit and dabbed some powder on her pasty face, Cassie went downstairs.

'This is my husband, Alex,' Mrs Denham said, smiling at a man who had grey streaks in his dark hair, and who had obviously just walked in, because he still had snowflakes on his shoulders.

'It's Miss Taylor, isn't it?' The man held out his hand, and Cassie sighed – another toff, she thought. But she took Mr Denham's hand and shook it firmly. At least he smiled nicely, and – just like his wife's – his eyes were kind.

Mrs Denham helped him take his coat off. She brushed the snow out of his hair with gentle fingers, and then she took his hands in hers and rubbed them, to warm them up again.

'How are you feeling, Alex?' she enquired, and Cassie heard concern, or it might have even been anxiety, in her voice.

'I'm fine, my dear,' said Mr Denham.

'You're better than you were this morning, then?'

'Yes, much better, thank you.'

'Good,' said Mrs Denham, but she didn't sound convinced, and Cassie wondered why.

Then they started supper, and it was a nightmare. Mrs Denham filled Cassie's plate with stew, and this was mostly orange lumps – carrots, she supposed, or maybe they were swedes or turnips, who could tell – and chunks of dark brown, chewy meat.

There was a dish of baked potatoes, and these didn't taste too bad, even though they were full of scabby bits. She couldn't eat the skin. It was too tough. She didn't know human beings could eat potato skin. At home, they gave their peelings to the scrawny chickens Mrs Gray across the road kept in her yard.

She sighed and thought how much she fancied a plate of fish and chips. A couple of bangers, or a nice pork pie.

The whole plate swam with gravy, and if there was one thing Cassie hated, it was gravy. Its slimy, greasy oiliness always made her feel like throwing up. But now she had to try to force it down. What was this disgusting greyish-yellowish-whitish stuff floating round in it, she wondered, poking at it crossly. It looked like lumps of snot.

Mrs Denham saw her prodding it with her fork. 'I hope you like pearl barley,' she said briskly. 'It's nutritious and it's very filling. We use a lot of it in soups and stews.'

'Yes, it's nice,' said Cassie, feeling sick.

'You should eat your potato skin,' chimed in the grumpy twin, who was gnawing at his own and talking with his mouth full. 'It's full of vitamins. It's good for you.'

Cassie gave the grumpy twin her meanest, dirtiest look.

He responded with a sort of grin, and a comment to the effect that he supposed it could go into swill for Mr Hobson's pigs.

'Who's Mr Hobson?' Cassie asked him.

'A smallholder in Charton,' Stephen said, when Robert

didn't bother to reply. 'He keeps pigs and goats and chickens, too. He and Mrs Hobson have a dozen children. The ones who live in Charton all work on the smallholding. Mr Hobson likes to get away from family life occasionally, and sometimes works for us.'

Somehow, Cassie managed to eat the horrid stew. The pudding which followed wasn't quite so vile. Jam roll boiled in a linen cloth, red and white and served with yellow custard, it didn't look particularly inviting, but didn't taste too bad.

She'd have loved a square or two of Cadbury's Dairy Milk, the chocolate which her granny had always bought her on her birthday when she was a child.

'Rob and I are going out tonight, Miss Taylor. Do you want to come?' asked Stephen, as she worried a back tooth with her tongue, attempting to dislodge a shred of meat.

'Where are you going?' Cassie asked him.

'Stephen, darling, give the girl a chance to settle down.' Mrs Denham gathered up the dishes and took them over to the Belfast sink.

'But she'll need to get to know her way around the district,' Stephen told his mother. 'You can't send her out tomorrow morning and assume she'll find the stables and the paddock and the road into the village by herself.'

'I suppose not.' Mrs Denham shrugged. 'But please wash the dishes before you do go out, and you must wrap up warm. It's freezing hard again tonight. I've never known a January like it. There's snow six inches deep in the top field. You'd think we were on Dartmoor, not in Dorset.'

Robert stood up and slouched towards the sink. He picked up the black kettle, poured hot water into the bowl of dishes, added a lump of soda from a jar and started scrubbing energetically.

Cassie took a tea-towel from the range. She dried

the plates and dishes, and then the other twin put them away, making up for his brother's silence with a stream of chatter.

'Why did you choose to come to Dorset?' Stephen asked, as he stacked the plates in wooden racks.

'I didn't choose,' said Cassie grimly. 'I told the recruiting office woman I'd go anywhere.' She shrugged. 'My granny was going on at me to leave the factory, and to get out of Brum. So I took the first job they offered me.'

'You've worked on farms before, though, haven't you?'

'No,' admitted Cassie.

'In a market garden, then?' asked Stephen.

'What's one of them when it's at home?'

'We asked for someone with experience.' Mrs Denham frowned. 'Miss Taylor, what exactly – '

'I had to get out of Smethwick, Mrs Denham!' Cassie met Rose Denham's gaze, and reddened. 'All right, I admit it. I don't know the first thing about farming. But I'll be quick to learn, I promise you. I do know how to work. I've spent the past two years in factories, doing twelve hour shifts, filling shells and making bits of aeroplanes and tanks. You'll get your money's worth.'

'My dear Miss Taylor, I intend to do so.'

But then Rose Denham smiled, and there was warmth and humour in her smile. Cassie decided, she's a tough old bird and she might talk like Lady Muck, but she'll be fair and decent.

So, fingers twisted, it would be all right.

'What's your first name?' Stephen asked. 'If you're going to live here for a while, we can't call you Miss Taylor all the time.'

'It's Cassie.'

'Cassie – that's unusual,' said Rose Denham, her dark eyebrows raised in arched enquiry.

'Yes, well.' Cassie shrugged. She wasn't going to tell them all the story of her life, or not yet, anyway. 'It's just a name.'

The twins and Cassie put on coats and scarves and hats and gloves, and then set off across the frozen fields. Stephen told her they were going to the nearest pub, which was in Charton, where she'd got off the train.

While they had been eating, there had been another fall of snow, covering all the footprints to the cottage, and making the whole world look new again. The clouds which must have gathered had blown away again, and now a round white moon shone from a purple velvet sky.

'It's so pretty!' Cassie cried, as she gazed delighted at the moonlit meadows, at the cotton-wool-topped hedges, and the stands of stark black white-rimed trees. 'We don't get snow in Birmingham. Well, that's a lie, we do, but it soon goes all mucky and it turns to slush. It's – '

'It's a bloody nuisance,' Robert growled, and glared at Cassie. Then he stomped off ahead, into the night.

'Holy Mother, what have I said now?' demanded Cassie.

'Nothing, Cassie.' Stephen sighed. 'I'm sorry, but Robert's been like this for ages, and we can't do anything with him. He wishes he was in the Western Desert, fighting Jerry – and so do we all.'

'How much longer will he be on leave, then?'

'I don't know,' said Stephen. 'But he has a medical next week, and I sincerely hope he passes it.'

'Me too,' murmured Cassie, but only to herself.

'The trouble is, he's bored,' continued Stephen. 'We've been at home too long.'

'So why *are* you at home?' asked Cassie.

'We've both been on sick leave since we copped it at Dunkirk. When we came out of hospital, they sent us back to Dorset. We've been here ever since. We help around the farm. Well, Robert does his bit, and more. But I must admit I'm not much use.'

'What happened to you?' asked Cassie. 'If you don't mind my asking,' she added hastily.

'I don't mind,' said Stephen. 'My mother's bound to tell you anyway, in vivid detail. It's her way of coping, droning on. But – in a nutshell – we were with the British Expeditionary Force. We got shot up in France. Then we were evacuated. We came home in separate boats, but both of them got hit by German planes.

'Robert had a broken arm, a bullet in his shoulder, and a piece of shrapnel in his chest that just missed his heart, but pierced his lung. Now, he's nearly fit, so he'll soon be going back to get blown up again. Me – well, I'm resigned to having a desk job.'

'Why?'

'I can't go back on active service. I got hit on the head, and now I have blackouts and epileptic fits.'

'We had an epileptic kid at school,' said Cassie, nodding. 'He had funny turns. He'd be standing next to you one minute, chatting away as natural as ninepence, but then he'd fall down, jerking. Sometimes, he'd wet himself. I was our class monitor, so I always had to get the spoon to stick between his teeth, to stop him biting off his tongue.'

'I wish you'd been here last Wednesday, then,' said Stephen, looking grave. 'I had a turn myself. When I came round again, the cat was curled up on my lap, purring and chewing something.'

'You're kidding!' Cassie cried in horror.

'So keep your spoon at action stations, yes? In fact, I feel a little strange right now.'

Cassie began to panic. But then she saw his grin. She pushed his shoulder, grinning back at him. This bloke might be a nob, she thought. But, like his mother, Stephen Denham was all right.

'How long have you lived in Dorset?' she enquired.

'Since I was ten,' said Stephen. 'In those days, there were five of us, my parents and my brother and my sister.'

'It must have been a bit of a squash while you were growing up, with all of you crammed into that small cottage?'

'We haven't always lived there. When we first came to Dorset, we lived in Melbury House. It was my dad's ancestral home, and it was big enough for half a dozen families. But we had a fire there, and we had to move into the cottage.'

'So that burned-down place I passed, when I came along the lane – that was *your* house, yes?' asked Cassie, shuddering. 'It must have been horrible for you, to lose your home like that?'

'Yes, it was rather rough on Mum and Dad, but the actual fire was exciting.' Stephen's dark eyes glittered in the moonlight. 'It's quite something, Cassie, to see a huge, great place go up like that, like some enormous funeral pyre. As it was burning down, the fire made great, red caverns – whole new worlds of scarlet, black and gold – and I remember wondering, what would it be like, to walk in fire?'

'You're giving me the shivers.' Cassie trembled. 'I hate it when the sirens go, and bombs start coming down, and you see the flames and know that some poor bugger's bought it.'

'Well, now you can relax a bit,' said Stephen, and he smiled. 'We don't get raids in Dorset. Or not here in the sticks, at any rate – believe you me.'

Robert couldn't believe it.

They had asked the Ministry of Labour for someone with experience. Someone who had worked on dairy farms. Someone who could turn her hand to anything. Someone who could take over from him when he was recalled to active service.

So who had turned up?

Some idiot girl who looked about fifteen. A skinny little creature, round-shouldered and with sparrow legs in wrinkled cotton stockings, who didn't look as if she would be able to lift a bag of flour, let alone a sack of cattle feed.

She had a sweet and very pretty face – he'd noticed straight away. So soon she would be smirking, flouncing, flirting all around the villages, making eyes at anything in trousers, at teenaged boys and fathers who hadn't been called up. She'd be annoying girlfriends, sisters, wives. She would be getting herself in trouble. She –

Stop that now, he told himself, as he ground his teeth and as the snow got in his boots, melting in chilly puddles in his socks. She's just a girl, an ordinary girl, and you don't know anything about her, perhaps she goes to church three times on Sundays and leads a blameless life.

She might be stronger than she looks.

I doubt it, said his other self. She'll be a liability, you'll see. We'll need a depth charge to get her out of bed these winter mornings. She won't be any good at milking, and she won't be any use with chickens. She'll be afraid of horses, and she won't be able to drive the pony trap.

She'll just get in the way.

He stumped into the pub and glowered at the barman. He wished he had the time and money to get drunk tonight.

Cassie enjoyed the walk across the fields.

The moonlight shining on the freshly-fallen snow made the whole place look like fairyland. Stephen told her silly jokes and helped her clamber over stiles and jump across the ditches. He caught her when she stumbled, which she often did.

When they reached the village, they were cold but glowing and went straight into the pub. As they pushed through the cosy, smoky fug, Cassie was still giggling at something he had said.

Stephen's brother was sitting at a table in the corner with his back to them, and from the shaking of his shoulders she thought he must be laughing. A dark-haired girl of maybe twenty, Cassie guessed, was sitting sideways on to him.

They turned to look at Cassie and their smiles froze on their faces. 'Come on, Cassie,' Stephen whispered as he pushed her forward. 'Rob's a miserable so-and-so, but he doesn't bite.'

Cassie saw the girl was wearing navy corduroy slacks, a soft, white jersey that had clearly cost a lot of money, and she had a gorgeous string of pearls around her neck. She wore bright scarlet lipstick which didn't really suit her, and was smoking, flicking ash on to the table top instead of in the ashtray by her side.

'This is Frances Ashford,' Stephen said, drawing up a couple more chairs and motioning to Cassie to sit down. 'This is Cassie Taylor, Fran. She's come to work for us.'

'Golly, how exciting.' Frances flicked some more ash off her glowing cigarette and stared at Cassie balefully. 'She doesn't look the bucolic type to me.'

'Come again?' said Cassie, thinking, Holy Virgin, are they *all* nobs round here? 'What do you mean by that?'

'You're tiny, and you don't look fit and strong enough for farm work.'

'I might be small,' said Cassie. 'But I've worked in factories making Spitfires, and I'm very strong.'

'How old are you, anyway – thirteen, fourteen, fifteen?'

'I'm nineteen,' muttered Cassie, thinking – what a cow. 'How about you, then – thirty, forty, fifty?'

'Ladies, ladies, please!' Stephen patted Cassie's shoulder. 'How about a drink? Cassie, I'm afraid it's gin or beer – or lemonade.'

'Gin,' said Frances promptly. 'Thank you, Steve.'

'A half of best,' said Cassie, who had never tasted gin. In Smethwick, only crones and tarts drank gin.

She scowled at Frances, who was muttering something to Stephen's grumpy brother. Obviously, she hadn't been brought up well enough to know that whispering was rude.

'Come on, sweetheart, smile. You'll need to get along with Frances,' Stephen murmured as he brushed past Cassie. 'She's the other land girl at Melbury, you see.'

Chapter Three

Cassie heard the insistent rattle of an old alarm clock going off in what seemed like the middle of the night. She became aware of someone coughing, heard them strike a match, and then she smelled the tang of cheap tobacco as someone lit their first smoke of the day.

A few minutes later, Mrs Denham was tapping on her door, telling her that it was time to get up for the milking. 'Put on a couple of your jumpers and your regulation breeches, then come down straight away,' she added briskly. Then she clattered off downstairs herself, and Cassie heard her fill the kettle.

Oh, Jesus Christ and all the blessed saints, she thought, as she splashed some water from the basin on her face and then began to pull her warmest clothes on hurriedly, they really do have cows.

Last night, she had been told so many stories, and been led up so many garden paths, that she hadn't been able to decide if she should believe the twins when they'd said their father's dairy herd was famous nation-wide.

After all, *she'd* never heard of it.

Mr Denham's Jerseys, which he'd bred himself, were coveted by farmers everywhere, Stephen had said proudly. They won all the prizes at the biggest agricultural shows.

'A female calf from Melbury is worth as much as any working horse,' his brother added, as he'd forced himself to speak, or rather grunt, between his gulps of beer.

'You'll see why, Cassie, when you meet our bull,' continued Stephen.

'Yes, you'll have your work cut out with Caesar.' Frances smirked into her gin.

Cassie was used to getting herself up and dashing off to work. So she was downstairs two minutes later, even before the twins or Mr Denham had appeared.

Mrs Denham handed her a mug of milky coffee. This must be the real thing, thought Cassie as she sipped it, not that coffee essence muck that looks like gravy browning and smells like dirty socks. She drank it very slowly, savouring each delicious mouthful.

As she was finishing her coffee, Robert slouched into the kitchen, swallowed down a mug of scalding coffee in two seconds flat, and Cassie followed him into the yard.

At the far end was a smart new building, much grander than the cottage, and from it came some loud and ominous sounds, like somebody in pain.

A moment later Frances Ashford rode into the yard, her bike wheels bumping on the frozen cobbles. 'Hello, midget,' she began, and grinned. 'You didn't run away, then. We were afraid we might have scared you off, that you'd be on the first train back to Birmingham this morning.'

'Did you?' Cassie tried her best to grin and sound relaxed and self-assured. 'I don't scare easily.'

'So I see,' said Frances. 'Rob?' she added, turning to the grumpy twin. 'What shall we do with Cassie? If we have to show her how to milk, she's going to hold us up. The lorry will be here before we've finished. She could feed the chickens, couldn't she?'

'Dad says she has to learn about the cows,' said Robert gruffly. 'When Steve and I have gone, you two will have to manage them between you, so she might as well get cracking.'

Robert glanced at Cassie. 'Go and put on a pair of rubber

boots, you'll find some in the porch,' he snapped, and then he strode away.

'Come on, midget, get a move on.' Frances clicked her tongue impatiently. 'We haven't got all morning.'

Cassie pulled on some rubber Wellingtons that were far too big – these toffs all have enormous feet, she muttered to herself – and then she scuttled after Frances.

She had never seen anything like it, or imagined it. As she followed the other land girl into the warm cowshed, rows of brown and golden cows all turned around to stare.

Shaggy-coated beasts as big as rag-and-bone men's ponies, with huge, brown bulbous eyes, they gazed with curiosity at Cassie, who suddenly felt sick and ill with dread.

She realised she was going to have to touch one. But she couldn't, it would bite her hand off, it would trample her to death.

'The churns are ready.' Stephen came in, blowing on his hands. 'Come on, you lazy devils, shift yourselves. The lorry will be here in an hour. Cassie, grab a bucket. I'll show you what to do.'

Cassie picked up a new-scoured metal bucket. She followed Stephen down the rows of cows, flinching as their tails swished her shoulders, and watching out for vicious, stamping hooves.

'This is Daisy,' Stephen told her, patting a golden-coated animal which was chewing placidly and watching them with interest. 'She's our friendliest, most docile cow. We called her after Daisy, our big sister.'

'Your sister's Daisy Denham?' whispered Cassie, as she eyed the munching cow with horror and disgust, looking at the bulging, swollen thing between its legs and wondering how on earth you got at it without being kicked to bits. 'Do you mean the film star?'

'Yes, she's been in a couple of films,' said Stephen carelessly, raking back his straight, black hair, then sitting down on a three-legged stool. 'We're very proud of Daze. There are lots of pictures of her on the sideboard in the sitting room. Didn't you notice when Mum showed you round?'

'Yes, I did.' But Cassie was so busy being terrified of all the cows that she didn't have time to be impressed.

Stephen stuck a metal bucket underneath the cow.

Cassie watched him squeeze the swollen thing. She saw the milk come spurting out in streams, and she heard Daisy sigh contentedly.

'Now you do it,' Stephen said. 'Cass, don't look so worried, she can't bite you, she's tied up. Sit down on the stool here. Get a bit closer, lean your head against her flank – that's right. Now, you just go on squeezing, until the bucket's full and Daisy's empty, and that's all you have to do.'

Cassie sat down. She braced herself. She groped for Daisy's udder, found a teat and yanked at it.

Daisy yelped and kicked the bucket over.

Cassie fell backwards off the milking stool.

Frances and Robert turned to stare. Robert glowered, but Frances laughed out loud.

I'll show them, Cassie thought. She sat down on the stool again, and shoved the bucket underneath the cow. Daisy shifted, stamped a bit, put one foot in the bucket, and then began to moo in – panic, irritation, anger, pain?

'Get out of the way, you idiot,' muttered Robert testily. 'There, there, girl,' he murmured, stroking Daisy's heaving side. 'Steve, take Cassie to feed the hens, all right? Fran and I can manage by ourselves.'

Stephen looked as if he was considering arguing, but Robert glared at him so angrily that he backed down again.

'Come on, Cass,' he said, and walked out of the shed with Cassie trailing after him.

24

Robert and Frances got on with the milking, both annoyed they were so far behind.

As he made his way along the row of lowing cows, who were all annoyed to be kept waiting and wanted him to know about it, he decided he'd been right about this idiot. They couldn't afford to keep a time-waster on this particular farm. He would probably tell his father later on today.

'Robert?' murmured Frances, as she was moving on to the next cow. 'You're very quiet today, even for you.'

'I was just thinking,' Robert said.

'Yes, I bet,' said Frances, and she grimaced. 'Let me guess – about our new recruit, our little pixie with the pretty face and cheeky grin. She'll never make a land girl.'

'I dare say you're right.'

Robert was used to Frances, who was always watching Stephen jealously. She'd been so disconcerted to see him come into the Lion last night with an attractive blonde girl on his arm.

Poor Fran, he thought, she doesn't know it's hopeless. Or she won't accept it, anyway. 'You don't need to worry about Cassie, Fran,' he said. 'She'll soon be on her way back home to Birmingham. Anyway, she isn't Stephen's type.'

'I'm sure I don't know what you're going on about,' said Frances, as she picked her stool up and moved on down the row.

'I'm his brother, Fran,' said Robert. 'So I know him best – and don't forget I know you, too. He won't be interested in whatsername, take it from me.'

When he glanced at Frances, she was scarlet in the face, but she didn't say any more. She just sat down and then got on with milking the next cow.

'It's just that they're so blooming big,' said Cassie, as she lugged two buckets of warm mash into the chicken run, where she was soon mobbed by hungry hens, all pecking crossly at her feet.

'They're actually quite small,' said Stephen, opening more wooden coops and letting out more chickens. 'Ayrshires and Holsteins, for example, are a whole lot bigger, and they're more aggressive, too. Jerseys are the gentle ones.'

'I must have hurt her, then.'

'I don't think you did, but sudden movements startle cows, and then they're liable to kick out. You'll get the hang of it, don't worry. Come on, Cass, we must collect the eggs.'

'I didn't think hens laid eggs in winter?'

'You thought right – left to themselves, they don't. But Mum's determined to encourage them to lay all the year round. So they get a better diet than we do, and thanks to our old generator their new coops are always warm and light.'

Cassie took a basket, went into a hen coop, and then began to fill the straw-lined pannier with freckled, new-laid eggs.

'Lay them in rows,' said Stephen. 'Then put layers of straw between the rows. If you just heap them up like that, they'll break and Mum will kill you.'

'I'm sorry, Stephen.' Cassie looked at him hangdog, then she sighed. 'I'm pretty useless, aren't I?'

'This is your first day, and once you've found your feet I'm sure you're going to be all right, so please don't worry.' Stephen smiled encouragingly. 'Everybody has to learn, and this is new to you.'

After the lorry had been to fetch the milk, after they'd washed everything down and left the cows all munching happily, the four of them trooped in to have their breakfast.

It wasn't true about the hens enjoying better diets than the humans, and Cassie cheered up at the sight of breakfast, for there were great big bowls of steaming porridge, plates of bacon, sausages and eggs, racks of toast, and coffee or tea to wash the whole lot down. You wouldn't have known there was a war on.

'Get stuck in then, midget,' murmured Frances, heaping crisp-fried red and golden rashers on to Cassie's plate. 'This is Sally,' she continued, grinning. 'She was one of Mr Hobson's pigs – a black one with a pretty little snout and curly tail. Next week, we'll be eating Bess or Patsy.'

'Stop it, Fran,' said Stephen.

But Frances took no notice. 'You must be hungry after all that work,' she went on slyly, making Cassie want to stick her tongue out at the bitch.

'How did you get on, then?' asked Mr Denham kindly, as he poured thick cream on to his porridge.

'Um – not very well,' admitted Cassie, who expected to be ratted on by Frances, then told to get the next train back to Birmingham. She hoped she'd have a chance to get her breakfast down her first. 'I wasn't any good at milking.'

'You did your best,' said Stephen, dipping his fried bread into his egg.

'You'll be all right,' said Frances, as she poured herself more coffee, making Cassie stare, astonished. So who would tell, she wondered. It was going to be Robert, obviously.

But Robert didn't speak. He just sat there, buttering his toast, then spreading it with honey from a jar.

The minutes ticked on by, and the Denhams talked of other things. Much to her relief, Robert didn't say she had been hopeless with the cows.

When he glanced up, she smiled at him in gratitude.

He didn't return her smile.

Somehow, with a lot of help and encouragement from Stephen, even though she got shouted at and bossed around by Robert, and Frances criticised her all the time, Cassie got through the day.

Looking at the twins in daylight, she observed that Robert was bigger, broader and no doubt much stronger than his brother, and that his sullen features were more regularly handsome. Too handsome, she decided ruefully. They were a distraction. They invited her to look at him, even when she didn't want to look. He should have a warning notice tattooed on his forehead, saying idiot women keep away.

Robert was the leader. Stephen looked to Robert for approval, but Robert didn't care what anybody thought of him.

'Frances lives at home,' Stephen explained, as they watched her cycle off into the frosty gloaming later on that afternoon. 'Poor Fran, her parents are quite elderly, and she's an only child, so she gets somewhat smothered. When her call-up papers came, Sir Stuart and Lady Ashford more or less insisted she should stay in Dorset. But I don't think she wants to be a land girl.'

'What would she like to do, then?' Cassie asked.

'She says she'd like to join the ATS. But Lady Ashford thinks the ATS is common, and Fran would meet all sorts of awful people, and so she's put her foot down.'

'Lady Ashford,' murmured Cassie, thinking blimey, was I supposed to curtsey? 'Do they live in that castle I passed on my way here?'

'Castle?' repeated Stephen, frowning.

'Yes, that big, square place with all those towers and lots of little windows. It's built of yellow stone.'

'Oh, you mean Charton Minster.' Stephen laughed. 'No, that's a boarding school for wayward boys. But, funnily enough, our mother lived there once, because her family owned it.'

'Did they?' Cassie looked at Stephen and it was her turn to frown. 'So why do you all live in this – um – '

'Hovel?' Stephen shook his head and sighed. 'As I believe I told you, once we lived in Melbury House. But after it burned down we had to move into the cottage. We hope to get the house rebuilt one day. But farmers didn't make much money in the 1930s. We didn't have the cash.'

'You must be doing better these days, though?'

'Yes, the war has made things easier, even though it's hard to get the labour. The country's growing most of its own food, and the government pays the farmers well. But in the 1930s, this country was importing almost everything we ate, and British farmers were going out of business every day. Dad was almost bankrupt by 1939. I honestly don't know how he held on.'

'But he managed it.'

'Yes, but he owes money to the banks. Mum is getting old before her time, and Dad's not well at all.' Stephen shrugged. 'That's enough family history, Cass. Let's go and have some supper.'

After he had thought about it for a little while, and realised it would be very difficult to get another land girl at short notice, Robert decided to give Cassie Taylor a chance to prove herself. After all, he thought, if I get rid of Cassie, they might send us someone even worse.

But, after she had given a couple of cows mastitis by tugging at their udders, he finally made his mind up. He ignored the little voice which told him he found her quite attractive, that if she wasn't here at Melbury, he'd miss her, wouldn't he?

Cassie had to go.

'I've written to the Ministry,' he said, as he and Stephen walked across the cobbled yard, a few days later that same week.

'I tore your letter up.' Stephen glanced at Robert, whose mouth had fallen open in surprise – for no one was allowed to cross Rob Denham, least of all his twin. 'You left the letter on the kitchen table, assuming Mum would post it when she went into the village. So I opened it, and then made an executive decision. Cassie's trying hard to be a land girl, and I think she ought to stay.'

'So Fran was right,' growled Robert.

'What do you mean?'

'You've fallen for a skinny little slum kid with a cheeky smile and pretty face. It doesn't matter that she's useless, worse than useless, and – '

'Now you're being stupid.' Stephen scowled at Robert, who glowered back at him. 'Yes, she's very attractive, but I haven't fallen for her, as you choose to put it. She's probably got a boyfriend, anyway. He'll be on a convoy, or in North Africa.'

'Or selling stolen goods on the black market, or in some prison cell, or – '

'Listen, Rob,' said Stephen patiently. 'It's damned near impossible to get a useful land girl. Mum's had half a dozen, and none of them have been a patch on Frances. Cassie's very skinny, I agree, but Mum is doing her best to feed her up. I think we ought to keep her on.'

'It's like I said, you've fallen for her, haven't you?'

'No, but someone needs to be on Cassie's side,' said Stephen, who was getting angry now. 'You scowl and glare and shout at the poor girl. She takes it on the chin and does her best. She's trying hard to learn. She doesn't shirk, she doesn't whine, she doesn't grumble, even when she's half dead from exhaustion. Once she's found her feet, she's going to be an asset here. You know it.'

'I suppose she's willing,' conceded Robert. 'Yes, she tries – I'll give her that.'

'As we're agreed, she's quite attractive, too.'

'If you say so.' Robert shrugged. 'If you like anaemic-looking, scrawny little blondes, which I can't say I do.'

'So let's give her another week, at least?'

'All right,' said Robert. 'But if she doesn't learn to milk a cow and do it properly by Wednesday week, she's on the next train home.'

Cassie was determined to show everyone in Melbury that she was every bit as good as Frances.

But Frances was a well-fed country girl, not an undernourished urchin from a city slum. Cassie was short, Frances was tall, Cassie was skinny, Frances was athletic. Frances worked quickly and methodically, and Cassie had to scramble to keep up.

At the end of every working day, Cassie had to force herself to have a proper wash, get tidied up a bit, to dab a little powder on her nose, then go down to the pub. There, she often fell asleep, either against a high-backed wooden settle, or lolling with her head on Stephen's shoulder.

She had to admit she wasn't anything like as capable as big, strong, strapping Frances, whose dark good looks attracted everyone's attention whenever they went into the village, or took the wicker panniers of eggs to Charton station in the pony trap.

As they drove home again to Melbury, they had to climb a couple of steep hills, and it was from the tops of these that Cassie got her first few glimpses of the English Channel – a thick blue line that curled around a headland, then merged into the sky.

She had never seen the sea before. She thought that when she had her next day off, she would go and take a closer look. She'd ask Stephen if he'd come along, to show her the way across the fields and down the winding lanes.

'You lived here all your life?' she asked, as Frances drove the pony trap to Melbury from Charton, one February morning.

'Most of it,' said Frances, as she shook the reins to make the pony pick his feet up. 'I'm not a country bumpkin, though,' she added, somewhat sharply. 'I was born in London, and when Mummy and Daddy married, they were very rich. They had a lovely house in Surrey, and they had a place in Berkeley Square. But in the 1920s, Daddy made some terrible investments, and after I was five or six they moved house rather often, to a smaller and smaller place each time. Nowadays, we live in a small cottage north of Charton, on a pittance.'

'Oh,' said Cassie, thinking that for someone living on a pittance, Frances had some really lovely clothes. Cashmere jumpers, velvet jackets, soft felt hats and elegant tweed skirts, all in the classic styles they sold in shops like Rackham's, shops where Cassie couldn't have afforded to buy the cheapest thimble, never mind a skirt or two.

Every night she wore a different outfit to the pub, and she had at least two strings of pearls, gold earrings, and several pretty brooches which were studded with glittering marcasite.

But Frances must have read her mind. 'We're the family paupers,' she continued. 'We exist on handouts from my father's brother, who's in manufacturing. My clothes come from my cousins, and that's why they're so old-fashioned.'

'It must have been quite awkward for you, always changing schools, and having to make new friends?' said Cassie, trying hard to find a neutral subject.

'I've never been to school.' Frances was staring straight ahead, her eyes fixed on the road. 'Mummy didn't think it was important for a girl to go to school. She didn't like me knowing other children. She thought they'd give me whooping cough or measles, and I'd die. She taught me French, and how to read, of course. But I'm very ignorant and stupid, as the twins will tell you. I'm no good at sums. I don't know much history or geography at all.'

'I only know a bit myself,' said Cassie ruefully. 'I can recite the names of all the kings and queens of England, and their dates. But much good that'll do me. It won't impress the cows. As for geography – I know the names of all the continents, and where the pink bits are all round the globe. But I don't – '

'Daddy says there won't be many pink bits left after the war is over,' interrupted Frances. 'He says there won't be any at all if Hitler has his way.' Then she glanced at Cassie. 'You're getting fatter, midget, and you don't look half so pasty these days. You've got a bit of colour in your cheeks. Mrs Denham's stews and pies are doing you some good, and you're not picking at them now. You're shovelling them down.'

'I get so hungry I could eat this pony, with mangel-wurzels on the side,' said Cassie. 'But I dream of fish and chips.'

'Talking about ponies, that reminds me,' went on Frances. 'Robert said I had to get you tacking this one up. Then, from tomorrow, you must take the reins, so you can take the eggs in by yourself.'

'You mustn't worry, midget,' she said, reasonably kindly, as Cassie's jaw dropped open. She was still scared of horses, even small ones, and she knew Frances knew it. 'You won't risk getting lost. The pony knows the way to Charton. So don't go running off with him to Smethwick.'

'I can't, because Mrs Denham's got my ration book,' said Cassie, and she laughed. 'I don't know where she's hidden it, but I dare say she's stuffed it down her drawers.'

Frances chuckled, too.

She's not so bad, thought Cassie. 'Frances,' she continued, 'when I have my next day off, I want to go and find the sea. Do you think Stephen would come with me to show me the way?'

'My goodness, how should I know?' Frances had sounded

pleasant, even friendly, when she'd talked about the pony. But now her tone was frosty, and her mouth was set in a hard line.

Moody bitch, thought Cassie. Miserable snob, she thinks she's far too good for me.

But, in spite of bloody Frances, and in spite of bloody Robert Denham, Cassie was determined to stick it out in Dorset, and to make it as a land girl.

The great shire horses that did most of the heavy work on all the local farms were still alarming, but as time went on she grew to love the docile little pony which was kept to pull the egg cart, and she'd almost stopped being scared of cows.

In fact, she really liked the Jerseys now.

Or most of them, at any rate.

There were some skittery, frisky ones who'd kick out without warning, but she was on to them. She grew to enjoy the early morning milking, sitting in the warm, cow-scented shed, listening to the streams of milk ping into metal buckets, and feeling the brown cow that she was milking grunt and sigh contentedly.

'You can go and feed the bull,' said Frances briskly, as she and Cassie came out of the cowshed one sharp morning. It had all gone very well today. Cassie had worked almost as fast as Frances, Stephen had told them jokes and made them laugh, and Robert had managed a half-smile or two.

They'd cleaned out all the stalls, they'd filled the mangers, so now they were ready for some breakfast of their own. 'I know you've never done it,' went on Frances, 'but I reckon it's your turn. The feed's kept in those bins,' she added, pointing to the store. 'There'll be a bucket somewhere, and the scoop is on the shelf.'

Stephen had gone back inside already. Cassie could see his boots lying in the porch. Robert was nowhere to be seen, and Frances now walked off towards the cottage, from which a smell of frying bacon wafted, scenting the cold air.

Cassie sighed, but did as she was told. She went to fetch the feed. Then she made her way across the yard to the converted stable where they kept the bull.

She found him staring out across the yard, swaying his great, horned head from side to side. Poor old thing, she thought, he was no doubt wondering what had happened to his breakfast. What a life, kept cooped up on his own. He probably wouldn't mind a bit of company now and then.

The bull was a lot bigger than the cows, but not enormous, and he stared at Cassie with a cow's brown, gentle eyes. Looking at those soft, dark eyes, she found she wasn't scared. So, opening the stable door, she went inside to fill his manger with the feed.

'Come on, old man, it's breakfast time,' she said. She saw him put his head down, saw the light glance off his horns.

She never knew what happened next.

Cassie became aware of someone slapping her very lightly on the face, first upon her left cheek, then her right.

A voice was calling out her name, telling her to wake up, Cassie, and it sounded pleading, anxious, angry, worried, frightened, all at the same time.

She blinked, opened her eyes, and saw that Robert Denham was glaring down at her, and that he was frowning furiously. He was more angry than she'd ever seen him yet. But there was something else in those dark eyes. Something even more alarming than his obvious fury.

'You stupid, idiotic girl!' he cried. 'What in the world possessed you? What were you bloody doing, letting out the bull?'

'I – I was going to feed him,' whispered Cassie, who was

feeling nauseous now. She must have bashed her head upon the cobbles. She could feel a lump, and it was getting bigger by the second. The frosty morning light had shattered into a hundred thousand little splinters, and they cut into her eyes. 'It – it was my turn.'

'You clot, who told you that?'

'I – Frances said – '

'Frances!' bellowed Robert, and a moment later she came running from the cottage, closely followed by Stephen and his mother.

'What's wrong with Cassie?' Frances asked.

Robert glared up at her, his dark eyes hard and very bright. 'Why did you tell Cassie she had to feed the bull?' he shouted, making Frances tremble. 'You were trying to get her killed, was that it?'

'No, it was a joke.' Frances was chalk white. 'Rob, you know she's scared of cows. I didn't think she'd go in with the bull.'

'You didn't think at all!' cried Robert. 'God, I've had enough of you,' he muttered. 'I'm sick and tired of all your bloody moods. You're a liability, and – '

'Robert, that's enough,' snapped Mrs Denham, as she hunkered down. 'Where does it hurt you, Cassie?' she demanded, in a much more gentle tone of voice. 'Listen to me, can you feel your feet?'

'My – my feet?' Cassie blinked. The light still hurt her eyes. But she found she could wriggle all her toes. 'My f-feet are fine.'

'Your arms?' said Mrs Denham. 'Come on, let me see you shake your fingers. Do it now!'

Cassie thought about it for a moment, but then she did as she was told. 'I don't think I'm hurt,' she whispered. 'It – it's just my head, and I feel sick.'

'All right, Robert, help her up,' said Mrs Denham crisply.

'Stephen, don't just stand there like a half-wit, go and catch the bull. He'll be half way to Dorchester by now.'

Robert slipped his arm round Cassie's waist. She groaned, but he was gentle and helped her to sit up. He let her rest a moment, and then he supported her while she rose unsteadily to her feet.

'I'm sorry, Cassie,' Frances whispered as she came round to Cassie's other side and put a steadying hand under her elbow. 'But I didn't think you'd be so silly – '

'Shut up, Fran, all right?' Robert glared at Frances balefully. 'You've had it in for Cassie from the start.'

'I haven't!'

'Yes, you have! Ever since that evening in the pub, when I told you we'd got a new land girl, and she was blonde and pretty, you've tried to make things difficult for Cassie.'

'Robert, that's not true!'

'Oh, for God's sake, Fran, you can't deny – '

'Do stop bickering, the pair of you!' Mrs Denham pushed her son away. She slipped her arm round Cassie. 'Let's get you inside and sitting down,' she said. 'Robert and Frances, come and eat your breakfast, then get on with your work.'

Cassie took a hesitant step forward, leaning heavily on Rose Denham's arm.

Robert watched them go inside the cottage. He was feeling sick himself. His heart was hammering, he was shaking, and he wanted to shake Frances Ashford too, until her eyeballs rolled around her stupid, thoughtless head.

I'm just in shock, he told himself. Anyone would be in shock if they had found a girl lying on the cobbles, pale as death. All I need now is half a pint of coffee. Then I'll be fine again.

But he found he couldn't stop trembling, and the bitter taste of dread and panic was making him feel ill. He didn't trust himself to think about how he might feel if Cassie had been badly injured, or if – God forbid – Cassie was dead.

He'd been so determined she should go. But now he was determined she should stay. He didn't know quite why, but told himself it was because he had a high opinion of anyone prepared to have a go. Cassie found farm work hard, exhausting, even terrifying, but stuck at it, all the same.

'Rob, are you okay?' Stephen walked into the farmyard, leading a confused and rather sulky-looking bull, which seemed more than ready to go back to its stable for its breakfast.

'Yes, I'm fine,' said Robert.

'You're shaking,' Stephen told him. 'You need to go and sit down.'

'I told you, I'm all right.'

Cassie sat by the range all morning, feeling ill and dizzy. Mrs Denham had tucked a blanket round her, and put a glass of water by her side and told her to take sips. But she wasn't offered any food.

Cassie dozed, opening her eyes occasionally to watch Mr Denham writing in his stock book, or Mrs Denham peeling heaps of vegetables, cutting up great slabs of meat and making floury dumplings.

Mr Denham didn't seem very well today, she noticed. He was rather breathless, and his colour wasn't good.

Mrs Denham didn't exactly make a fuss of him, or treat him like an invalid. But, as she went about her work, as she walked in and out, she would touch his shoulder, and he would sometimes catch her hand and hold it for a moment, and both of them would sigh.

Cassie wondered what was wrong with him, if it was serious. He didn't do much work around the farm at any time, unlike Mrs Denham, who worked hard all day.

By late morning, Cassie felt less dizzy. She knew that she was getting better when the smell of cooking stopped making her feel ill, and made her hungry.

'How are you feeling now?' asked Robert, when everyone came in to wash and have their mid-day meal.

'A lot better, thank you,' Cassie told him.

'Good,' said Robert, crouching down so that their eyes were level, and to Cassie's surprise he almost managed to crack a smile.

She looked at him, into his eyes. She saw herself reflected there. She remembered he'd told Frances she was pretty. 'I'm sorry I was so stupid,' she told him.

'Oh, don't fret about it,' Robert said, and suddenly he smiled properly.

It changed his face completely. It made him look as friendly and as likeable as Stephen. But there was something else there too, something irresistible, and Cassie knew she'd have to watch it now, or she would be in real trouble.

'Get Cassie to the table, Rob,' said Stephen, sitting down himself and sawing off a hunk of bread. 'Come on, Fran, cheer up. You didn't kill her this time, even though you tried.'

Chapter Four

'It wasn't true, you know, what Robert said.'

Frances was wheeling her bike across the yard the following evening, ready to go home. She and Cassie had worked very hard that day, doing all their usual jobs, and cleaning out the calf stalls and polishing all the horses' tack, as well.

Cassie was feeling more or less all right again, except for the still-tender bump on the back of her head, and that was going down.

When she'd got up that morning, she'd insisted she was fit for work. She knew this had surprised and pleased the twins. She had long suspected they thought she was a layabout, a lazy city slacker. Well, she would show them, she'd decided – and she had, even though she ached all over and had bruises everywhere, even though she'd had to make a superhuman effort to get up and out of bed.

'What wasn't true?' she asked.

'What Robert said about me having it in for you,' said Frances, going red.

'Oh, Fran, don't worry about Robert!' Cassie grinned. 'Miserable so-and-so, he's mean to everybody, you know that. Listen, you've been great.'

'I jolly haven't!'

'Yes, you have, you've taught me such a lot, and you've been so patient with me when I've mucked things up. I was daft, to go in with the bull. I won't do that again.'

'You mind you don't,' said Frances. 'Where's Steve tonight?' she added, looking round.

'He's gone to bed,' Cassie replied. 'Mrs Denham came out just now and told me. She said he was looking rather green, and she was afraid he'd have a turn. He sometimes gets them when he's had a shock, she said, and I shocked everybody yesterday! So she's sent him up to sleep it off.'

'Poor Stephen,' whispered Frances, and Cassie saw her redden again, and suddenly it all clicked into place – the moods, the sarcasm, the touchiness.

'You like Stephen, don't you?' she said gently.

'I like both the twins,' said Frances, but she turned away from Cassie's gaze. 'I've known them for ages, Cassie, ever since we moved here, and they're family friends.'

'But you like Stephen best. So, that first night, when Rob went on ahead of me and Steve and told you I'd arrived, and then we came into the pub, and we were laughing, you decided – '

'What would *you* have thought?' demanded Frances. 'Rob came in all cross and said they'd sent some slinky glamour girl to work at Melbury, that she looked like the bloody fairy on the Christmas tree, and wouldn't be any good at milking cows, he'd bet his life on it. I had the very devil of a job to cheer him up and make him smile again. Then you two came in giggling at something, you were blonde and pretty, and Stephen had his arm around your waist – '

'You idiot, Stephen had been stopping me from falling in the mud. My shoes weren't made for tramping across fields.' Cassie couldn't believe what she was hearing. 'Frances,' she said kindly, 'I'm not pretty. I'm pasty, short and skinny. My hair's the colour of dirty straw. It's certainly not blonde.'

'But you're not a big fat pudding, are you?' Frances was busy picking at the rubber on her handgrips. 'Mummy's always going on at me, saying she can't imagine how she produced a lump like me, when she's so slim and dainty. She says I'm fat because I'm far too greedy, and I ought to diet. But I get so hungry when I'm working on the farm, and it's not as though I'm always stuffing, but Mummy watches every single mouthful, and – '

'Oh, Fran, don't be ridiculous. You have a gorgeous figure. The men all fancy you – you know they do!' Cassie looked at Frances earnestly. 'I'd give anything to have your English rose complexion, your beautiful white teeth, your lovely, long dark hair. Look, we can't stay out here chatting now. We're going to freeze to death. But can't we be friends?'

'If you want friends like me,' said Frances bleakly. 'If you're that desperate.'

'Mother of God, I'm desperate, believe me,' Cassie told her, grinning. 'Go on, Fran, you'd better get off home. Or else your mum will think a German airman came swooping down and grabbed you.'

She held out her right hand. 'Shake?' she said, and – after a short moment's hesitation – Frances shook.

'Okay,' she said. 'We're friends.'

The letter which arrived the following morning changed everything again.

Soon after Cassie had arrived in Melbury, Robert had gone into Dorchester to have his medical, and a few weeks later he was told he'd been passed fit. He'd be going back on active service, to have another bash at getting killed, as Stephen put it.

Cassie didn't want to think of Robert getting wounded, much less getting killed. She didn't want to like him, but she did. She didn't want to dream about him, but he walked into her dreams regardless, and made himself at home inside her head.

She had to stop herself from looking, staring, grinning like an idiot when Robert glanced her way, from talking to him when she didn't need to say a word. He made it worse by helping her occasionally, by buying her a pair of boots which actually fitted when he went into Dorchester with Stephen, by stirring precious sugar into her morning coffee because he knew she liked it.

She'd never had a boyfriend and had never touched a man, except to shake his hand. But now she found she wanted to touch Robert, to run her fingers through his dense, dark hair, to stroke his forearm, to sidle up to him and brush against him.

Since he'd had that letter, he wasn't sulking any more. In fact, he joked and whistled all day long, so she couldn't even tell herself he was a miserable thing.

He'd always worked methodically, and he had more stamina than his brother, but now he worked much harder, obviously keen to get the place into good shape before he went away.

'Look out, here comes the jolly farmer,' Cassie said sarcastically, at the end of one cold, dismal day. Stephen, she and Frances were in the cottage porch, all pulling off their Wellingtons, and Robert was coming towards them from the barn.

It had rained incessantly all day, a freezing winter downpour that had soaked them through and through. Stephen had a streaming cold, Cassie had slipped over on a slick of muck and hurt her knee, and Frances had been kicked hard by a cow.

But Robert had been cheeriness itself, had told them to buck up and think of England, reminding them that moaning wasn't going to beat the Jerries.

'He's worse than a Boy Scout,' croaked Stephen, as he eyed his brother balefully. 'Baden-Powell would be so proud of him.'

'I'd have him shot,' growled Frances.

'What's all this, then? Why the gloomy faces?' Robert asked them, as he joined them in the porch and grinned encouragingly.

'We can be gloomy if we like,' said Cassie scowling and rubbing at the bruise on her sore knee.

'But Cassie, if you smile, you'll feel much better.'

'Just listen to him,' said Cassie sourly. 'Well, Mr Ray of Sunshine, *you've* changed your bloody tune.'

'What's that supposed to mean?'

'What are you all arguing about?' Mrs Denham came out of the cottage. 'Supper's ready now, so come and eat it while it's hot. Frances, dear, your father phoned this afternoon to say he's coming over in the car to take you home. Your mother doesn't want you cycling back in all this rain.'

'Why not, she's waterproof,' said Robert.

'Shut up, Rob,' growled Stephen, making Frances smile gratefully at him. 'You're driving everybody up the wall with all this we're-British-and-so-we-can-tackle-anything routine.'

But Robert took no notice of his brother and became more cheerful and more boisterous day by day, reminding Cassie of a Labrador or other large and friendly dog which had too much energy and wore its owners out.

'Put me down, you bugger!' she gasped one supper-time, as Robert picked her up, then turned her upside down and carried her head first into the cottage.

'You need to learn some manners, Cassie,' Robert said, and laughed at her discomfiture. 'You shouldn't call me names. You shouldn't say my singing's like a crow with tonsillitis and always out of tune.'

As Cassie went on squawking, Mrs Denham came into the kitchen, and stared in disbelief. 'What on earth do you think you're doing, Robert?' she demanded. 'Put Cassie down at once!'

Robert dumped Cassie sideways on a chair.

Cassie glared at him. But then she met his dark brown gaze, and thought, he's the man who said I was a slinky glamour girl, who said that I was pretty, even when he didn't want to like me.

'You watch yourself,' she muttered, aware that she was blushing like a pillar box. 'You mind yourself, all right?'

'Or you'll do what?' He grinned, then reached across and tweaked her hair, pulling a stray ringlet straight, then letting it spring back into a curl.

Cassie slapped his hand away and bared her teeth at him. 'Something you won't like, you wait and see.'

'Robert, jolly well behave yourself,' snapped Mrs Denham, putting an iron pot in front of Frances, who was having supper at the cottage. 'If you've finished gawping at this pair of idiots, Frances, maybe you'd be good enough to serve, since they apparently can't help themselves?'

Cassie found she couldn't help herself.

She was watching Robert all the time. She hoped he wouldn't notice she was looking, but also hoped that he would soon be taunting, teasing, even tipping her upside down and making Mrs Denham glare and frown at him again.

In church on Sundays, she listened to him singing. He was a good singer, in spite of what she'd said, and he was never out of tune. She didn't know the hymns at first, of course, but after a few weeks at Melbury she got the hang of most of them and joined in with the others.

She supposed she shouldn't really be in church at all. Or not in this one, anyway. When she'd first arrived in Melbury, she knew she should have asked where she could find the nearest Catholic church. But it was now a bit too late for that, and she soon decided it didn't really matter anyway.

The service was peculiar, but she found she liked the words so much that she was mouthing them, telling herself that if she didn't say the words out loud it didn't count.

She somehow didn't think that Father Riley would agree.

'Daydreaming, are you, midget?' Frances asked, as they polished harness one cold morning, Cassie rubbing it reflectively and wishing Robert would come and look for them, tell them to do something else, would speak to her again. It had been three hours or more since they had met at breakfast, and she wondered where he'd gone. 'What's the matter, Cassie?'

'What?' Cassie started guiltily. She rubbed the halter she was holding even harder, as if she was trying to polish it away.

'Only you've just gone all red.' Frances grinned. 'I think you must be coming down with something.'

'I hope I'm not.' Cassie cleared her throat and also hoped she'd manage to sound casual and artless when she spoke again. 'Where are the boys this morning?'

'They've gone to Dorchester with Mr Denham. He had to see a lawyer about some access rights along the road going into Charton. Didn't you hear them talking while we were having breakfast?' Frances giggled. 'Or were you in a daydream then, as well?'

Robert couldn't wait until he was recalled to active service, could rejoin his unit, and could see his men again.

But he was reluctant to leave Melbury, his family and England – oh, and to leave Cassie too, a voice inside his head reminded him. You're going to miss Cassie most of all.

Somehow, she had got inside his heart, inside his soul, and he didn't quite know how or why. She wasn't anything like the other girls he'd met at dances, girls with whom he'd flirted, girls he'd kissed.

Cassie was definitely not a flirt. She didn't smirk, she didn't stick her chest out, she didn't stare at men with big, wide eyes. She didn't do that thing with cigarettes – she didn't lose her matches so men had to light her Woodbines while she gazed into their eyes, either looking soulful or ridiculous, depending on the girl. She didn't smooth her skirt over her hips to draw attention to her shape.

She never traded on the fact she was a woman, and expect to be excused the heavier jobs, or helped to do her work.

She just got on with it.

As he lay in bed one night, just a matter of feet away from where she must be sleeping, he wondered what she'd feel like if he took her in his arms.

All bones and angles, he supposed – prominent shoulder blades and small, sharp elbows. These wouldn't hesitate to jab him in the ribs if she thought he was trying to do anything he shouldn't.

She wasn't quite as skinny as when she'd first arrived. His mother's cooking had succeeded in fattening her up – not very much, he had to admit. But she didn't have the sort of figure which would ever put on any serious fat or muscle.

He'd met lads like Cassie when he had been in France. Boys from the big cities who were small and thin and hollow-chested, but who'd had lots of stamina and were not afraid of work. A couple of them had pulled him into that little boat when he had been wounded at Dunkirk.

Bob and Dave from Manchester, two wiry little blokes they'd been, and they had saved his life. If Cassie had any brothers or male cousins, he was sure they'd be like Dave and Bob.

He lit a cigarette and stared up at the ceiling, which was washed by moonlight. She was just a girl, he thought, a cheeky, forward, gobby little madam who happened to be a damned good worker, too.

He blew a smoke ring, watched it drift across the room.

He didn't understand it, but he found he wanted to be close to Cassie Taylor.

He was very tired tonight, but knew he wouldn't sleep.

'You're looking rather bleary-eyed this morning,' Frances told him, as they went in for breakfast after they had milked the cows.

'He's sickening for something,' Stephen said.

'No, I'm not,' said Robert.

'You probably need a dose of castor oil.'

'Shut up, Steve,' said Robert testily.

'Cassie, what do you think?' Frances asked. 'Castor oil or Epsom salts, which would you recommend?'

Cassie glanced at Robert, blushed and turned away.

'She's coming down with something, too,' said Frances, as she grinned at Stephen. 'Whatever could it be?'

'I wonder,' Stephen said.

As the day wore on, Robert took every opportunity to brush her arm with his, to hold her steady as she climbed the ladder to the hay loft, to help her tack the pony up, to be back to back with Cassie while they did the evening milking, smelling her delicious Cassie scent of soap and something else which he could not identify, but which made him want to touch her, hold her – kiss her on her pretty little mouth?

He couldn't help but tease her, taunt her, make her call him names, and he'd grown to love the sweet sensation as his heart beat faster when she grinned at him.

He told himself repeatedly that he liked the girl because she worked so hard and didn't grumble. But he knew this wasn't the whole story.

Maybe it was just as well he'd soon be going away.

The weather was getting gradually warmer, and the evenings lighter.

It didn't get dark until long after all the work was done, so Cassie had time to go for a walk after she'd had her supper, to sit on a stile and daydream, or stroll along the headland and watch the waves roll up on to the beach.

The seascape was so huge, so vast that she could hardly take it in. Sometimes, the waves were angry, with foam-flecked breakers crashing like thunder on the shingle beach. But, on other days, it was all so peaceful that it almost made her cry, to think there was a war going on, and people were doing awful, ugly things, when God had made the world so beautiful.

The shingle beach itself was out of bounds. All along the tide-line there were tank traps, concrete bollards and thickets of barbed wire, for when the Germans came.

But did they mean to come?

'I doubt it, Cass,' said Robert, who'd just happened to join her as she walked along the headland one clear evening. 'Of course, they should have followed us as we came home from France. They could have walked it, back in 1940. We couldn't have stopped them even if we'd tried. But things are different now.'

He turned to Cassie, who hoped she wasn't blushing, because she knew he'd tease her if she blushed. 'Cass, you're different, too. You look much better these days. There are roses in your cheeks, and you've put on a bit of weight. I'll swear you've grown an inch or two, as well! Do you like being a land girl?'

'Yes, I do,' said Cassie. 'I thought it would be boring. But most days, it's fun. I love the chickens and the cows. I don't know if I'll stay in Melbury for the whole duration. I'd like to see a bit more of the world. But, one day, I'll come back to work in Dorset.'

'You mean, work on a farm?'

'Why shouldn't I?'

'No reason, Cassie, so don't look at me like that, all narrow-eyed and all suspicious.' Robert smiled and Cassie's heart did cartwheels of delight. 'I was only asking.'

'All right, but it's time I was getting back again,' she told him. 'I need to write a letter to my granny before I go to bed.'

'I'll walk back with you – that's if you don't mind?'

'I don't mind at all.' Then Cassie thought, please take my hand, please take me in your arms – no, don't, it would be pointless, it would only make me sad.

'What did you say?' asked Robert.

'I didn't speak,' said Cassie.

'But your lips were moving.'

'You're imagining things.'

As well as farming, Cassie was getting interested in gardening and in horticulture, too. Before she'd come to Dorset, she'd never really thought about where food was actually grown, or wondered how it ended up in shops.

They'd had allotments back in Smethwick, but she had never seen one. She hadn't had a father or an uncle to take her digging potatoes, planting carrots, picking beans. Lily Taylor's little terraced house had had no garden, just a brick-paved yard in which there was a mangle and an outside lavatory shared by the whole row.

The Denhams' kitchen garden, with its long, straight rows of currant bushes, cloches protecting delicate and over-wintering crops, raspberry canes and funny-looking plants she didn't know the names of yet, was a revelation. Cassie liked to work there, listening to the birdsong, and feeling the warm, spring sun upon her face.

One Monday evening, Robert found her hoeing carefully among the just-emerging broad bean plants, where the weeds were springing up as well, and humming to herself.

'Hello, Cass,' he said, and smiled.

'Oh, it's you,' she said, and then she grinned. She couldn't help herself.

'You don't have to work all day,' he said, taking the hoe out of her hands and walking down the row towards the path.

She followed him. 'I like it – gives me exercise,' she said. 'All right, hoeing weeds is work to you, but it's a novelty for me. You can't imagine what it's like, living in a city where the sky's a dirty grey, where the grass is yellow, where the canals are full of muck and rubbish. Dorset's a paradise compared to Brum.'

'I grew up in India. Dad was in the army and he was based in Delhi, so I know what it's like to live in cities,' Robert said. 'Cassie, you're a conscientious worker, but you mustn't overdo it. We don't want to work you half to death.'

'Why should it bother you?' she asked him.

Then she felt herself go red. She hadn't meant to sound so rude and so aggressive, but he got her so confused she couldn't help herself. 'You're going off,' she added. 'You're going to get yourself smashed up again.'

'I don't *want* to get smashed up,' said Robert. 'I hope I won't get hurt. But if I do – well, I'm in the army. It's my job.'

'Why do men like fighting?'

'I don't know if we like it, but it's something most men have to do at some point in their lives.'

'You could all be pacifists instead?'

'I don't think so, Cassie.' Robert shrugged. 'It's not the way most men are made. Do you admire the pacifists?'

'Yes, I knew a few of them in Brum, and they were all good blokes. There were these two brothers, they were Quakers, they were in the Heavy Rescue. Some of their mates drove

51

ambulances, others worked in hospitals as porters, and some of them were firemen.'

'So they're doing their bit, and I respect anyone who does their bit,' said Robert gravely. Then he smiled his lovely smile again, and – miracle of miracles – he took her by the hand. 'Come on, Cassie, leave your weeds. It's nearly time for supper.'

As Cassie's heart beat twenty to the dozen, Robert's smile grew wicked. 'There's bound to be another pot of Mum's delicious stew, with lots of that pearl barley you've come to like so much.'

'Yes, I have,' she said. 'So you can just stop mocking me. The food you country people eat isn't what I've been used to having. I never had your sort of meals while I was growing up. But now I've got a taste for them.'

She'd got a taste for Robert, too. She let him hold her hand a moment longer, then she thought that somebody might see them, and so she shook him off.

She sneaked a glance at him. Yes, he was tall and dark and handsome, he looked like a film star – and he knew it, too. My granny warned me about men like him, she thought. Nobs who think all working girls are tarts, and up for anything.

You keep a grip, girl, don't you give away your heart.

But as they walked back to the cottage, she could still feel the warmth of his broad palm against her own, still feel a silly, happy smile playing round her lips. More than almost anything, she wanted him to hold her hand again.

'I've got my marching orders too,' said Stephen, as they rolled out the churns and waited for the lorry one March morning.

'Oh, Steve, where are you going?' Frances looked suddenly stricken, Cassie noticed, ashen-faced and fearful.

'Only up to London. I'm being seconded to the General Staff, and I'll be working in an office.' Stephen winked at Cassie. 'You wouldn't know it just to look at me, but actually I'm pretty good at reading, writing, all that kind of thing. I'll make sure the army gets its bombs and shells and bullets, that there are plenty of lorries, tanks and guns.'

'Basically, he's going to run a quartermaster's stores,' said Robert, laughing as his brother punched him, falling back and groaning as if he was really hurt.

'When will you be leaving?' Frances whispered.

'I think it's Friday week.'

'But what about us?' said Cassie, frowning. 'We can't manage everything between us.'

'Dad's going to get Mr Hobson from the village to help out,' said Stephen reassuringly. 'So you'll be all right.'

'But Mr Hobson is so old,' objected Frances.

'He's going to bring one of his sons with him. Daniel Hobson's backward, so he won't be called up, but he knows his way around the cows.' Robert smiled his most beguiling smile. 'Ladies, will you write to us?'

'If you'll write back,' said Cassie. 'I haven't got time to sit around and write to people who will use my letters to wipe their arses on.'

'What a suspicious mind you have,' said Stephen.

'As if we would do anything like that.' Robert laughed at Cassie's frown. 'I'll write back,' he promised. 'Cross my heart and hope to die. We're going to miss you, aren't we, Steve?'

'You can't wait to get away,' said Cassie, but only to herself. She understood that he was restless, for she was restless, too.

In spite of liking being in the countryside, and working on the farm, and having all these new experiences, she also missed the hustle and the bustle of the town.

She didn't miss the dirt and smoke and grime. But she

missed the noise, she missed the rush, she missed the shops and trams, the streets and crowded buses, the glamour and excitement of going to the cinema and to the local dance hall with the girls with whom she'd been at school, because she loved to dance.

She missed the food, especially the Italian hokey-pokey, the meat-and-jelly-filled pork pies, and the golden, fresh-fried fish and chips.

She missed her granny. She worried about Lily all the time, and hoped she wouldn't get caught in a raid. Lily didn't seem to think she was in any danger. She thought that if she said her prayers and lived a holy life, she'd be all right.

Cassie said her prayers for Lily, too.

She didn't know what she'd do if Lily died.

'I think Robert likes you,' whispered Frances a week later, as she and Cassie did the washing up after they'd all had their mid-day meal. Mr Denham was having forty winks, the twins had gone to town to buy some stuff they'd need before they went away, and Mrs Denham was outside on the drying green, getting her washing in.

'He likes you, too,' said Cassie.

'You know what I mean,' said Frances, blushing.

'He's been cooped up here for months and months,' said Cassie, knowing she was reddening too. 'He's been like an eagle in a cage. He hasn't had a chance to spread his wings. Frances, he's a cock, and I'm a hen, and so it's only natural – '

'Oh, Cass, you say the most outrageous things,' said Frances, laughing.

'Well, I'm not trying to be out-whatsit, don't you even think it.' Cassie scrubbed a saucepan with unnecessary force. 'Frances, listen – don't misunderstand me, don't take this the wrong way. The fact is – I like everybody I've met here in Dorset. You've all been good to me. But you're a bunch of toffs, and I'm a guttersnipe from Brum. Men brought up like Robert don't value girls like me.'

'That's nonsense, Cassie.'

'No it's not,' snapped Cassie.

'How do you know, then?'

'I might tell you one day.' Cassie pulled the plug out, let the water gurgle down into the old zinc bucket underneath the sink.

'Gosh, that sounds mysterious.'

'Frances, Stephen told me that you wanted to join the ATS,' said Cassie, wishing she hadn't got into that previous conversation.

'Yes, I did. But Mummy said – '

'How old are you, Fran?'

'I'm twenty-two.'

'So you're officially grown up. Frances, listen – it's *your* life, not Mummy's. Why don't you do what *you* want, for a change?'

'I suppose I don't want it quite enough,' admitted Frances, shrugging as she hung a couple of damp tea-towels on the plate rack. 'It's so much easier, doing what my mother says. I'm a coward, too. I wouldn't want to leave my home and to go off on my own.'

'Well, I don't want to bury myself in Melbury all my life.' Cassie grinned. 'So why don't I come with you?'

'Cassie, if we leave, poor Mrs Denham is going to be stuck,' said Frances gravely. 'Perhaps we ought to stay?'

'Oh, don't make excuses, Fran,' said Cassie. 'All she has to do is get on to the Ministry of Labour, or put an advert in the *Farming Times*. She'll easily find new girls for Melbury.'

'Do we dare?' asked Frances.

'Let's find out what's available,' said Cassie. 'On our next half day, we'll both go into Dorchester and go to the recruiting offices. We can make enquiries, and see where we'd fit in.'

'My mother had better not find out,' said Frances.

'Well, I'm not going to tell the mean old maggot.' Cassie grinned again. 'She doesn't sound like the sort of person who would speak to me in any case, unless I was her charlady or serving in a shop.'

'Well, that's just Mummy, isn't it?' Frances shook her head. 'It's funny, don't you think, how things work out?'

'What do you mean?'

'You and Robert – may I be your bridesmaid?'

'Oh, don't be ridiculous,' said Cassie, going scarlet. 'I know you like to tease me, Fran. You don't mean any harm, but sometimes you take things too far.'

Cassie wished she didn't still dream of Robert every night.

But, once she'd closed her eyes, he came and took her hand, and then he pulled her into his embrace, and they were kissing, more than kissing, and she woke up horrified by what they'd done – or almost done. She remembered Father Riley's lectures to her confirmation class, when he'd talked extensively about all kinds of sin.

As the time for him and Stephen to remain in Dorset ticked away, she almost wished he would go sooner. Then she might have some peace.

It was so difficult, seeing him all the time and wishing he would brush her hand, would touch her hair, and it was so embarrassing to start grinning like a halfwit whenever he happened to glance in her direction.

Everyone must have noticed she was making a right old exhibition of herself. So perhaps it would be better if *she* was going away?

As she thought about it, the more it seemed desirable, and – what was more – achievable. So what she was a woman, not a man?

She'd have liked to have adventures, too.

Chapter Five

After the twins had gone, it was so quiet.

Mr Hobson and his son were silent and methodical as they went about their work. Daniel didn't speak at all, and Mr Hobson didn't approve of chatter. He shook his head at Cassie if she talked or sang while she was milking.

'You'll upset them cows, the way you carries on, warbling away the way you do,' he muttered darkly. 'You ain't no Gracie Fields or Vera Lynn, and that's a fact.'

But Cassie didn't care if Mr Hobson didn't appreciate her warbling. She went on singing to the Jerseys, especially the songs which Rob and Steve had sung to them, a mix of big band numbers she'd heard on the wireless, and the hymns they all sang every Sunday in the local church.

After a long, hard winter, spring was here at last. People and their animals were shaking off the sluggishness of all those cold, dark days, and everyone was getting on with life.

Or giving birth to it.

There were two new babies in the village, and there were skipping lambs in all the fields. There were several dozen new pink piglets in Mr Hobson's pens, six of the cows had calved, several of the hens had fluffy broods of golden chicks, and there were fragrant yellow flowers growing on all the banks.

'Primroses,' said Frances, who couldn't believe that Cassie had never seen a primrose in her life. 'They grow like weeds all over Dorset.'

'What about those things that look like primroses, but smaller and with lots of little flowers on every stem?'

'They're cowslips, and those other yellow flowers are daffodils.' .

'I know what a daffodil looks like,' Cassie muttered, huffing rather crossly. 'Do you think I'm ignorant or something?'

'God, perish the thought,' said Frances, laughing. 'Cassie, isn't it a lovely day? You'd never know there was a war on.'

Cassie nodded. On a blue and gold spring day like this, if you didn't listen to the wireless, if you didn't go down to the beach and look at all that concrete and barbed wire, it was almost possible to forget.

Mrs Denham had got hold of dark blue paint from somewhere, and she'd spruced up her front door.

About time too, decided Cassie, who thought she'd never understand the posh squad's lackadaisical and easy-going ways. Lily Taylor washed and cleaned and polished all day long. But Rose Denham's stone-flagged kitchen floor often didn't see a mop or broom from one week to the next.

'Three more people looking for work,' she said one April morning, as they were having breakfast and she was busy opening the post.

'Anyone with any experience, though?' asked Mr Denham, looking up from his *Farming Times*, and wheezing like an ancient pair of bellows as he lit another cigarette.

'Yes, two girls in their twenties who are on farms in Devon at the moment, but want to be near their parents' homes in Dorset. They say they're used to dairy herds and heavy horses. So I think they'd be ideal for us.'

Mrs Denham looked at Cassie and Frances. 'But we don't need them, do we? So they'll have to stay in Devon. Or join the ATS. I heard on the Home Service the government wants more women in the army.'

Cassie glanced at Frances, raised one eyebrow.

But Frances shook her head.

'But *why* can't we leave?' demanded Cassie, as they mucked out the shire horses' stables, later on that morning.

58

'I think it would be very mean,' said Frances. 'Mrs Denham's such a good employer, and she's been so kind to us.'

'Fran, she gets her money's worth!' cried Cassie. 'All right, she feeds us properly, she doesn't overwork us, but she makes flipping sure we earn our wages, every single penny of them.'

'But I thought you liked it here in Dorset?'

'Yes, I do,' said Cassie. 'But Frances, think about it – Dorset isn't going to go away, and there's a great big world out there.'

'Yes, and lots of horrid things are going on in it. Cassie, Mr Denham isn't well.'

'Mr Denham's past it.' Cassie shrugged. 'Mrs Denham runs the place, and all Mr Denham does is sit around, and do the books, and read the *Farming Times*.'

'I suppose she could have those girls from Devon,' said Frances thoughtfully.

'Yes, she could,' said Cassie. 'She's got Mr Hobson and his son. They do as much as Steve and Rob, or more. If she has a couple of girls, as well – '

'She'll be all right.' Frances looked suddenly wistful. 'It would be quite nice to have adventures, and to see a bit of life.'

'Of course it would.'

'We'll talk to her on Friday evening, shall we?' Now, her growing excitement blobbed two spots of pink on Frances's pale cheeks. 'When Mr Denham goes off to his farmers' meeting at the village hall.'

On Friday evening, Cassie ate her supper very quickly. She forked up every single grain of barley and then mopped up her gravy with some of Mrs Denham's fresh-baked bread.

Frances was staying to supper too and, after she'd finished her raspberry jam and roly-poly pudding, she told Mrs Denham to put her feet up for a change.

'Cassie and I will go and get the washing in,' said Frances casually. 'We'll do all the pots and pans, and have a tidy up.'

Rose Denham looked from one girl to the other. 'Oh, I see,' she said, and smiled at them.

'I'm sorry, Mrs Denham?' said Cassie, blushing.

'It's time to go and have adventures, is it?' Mrs Denham pushed her empty pudding bowl aside. She ran her fingers through her long, dark hair, looping back some errant strands and pinning them up again. 'I was thinking yesterday, it's been a long time coming.'

'Adventures, Mrs Denham?' repeated Cassie glibly, aware that she was going even redder in the face, embarrassed to be so easily found out.

'I don't think I'm mistaken, am I, Cassie? You've both been so restless since the boys went back. I don't think it's natural for two young girls like you to want to spend your lives stuck on a farm, out in the middle of nowhere, milking cows.'

Mrs Denham stood up then, brushed the crumbs from off her pinafore, and went to fill the big black kettle. 'So, Fran and Cassie, which is it to be? The Wrens? The WAAF? The ATS?'

'Mother of God, they don't have my sort in the Wrens,' said Cassie, laughing and wrinkling her nose. 'The Wrens is just for nobs. Frances would be all right, of course. She's pukka, aren't you, Fran? Your old mum might let you join the Wrens?'

'Oh, do shut up, midget,' said Frances, not unkindly. 'Mrs Denham,' she continued, 'we quite fancy being in a battery, so we could help to shoot down German planes. Or we could ride motorbikes, delivering dispatches. Or we could drive lorries. We think we'd like to move around a bit.'

'It'll have to be the ATS, then,' Mrs Denham said. 'But

Frances, I'm not sure if Lady Ashford's very keen on lady soldiers? I can't imagine she'd want you to be one! What about your granny, Cassie? Didn't she want you out of danger's way?'

'Mrs Denham, could you write to Mummy?' Frances looked beseechingly at Rose Denham. 'She would listen to you. Maybe you'd write to Cassie's granny, too?'

'I should suggest you leave the safety of the farm, to go and risk your lives in ack-ack batteries, or driving through the blackout?'

'Well – '

'Oh, Fran, don't look at me like that!' Rose Denham smiled again and shook her head. 'I wasn't always old, you know,' she added. 'When I was your age, I wanted to have adventures, too.'

'So did you, Mrs Denham?' Frances asked.

'Yes, I became an army nurse,' Rose Denham told them. 'I served all over France, and then I went to Russia. Very well, I'll write to Cassie's granny and Lady Ashford later on tonight. But, if I were you, girls, I'd get your applications off right now. I dare say you've been to get the forms?'

'Well actually, Mrs Denham,' admitted Cassie, shamefaced, 'we got them yesterday.'

Frances came to work a few days later to report that Lady Ashford had taken to her bed, and also that her father was going on and on about their daughter being ungrateful and unkind.

But Lily Taylor's letter to Rose Denham was very fair and reasonable, considering the fuss that Cassie had been almost sure her grandmother would make. All Mrs Taylor said was that she'd like a visit from her granddaughter before she took her posting up, wherever it might be.

'You'll have time off for that, of course,' said Mrs Denham. 'Frances, when Cassie goes to see her granny, maybe you should go along, to keep her company?'

'Yes, Frances, come and meet my granny,' Cassie said. 'I'll take you to a café for a decent meal,' she added, after Mrs Denham had left the kitchen and gone to see her hens. 'We'll have some big, fat bangers, with a pile of mash. Or fish and chips. Or a piece of haslet. Or a nice pork pie.'

'They don't waste any time,' said Frances, showing Cassie the official-looking letter telling her to report for a medical on Monday week, at the army camp in Dorchester. 'I thought it would be ages before we got replies.'

'Well, there *is* a war on,' Cassie said. 'I've got a letter, too,' she added. 'So we'll ask Mrs Denham if she'll let us have next Monday off. If we do the milking, get the churns all ready for the lorry, then go and feed the chickens, we can scoot off and make a day of it. We could have our dinner in a café. Go to the flicks, perhaps.'

'What if we fail our medicals?' asked Frances. 'We won't feel like going to the cinema if we fail.'

'We'd better flipping pass then, hadn't we?' said Cassie. 'I'd like to go and see that film about the Battle of Britain, starring Dawn Adaire and Ewan Fraser. I think he's really cute.'

'He's married, actually, to Rob's and Stephen's sister,' Frances said to Cassie, and she grinned. 'Sorry, midget, he's been nabbed already.'

'He's Daisy Denham's husband?'

'Yes.'

'Why didn't you say?'

'I thought you knew. There's a photograph of him and Daisy in the sitting room. They're at a premiere or something, and they're dressed up to the nines. They're gazing at each other in that soppy sort of way that people do when they're in love.'

'I'll go and have another look some time.'

'It's from Robert,' Cassie said, opening the letter that came the following morning, just as they were going to feed the hens.

'What does it say?' asked Frances.

'You can read it, if you like.' Cassie passed the single sheet to Frances. 'He says he's bored, stuck in some camp in – Camberley, I think it is, his writing's bloody awful – and he can't wait to go back overseas. He's training new recruits and taking courses in explosives and in deto-something.'

'Detonating,' Frances told her, as she read the letter. 'He's learning about fixing charges, about laying wires and setting mines. Ooh look, Cass, he sends his love!' Frances grinned. 'I think he's getting serious.'

'Oh, don't be daft,' said Cassie, reddening. 'Love from whatsisname, it's just what people say in letters. So have you heard from Steve?'

'Yes, I had a postcard, a couple of days ago.' Frances shrugged. 'Cassie, we're just friends. I do like Stephen, very much, but I know he doesn't fancy me.'

'Or he might think you wouldn't fancy *him*, now he's sort of – after he got hurt.'

'I met Stephen long before he ever joined the army, let alone got hurt, and he's always treated me like a sister. It's never going to change.'

'You don't know that, and anyway – '

'Just leave it, Cass – all right?'

'We both passed, Mrs Denham,' Frances told Rose Denham, one week later when the letters came.

'You're both A1?' asked Mrs Denham.

'Frances is A1, but they've told me I've got to try to put some weight on, and I have to get my teeth fixed. I need a couple of fillings,' muttered Cassie, probing a back cavity with her tongue. 'The army dentist's going to do them. I've never had a filling. What's it like, Fran? Do you know?'

'It's agony,' said Frances. 'The dentist has this great big drill, he tips your head back, and it feels like somebody or something is boring through your brain. It's – '

'It's nothing, Cassie,' said Rose Denham. 'The dentist gives you an injection first, to dull the pain, and so it doesn't hurt at all. Frances, don't be mean.'

'Sorry,' said Frances, grinning.

'Just you wait,' said Cassie, narrowing her eyes.

'We have to report for basic training as soon as you can spare us, Mrs Denham,' went Frances. 'We've got to do a six week course, then we'll be posted somewhere.'

'I suppose I'll have to write to those two girls in Devon,' said Mrs Denham, sighing. 'I hope they haven't found other jobs just yet.'

But Rose Denham's grey eyes sparkled brightly, and Cassie could see that she wished she was going with them, to have some adventures of her own.

Robert was sick and tired of Camberley.

Once he'd convinced the army he was fighting fit again, he had expected to be sent back overseas. Instead, they'd sent him to a training camp, given him three dozen new recruits, and ordered him to turn them into soldiers.

So he was spending all his time in drilling, marching, getting a bunch of idiot civilians to listen to orders yelled at them by red-faced sergeant-majors, and to obey these orders without thinking.

It was as bad as training land girls, but none of the

recruits was anything like as pretty as a land girl. Or as one particular land girl, anyway.

He hadn't meant to fall for Cassie. He still didn't quite know how it had happened. When she had been tossed by Caesar, maybe? When she hadn't made a fuss? When she'd got up the following morning, obviously aching everywhere, and with a lump as big as a Jaffa orange on her head, but carried on as normal?

Or when he'd found her hoeing in the vegetable garden, humming to herself and looking so contented as she worked? When she'd looked up and smiled at him, the late evening sun reflected in her gorgeous violet-blue eyes?

He'd signed the letter he had sent to Cassie with his love. Maybe, on reflection, that hadn't been very wise?

Well, it was too late now.

Cassie and Frances had signed all the forms, and so it was too late to back out now. They were in the army, and there for the duration.

The basic training came as a big shock. The girls were up at crack of dawn, to do PT in cotton vests and hideous khaki army bloomers, while squads of male recruits stood gawping, leering or passing ribald comments, until their sergeants yelled at them and threatened to put the buggers on a charge.

Endless uniform and kit inspections, square-bashing and more PT filled up the weary days, and Cassie fell into her bunk each night exhausted, dead to the world until reveille woke the company up the following morning.

But by the third week of their training, Cassie was feeling better and fitter than she ever had in all her life. While working on the farm, she'd started to develop a bit of muscle tone, and these days she was very pleased to see her skinny sparrow legs were shaping up a bit, and that she seemed to have a sight more bosom now she'd learned to stand up straight and tall.

Well, taller, anyway.

Thanks to the army dentist, she could now chew her food effectively. Thanks to the army hairdresser, her fair hair looked much glossier and less straw-like now she had had a decent permanent wave.

When their mid-course leave came up, they arranged to go to Birmingham. 'Mummy says I'm insane,' said Frances, as they stood on the station platform waiting for the train. She smoothed down the lapels of her new uniform, and fiddled with her hair, which she'd had cut short and now curled softly round her ears.

'Mummy's probably right,' said Cassie, grinning. 'You should have stayed at Melbury, milking cows and feeding chickens and being bored out of your mind.'

The train came roaring in. They got a whole compartment to themselves. Mrs Denham had made a cake to take to Cassie's granny, and Cassie put the box up on the rack.

'Of course you're not insane, you're patriotic.' As Frances frowned and chewed her lower lip, Cassie jerked the leather strap that held the window closed, and let in some fresh air. They sat back in their seats and looked at one another, and then they burst out laughing.

'We've escaped,' said Cassie.

'We're going to have adventures,' giggled Frances.

'The war's as good as won.'

Cassie took out a pack of Passing Clouds, tossed a cigarette up in the air, and then she caught it neatly in her mouth, a trick she'd learned from Robert. 'You want to watch it, Adolf. *We're* in the army now!'

When they arrived in Birmingham at last, it was a novelty for Cassie to see Frances Ashford looking so bewildered.

Cassie was used to picking her way through streets of damaged houses, broken pavements and flattened factories. But Frances had never heard a bomb go off, let alone seen what bombs could do, first hand.

'You see, you country bumpkins had it easy,' Cassie said to Frances as she took her friend along the roads where she had lived most of her life. In Redland Street, there were some houses missing, and only six or seven were still unscathed.

'Yes,' she continued, as Frances stared in horror, 'you lot watch the newsreels at the flicks, and listen to the wireless, and you all say how dreadful, bleedin' Jerry, stuff like that. But you don't smell the burning. You don't feel the terror when the planes come over, and start dropping bombs on you.'

'You're right,' said Frances, quietly. 'You people in the cities, you've all been so brave.'

'It's not like we had much choice,' said Cassie.

'I wonder where they'll post us, Cass?'

'Oh, right in the thick of it, I shouldn't wonder.' Cassie shrugged her shoulders. 'If we volunteer for ack-ack training, we'll be going to Portsmouth, Wolverhampton, Coventry – somewhere nice and dangerous like that. Here we are then, home sweet home. You'd better brace yourself.'

'But what – '

'You'll see.' Cassie got out her key. But as she put it in the lock, the front door opened, and there was Lily Taylor on the threshold, with tears in her eyes.

'Hello, Granny.' Cassie hugged her granny tightly, told her not to cry, and then stood back to look at her with Frances Ashford's eyes. She saw a bird-boned, grey-haired woman in a snow-white apron, a neat, dark blouse and skirt, and carpet slippers on her arthritic feet. 'Fran, this is my granny.'

'Good afternoon, Mrs Taylor.' Frances smiled. 'I do hope you're well?'

'I'm middling, miss, just middling, that's all.' Lily shook Frances Ashford's proffered hand. 'It's nice to meet you, and it's very good of you to come with my Cassandra. Well, girls, don't just stand there on the doorstep, like cheese at fourpence ha'penny. Come into the parlour.'

'Welcome to the holy of holies,' whispered Cassie softly, pulling a wry face.

'I beg your pardon?' Frances frowned.

'Oh, come on,' said Cassie, and dragged her friend inside.

It hadn't changed a bit. In spite of all the bombing, which shook other people's precious ornaments off their shelves and brought their plaster down, Cassie saw Lily Taylor's house looked just as it had always looked for nearly twenty years.

A gallery of religious pictures covered all the wall space, and on every surface stood statuettes of saints and martyrs, holy water flasks, small shrines and rosaries. 'My gran's a Holy Joe,' mouthed Cassie, shrugging as Frances stared.

'What do you think, miss?' Lily Taylor asked, brushing some invisible specks of dust off two little statues of the Virgin Mary and Saint Bernadette, which she'd been sent from Lourdes.

'It's very nice,' said Frances.

'Come into the back, miss,' Lily said, and Cassie rolled her eyes.

The little room behind the parlour was a shrine to Cassie's mother. There were brown-tinged photographs of Geraldine from when she was a baby until when she was a bride. There were clothes and personal possessions, brushes and combs and dolls and books and trinkets.

There were First Communion cards and brittle, faded nosegays, spill tins she had covered with patterned paper, and papier-mâché egg cups she had made.

Cassie had heard the story so many, many times, and now

she braced herself, knowing she'd soon be hearing it once more. How widowed Lily Taylor's only child, the beautiful and pious Geraldine, was courted by an older gentleman of independent means, who'd walked into the sweet shop where Geraldine was working, and been smitten.

How she'd become engaged to marry him, and how they'd had a quiet but lovely wedding at St Saviour's Roman Catholic Church, just up the road. Then they'd moved into a house in Bromsgrove, and a few months later Geraldine was expecting their first child.

But just before the baby came, its father had cleared off. It turned out he was married to someone else. He had a wife and family in Halifax, or so the police had told them. He'd been had up for bigamy once already, in 1917. But, added Lily, and this was the worst blow of all, he was not a Catholic.

Geraldine had died a few days later, giving birth. 'But it was the shame that killed my daughter,' Lily said to Frances, dabbing at her eyes.

The baby lived, and was baptised Cassandra, the name her mother had chosen for it if she had a daughter. She'd always had her nose in books, said Lily, and she'd probably found the baby's name in one of those.

Broken-hearted, Lily had found her personal tower of strength in Father Riley. The local priest assured her that her daughter's soul was in no danger of the everlasting fire.

'But that dirty Protestant – he'll burn in hell for all eternity,' Lily added, fiercely. 'No offence to you, miss, if you're one of them yourself – a Protestant, I mean,' she went on quickly. 'I'm old enough to know there's good and bad in everyone. Like that Mrs Lee from down the road, she's a Presbyterian from Belfast, but a nicer, kinder sort of woman you couldn't hope to meet.'

'Granny, shall we have some tea?' asked Cassie. 'Look,

we've brought a cake, with real eggs inside it, and real strawberry jam, and there's a bit of sugar on the top.'

'Your granny's sweet,' said Frances, as they sat on the tram going back into the city centre where they would catch their train.

'Sweet but crazy.' Cassie's grin was wry. 'She prays to the Virgin every day to keep her house from harm. She hasn't bought it yet, so now she reckons there's a holy brolly over 40 Redland Street, protecting it from twenty-pounders and incendiaries.'

'I didn't know you were a Roman Catholic,' went on Frances. 'When you were at Melbury, you came to the village church with us, and now you're in the army, you go to church parade with all the Church of England lot. I didn't think Roman Catholics went to other people's churches.'

'I don't know if I am a Roman Catholic any more,' said Cassie, sighing heavily. 'I don't know what to make of all that holy water and holy pictures stuff. Quite honestly, I just don't know if I believe in any God at all. But now you've seen my granny and where I came from, you'll understand why it would never work with Rob and me.'

'Why do you say that?'

'Oh, for heaven's sake, Frances!' Cassie cried. 'He's an officer, I'm a private. He's a toff and I grew up in squalor in a city slum. He's Church of England and I'm a Roman Catholic. Well, I am in theory, anyway.'

'So?' said Frances. 'None of that would matter to me, and if I happen to meet a lovely Catholic chap myself – '

'Your parents would disown you. I reckon they should be prosecuted, Fran. It's nothing short of criminal, having a child, and letting her grow up to be as ignorant as you.'

'What do you mean by that?'

'I don't suppose you know what people do to get a baby?'

'Well, as a matter of fact, I do,' said Frances huffily. 'Robert and Stephen told me years ago. Their mother explained it all to them, and they explained to me. Mrs Denham might be very strict, and I agree she looks a bit old-fashioned, but in some ways she's extremely modern.'

They arrived back at the barracks just before their passes were going to run out. Frances was finding it quite hard, thought Cassie, sharing a wooden barrack hut with thirty other girls, most of them from backgrounds very similar to Cassie's own. So while Cassie got on well with all the other women, they mocked Frances and her accent, and called her Lady Muck.

'Don't take any notice,' Cassie said, whenever Frances got upset. 'That Doreen Jackson, who was teasing you for being posh, she came back from leave last week with lice as big as blow-flies. They'll have her in the fumigation unit when they notice.'

'But they've *all* got it in for me,' wailed Frances.

'No, they haven't, Frances, don't be such a mardy baby. Just try to go along with them and you'll be fine, you'll see.'

Cassie grinned encouragingly. 'The officers have noticed you're a nob. Soon, you'll be getting your first stripe. Then you'll be off to train to be an officer yourself, and you'll be able to put the likes of Jackson in the glass-house. You can get her cleaning the latrine block with a toothbrush, or scrubbing lumps of coal.'

'But they all tease me when I kneel down at night to say my prayers,' said Frances sadly.

'Just glare back at the bitches, that's what I would do,' said Cassie firmly. 'Then say your prayers as normal.'

'It's all right for you.'

But with Cassie to buck her up and to assure her she was doing fine, Frances managed to cheer up a bit. When Doreen Jackson started mocking her again, Frances said that Doreen should go and boil her head – or dunk it in some paraffin, at least – and all the others laughed.

'I wonder where we're going to be posted?' Cassie asked, on the day that they were due to finish their basic training.

'Anywhere, the sergeant says.' Frances looked at Cassie anxiously. 'Cassie, I do hope we'll be together.'

'We've both asked for battery or drivers' courses,' Cassie reminded Frances. 'So with a little bit of luck we might be.'

They went to get their post.

'Some holy medals from my granny,' said Cassie, shaking the envelope to make it clink. 'A letter from Father Riley to remind me to stay pure – '

'Who's the third one from?'

'I dunno,' said Cassie, going red but grinning – she couldn't help herself. When she heard from *him*, it made her day.

'What does he say?' asked Frances.

'The usual stuff – he's bored, he's tired of drilling, marching, training new recruits, and he can't wait to go back overseas. But before he does – '

'He what?'

'He wants to see me.'

'Does he?' Frances beamed. 'I told you so!'

'You didn't.'

'Yes, I did,' said Frances. 'So, when are you going to meet, and where?'

'He's hoping he can get some leave quite soon, and asks if I could go to London.'

'So write back and tell him yes, you could!'

Chapter Six

'He needn't think I'll jump through hoops for *him*,' said Cassie, as she and Frances got their breakfast porridge from the cookhouse counter, three days later.

'Quite right, Cass – why should you?' Frances said.

But Cassie didn't miss her grin. 'If he *does* get leave,' she added crossly, 'how would I get to London, anyway?'

'I don't suppose you could hitch a lift, or catch a train, or something?' Frances shrugged. 'It's not as if you're dying to see him, is it?'

'No,' lied Cassie, but she knew she was blushing as she carried off her tray.

'What's all this, then?' asked a girl from Swansea, reaching for the salt and looking curiously at Cassie. 'Why are you all red?'

'Cassie's got a date, but she's pretending she doesn't want to go,' said Frances, starting on her porridge.

'Who's the bloke?'

'He's a lieutenant in the Royal Dorsets.'

'She's going with an officer? Ooh, my word, there's posh!' The girl pushed up the end of her snub nose, and all the others sniggered.

'After *he's* had his hands inside your drawers, you won't be speaking to the likes of us,' put in her friend.

'You two had your postings yet?' enquired another girl.

'We're both off to driving school,' said Cassie, relieved to change the subject.

'In Luton,' added Frances. 'It's a three day course. They're desperate for ATS to drive the army's lorries.'

'They reckon you can learn to drive a lorry in three days?'

'It can't be very difficult,' said Cassie. 'You just go backwards, forwards – '

'Then you drive into a ditch!'

On an airstrip outside Luton, twenty ATS girls from various army barracks all around the country stood on the tarmac in the morning mist, eyeing four Bedford trucks parked side by side, a hundred yards away.

'Any of you lovely ladies ever driven before?' enquired the grim-faced sergeant instructor, scowling at them all in obvious scorn.

'Yes, I have, Sergeant Brent,' said Frances promptly. 'I've driven Daddy's Morris since I was seventeen. I can drive an Austin van, as well.'

'Oh, I say, can you really, Lady Muck?' The sergeant grinned, and Frances blushed bright red. 'Maybe you'll end up teaching me a few things I don't know.'

'Sarcastic bugger, take no notice,' whispered Cassie.

'Who asked your opinion, Fairy Fay?' Sergeant Brent glared angrily at Cassie. 'You speak with my permission, understood? Otherwise, you button it. I dunno why they've sent you here, I'm sure. You're far too short to see out of a lorry. You'll look like bloody Chad in that cartoon, tryin' to see over that brick wall.'

'We can sit her on a cushion, sarge,' the corporal standing beside the sergeant said, and he winked at Cassie conspiratorially.

'Jesus, give me strength,' the sergeant muttered. 'All right, girls, this way. Quick march, at the double, pick your feet up. Shoe leather costs money, so don't wear it out by scrapin' it along the road. Whoever taught you shower to march, was they a cripple, too?'

Cassie pulled a face behind his back.

'This thing here's a truck,' said Sergeant Brent, slapping

a Bedford lorry on the bonnet. 'Inside, you got the steerin' wheel, an' gears an' brakes an' stuff. Outside, you got the engine. You have to make 'em all co-operate.'

Cassie listened carefully, determined not to fuck it up as the sergeant confidently predicted they all would. She was put in Corporal Benson's group and, when it was her turn behind the wheel, she found to her relief that she could reach the pedals – just.

As Corporal Benson climbed into the cab, she tapped the pedals lightly with her shoe, getting the feel for where they were – accelerator, brake, she thought, accelerator, brake, and don't get them mixed up.

'Now, if you're sitting comfortably, just put her into first,' the corporal said, and lit a casual cigarette. 'Clutch right down, your other foot on the gas, then ease the gear stick to your left. Just push it, love – don't shove.'

Cassie put her foot down on the clutch, engaged the gears, released the hand brake and prayed to the God she didn't know if she believed in: make the bastard move.

The bastard did.

'The fairy's done all right today, and Lady Muck's not bad, but the rest of you are bleeding hopeless,' said the sergeant, at the end of a long twelve-hour session that had left some girls in tears. The Bedford trucks had had their paint scraped off, their gears ground down to iron filings, and the rubber burned off all their tyres.

'Grayson, Taylor, Lucas, Ashford, Penfold – you'll report for duty again tomorrow morning, six o'clock, an' no one's to be late. We've got a war to win. The rest of you are useless, so I'm getting shot of you before you cause a fatal accident. Or bugger one of the army's precious lorries, which would be ten times worse.'

'We did it!' As Cassie and Frances fell out with the others, and walked towards the hut where they'd be sleeping while they did the course, they grinned at one another.

'But we've got to strip an engine down tomorrow morning,' said Frances doubtfully.

'So, how hard can it be?' Cassie shrugged and smiled encouragingly. 'I know all there is to know about engines, anyway. I used to help to make them. Well, I made them for tanks. I don't suppose a lorry's very different.'

It wasn't, and Cassie got on very well. By the end of the intensive three-day course, Sergeant Brent had laryngitis and Corporal Benson said he was putting in for a transfer to the Catering Corps, but all the girls had passed. Now they'd be sent off to another army camp, to train to be army drivers, couriers, chauffeurs, driving anything from motorbikes to three ton army trucks.

'Well, are you going?' Frances asked, when Robert wrote again and said he'd finally got some leave from Camberley.

So could Cassie get away and spend a couple of days in London? She could stay with his sister, Daisy Denham, and her husband Ewan Fraser, in Park Lane.

'You mean she's going to stay with Daisy Denham?' asked Jess Penfold, when Frances told the others all about it – that Cassie was going to London to see Daisy's little brother, and would meet his actress sister, and her famous film star husband, too.

'You mean *the* Daisy Denham?' demanded Alice Lucas. 'The one who's in those London shows?'

'Yes, I suppose,' said Cassie carelessly.

'You lucky cow!' cried Linda Grayson.

'Cass, get me her autograph?' asked Alice.

'All right,' said Cassie, yawning.

But inside, she was scared.

This was all too much.

She was really dying to see Robert. She'd stopped bothering to deny it. But she had never been to London, and she'd never met anybody famous. As for actresses – weren't they really bitchy, didn't they lie in bed until mid-day, didn't they get divorced every five minutes?

'Cassie Taylor, the CO wants to see you, now.' A corporal tapped her on the shoulder, shaking her out of her worried daydream. 'Leave your porridge.'

Cassie was marched across the parade ground, trying to work out what she'd done wrong – had Corporal Benson grassed on her for cheek? Or had her overalls been dirty? Or had she let her hair grow so it brushed her jacket collar? Or were her badges less than shining bright?

'Good morning, Private Taylor.' As Cassie stood to attention on the lino, quaking in her shoes, the army captain looked up from his desk.

He smiled at Cassie kindly. 'Stand at ease,' he said. 'Thank you, Corporal Howard, you needn't stay. Well, Private Taylor, I've heard great things of you, and you're in line for your first stripe.'

'Congratulations, you deserve it,' Frances said, and grinned.

'Jolly well done, Cassie.' Alice patted Cassie on the shoulder.

'You were the best of all of us,' said Jess.

'So you'll soon be off, then?' Linda asked.

'Yes, it looks like it,' said Cassie, wondering where she'd put her sewing kit. She was sure she'd left it on the night-stand. Some thieving so-and-so must have borrowed it.

'Where will you be going?' Alice asked.

'Aldershot,' said Cassie.

'That's not too far from Camberley or London,' Frances told Cassie, beaming. 'So even if you find you can't get any leave, Robert will be able to get himself to Aldershot to see you.'

'Do you think he might?'

'He'll be there,' said Frances. 'I would put money on it.'

Later on that day, when she and Cassie were by themselves, Frances coughed and cleared her throat, like people often did when they had something difficult to say.

'Listen, Cassie,' she said impressively, 'you will be nice to Robert, won't you? I mean, you won't be smart with him? Or laugh at him? He'll be going away, remember, and he might get killed. He likes you very much – '

'Well, Fran – there's nice and nice,' said Cassie. 'I'm not going to be so nice to Robert that I end up like my mother. It would kill my granny.'

Cassie arrived in Aldershot on a damp June evening.

The train was very late. Mid-way through the journey, the engine had packed up, so it had had to be towed off, and it had been ages before a new one came. The passengers had been stuck in a siding for three hours or more. They were desperate for a cup of tea, but had to make do with smoking, playing cards, and looking at each other.

Now, glancing at the station clock, Cassie saw she'd been expected at the local barracks hours ago.

The other passengers were civilians, and they were all going into town. It didn't look as if she'd get a chance to cadge a lift. So she asked a porter for directions, was told about a short cut that would take a mile off her walk, and then she set off on her own.

Shouldering her kitbag, she started slogging down the road between high, flowering hedges, enjoying the sweet scents of summer, but longing for her supper.

It was almost dark. Moths were fluttering softly round her head, bats swooped low to dart at flying insects, and ahead of her she saw a family of rabbits sitting boldly in the road, the young ones playing while their elders nibbled at the verge.

All was peace and beauty. She couldn't believe she'd once been happy living in a city, breathing dust and smoke, without a single blade of grass in sight.

'Carry your kitbag, miss?'

Startled, she turned to see a tall, broad figure a yard or two behind her, his cigarette glowing red and threatening in the deepening twilight.

'It – it's all right, I can manage,' stammered Cassie, clutching at her kitbag nervously.

But now, the empty countryside was suddenly a place of fear and dread. At once, the rabbits scattered, disappearing in the undergrowth. Cassie hoped she was getting near the barracks, where somebody might hear her yell if this bloke tried it on.

'Oh, don't be so daft. Come on, let's have it.'

The man reached for her kitbag, and Cassie was about to kick him hard where it would hurt, when the yellow moon lit up his features, and she saw he was grinning.

'Rob, you stupid bugger!' She glared at him in fury, angry that he'd made her panic, thrilled to see him, knowing she must be blushing like a pillar box, and ready to take a proper swing at him. 'How long have you been following me?'

'Since you left the station. I'd been in the buffet all day long, waiting for your train. But then, when you got off, I'd gone across the road to buy another pack of cigarettes, and so I missed you. A porter said he'd seen an ATS girl, she'd marched off up the road all by herself, so I hoped she'd be you.'

'How did you know I'd come today?'

'Frances wrote and told me.'

'Bloody Frances!' Cassie cried, vowing that when they met again, she'd settle Frances Ashford's interfering hash once and for all. 'Why can't she keep her nose out of my business?'

'You know Frances,' Robert said, smiling and hefting Cassie's kitbag. 'What the hell is in here, Cass? A hundred tins of spam?'

'All my stuff, and spares for a motorbike the sergeant back in training camp asked me to take for him.'

'They weigh a ton,' said Robert, frowning. 'Lazy sod, he should have had them properly requisitioned, then sent them down by train – not asked a little thing like you to carry them for him.'

Robert and Cassie walked along the road. Now, Cassie was very glad there was nobody else about, that there was no sign of the barracks, that the only artificial light was from the glow from Robert's cigarette, and that there was a moon.

'How have you been getting on?' asked Robert. 'Fran said you were doing really well, that you were the star student on your course, and that you passed out top.'

'She did all right herself,' said Cassie, blushing.

'So now you'll be based in Aldershot? You're going to be a driver?'

'Yes, that's what it looks like.'

'Excellent,' said Robert, and he laughed. 'As soon as I'm a colonel, I'll put in a request for Private Taylor to drive me all around. Then we can go on secret expeditions.'

'It's Lance Corporal Taylor now, if you don't mind!' cried Cassie, mortally affronted. 'Look – I've got a stripe.'

'My goodness, so you have.' Robert smiled, and then reached out to trace the single chevron sewn on Cassie's sleeve. 'Well done, you're a clever girl.'

'I'm going to be a sergeant soon, you wait and see.'

'I'm sure you will.' Robert's palm slid down the rough material of Cassie's khaki jacket, and then he took her hand. He pulled her round to face him. 'But I think we've been waiting long enough.'

He put her kitbag down on to the road.

He threw his cigarette away, and then he took her in his arms, wrapping her inside his army greatcoat so that she was warm against his chest.

Cassie raised her face to his, and to his delight she let him kiss her on the temples, then the mouth, following his lead at first, letting him demand and set the pace.

But very soon she was demanding on her own account, putting her hand behind his head and kissing him herself, encouraging him to kiss her harder, pulling him closer, closer, closer, until he could feel her body pressing up against him, tantalising him.

'You smell delicious, Cass,' he said, as he entwined his fingers in her hair.

'It's just Amami setting lotion, everybody uses it.' Cassie smiled seductively at him. 'You smell gorgeous, too,' she said. 'I love the smell of cigarettes on men.'

'I smoke too much. It makes me cough and wheeze, but I find I can't do without a fag.'

'Well, you don't need one now,' said Cassie, kissing him again.'

She was right – he didn't need anything but Cassie now. But, even though she was exciting him, even though he knew he hadn't felt like this before, he also knew he had to stop himself before things went too far.

'We must get you to barracks,' he said softly, as he let her go, reluctantly but knowing he had no choice.,

He found her cap, which had been knocked off and landed upside-down in a deep ditch. He straightened Cassie's jacket, brushing his hands across her chest, which made him want to kiss her more, to kiss and kiss forever.

'I suppose so,' Cassie said.

She knew her speech was slurred. She must be drunk, she

thought, but not with alcohol, with happiness. She couldn't help the silly little smile that played around her mouth. She didn't want to lose this lovely, floating feeling.

'Come on, love, duty calls.' Robert picked up her kitbag. 'They'll be wondering what's become of you. They'll know the train's come in, and soon they'll be sending out the redcaps, to search in all the bushes.'

'You're so flipping organised,' slurred Cassie, as she smoothed her skirt, and tucked her hair behind her ears.

Then it began to rain, and with the downpour she came back to reality. 'All right, Rob,' she said bitterly, 'I get it. You've had your bit of early evening fun, so now I can bugger off to barracks. You'll go back to London, have a pint or two, go picking up some other bird – '

'I'll go back to London, certainly, but I won't be picking up some bird, as you so elegantly put it.' Then Robert took his greatcoat off, and draped it over Cassie's narrow shoulders. 'Come on, Cass. You'll get soaked, and so will I. We need to get you to the barracks, and out of all this rain.'

Robert took her hand and started walking, so Cassie was obliged to go with him.

Chapter Seven

'Jesus Christ, look what the cat dragged in,' said the NCO on duty, grimacing as Cassie appeared at the guardroom door, soaking wet and shivering in the twilight. 'Where've you been till this time, eh? We was expecting you at three o'clock this afternoon.'

'She was delayed.' Robert loomed out of the murk, dumped Cassie's kitbag on the guardroom floor, and then stood there dripping on the clean cement. 'Lance Corporal Taylor is attached to Transport Corps,' he added, as the startled NCO came briskly to attention. 'You'll need someone to take her to her quarters.'

'Yes, sir,' rapped the guardroom sergeant, as he saluted Robert, but managed to give the pair of them a dirty look, as well.

A minute later, Cassie was being marched across the square, lugging her heavy kitbag. She glanced over her shoulder, anxious to see if Robert was still there. She couldn't make him out, so she supposed he must have gone. He'd have a long, wet hike back to the station.

But what on earth had she been doing, smooching in the darkness with him, when she was on duty? If this was what men did to you, she thought, if they made you lose all track of time and totally forget yourself, she didn't wonder girls got caught, that girls had little accidents. She must make sure he didn't catch her off her guard again.

'So you're an officer's floozy, eh?' the corporal muttered, as he marched Cassie to her wooden hut. 'I know your sort. Officers' groundsheets, right? The ATS is full of girls like you, too stuck up to go with blokes like us.'

Cassie didn't comment.

'You deaf as well as dumb, then?' The corporal sniffed in scorn. 'You ain't goin' to like it 'ere, milady,' he continued. 'The girls in your block, they're all really rough – a load of thieves and tarts. They'd slit your throat for half a crown.'

Oh, don't you worry, corporal, I know rough, thought Cassie, although she didn't think it wise to say.

He hadn't seen the street where she'd grown up. He hadn't seen the teenaged tarts who'd slouched and smoked in doorways, seen the gangs of kids who'd wrestle you to the pavement, yank your shoes off, then sell them down the market for a couple of bob.

If it hadn't been for Lily Taylor, she'd have been a thief or tart herself.

In spite of what the corporal said, Cassie soon made friends and settled down.

'The girls I mess with are all right,' she wrote to Frances. 'There are lots of them from the big cities, and most grew up in little terraced cottages, like me. The drivers are all nobs, though. They drove Daddy's car before the war, and Daddy's chauffeur taught most of them to drive.

'But they're very interested in Rob, and it's all round the barracks that he met me at the station, walked me here, and then cleared off into the night.

'I've told them all he's Daisy Denham's brother. So he'd better introduce us, and I'd better get her autograph, or else my name here will be mud.'

She didn't manage to get any leave. But then, she thought, she'd only just been posted, and she couldn't expect it. All the same, she wished and wished and wished she could see Robert, hug him, kiss him, talk to him, and feel the warmth of him.

But her other self insisted it was best she didn't, that

nothing but hurt could come of it, that men like Robert Denham never meant what they said to girls like Cassie.

She had a few days' training, driving and stripping down the engines of the big black staff cars in which the senior officers got ferried round the country.

Then she was given her first job, taking a visiting colonel back to London, and bringing a brigadier to Aldershot the following morning, staying in a requisitioned billet overnight.

This could be her chance. She asked if she could spend the night with her mother's cousin who lived in Hammersmith, a place she'd heard of through the other drivers, and knew was part of London.

She was informed she could, provided she left the car itself in an army garage in Piccadilly, and was there herself at nine o'clock the following morning.

'So that would be perfect, if you could come to meet me. If you aren't too busy, or canoodling with other birds,' she wrote to Robert.

'All the birds are hiding in the bushes, so I suppose I must make do with you,' said Robert's postcard and, instead of being offended, Cassie found she was elated.

'This is stupid,' said her other self, as she washed her underwear in Lux flakes stolen from a driver who was off on leave, and as another girl, who had been a hairdresser in Civvy Street, Amami-waved her hair.

As she showered herself with someone else's Coty L'Aimant talc, and as she practised painting a perfect Cupid's bow with the hut corporal's lipstick, she told herself she was a fool.

Shut up, shut up, she told this other self.

On the morning she was going to London, she was up and smartly turned out hours before she had to leave, impressing both the visiting colonel and her own CO.

'Your first time in London, I believe. I hope you know the way?' the colonel asked as she saluted and as he stared at her legs.

'I have directions, sir,' she said politely.

'Then let's hope you can follow them.'

Cassie held the door open and the colonel got into the car. She put on her brand new driving gloves and then they drove away.

To her relief, the whole thing was a doddle. There was hardly any other traffic on the roads, and the colonel dozed most of the way, so she could concentrate on driving. Although the road signs had been taken down, she soon discovered the directions she'd been given were all excellent. She didn't lose her way.

The London traffic was a challenge, but she found most other vehicles gave way to the Humber, waving her through at junctions, and waiting patiently on the rare occasions that she stalled.

She dropped the colonel off at his HQ in Oxford Street, drove the big black car to Piccadilly, found the army garage down a side street, then walked to the Lyon's Corner House where Robert had suggested they could meet, and there she saw – the twins.

She hadn't expected it to be the twins.

But, as she thought about it, she realised Robert would want to see his brother before he went away. She felt mean and cruel for wishing Stephen wasn't there, especially when his face lit up as she walked up to them.

'Just look at you!' cried Stephen, who now jumped up and kissed her on the cheek, and then stood back to stare, amazed. 'Gosh, don't you look smart! You've filled out, as well. I honestly wouldn't recognise the skinny little urchin who turned up at the cottage – when was it, Rob? Six months ago?'

'At least.'

Then Robert smiled at Cassie, and her heart turned somersaults of joy. 'Come and sit down,' he added, standing up and pulling out a chair. 'Miss, may we have more coffee, and another plate of cakes?' he asked a passing waitress, who blushed and grinned at him.

'How are you getting on?' asked Stephen.

'Oh, I'm doing fine.' Cassie took a cake, a sorry-looking yellow thing, piped with ersatz cream and blobbed with runny, scarlet jam. 'I've passed lots of tests, and now I'm driving lorries, jeeps and staff cars.'

'You're a marvel, aren't you?' Robert shook his head. 'You learned to drive in what was it, a fortnight?'

'It was three days, to be exact,' said Cassie carelessly, as she licked the jam off her cream cake.

'That's even more astonishing, and now they're letting you drive the army's most expensive vehicles into London.' Robert picked up another cake himself. 'You didn't have any little prangs?' he added, grinning wickedly.

'No, I did not!'

'Put in a request to come to London, and then you can drive me,' suggested Stephen. 'Since I got my head bashed in and go doolally sometimes, they won't let me drive myself.'

'I saw her first,' said Robert, as he draped one arm round Cassie's shoulders. 'When I'm a colonel, Steve, she's going to drive *me*.'

'We'll toss for it,' said Stephen. 'We – '

'Shut up, Steve,' said Robert, 'and have another cake.'

They drank their coffee, ate their cakes, then Robert said it was time to go and see Daze, who was expecting them for dinner.

Dinner?

Cassie's heart began to pound. This is where I muck it up, she thought. She was all right, sitting in a café with the twins, with lots of other, ordinary people. But now, she was going to meet their famous sister, and she would be out of her depth, she knew it.

She should not have come. She didn't know how to behave with nobs. She wouldn't like nob food. She wouldn't know which fork to use for what. She knew she'd be so nervous that half her dinner would end up in her lap, and there would be loads of stuck-up servants who would sneer.

But Rob and Steve were getting up and putting on their hats. They linked their arms through hers, they took her into custody, and then they marched her off to meet her doom.

They soon reached a smart apartment building in Park Lane, sandbagged and heavily pock-marked from the effects of bombing, but an impressive mansion all the same.

They went inside and up some marble stairs.

When they rang the bell to the apartment, some old butler – or Cassie supposed the bloke must be a butler, since he was all dressed up like Charlie Chaplin in striped trousers and a tail coat – came to the door at once.

'Good afternoon, Mr Denham,' he began, 'and Mr Denham, too. Miss Denham is expecting you.'

'Hello, Mr Reeves. Come on then, Cass,' said Robert, taking Cassie's hand and pulling her inside the flat.

The butler took their hats and gloves, then led them to a vast and handsome sitting room, done out in pale wood, with a huge Turkey carpet on the floor. A pretty, fair-haired woman was sitting by the window, writing at a little desk.

'Hello, Daze.' Still holding Cassie's hand, Robert strode across the room, kissed his sister briefly on the cheek, then slumped on to a sofa, dragging Cassie down beside him. 'This is Cassie, Daze. She used to work for Mum at Melbury, but now she's in the ATS.'

'Good afternoon, Miss Denham.' Cassie struggled to her feet again, went over to Miss Denham, and held out her right hand.

'Good afternoon.' Miss Denham shook Cassie's proffered hand, and smiled at her politely. 'It's Daisy, please,' she said.

'Where's Fraser?' Stephen asked his sister.

'Oh, he's got a special matinee, but he'll be here for dinner,' said Daisy Denham calmly. 'Then I thought we'd all go to a club.'

Daisy stood up then and smoothed her smart tweed skirt, which Cassie could see had cost a lot of money. It fitted to perfection, and didn't sag at the back or round her knees. 'Cassie, do you like to dance?' she asked.

'I – er – yes, I love it,' faltered Cassie.

'Then you must dance with Ewan.' Daisy ruffled Robert's hair. 'Poor Ewan, he was hopeless when he was Robert's age, but now he's wonderful. So he'll be a better partner for you than this awkward lump.'

Robert made a face at Daisy.

Stephen helped himself to whisky from a glass decanter.

Robert put his feet up on the sofa, then told Stephen to pour him a whisky, too.

Cassie stood and stared.

'I expect you'd like to make yourself respectable?' said Daisy suddenly.

'Sorry?' Cassie jumped and thought, what's wrong with me – have I got something down my front, or have I smudged my lipstick?

But Daisy was already at the door, so Cassie followed her along a passage to the most gorgeous and luxurious bedroom she could have imagined, frilled and draped like something in a film.

'I do hope you'll be comfortable,' said Daisy, opening another door. 'Just through here's a shower, but if you wish to have a proper bath, the bathroom's down the passage.'

'It – it's all lovely, thanks.' Cassie put down her shoulder bag and gazed out of the window at a beautiful green park, which was these days one enormous vegetable patch, but made a pleasant outlook, all the same.

She hadn't known real people lived like this.

She had a wash in the luxurious shower room, marvelling at its golden dolphin taps and giant seashell of a porcelain basin. Then she put on more lipstick, combed her hair, and went to make a fool of herself at dinner.

But dinner didn't turn out to be so bad.

Daisy's famous film star husband hadn't yet appeared and, to Cassie's great relief, the food was recognisable as standard meat and vegetables – it wasn't something strange. Also, you could help yourself – you didn't get it dumped on to your plate.

There was just one servant, a woman dressed in black. She put all the dishes on the sideboard in the dining room, and then she disappeared. She'd had to go on fire-watching duty, Daisy said.

The butler had gone fire-watching too.

Robert and Stephen filled their plates, and Daisy talked and ate at the same time. No one seemed to care which fork you used.

Daisy had changed for dinner. She was looking beautiful, in a low-cut, dark red satin dress – far too posh for eating a bit of dinner in, thought Cassie. But Daisy was an actress, so perhaps she was allowed?

Then they heard the front door slam, and Daisy's husband walked into the room.

'Och, here's Macbeth at last,' said Stephen, grinning like a monkey and spitting out some crumbs.

'Hello, Ewan darling.' Daisy kissed the man, and he kissed Daisy, and Stephen made a face. 'Good matinee? I'm afraid the brats have come to cadge some dinner. But at least they've brought their pretty friend.'

Daisy's famous husband, Ewan Fraser, whom Cassie had

had a great big crush on since she was sixteen, turned out to be very nice, and very natural as well – not at all stuck up. He had bright red hair, a Scottish accent, and he smoked all through dinner, stubbing out his fag ends on his plate.

He too talked with his mouth full, telling them about his matinee, saying they'd had a decent house, whatever that might mean, and that some woman called Lizzie was divorcing Richard, and that Ewan wasn't surprised, because poor old Richard was a drunkard and a fool.

'Aye, the demon drink,' said Ewan, and shook his chestnut head. 'It's been the ruin of many a puir wee man.'

'God, you're such a Presbyterian hypocrite,' Stephen told him, knocking back some more of Ewan's whisky. 'You're always going on about – '

But he didn't finish, because now Ewan quelled him with a flash of his green eyes – the look which had the bad guys shivering and shaking in his films, and now shut Stephen up as well.

Ewan wasn't anything like the English toffs and nobs he often played in films. He talked so posh in films, and he must wear a wig in them, thought Cassie, or he must dye his hair.

'So, where do you come from, Cassie?' Ewan asked, his eyes still twinkling bright.

'Birmingham,' said Cassie, thinking blimey, can't you tell?

'I was once in rep in Birmingham,' said Ewan, blowing a perfect smoke ring. 'A filthy, dirty place it is, canals and smut and smoke and factories, as I recall. How did it manage to produce a bonny lass like you? I remember, back in '36 – '

'Oh Jesus Christ, he's off again – when I played with Noel Coward, when I kissed Vivien Leigh,' groaned Robert, helping himself to pudding, and putting the serving spoon down on the cloth.

'Where are we going tonight, Daze?' Stephen asked.

'We'll get a taxi to the Florida, but if no one interesting is there, we'll go to the 400,' Daisy told him.

'But Cassie hasn't got a frock,' said Robert.

'I could go in uniform, don't worry,' said Cassie hurriedly, for she was scared of being left behind.

'I think we ought to find you something, dress you up a bit,' said Daisy, standing up and holding out her hand. 'Come on, I must have something that will fit you. I know – there's my violet calf-length tulle. It will be full-length on you. The colour will match your eyes.

'Robert and Steve,' she added briskly, 'Mrs Jimp's not here, so you two do the washing up.'

'What, just us?' said Stephen.

'Why can't Fraser help?' demanded Robert.

'Because he pays for everything, you're a pair of parasites, and you've drunk all his whisky.' Daisy narrowed her eyes at both the twins. 'Come on, brats, jump to it.'

'Aye,' said Ewan, leaning back and lighting up again. 'Off you go now, boys – do as your sister tells you.'

Grumbling, Robert and Stephen began to clear away.

Cassie looked at herself in the glass and didn't believe her eyes. She looked so lovely, so sophisticated. She looked like a lady – like a toff, in fact – not like a Brummie slum kid from a street behind a tannery.

Daisy had zipped her into the blue dress, pulling it in under her bust, pinning and tacking to make it fit her like a second skin. She'd done Cassie's face and hair, painted her mouth and nails bright scarlet, and she'd found a pair of lovely high-heeled silver slippers, which she'd stuffed with cotton wool to make them fit her guest's small feet.

'I feel like Cinderella,' whispered Cassie, goggling at the amazing transformation in the dressing table mirror.

'You look very sweet.' Daisy surveyed her handiwork.

'You have good bones, your posture's excellent, and you have lovely eyes. If you wore your hair a little longer – you could put it up while you're on duty – and used a bit more make-up, you'd always look divine.'

Cassie blushed and looked down at her scarlet-varnished nails. 'It's very kind of you to dress me up,' she said. 'I mean, someone like you. I wouldn't expect it. I – '

'Someone like me?' repeated Daisy, frowning. Then she realised what Cassie meant, and laughed. 'Oh, you've got it wrong, love. I'm no lady. I'm a Cockney. I was born in Bethnal Green.'

'But I don't understand,' said Cassie, puzzled. 'You're Robert's sister, aren't you?'

'I'm adopted.' Daisy took Cassie's hand and helped her up. 'My mother wasn't married, and Mr and Mrs Denham took me in. Phoebe – she's my natural mother – she went to America when I was just a baby, and she lives in New York City now. I see her often, or at least I did, before the war. So Phoebe is my mother, but darling Rose will always be my mum.'

'How did you come to be an actress?'

'I'd always liked to sing and dance, and I was a proper little show-off when I was a child. I wanted everyone to look at me! When we left India and went to live in Dorset, I nagged and bullied Rose until she let me join a down-at-heel provincial theatre company, when I was fifteen.'

Daisy smiled and shook her head. 'Poor Rose and Alex. I was such a horrid brat, but they've always been the best of parents. Come along now, darling. We must go and show you to the boys.'

'Cass, you look unbelievable,' said Robert.

'You're like a princess in a fairy tale.' Stephen spun her round and made her billowing skirts fly out in clouds of gossamer and gauze. 'It never ceases to amaze me, how you girls can change your faces.'

'But I don't look all that different, do I?' Cassie asked them, anxious now.

'No, just much more beautiful,' said Ewan gallantly.

'Well, that's all thanks to Daisy, because she did my make-up.'

'Of course, old Daze knows all the tricks.' Robert picked up the evening wrap his sister had found for Cassie to borrow and put it round her shoulders. 'You smell delicious, too.'

'It's Arpège by Lanvin,' Daisy told him.

'I didn't think it was Vim,' said Robert, grinning. 'Let's go and show you off.'

'Stephen, love,' said Daisy, 'could you go and find a taxi?'

In the taxi, everyone was crammed up close together, and Cassie let herself dream for a moment, to imagine these good-looking, generous people were her real family.

The twins teased Daisy for a while, then made sarcastic comments about Ewan's latest film. This was some Elizabethan costume drama in which he had had to wear a velvet doublet, a codpiece and silk stockings.

'At least he has the legs for stockings,' Daisy told them, sticking up for Ewan.

'Yes,' said Stephen, grinning. 'The world will be a better place for seeing Fraser's knees.'

Ewan shook his head and lit an expensive-looking black cigar, glancing briefly at the twins as if they were a couple of scruffy little kids he'd caught stealing apples but couldn't be bothered to clip around the ears.

Then the conversation turned to Denham family matters, and Cassie pinned her own ears back.

'What's all this about Mum and Charton Minster?'

Robert asked his sister as they bounced and bumped over the potholes, and the taxi's mostly blacked-out headlamps threw narrow beams of silver on the dirty, rutted streets.

'Well, she wants to buy it back,' said Daisy. 'It's going to rack and ruin, the roof is falling in, but that sod who owns it won't pay for the repairs.'

Daisy shrugged inside her satin wrap. 'The kids who live there now are hopeless cases,' she continued. 'They're boys from prisons and reformatories, all of them bad lots. They're wrecking it inside, so Mrs Hobson told me. One of her grown-up children does some casual gardening there, and he's appalled at how the kids behave. But Mum thinks she could save the place.'

'But she can't afford to buy it, can she?' Robert put his arm round Cassie, hugged her tight, and Cassie snuggled warmly up against him.

'I was thinking I could help her out.' Daisy shrugged again. 'It's partly down to me she lost it in the first place.'

'But would she *let* you help her out?' asked Stephen. 'You've tried to give her money before, but she would never take it.'

'What would she do with Charton Minster, if she got it?' put in Robert.

'God only knows. Maybe she and Dad could go and live there.' Daisy lit a cigarette, inhaled and blew out smoke. 'It means a lot to Mum, and if she wants it, I'm going to see she gets it.'

'That's fighting talk, my darling.' Ewan Fraser hugged his wife. 'I know who I'd put money on. Well, chaps, it looks like this must be the Florida.'

They got out of the cab. Ewan paid the driver, and then they went inside the club. Cassie saw there were several girls in various forces' uniforms, but these looked like drab sparrows compared with those in evening gowns of emerald, ruby, gold. The men wore uniform or black, blending into the smoky background as the women swooped and fluttered, like so many birds of paradise.

Daisy and Ewan knew everyone, it seemed, and spent the first ten minutes walking round, kissing and being kissed. But then they got a table.

'Champagne, Cassie?' Robert took the bottle from the bucket and poured an ice-cold glassful.

'Not too much, Rob,' Daisy cautioned him. 'She isn't used to it.'

'Oh, don't be such a rotten spoilsport, Daze,' said Robert, frowning. 'Go on, Cassie, try it. Do you like it?'

'It's a bit like Tizer.' Cassie took another sip. 'I like the way the bubbles go up my nose.' Then she took a hearty swig, and giggled. 'Blimey, Rob, it's got a kick to it! But it's delicious.'

'That's my girl.' Robert topped up her glass, and from then on he kept it full, in spite of Daisy's frown.

After they had listened to a black girl in a gorgeous silver sheath dress singing jazz, Ewan said it was time to make a move, and that they should go on to the 400.

This turned out to be a dimly-lit and claustrophobic cavern, the walls of which were draped with blood red silk, with red plush seating and a wine red carpet. 'What do you think?' asked Stephen.

'It's very red,' said Cassie, hiccupping and giggling and wondering why she felt so very strange – floating outside herself and seeing lots of flashing colours, glittering lights. As she'd stumbled from the taxi, she'd been very glad to cling to Robert for support.

Now, she stared in wonder at the women, most of whom were laden down with jewels and wearing fabulous evening frocks. They danced with handsome officers, tossing back their perfumed hair and laughing at their escorts' jokes.

They sat at little tables lit by just one glowing candle, flirting while they drank champagne. This is what I want, thought Cassie. This is how I want to live.

Ewan didn't care how much he spent. He smoked the best Havanas, ordered bottle after bottle of champagne, and later there was caviar, served with ice on dainty little plates.

Cassie tried a mouthful. 'I don't think I like this,' she said, and puckered up her face. 'It's much too salty, and it's slimy. It makes me think of fish paste that's gone off.'

'Then we'll no' be wasting it on *you*,' said Ewan grimly, and took her plate away. But then he smiled to show he wasn't cross, and Cassie giggled back at him.

Cassie danced with Robert, Ewan and Stephen, and then some more with Robert.

Then the room began to spin.

'We need to put this girl to bed,' said Daisy, as Cassie slumped down next to her and yawned behind her hand.

'Yes, I'm really sleepy.' Cassie turned to Robert, fell against his chest, gazed up at him. 'Your sister says we have to go to bed.'

Stephen and Ewan stood up at once. 'Come on, Cass, let's get you home,' said Stephen.

'No, I don't want you and Ewan, I want to go with Robert,' Cassie told them, hanging on to Robert.

'Get her in a taxi, Rob, and take her home,' said Daisy. 'Mrs Jimp will be back now, and she'll put Cass to bed.'

So Robert picked up Cassie's wrap and then he helped her totter to the exit, holding tightly on to him.

The doorman found a taxi, and between them he and Robert helped a very drunk but merrily giggling Cassie into it. Robert was aware of thumps and bangs – a raid was going on somewhere – but all Cassie seemed to feel was happiness and calm.

She laid her head on Robert's shoulder, and he put his arm around her waist. 'Rob, I'm having such a lovely, lovely time,' she whispered, as she snuggled up to him and hiccupped. 'I've never been so happy in my life.'

'Oh, Cassie, you're so sweet,' said Robert, laughing.

'What's that supposed to mean?' demanded Cassie, frowning.

'You're sloshed, my darling.' Robert held her as the taxi lurched over the ruts and bumps. 'You're in the middle of dirty, dangerous London, in an air raid, but you're having a lovely, lovely time. You're sloshed, but very sweet.'

The flat was dark and chilly after the light and warmth of the 400. After he'd checked the blackout curtains, Robert put on some lights, and Cassie blinked because they were too bright.

'Got to go to bed,' she muttered as she kicked off Daisy's silver shoes, then staggered off along the passageway.

'Yes, you must,' said Robert, catching her as she fell against the dado rail and scraped her elbow painfully, then righting her again.

'Robert, you come with me.' Cassie wound her arms around his neck and kissed him on the mouth. 'Come and tuck me up and cuddle me?'

'Oh, Cass, I can't do that,' said Robert.

'Why not?' pouted Cassie.

'You don't know what you're asking me, that's why.'

'Of course I do.'

'Just the same, you need to sleep it off, all by yourself.'

'But I'll be so lonely.' Cassie rubbed herself against him, smiling up at him with big, round eyes. 'Robert, will you come and put my light on?'

'Yes, all right,' said Robert, then half-walked, half-carried Cassie to the bedroom.

'You'll have to help me get undressed,' she whispered.

'I'll see if Mrs Jimp is back from fire-watching yet, then she can help you into bed.'

'But I don't want Mrs Jimp,' sulked Cassie. 'Robert, the only one I want is you.'

Then Cassie sat or rather fell down on the bed. She flopped against the lacy pillows. 'Rob,' she whispered softly, 'will you take my stockings off for me?'

'You must take them off yourself.'

'But I can't,' said Cassie. 'You do it, Robert – please?'

So Robert did as Cassie asked him, rolling down her fine silk stockings, carefully turning them around her ankles so as not to ladder them, then slipping them off her feet. She had such tiny little feet, he noticed now, and the urge to kiss them was almost overwhelming.

But he didn't – couldn't – it would not be fair.

'I love you, Rob,' said Cassie, as he stroked her ankle. 'I love you more than anything.'

'Oh, sweetheart.' Robert sighed. He smoothed her hair back from her forehead. 'I've been such a fool. I shouldn't have made you drink all that champagne. You've gone a really ghastly shade of green. I think we need to get you to the bathroom.'

'Why?'

'You're going to be sick.'

Chapter Eight

Cassie couldn't remember very much about what happened next that evening. She had some vague, embarrassing recollections of being in a cold, white bathroom, making awful noises, and then of someone putting her to bed.

Later on, she must have dozed a while, she thought, because she woke up lying in a little pool of dribble. Both of her eyes were glued together with mascara, and she felt very ill.

The blackout curtains were still closed, but the bright morning sun had somehow found its way between the curtains and the window sill, and a shaft of light had sliced the room in two. The tiny gilt alarm clock on the bedside table said the time was half past eight.

'Holy Mother of God!' Cassie started up, fell out of bed, scrambled to her feet again and grabbed her army uniform, which – thank you, Blessed Virgin – someone had put neatly on a hanger and hung up from a hook behind the door.

She tore off Daisy's crumpled evening dress, and started pulling on her shirt and skirt and horrid lisle stockings, fastening her suspenders and buttoning her jacket.

But – Holy Mother – where had she left her cap? On the sofa in the sitting room? Or had the butler hung it on the hallstand when he'd hung up Rob's and Steve's? Please, God, let it be there!

'What's all the rush?' asked Daisy's husband, who was in the dining room, reading the morning paper, eating toast and drinking coffee. Ewan was in uniform today. Perhaps he was in ENSA? 'Sit down, Cassie,' he continued calmly. 'What would you like for breakfast?'

'I ought to be in Piccadilly! I have to take a bridagier

to Alsherdot. Please, is there any coffee?' she gabbled, wondering why she felt so bloody awful and couldn't seem to make her words come out the way they should – was she sickening for something, maybe? Did she have any spots?

'A bridagier, eh?' Ewan Fraser smiled and poured some coffee, and Cassie drank it greedily, because her throat was parched.

'Where's Rob today?' she croaked.

'He went out with Stephen, but they'll be back at lunch time. We thought you'd sleep for hours.' Ewan took some toast out of the rack, spread a curl of butter on it, handed it to Cassie. 'You need a prairie oyster, lassie – that'll set you up.'

'Or kill you off.' Daisy came in then, and she was also wearing uniform, dark green with smart red piping. But, unlike Cassie, Daisy was immaculately groomed and ready to start the day.

'Good morning, Cassie,' Daisy said. 'Pour her out another cup of coffee, could you, darling?' she continued, as she kissed her husband on the cheek. 'Black, with a little sugar in it, if we have some left. She ought to have a glass of water, too.'

Ewan nodded, fetched a glass of water, and Cassie drank it down.

'Come on, love,' said Daisy. 'Let's get all that varnish off your nails and I'll repair your face.'

Cassie made it – just.

As she skidded round the corner from the Ritz hotel and ran towards the garage, she met her passenger going in.

The brigadier was a thin, sour-looking man who carried a bulging briefcase. His trousers were very sharply pressed, his boots gleamed like new conkers, his neat moustache was newly trimmed, and all his buttons shone. A stickler, she thought, a bloody stickler – that's all I flipping need.

'You're late,' the officer observed, looking Cassie up and down with obvious disapproval.

'I'm sorry, sir,' said Cassie. 'Good morning, sir,' she added, just about remembering to salute.

'It doesn't look as if it's good for you.'

As Cassie opened the door for him to get into the car, the brigadier scowled crossly at his driver. 'Straighten your tie, Lance Corporal,' he rapped. 'Tie your shoelaces, and try to be a credit to your service.'

Cassie checked the water, oil and petrol, took the pressure of the tyres and pumped them up again. She got the engine running, got into the cab and carefully reversed out of the garage. She drove the ponderous Humber staff car along Piccadilly and set off for Aldershot.

She couldn't believe she'd got it all so wrong, made such an exhibition of herself, and ruined her whole life. She wouldn't see Rob again, of course. His leave was almost over, and soon he would be going overseas, where he was likely to be killed.

As for Daisy, who had been so kind – Cassie had paid her back by spilling champagne on her expensive dress, getting make-up all over her sheets, and being sick in her bathroom.

As she made her slow way back to Aldershot, head throbbing, throat as dry as the Sahara, she couldn't believe she could have been so stupid, so unutterably awful. They reckon breeding always shows, she thought, and now they'll know that I've got none at all.

'Did you get her autograph for me?'

'What was her house like?'

'Does she have a sunken bath?'

'Does she dye her hair, or is she naturally blonde?'

Cassie had originally planned to tell the others all about it, down to the last detail – to reveal all Daisy's beauty secrets, to describe her home, her husband, servants, the contents of her wardrobes, everything.

But now she saw that this would be the most mean-minded thing to do, and a huge betrayal of Daisy's kindness.

'She's got a posh apartment in Park Lane,' she offered lamely.

'Yes, I know, it said so in the *Mirror*,' said a girl from Hull, who kept a scrapbook about Daisy and other British stars. 'But what's it like inside? Does she have a marble bathroom, does she have gold taps, and big, gilt mirrors on the walls? Does she wear a satin dressing gown, and did you get a photograph for me? You promised me you would.'

Cassie told them Daisy certainly didn't dye her hair, that she was in the WVS, and that she looked very glamorous in her green tweed uniform.

Then she went and sat down on her bed, and wrote a letter of thanks to Ewan and Daisy. She said that she was sorry from the bottom of her heart for all her bad behaviour, and she was ashamed. She added that they couldn't think any worse of her than she thought of herself.

She couldn't bring herself to write to Robert. He must have been disgusted to find that she was nothing but a drunken, maudlin slut, a silly cow who couldn't hold her drink.

He had called her darling. She was almost sure he had. But now one thing was certain – he wouldn't call her darling any more.

She would have thought it couldn't get any worse. But a few days later on, it did. One of the toff drivers caught her coming out of the shower room, and she pinned Cassie up against the wall.

'So, you met Daisy Denham?' began Lavinia Mayne, her spiteful, thin-lipped mouth curved in a sneer.

'So, what's it to you?' demanded Cassie.

'It's just that you were seen at the 400. Or anyway, I

imagine it was you. My cousin was also there that night, and said there was a ghastly, common woman with Miss Denham and her husband, slobbering all over some young Royal Dorsets officer, and getting roaring drunk.'

'Yes, that was me all right,' admitted Cassie.

'Well, I just want to say, I think you're awful.' Lavinia tossed her fine, patrician head. 'I don't know what Luigi can be thinking of, letting people like you into the club.'

'Get out of my way,' said Cassie flatly.

'I think you'll find that I'm not in your way.' Shuddering theatrically now, Lavinia stepped aside. 'Some men like a bit of rough,' she called as Cassie left the shower block, 'especially if they're going overseas. It gets them in the mood for foreign women, who will do anything.'

The next few days were horrible, with whispering and gossiping and giggling to endure, all made much worse for Cassie by the knowledge she deserved it.

'So I burned my bridges,' she told Frances, when she was finally feeling strong enough to write a full account of that disastrous, hideous night. 'I really mucked it up. I dare say all the Denhams hate me now.'

'Oh, don't worry, midget, they won't hate you. It was just bad luck.' Now posted up to Chester, Frances wrote back straight away. 'Champagne can be very tricky stuff,' she added wisely. 'I remember having some at a wedding, when I was seventeen, and it knocked me for six! You think you're stone cold sober, then suddenly – wham – it hits you, and you're rolling drunk.

'You'll know better next time. I think Robert taking off your stockings, and him looking after you while you were being sick, is really rather lovely. What a perfect gentleman!'

Yes, and what a pity I'm not a lady, reflected Cassie sadly.

But then she made a vow. She would stop swearing, stop trying to act tough. She would learn to be a proper lady, in thought and word and deed, and she would never touch champagne again.

Almost a whole week went by before she had the letter she was dreading. The pale blue BFPO envelope looked absolutely harmless, but Cassie held it gingerly, as if it was a hand grenade and likely to go off.

She spent the day on motor maintenance, lying under lorries, changing tyres and cleaning spark plugs. All that time she worried about her letter, and wondered what it said. He didn't want to see her any more, and anything between them was all over, obviously.

But how would he say it?

She finally couldn't stand it any longer, and when she was queuing up to get her supper, she tore the letter open.

'My dearest Cassie,' it began, which was a big surprise. *'I hope your headache's better! I'm sorry that I missed you and didn't get a chance say goodbye. I didn't realise you had to drive a bridagier to Alsherdot so early in the morning. I hope you got him there!*

'I've still got a few days leave before I go abroad. If you like, I could come down from London and pick you up at barracks. We could go and have a drink somewhere. What do you think of that?'

As long as it's just lemonade, thought Cassie, wincing in embarrassment at the very thought of anything remotely alcoholic.

'Do you have any photos of yourself?' continued Robert. *'If so, could you spare a few for me? I'm sending you a cutting from the* Sketch. *You'll see some hack photographer had nothing else to do that night, and snapped us at the Florida.*

'Look after yourself, my darling Cassie. I'll hope we'll meet again before too long, and in the meantime, I send you all my love.'

He sent her all his love!

Suddenly, Cassie felt beatified. She understood the power of holy relics, for she held one in her hand. As the queue for supper shuffled forward, she felt she'd been renewed, redeemed, reborn in Robert's name.

She read the letter through again. She looked at the smudgy, smeary photograph, saw that it was captioned *Miss Daisy Denham, Mr Ewan Fraser and their party at the Florida Club last night.*

There was dear old Stephen drinking whisky, and there was Robert smiling, and he had his arm around her shoulders, and – oh, thank you, God – the picture had been taken before she had got drunk.

I'll learn to be better, nicer, kinder, Cassie told herself. I'll be the sort of girl he thinks I am, and I'll deserve him.

'Come on, Dolly Daydream,' said the cookhouse orderly who was dishing up. 'Do you want sausages in batter, spam and mash, or cheese and onion pie?'

Cassie couldn't trust herself to send him anything longer than a sentence on a postcard. Saying she was sorry could come later, she decided. All she told him there and then was she'd be off duty Wednesday evening.

To Cassie's huge delight, the vile Lavinia and her vile best friend, the Honourable Antonia Something, were both walking into barracks just as Cassie happened to be walking out of them, and as Robert came along the road.

As they heard his footsteps, both the women turned to glance behind them. When they saw a tall, dark, handsome officer, they smirked and started preening, smoothed their jackets round their hips and fiddled with their hair.

'Good evening, ladies,' Robert said, and Cassie realised from the way he looked at them that it was an effort not to laugh. 'Cassie, what good timing. I was worried I was late.'

The look Lavinia gave Cassie would have curdled milk.

As Robert held out his arm and smiled at Cassie, she heard Antonia hiss.

'Good friends of yours?' asked Robert as they walked down the road towards the town.

'No, Rob, they hate me,' Cassie said. Then, before he started to ask why, she stopped and looked into his eyes. 'I'm sorry, Rob,' she said.

'You're sorry?' She'd never seen a face blanch quite so quickly, as all the natural colour drained away. 'You mean – '

'Yes, Rob – I mean no!'

Cassie realised what he'd thought she meant, why she had sent him that curt sentence on a postcard, and now a torrent of words came pouring out. How she was sorry for behaving like an idiot, how she was mortified, how she'd been sure she'd never hear from him again, how relieved she'd been to get his letter, how she'd never meant to get so drunk –

She stopped, and took great gasping breaths, and she was astonished to see he was breathing heavily as well.

'I thought you meant,' he said, 'I thought you were telling me you'd changed your mind about me. I thought – '

'No, Robert – no!' She grabbed him by the shoulders, shook him hard. 'I didn't mean that at all! I just meant I'm sorry to have behaved so badly, to have embarrassed you in front of Daisy, to have been such a stupid, drunken fool – '

'Oh, Cassie darling, don't worry about that!' Robert started laughing. 'You should have seen me the first time *I* got drunk! I thought I'd never hear the end of it from Mum and Dad.'

'What happened?'

'Steve and I were fifteen, sixteen – I'm not sure exactly, but about that age – and we and some other chaps from school managed to get hold of half a dozen flagons of strong cider.

'We drank the lot, and – God, we were so ill. You think *you* were embarrassing! But let's not talk about it any more. There's a little pub just down the road, and they're bound to have some lemonade or ginger ale or soda water.'

The pub was quiet and almost empty, apart from three or four old men who were sitting playing dominoes. They all looked up and smiled and nodded, then looked away again.

Robert went to the bar and bought some drinks – a glass of blameless lemonade for Cassie, and a pint of beer for him. Cassie found she didn't want to talk. All she wanted was to sit with Robert, holding hands with him. It seemed this was all he wanted, too.

I'll remember being here, she thought, how I felt so contented in this little pub, how we sat feeling comfortable together, how we didn't have to chatter on, because there was no need. We understood each other perfectly.

'Be careful, Rob,' she said, as they walked back to Cassie's barracks in the moonlight. 'Stay safe, and come back home to me.'

'I'll do my best.' Robert had his arm around her shoulders, and now he pulled her close. 'I'm always very careful, actually.'

'You go on being very careful, then.'

'Cass, I'm coming back to you, I promise.' Robert kissed her lightly, then more deeply, and she clung to him, unwilling to let him walk into the night, but knowing he had to go.

She watched him walk off down the road again and thought her heart would break.

There was a yawning gap before she heard from him again, and Cassie had to fight down her despair, to keep the faith. Then two letters came at once – but these were very short, a bit of hasty scribble which she could hardly read.

She did her best to keep her vow of saintliness, but this

was very difficult, especially when the bitch Lavinia and her stuck-up friends kept on making horrible remarks about certain people who got drunk in nightclubs of which they were not members.

But Cassie's virtue was eventually rewarded, and letters started coming all the time. They smelled of dust and spices, said he missed her, and couldn't wait for them to meet again.

Then, in September, Cassie heard from Stephen.

When she first saw the writing on the envelope, and realised it had been posted on the UK mainland, she felt it was the birthday of her life and all her Christmases in one.

But it was not from Robert, after all. The handwriting was similar, but it was not the same.

'A missive from the other twin,' wrote Stephen, as if he had divined her disappointment. *'We're planning a little party, Fran and I. We wondered if you'd like to come along. Dad's not very well, but it's their wedding anniversary soon, and Mum's afraid that it might be their last. We've both got a few days' leave, and so we're going to Dorset.'*

Cassie was surprised, then touched – and also sad, for Mrs Denham's sake. Poor Mr Denham, he'd never looked particularly well. But she hadn't thought he might be dying.

She asked for three days' leave, and got it.

Stephen and Frances met her off the train, and Stephen took her kitbag.

'Oh, Stephen, Fran – it's great to see you!' Cassie cried, and realised she meant it. 'Gosh, I've missed you!'

'It's great to see you, too,' said Frances, grinning. 'My goodness, midget, you look very smart! You've had your hair done, haven't you, and what about that lipstick?'

'I'm trying to be a credit to my service,' Cassie told Frances primly, smoothing her lapels, then picking up a cardboard box with holes punched in the sides. 'Steve, how are your parents?'

'Dad's going downhill fast. It's his lungs, the doctor says, it seems they're packing up. They think he's got a month or two at most.' Stephen shrugged dejectedly. 'I don't know how Mum's going to cope alone.'

'On the farm, you mean?' Cassie touched his sleeve in sympathy. 'Steve, you don't need to worry. She's always seemed quite capable to me.'

'I mean, inside herself.' Stephen slung Cassie's kitbag on his shoulder. 'They haven't spent a night apart for almost twenty years, except for when Dad was in hospital, and that was back in 1930-something.'

'Oh, I see,' said Cassie, wishing she could unsay what she'd just said, which now seemed insensitive and mean.

'But we're going to make these few days special,' added Stephen. 'We'll have a party we can all remember.'

'Cass, what's in that box?' demanded Frances.

'It's just a little present for Mrs Denham,' Cassie said mysteriously.

Mrs Denham had really pushed the boat out, Cassie thought.

Every piece of furniture in the cottage had been polished, the range had been black-leaded, and she must have stockpiled food for months, to make a spread like this.

She'd even got dressed up and had her hair done, and Cassie saw how beautiful Rose Denham must have been when she was young – how beautiful she was today, in fact. She could understand how Mr Denham must have fallen for her all those years ago.

'Hello, Cassie,' said Mrs Denham brightly, welcoming her former land girl with a generous hug. 'Goodness, Alex, look! She's got a stripe already. You must be doing well!'

'She's driving senior army officers all around the country,' Stephen told his mother. 'She brought my colonel back from Halifax last week. They all ask for Cassie, actually.'

'No, they don't,' said Cassie, blushing scarlet.

'Well, they should,' said Frances.

'I brought you this,' said Cassie, still blushing and handing Rose the cardboard box. 'I thought he would be company for you.'

'Oh, Alex, Stephen, look!' Mrs Denham opened up the box to find a sleepy puppy lying on a bed of straw. 'Oh, aren't you beautiful!'

Cassie smiled, relieved.

The chocolate Labrador looked up at Rose Denham, sniffed the strange new human smell, but then he wagged his tail. She stroked him with a gentle hand, and then she picked him up.

He snuggled up against her, licked her face and whickered.

'I expect you're hungry,' said Mrs Denham kindly. 'Come along inside, let's find you something nice to eat.'

Cassie saw she'd brought the perfect gift.

'I didn't know if I should get your mum a dog,' said Cassie, after the party which had been attended by almost the whole village. The weather had been kind, and so they'd taken tables, chairs and trestles out into the stable yard, and organised some games with little prizes for the village children.

Everybody had enjoyed themselves, eating, drinking, having fun, and for just one afternoon the war had been forgotten.

Daisy and Ewan had to leave to go straight back to London because they were both on stage that night. Frances took her parents home, and Mrs Denham helped her weary husband up to bed. Cassie and Stephen helped a couple of women from the village wash the dishes and clear the last few bits of mess away.

'I mean,' continued Cassie, 'she'll have to feed him,

exercise him, train him, as well as all the stuff around the farm she has to do. But I think he's a lovely little thing.'

'Where did you get him?' Stephen asked.

'One of the driver's mothers is a breeder of chocolate Labradors. She said he's a pedigree.' Cassie shrugged. 'Of course, *I* wouldn't know! Steve, he was so quiet and good while we were on the train. He didn't whine or bark.'

'Mum had a chocolate Labrador when she was a girl at Charton Minster,' Stephen said. 'She's thrilled to have a puppy, I can see, and I wish I had thought of it. She's going to call him Tinker.'

'If that's all then, Mr Denham?' said one of the village women.

'Thank you, Mrs Lyle and Mrs Croft.' Stephen smiled his gratitude. 'Make sure you take some cakes home for your children?'

As the village women left, Stephen swept up the last few crumbs and then leaned on his broom. 'Cass, you won't hurt him, will you?'

'Rob, you mean? Of course I won't.' Cassie looked at Stephen. 'What do you take me for, some kind of trollop? Out of sight and out of mind – is that what you're saying?'

'Now, Cass, don't get annoyed.' Stephen shrugged and looked apologetic. 'It's just that Rob takes everything so seriously, and when he gets upset – well, you know what he was like when you first came to Melbury. When he was worried the army wouldn't have him back.'

'Yes, I remember,' Cassie said. 'But I didn't chase after him, you know. When I first began to think Rob liked me, I didn't want him to know I liked him back. I mean, I'm not exactly the sort of girl your mum must want for Robert.'

'Mum's not that kind of person, Cass,' said Stephen. 'You know her well enough to know she's not a snob.'

'No, but she – well, anyway. I won't hurt your brother,

Steve. I promise, hand on heart. When Rob comes back, it will be the best day of my life.' Cassie smiled at Stephen. 'It's been so lovely to see you and Frances.'

'Yes, dear Frances.' Stephen pulled a face. 'Salt of the earth, is Frances. A pity there aren't more like Frances, eh?'

The following day, the three of them walked along the lane to Charton, Frances and Stephen striding on ahead, Cassie dawdling, pulling at grass stalks, eating blackberries, and enjoying autumn in the countryside, something she'd not experienced before.

They passed the ancient Minster, glowing golden in the sun.

'It's empty now,' said Stephen.

'I thought it was a school for boys?' said Cassie, who had just caught up.

'It was, but rain was getting in, the owner wouldn't repair it, so the boys have gone elsewhere.'

Cassie looked up at the roof. She saw some of the weathered grey stone tiles were cracked or missing, and a chimney stack was leaning at an awkward angle.

'It looks like the enchanted castle out of *Sleeping Beauty*,' whispered Frances.

'It looks more like the ogre's lair to me,' said Stephen, grimacing.

'Steve, have you ever been inside?' asked Cassie.

'No, but Daisy often used to say she wished we were locked up there with all the other hooligans.' Stephen grinned, remembering. 'Poor Daze, as kids we used to drive her mad.'

'What's Daisy going to do?' asked Frances. 'Cass was telling me she'd like to buy the place and give it to your mother.'

'You never know with Daze, but now the place is empty,

she says she's going to make the bloke an offer, although she's almost sure he'll turn it down.' Stephen shook his head. 'There was some village gossip once, along the lines this chap was Daisy's father – that he seduced her mother when he was in London, during the last war. Then he smarmed up to Mum's old man, and somehow got his hands on Charton Minster, so he must be a nasty piece of work.'

'Have you ever met him?'

'No,' said Stephen, 'and he had a stroke a few months back, so he doesn't go out any more.'

'Why won't he sell the Minster?' Frances asked. 'It can't be any use to him.'

'Maybe he likes upsetting Daze and Mum.'

As they were walking back to Melbury, Stephen fell into step by Cassie, leaving Frances to go on ahead. She wished he wouldn't walk so close, almost pushing her into the hedge, but she didn't want to make an issue of it, or shove him away.

As they climbed a stile, Cassie stumbled.

Stephen caught her hand, and then he held it longer than he needed, and she could feel his gaze upon her face.

'Stephen,' she said gently, as she tried to pull her hand away.

'I know, Cass,' he said, and sighed, 'wrong twin.'

Chapter Nine

January 1943

Robert lay on his stomach among some thorny bushes, scanning the Tunisian hills and wadis through his field binoculars.

A German unit was supposed to be dug in on the hillside opposite. But, stare as he might, he couldn't make it out. Fritz must be well camouflaged, he decided. If Fritz was there at all ...

Suddenly, a shell exploded fifteen feet away, and then another, closer this time. So, even though he couldn't see any Germans, they'd obviously seen him. They'd spotted the light reflecting off his lenses, he supposed.

You fool, he told himself. You shouldn't have used binoculars! Now, it was time to go. He inched back down the hillside, accompanied by angry bursts of red and purple fire that made the orange dust spurt up all round him, crawling on his belly like a lizard until he was out of sight of the ridges held by German gunners.

Then he lit a welcome cigarette, inhaling deeply, and began to make his way back to the British camp.

Earlier that day, his men had been attacked by German Stukas dropping bombs on them and on some London Irish, who were next to them in line. The planes had killed four Royal Dorsets, and wounded seven more.

The British anti-aircraft guns in batteries further back had brought a couple of German bombers down, but now the British guns were silent. So what were they doing? What was going on?

As so often happened, he didn't know and wasn't likely to find out. All he and his platoon could do was lurk here like a nest of new-born leverets, ill-concealed amidst the vegetation, hoping a fox or eagle in the shape of a Stuka wouldn't spot them and swoop down on them.

As he made his way back down the hill, he passed a couple of Arab homesteads, which had been shelled and burned by enemy fire. Some Highlanders were using one of the houses as a makeshift operations post, and they had trashed the place, destroying the little garden round the house, and using all the furniture for firewood. As a farmer's son himself, he pitied the Arab farmers who'd got caught up in this, who'd had their land invaded by columns of men in khaki and their war machines, who'd had their livestock killed and crops destroyed.

He scratched an insect bite that had made one arm swell up, so now the skin was red and tight and shiny. He ought to go and see the medical officer, he supposed. In this awful climate, almost every scratch or bite was liable to go septic. So maybe he should get a shot of something.

'You all right, Mr Denham?' asked Robert's middle-aged sergeant, who had come to look for him.

'Yes, I'm fine,' said Robert, slithering down the last few feet of scree. 'Did you get the wounded men away?'

'Yes, sir,' said the sergeant. 'They'll be at the aid post now. We buried all the other poor bastards down there in the valley.' He glanced up at the hill. 'See anything up there, sir?'

'They must be directly opposite, but they're jolly well dug in and hidden. They had a pop at me.'

'You take too many risks, sir,' said the sergeant. 'I know you're bored, but there's no point in going looking for trouble, if you don't mind my saying.'

It's better to go and look for it before it comes to look for you, thought Robert, but he didn't say. Sergeant Gregory was a conscientious NCO who wanted to get as many men as possible through this and home again. Robert had the

116

same intention, but – as his sergeant realised – he was bored. He wouldn't have minded action now and then.

The African night descended like a black velvet curtain embroidered with a million little stars. Once in a while, a few white shells burst overhead, adding to the brilliance above. Robert and his platoon were all in trenches, as they'd been for nearly two weeks now. Bored out of their minds, but sometimes getting scared out of their wits, they waited for an order to advance, retreat, do something, anything.

Robert put a third of the men on guard. The others dozed, wrote letters, cleaned their rifles, smoked, played cards and brewed up endless cans of tea on little fires. The stars shone bright, so bright that it was possible to read.

But no one felt like reading.

The sergeant sat on a pile of kitbags, staring into space.

'You seem a bit distracted, sergeant,' Robert said, hoping his sergeant wasn't getting wind up, because he was an excellent NCO, if a bit outspoken on occasions.

'Just had a letter from back home, sir,' said the sergeant, as he stared into the fire. 'Our eldest daughter, Nell – she's misbehaving, hanging around with spivs and undesirables, and her sisters always copy Nell. The missus doesn't know what to do. So she wants me to sort it out. As if I can do anything out here.'

'You could write to Nell, perhaps?' said Robert. 'I don't mean any stern, Victorian father kind of stuff. But ask her to keep her mother's spirits up, remind her she's the eldest, and she needs to look out for her sisters – that should bring her to her senses.'

'You reckon, sir?' The sergeant grimaced, shook his greying head. 'You're not married, are you, sir?' he asked.

'No,' admitted Robert.

'Got a girl, sir?'

'Yes.' At the thought of Cassie, Robert smiled. He was so glad they'd had the chance to meet again before he'd come to Africa, glad they'd had their walk together, glad they'd sat companionably in that Surrey pub, and glad they'd had a chance to kiss goodbye.

He shouldn't have let her drink so much the night they were in London. Poor Cass, she'd been so ill. He'd never seen anybody be so sick.

He had two letters in his pocket which he hadn't opened yet. One of them was from Stephen, and the other was from Frances. He might as well glance through them, he supposed. He hadn't anything else to do.

He opened the letter from his brother first, and what he read there made him catch his breath.

'Something wrong, sir?' asked his sergeant, looking at him, concerned.

'My – my father's dead.' As the initial shock wore off, Robert took a few deep breaths, and eventually he felt his heart slow down and the life blood flow back into him.

As he'd started reading Stephen's letter, and saw his brother said he had bad news, he'd dreaded it would be Cassie who was hurt – or had even died.

Now he felt very guilty because he was relieved.

'I'm sorry, sir,' the sergeant said, sounding as if he meant it. 'It's hard, to lose somebody back at home, while we're stuck over here.'

'Thank you,' Robert said. 'But Dad was ill,' he added. 'We'd been expecting it.'

Later, he forced down steak and kidney pudding they'd boiled up in a tin, then tried to snatch some sleep.

He drifted in and out of consciousness, dreaming of when he was a little child, of when they'd lived in India, and of his father teaching him to ride.

Of summers in the Himalayan foothills, where he and

his brother and their father had gone on exciting, all-male expeditions. Of his big sister Daisy, pirouetting round their bungalow in a new white frock made for an engagement at an army garrison theatre, where she invariably stole the show.

When he woke up he realised there were tears in his eyes. How would his mother cope, he wondered? She and his father had always been so close, so very much in love, so how would Rose survive a loss like this?

He got up, walked around the camp, talked briefly to the sentries he had posted earlier, smoked a couple of very unpleasant Libyan cigarettes, and then lay down again.

Soon, he was dozing fitfully, and dreaming he was in an army lorry and driving down a street in some strange city full of towers and domes – Delhi, it might have been, or possibly Bombay.

Then he saw Cassie wearing Daisy's cocktail dress, silver shoes and heavy, mask-like make-up, looking like she'd looked that night they'd all gone out in London.

But she wasn't in Daisy's flat, or at the Florida or the 400. She was standing in the doorway of a bombed-out building with men in cheap but flashy clothes, men who looked like spivs, and she was laughing. He could hear the crump of falling bombs, but she was obviously having a good time.

One of the spivs was hugging Cassie round the neck, and he had Stephen's face.

Cassie passed a few more driving tests for different kinds of vehicles. She was rewarded with a second stripe. She thought, if only Robert would come home, life couldn't get any better.

Of course, things could be better generally. The Allies could actually defeat the Germans and Italians. But that was bound to happen some day, surely? Now the Americans had come in on the Allies' side?

But when the war was won, things would go back to normal. There'd be no excitement, everything would be dull again, and she'd go back to Smethwick.

She'd be a shop assistant, cleaner, factory worker, making or packing sweets or cigarettes. Or she'd work in the local Chinese laundry, like she had when she'd left school, where her hair would go all lank and frizzy in the steam, where her hands would end up red and roughened, where she'd be shouted at by Mr Wong.

Or she'd get married to some local boy, a grown-up version of a snot-nosed kid who'd shared her desk and pulled her hair and pinched her black and blue at St Saviour's Elementary School. She'd live in a little terraced house like Lily Taylor's, have half a dozen wailing brats, get stretch marks, piles and possibly a prolapse, and all the other gruesome female ailments which the married women talked about as they came home from church.

She was now a corporal. One day, she might make sergeant, then she could boss the likes of vile Lavinia and Antonia about. She didn't want the war to end just yet.

Frances wrote to tell her Mrs Denham's husband had just died, so Cassie put in for a pass to go to Mr Denham's funeral. She got a lift to Dorchester, and then she caught a bus to Charton. When she arrived at Charton's little honey-coloured church, she saw it was packed with people from the village, many of them in tears.

Stephen and Fran had both got leave, and Daisy came, of course. But Ewan couldn't make it – he was touring somewhere in the Midlands, Daisy told them, organising ENSA shows for troops.

'I'm so glad you could come, my little sparrow,' Daisy said to Cassie. 'It means a lot to Mum, to see so many people here.'

Daisy was looking very glamorous in a black wool suit,

black furs, gleaming black high heels, and a black velvet pillbox hat trimmed with black ostrich feathers. But when she put her veil up, after they'd had the service and filed out of the church to watch the actual burial, Cassie saw Daisy's face was streaked with tears, that her black mascara had pooled in purple puddles, and that her nose was running like a child's.

While Mrs Denham stood dry-eyed and sorrowing, like an image of the Virgin, Daisy cried and cried.

'I'm so sorry, Daisy.' Cassie didn't know what to do or what to say in the face of such tremendous grief. 'He was nice, your dad,' she added, lamely. 'He was always very kind to me.'

'He was k-kind to everybody, Cassie, that's why everybody loved him,' Daisy sobbed, and then burst into storms of tears again.

'Come on, Daze, old girl.' Stephen looked pale and wretched, but he was not yet in tears. He put his arm round Daisy's waist, and let her rest her head against his shoulder. 'Remember you're a soldier's daughter, eh?'

'Y-yes, I know,' sobbed Daisy. 'D-dad would be ashamed of me, carrying on like this. He'd tell me to brace up, shoulders back, and all that sort of thing.'

She rummaged in her handbag, found her little golden compact and put some dabs of powder on her nose. 'My God, I'm going to look a fright this evening,' she continued, patting with a little lace-edged hankie at her red and swollen eyes.

'You should have let your understudy go on, and stayed with Mum tonight.'

'Well, I did think about it.' Daisy tried to smile. 'But Dad would have told me to get on with it, play up and play the game. I'm not due on stage for ages, anyway. I'm in variety at the Theatre Royal tonight, and I'm on at nine.'

'Cassie, would you like to stay the night?' Mrs Denham left a group of villagers who had all been offering sympathy, and now she walked up to her son and daughter. Cassie saw she hadn't slept, that there were big, black circles underneath her tired, grey eyes, and she was as pale as death herself. 'You could have Stephen's room – he's going back tonight.'

'Thank you, Mrs Denham.' Cassie watched the final mourners hurrying away. It seemed there was to be no funeral supper, no going back to the bailiff's cottage for sandwiches and cake. Stephen had said his mother couldn't face it.

'I'll cook the evening meal,' said Cassie, 'and I'll help Tess and Shirley with the evening milking.'

'Bless you, Cassie dear,' said Mrs Denham, then her shoulders slumped and she began to cry.

Cassie went with Frances, Stephen and Daisy to the station. Tinker had decided to go with them, and now he was nosing in the dry, brown bracken, and sniffing dozens of exciting smells.

Stephen still looked white and miserable, and Cassie hoped he wouldn't have a turn. She remembered Mrs Denham saying strong emotion sometimes brought them on.

'I've volunteered to go to abroad,' she told them, as they waited for the London train.

'Oh?' said Frances, and now she looked astonished. 'What does your granny think of that?'

'I haven't told her yet.'

'Where exactly do you hope to go?'

'The other drivers reckon they might send us to North Africa,' Cassie replied, and then she shrugged. 'We'd be based in Egypt, but then we could be sent to Libya. Or even Palestine.'

'Africa's quite big, you know,' said Frances. 'You're not exactly likely to run into him.'

'I didn't think I would!' cried Cassie, blushing.

'Wherever you go, be careful.' Stephen glanced down the line and saw the London train approaching, so he kissed Frances lightly on the cheek, and then he turned to Cassie.

'Goodbye, Stephen.' Cassie hugged him, but made sure she turned her face away, so Stephen couldn't kiss her if he tried. She didn't want to kiss him or be kissed. He'd been so kind when she had first arrived in Melbury, and she wanted him to be her friend – but no more than her friend. Frances, she thought, you should be kissing Frances, she's the one who loves you.

'You look after yourself, my sparrow,' Daisy said, and then she enveloped Cassie in an Arpège-scented, warm embrace. 'Come and see us in London, will you, if you have the time?'

'I'll try,' said Cassie.

'Good,' said Daisy, standing back and tweaking one of Cassie's curls so that it sat just right. 'We'll go shopping, shall we, and buy you something pretty? We should celebrate that nice new stripe.'

'You're going to stay with Mrs Denham, then?' asked Frances, as Stephen's and Daisy's London train went steaming down the line, and she and Cassie waited for the one to Chester.

'Yes, I got a thirty-six hour pass.'

'She's made her mind up you're going to marry Robert.'

'I don't know why.' Cassie felt the blood rush up her neck and flood her cheeks, warming her face in the still, frosty air. 'We're only friends, like you and Steve.'

'I don't think Stephen wants to marry *me*.'

'Well, he just kissed you, didn't he?' asked Cassie.

'I suppose so.' Frances shrugged. 'But – '

'There you are, then.' Cassie smiled. 'Stephen likes you,

Fran. He thinks you're great. Salt of the earth, he said you were – and then he said it was a pity there weren't more girls like you.'

'He did?' said Frances doubtfully.

'Yes, Fran – cross my heart and hope to die.'

Cassie looked down the line. She didn't want to have this conversation. 'Look, Frances, here's your train.'

'Cassie, write to me from Africa.' After she had got into the carriage, Frances tugged at the leather strap and then let down the window. 'Let me know what happens, and listen, midget – you take care.'

'Of course I will,' said Cassie. 'You take care, as well. Look after Steve, all right?'

'You take care, my girl,' said Lily Taylor solemnly.

'Yes, Granny,' Cassie said, for what seemed like the hundredth thousandth time.

After she'd been vetted, prodded, had all manner of injections, and been passed fit for service overseas, Cassie had four days' embarkation leave.

She'd been very tempted to spend one of them in London seeing Daisy and going shopping. How wonderful it would have been, she thought, to go to all those famous London shops with a famous actress, have people bowing, scraping, opening doors and calling taxis for them as if they were royalty. But in the end she'd gone to Birmingham to spend the whole time with her granny.

There, she helped to purify the shrine, listened to hours of good advice doled out by Father Riley, and felt slightly guilty because Lily didn't want her to go sailing off to Egypt, and she said so, many times.

'Granny, I'll be all right,' insisted Cassie as she polished up a statue of the Blessed Virgin. 'It's not as if I'm going into battle. I'll just be driving trucks.'

'Mind you go to church, if they have any Catholic churches in those heathen places.'

'Yes, I'll go to church,' said Cassie, crossing her fingers underneath her apron so the promise didn't count.

'If Our Lord had meant us to go visiting foreign parts, he would have shown us how to walk on water,' added Lily crossly. 'You were born in England, and that's where you should stay – it stands to reason.'

'Granny, other people go abroad, and most of them don't come to any harm.'

'Mrs Murphy's son, he's in the Navy, but he's seasick all the time, and I expect you will be, too,' said Lily, with the grim satisfaction of someone who was always right. 'You'll heave your heart up and you'll pray to all the saints, but they're going to think it serves you right and take no notice.'

I couldn't be any sicker than I was that night at Daisy's place, and I got over that, thought Cassie wryly.

'Say your prayers each night,' continued Lily.

'Yes, of course I shall.'

'Just remember, child, you're all I've got.'

'I know that, Granny.' Cassie put down her duster and hugged Lily round her bony little shoulders. 'I'll come back to you.'

'We ought to go and see your mother before you leave,' said Lily, as they ate their breakfast the next morning. 'You'll need to ask her blessing.'

So they spent that gloomy winter morning visiting poor Geraldine, Lily tidying up the grave and talking to her daughter, Cassie standing there embarrassed as her granny chatted to her mother, hoping nobody she knew would see them. It had dogged her childhood, the awareness that the whole of Smethwick thought that Lily Taylor was completely round the bend.

'Cassandra's here,' said Lily suddenly, startling Cassie out of dreams of Robert. 'She's going away, she's going on a ship to somewhere hot, but she'll come back to see you soon.'

As Lily talked to Geraldine, Cassie bowed her head and tried to think of something she could say to a mother she had never known.

It was so exciting, going on board ship and sleeping in a bunk and having a little porthole window from which she could see the cold, grey water.

But soon Cassie wished that she had listened to her granny's good advice, and stayed in dear old Blighty.

It had been all right in the Channel. The sea had been quite choppy, but it hadn't been *too* rough. Seamen, troops and ATS had all been in good spirits, looking forward to their great adventure, and hoping they would see the Pyramids and the Sphinx.

Cassie had thought, there's nothing to it, being on a boat. People who say it takes a couple of weeks to get your sea legs, and everybody's ill, just want to make you scared.

But now the wind was blowing hard, pushing up the waves until they were great walls of water, and Cassie was so ill she thought she'd die. She grasped the holy medals which her granny had hung around her neck, and prayed to God, his Virgin Mother, and any saint who might be listening, to save her life.

But whichever saint was now on duty, and responsible for sailors being tossed around in storms while in the Bay of Biscay, took no notice. The whole convoy, troopships, corvettes and destroyers alike, was tossed about like toys in a child's bath.

'So you've never been to sea before?' enquired a red-haired, grey-eyed Scottish girl, who'd also volunteered to go abroad, and for some reason wasn't being sick.

'No,' said Cassie, hating her for looking so flipping pink and healthy. The girl was lounging against the rail and cheerfully eating something from a dish. It smelled like bacon and tomatoes, and Cassie felt the bile come pumping up into her throat again. Then she was sick again and yet again. 'I wish I'd never come,' she groaned, as she clung to her medals and cursed her wretched fate.

She prayed and prayed for calm, for the storm to die down just a bit. But the storm got worse.

Soon, they were being stalked by German U-boats, and rocked by exploding mines that damaged several of the vessels. But the convoy battled on, each ship a heaving cesspool of injured, sick, and sometimes even dying.

When at last they'd passed the Straits, and got into the Med, the sea was calmer. But there were many other hazards now. Italian bombers strafed the convoy, and by the time the troopship in which Cassie was a passenger was lying off Algiers, its many decks looked like a battlefield, with wounded soldiers lying in groaning rows on makeshift stretchers, and lots of others being ill below.

Some ATS girls had been slightly wounded, too. A few of them had been more sick than Cassie. Then one got hit by shrapnel and was badly hurt, so she would be going straight back home to England.

Cassie realised she was in a battle zone, that perhaps all this would not be an exciting new adventure, after all.

Maybe she had signed her death certificate, instead.

But then the wind came out of Africa, a fresh, clean breeze that blew away the acrid taint of sickness. As she leaned upon the rail and watched the coast come nearer, keeping her eyes trained on a line of purple hills that closed the far horizon, Cassie felt much better.

This foreign wind smelled sweet, she thought, and sniffed it gratefully. It smelled of Robert's letters, dry and crisp and scented with lemons, mint and thyme.

Closer to the land, it didn't smell so lovely. In fact, it stank of fish and sewage. But now the ships were safer, lying under the protection of the British guns.

When they docked at Algiers to let some soldiers disembark, little brown-skinned boys came swimming out and clambered up the sides of the huge vessel, shouting to the passengers, grinning and demanding to be given cigarettes or baksheesh.

The soldiers didn't give them anything. Instead, they hit them, knocked them down into the sea, but the boys came back, swarming up the sides like ants, and Cassie was dismayed to see the soldiers smash the children's fingers with their rifle butts. She hadn't realised ordinary men could be so cruel.

Cassie and nine other ATS girls were going on to Alexandria. The periscopes of U-boats dogged their progress. When Italian bomber planes went screeching overhead, she clutched her holy medals, and she prayed.

She had told Frances she didn't know if she believed in God. But now she recognised the truth of the old saying from the previous conflict – there were no atheists in trenches.

Or on troopships in the Med.

She thought of Robert constantly. She wondered where he was, and if he was in action, if he was in danger, if he had been wounded. She didn't allow herself to wonder if he might be killed.

'Blessed Mother, please keep him safe,' she prayed.

She hoped her prayers might be answered, especially since nowadays she wasn't asking for anything for herself.

Thanks to the corvettes which kept the German submarines at bay, the convoy got to Alexandria more or less unscathed.

Cassie and the other drivers, smartly turned out in their tropical kit and lugging heavy kitbags, were quickly disembarked, loaded on to an army truck, and taken to their quarters.

'We're going to see the Sphinx,' said one girl, happy to be off the ship at last.

Cassie wasn't bothered about the Sphinx. She was looking forward to eating something tasty, and not seeing it come up again.

'Look at all the bugs!' exclaimed the red-haired Scottish girl, as she stared in horror at the squalid bedrooms in the white-washed villa which had been commandeered for their quarters.

'Look at these beds!' added another girl. 'They're absolutely crawling!'

'We'll need to burn these mattresses,' said Cassie, eyeing the iron bedsteads with distaste, and wondering how many thousand bugs could be in all the nooks and crevices. 'We could have a bonfire in the courtyard. We'll stuff the cracks in all the bedsteads with cotton wool we've soaked in paraffin, and then set fire to it.'

'How do *you* know what to do?' enquired the Scottish girl, suspiciously.

'I – I just know,' said Cassie.

She wasn't going to tell them she'd seen even bigger bugs in Birmingham, or that where she came from the paraffin-and-cotton wool routine had been a regular event.

'Settling in then, ladies?' asked a harsh, deep voice.

Cassie turned to see the owner of the voice was almost six feet tall. She had close-cropped grey hair, and wore a well-pressed skirt and jacket made of khaki drill, with major's crowns upon the epaulettes.

A dark-haired female sergeant accompanied the major, and now she brought the new girls to attention.

'I'm Major Sheringham,' the officer continued, as Cassie and the others stood as stiff as ramrods, staring straight ahead. 'I'm your new commanding officer. Welcome to Alexandria.

'Now, let's get one thing understood. Do right by me, girls, and I'll do right by you. You'll find I'm firm, but fair.'

She smiled down at Cassie. 'Corporal, you don't look big enough to drive a three-ton truck. But right now I need a girl to run my special errands, and I think you'd be ideal for me.'

Chapter Ten

The major told her sergeant to carry on, then left.

'Looks like she means to have you, Corporal Taylor,' said the sergeant, grinning. She told the new girls she'd been with the unit from the start, and so she knew the major very well.

'Our Annie Sheringham,' she added, 'she's always had a fancy for skinny little blondes. You mark my words, my girl. She'll be in your knickers before you know what's hit you.'

Cassie shuddered. Since she'd joined the army, she had realised some girls liked other girls. Good luck to them, she'd thought, it takes all sorts.

But she herself had never had the come-on from a woman, let alone an officer, and that would be one order she would definitely have to disobey.

Then she would be court-martialled.

Then she'd be on the next ship back to Blighty.

Well, she told herself, that would please my granny, anyway.

The new girls had three days to settle down, to get their land legs back, to look round Alexandria, and to get used to the heat.

Anxious to avoid the major, Cassie joined in all the expeditions to the souks, she went to see the harbour, she walked along the promenades, she visited the catacombs, the churches and the mosques, and she went to see the Roman ruins.

But her delight in this new, fascinating foreign place was tainted by the dread of getting a sudden summons from the major to come and run a special errand – whatever that might mean.

'Sergeant Payne was kidding you, you gormless Brummie clot,' said Jane MacFarlane, the red-haired, grey-eyed

Scottish girl who had been so healthy on the boat. 'God, don't you know anything?'

Jane knew flipping everything, thought Cassie. She had settled down in Alexandria straight away. She had lived in Egypt as a child, she had informed the rest of them, when Daddy was in the diplomatic service. She'd noticed Cassie pussy-footing around and looking nervous, and finally she'd managed to get her to admit what she was worrying about.

'The major's got a girlfriend,' Jane continued, laughing. 'A horse-faced, black-haired woman from the shires. I saw her yesterday. She was in Annie's office. Cass, she's got a bosom like a bolster, and she looks like she could play at Twickenham. So, if Annie fancies toff brunettes with thighs like rugby centre-forwards, she's hardly going tae take a shine to undernourished little blondes like you.'

Cassie was relieved, but – undernourished little blonde, the nerve of it!

She ached to smack the snooty Miss MacFarlane – or pull rank and put her on a charge for insolence. She couldn't wait for training to begin.

She'd show the lot of them.

Rolling down her mosquito net that evening, she noticed Jane MacFarlane whispering to another girl, and heard them both start giggling.

She thought, just let them wait.

She lay down on her stomach and began to write a letter to Robert, telling him all about the voyage from England, and saying she was very glad to be on land again.

She'd already written once, a short and dashed-off note to say she'd got there in one piece, but now she wrote and wrote, pages and pages, pouring out her heart to him.

Robert wondered when the post would come, and if there'd be a letter from Cassie soon. Steve had written to tell him she'd applied for service overseas, and Robert found he didn't like the thought of that at all.

'She seemed very keen to get away,' Stephen had said. 'I think she's either planning to track you down, or to sort out Rommel all by her little self.'

Robert didn't appreciate his brother's flippancy. Cassie on a troopship was a horrifying thought. The Mediterranean was so bloody dangerous for shipping. If the Italian air force didn't get you, the chances were the German navy would. Also, why was Steve so well-informed? Why hadn't Cassie written to him herself?

Letters go astray, he told himself – you know they do.

But Stephen had liked Cassie from the start, from the first day she'd arrived in Melbury, and Cassie obviously liked Stephen, too. Stephen was in England, where Cassie was – presumably – at least for the time being?

He wished he could get that stupid dream out of his head.

When he finally got a letter saying she was in Alexandria, it was very short and to the point, merely telling him she'd arrived there safely, where she would be living, and adding she would be writing soon to tell him all about it.

He waited for more letters anxiously, and they arrived – from Frances, Stephen and his mother. But Cassie didn't write to him again.

At six o'clock the following morning, the new girls were paraded for the major, then kitted out in short-sleeved khaki overalls, which did less than nothing for their figures.

Then they were piled into an army truck and driven into the desert, a chilly, bleak and barren emptiness that made them shudder, and wonder why they'd volunteered for service overseas.

'You'll all be trained to drive a breakdown lorry,' their instructor told them, as she looked her shivering, nervous charges up and down. 'Vehicles have lots of accidents, they get blown up, or else they just conk out, and it'll be your job to go and find them, then bring them home again.

'You'll be delivering them, too – moving jeeps and lorries and other kinds of transport all around the Middle East. So, first of all, you'll need to get your bearings. You'll need to get used to living in the desert. I'll teach you some survival skills today.'

People *lived* in the desert? As she gazed across the almost featureless wastes of grey-brown sand, Cassie thought she'd never find her way around this howling wilderness.

The maps the girls were given all looked useless. They seemed to bear no relation to the landscape, which was made up of rocks and scrub and endless drifts of sand. This sand got whipped up by the wind to end up in your eyes, your ears, your clothes, your food, your hair. But somehow, everyone survived that first, long, tiring day.

'God, it's getting bloody cold,' said one girl, as they put their tents up for their first night in the desert. 'I thought it was always hot in Egypt.'

'So did I,' another girl said, shaking out her groundsheet – they'd been told to do this all the time, in case of scorpions and other things that bit. 'In all the pictures in my Bible, it looks boiling, with everyone in long white robes or little pleated skirts.'

'They got it wrong,' said Cassie, and she shivered. She glanced at Jane MacFarlane, who was getting in a tangle with her guy ropes. 'But I dare say Miss Know-It-All MacFarlane could enlighten us? Jane, why is it so hot here in the daytime, and why is it so flipping cold at night?'

But Jane did not enlighten them. 'I didnae think that we'd be doing stuff like this,' she muttered, as she shook the sand out of her hair. Although she hadn't been sick on the boat, reflected Cassie, now she was looking very sick indeed.

'I volunteered for motor maintenance duties,' she continued, anxiously. 'I've no sense of direction. I cannae find my way to my own bed on a dark night. How am I going tae find my way round here?'

Cassie knew real panic when she saw it. 'They said in Alex that we always drive in convoys,' she told Jane. 'So you just make sure you're not the last one in the convoy – that's all you have to do. If you follow me, and I get lost, at least we'll both be lost together.'

'MacFarlane, Corporal Taylor?' Sergeant Payne glowered angrily at Cassie. 'Taylor, you should be putting up your tent, not gossiping. You're an NCO. God alone knows why, but you could *try* to set a good example to the other girls.'

It took a while to get her bearings, but Cassie soon began to memorise the features of the rough terrain. She noticed little differences in similar piles of rocks. She could find the roads, even when obscured by wind-blown sand. She found that she could reproduce the landscape on a map inside her head.

On night patrols, she couldn't help but notice all the different constellations. She'd heard of wise men following stars, of course, but hadn't supposed that it was really possible to steer yourself by pinpricks in the sky.

You couldn't see stars in Smethwick, anyway. There was too much smoke from all the factories and other industries. But, out here in desert, the night sky was crystal clear, and studded with little clusters of friendly, glowing lights. She knew they would always lead her home.

She passed the various tests of skill with ease. She mastered driving all the different vehicles used in deserts. She learned how to deal with all the usual things which could cause breakdowns, and how to hitch a conked-out vehicle to her breakdown lorry, then drive it back to base.

She was soon leading convoys, taking jeeps to Cairo, and bringing lorries from Port Said.

'I've never met a girl like you,' one of the male sergeants at a transport depot told her, grinning. 'You women, you don't usually have a good sense of direction. But *you* seem to find your way around.'

'I'm a freak,' said Cassie, grinning back.

'You'd need to be, to want to come out here, then drive all round the bloody Western Desert, when you could be tucked up in your bed in dear old Blighty.'

But Cassie liked the desert. She grew to like the major, too. The CO stuck up for her girls and, even though she worked them hard, she saw to it they got their rest, as well.

Major Sheringham always noticed when a girl was sick, depressed, upset or merely lonely, and got her sent back home, transferred or, if it was necessary, discharged.

She was kind to Cassie, but in a motherly sort of way. Soon it became important to Cassie she should please the major. So, far from dreading being in the major's company, Cassie enjoyed her running errand days, when she could wear a clean, smart uniform, not those awful khaki dungarees, and when she could drive the major and her own superiors all round Alexandria in a big black Humber staff car.

When the troopships and supply ships came, bringing letters and presents from Britain, everyone in the unit got excited. But Cassie's post was mostly rather dull. It was made up of yet more holy medals and more prayer cards from her granny, reminders to stay pure from Father Riley, gossipy little notes from Frances, and the occasional letter from Stephen Denham.

The sight of Stephen's writing made her feel uneasy, although she didn't know why. She was fond of him, she wished him well, but – oh, she didn't understand it, she didn't know what to make of Stephen.

She hadn't heard from Rob for several weeks. But she tried not to worry. She told herself that things were going well along the coast. The Germans were hanging on and hanging on, but soon they'd be defeated – everybody said so.

Field Marshal Rommel, whom the soldiers called the Desert Fox, was on the run.

If Robert had been hurt or worse, somebody back in England would have surely written to let her know? Meanwhile, she kept the faith and wrote a letter almost every day, telling him what she was doing and saying she hoped they would be able to meet in Alexandria some time soon.

Then, at the beginning of June, when she was almost ready to despair, she finally heard from him.

'I have some leave,' wrote Robert on a Forces postcard. 'So I'm hoping to get a lift to Alex and to see you on the seventeenth.'

'I never thought you'd make it,' Cassie told him, gazing up at Robert in delight.

Jane MacFarlane had opened the front door to him, and she'd called to Cassie with a giggle in her voice that there was some man here who was asking for a Corporal Taylor. Cassie had assumed it was the major's runner with instructions for the following day. But it was not the runner – it was him.

Robert was standing in the hallway of the white-washed villa, his tall shadow blocking out the sun, but she still couldn't believe he might be real. She was afraid that if she touched him, he would vanish in a puff of smoke.

On the day he'd told her he hoped to be in Alex, she'd been driving Major Sheringham all around the town. After she'd put the car to bed, she'd hurried back to the villa, had a bath and washed her hair, then got another girl to trim and set it.

She didn't know why she was going to so much trouble. She had convinced herself he wouldn't come, that something would prevent him.

But here he was, all tanned and handsome, looking really marvellous in his tropical khaki drill. It was very shallow of her to notice he had perfect legs for shorts, of course she realised that – but seeing him look so gorgeous only added to her happiness.

'So you managed to get your lift,' she said, unable to stop grinning like a cat who's lapped up half a pint of cream.

'Yes,' said Robert, but he wasn't smiling back. 'Cassie, you hardly ever wrote to me.'

'I did write!' She stared at him, astonished. 'I've written to you nearly every day! Why didn't you write to *me*?'

'I did write to you.' Robert looked at her intently, studying her face. But then – to her intense relief – he cracked a sort of smile. 'I suppose some letters must go astray?'

'Yes, they must!' cried Cassie. 'I bet there are Forces postal depots all over the Med full of sacks of undelivered mail.'

'Perhaps,' said Robert.

'There's no perhaps about it!'

'Cass, don't look at me like that. You say you wrote, and I believe you.'

'I should think so, too.' But Cassie was still annoyed with him. How could he dare to think she hadn't bothered to write? 'I wrote you dozens of letters, Rob,' she said. 'They'll probably all turn up at once some day.'

'I dare say they will.' Robert shook his head. 'I'm sorry, Cassie, I'm such an idiot sometimes,' he added ruefully. 'I'm going to be here for a week. Do you think you could get some leave?'

'No, but I'll sort something out, don't worry.' Cassie

grinned at him – she couldn't help it. 'Helen Crane's been having an affair with a married captain. I've been doing all her motor maintenance, so she owes me half a dozen favours.'

'Good, let's call them in.'

'Where are we going?' Cassie asked, as Robert picked her hat up from the table in the hallway and put it on her head.

'We'll have something to eat, and then – we'll see.'

They walked from Cassie's billet into the old part of the city, dodging a dozen hawkers selling everything from genuine Middle Kingdom artefacts to ersatz versions of American cigarettes.

Robert stopped on a corner to give some street kids money, and soon he had a whole tribe chasing after him, all shrieking for baksheesh.

'They think you're Father Christmas,' Cassie told him, as the grubby, chattering column grew in length and volume.

'Poor little sods,' said Robert. He took more change out of his pockets, dividing it between the ten or fifteen ragged children who had followed him.

'That's more than enough, Rob,' Cassie told him, for by now she was almost immune to children begging on the streets, and had learned that the best way to help them was to give to missions where they were clothed and fed. 'Go on, you lot, hop it,' she told the clamouring children, as they grinned and jabbered and held out their skinny hands for more.

'Baksheesh, British officer, baksheesh!' exclaimed a lanky ten-year-old in a dirty tunic, jumping up and down in front of Robert.

'No, that's all you're getting,' insisted Cassie, and she clapped her hands at them. 'Go on, clear off – shoo!'

Eventually, the children shooed.

They turned another corner to find a row of traders

with their goods laid out on carpets on the pavements. As Europeans in business suits and Allied servicemen and women walked by, the men called out to them.

'You buy a present for your pretty lady?' one of them demanded, as he grabbed at Robert's sleeve.

'No, thank you.' Robert shook him off.

'Your man, he's mean.' The trader grinned at Cassie, revealing stumps of brown-stained, rotting teeth. 'You find a nice man, plenty money, *he* buy you presents – yes?'

Cassie laughed, and stopped to look at the stuff the man was selling – earrings, necklaces and silver bangles. 'Those silver ones are pretty,' she told Robert, pointing.

'They sell stuff like that in the bazaars in India,' said Robert. 'But it isn't silver, it's some sort of alloy. Cassie, darling, if you'd like a bangle, I shall buy you one, but from a proper jeweller's shop.'

'Bangle, bangle, lady wants a bangle!' cried the trader, scooping up a pile of them and trying to push some on to Cassie's wrist. 'My bangles, solid silver, very good!'

'How much?' asked Cassie. Poor bloke, she thought, he's just like all the rest of us, trying to get by and make a living, and what's the harm in that?

The man considered for a moment, eyeing Robert up and down, and then he named a price.

Robert worked it out in English money.

'That's about a shilling for a dozen, or a penny each,' he said, and laughed. 'Come on, Cassie, you don't really want a penny bangle. Let's go to a real jeweller, eh? They'll still be open.'

'Buy me just one.' Cassie smiled at Robert. 'Just one penny bangle?'

'Just one?' echoed the trader, eyeing Robert mournfully.

'Just one,' said Robert firmly, and gave the man some money. 'It's all right, keep the change.'

The man looked puzzled for a moment. But then he understood, and shoved the money deep inside his robe. Salaaming like a puppet on a string, he called down all the blessings of the Prophet on the generous English officer, wishing him long life, a pretty wife and many sons.

As Robert and Cassie walked on down the street, the other hawkers shouted out to them, offering them even better, even cheaper jewellery.

But Robert hustled Cassie on. 'You mustn't wear that thing,' he said. 'It's bound to tarnish. It'll make your wrist go green.'

'I'll take the risk,' said Cassie, and she slipped it on. 'My penny bangle,' she said smiling, as she turned it round and round. 'Look, Rob. It's very pretty. Do you see these little patterns?'

'I tell you, it'll make your arm fall off.' Robert took Cassie's hand. 'Come on, let's find a jeweller.'

'How long will the army be in Africa?' asked Cassie, as they came out of a jeweller's shop, where Robert had bought a heavy silver bracelet that fitted perfectly.

'Not much longer,' Robert said. 'The desert war is over, the Germans are defeated. Some Italian units are still holding out, but they must know they're beaten.'

'Where will you be going next, I wonder?'

'Italy,' said Robert. 'It's all hush-hush, of course, so absolutely everybody knows. The Yanks and us, we chase the Axis armies back to Rome, then to Berlin. Or anyway, that seems to be the plan.'

'I could come to Italy,' said Cassie.

'What would you do in Italy?'

'I'd earn my keep, don't worry. I could drive an ambulance, a jeep, a three-ton truck. Anything, in fact, except a tank. I've passed all the tests.'

'They probably won't want ATS girls. Cassie, this won't be a Sunday picnic. It's going to be a real hard slog, making our way up Italy. There won't be any jobs for women anyway, except for nursing staff.'

Robert smiled affectionately at Cassie. 'You stay here in Egypt, where you're safe. When I get leave, I'll come to Alex, and I'll take you out, all right?'

But Cassie was already plotting, scheming, wondering, how she could get to Italy. She would ask the major. Annie Sheringham was sure to know.

They went to a city restaurant which was full of Allied army officers and their civilian women, French girls in couture gowns all dolled up to the nines, dark-eyed Lebanese businessmen in suits all doing deals, and shifty-looking gentlemen of indeterminate extraction, together with a sprinkling of service girls in uniform, all of them with men.

'What would you like to eat?' asked Robert, as he looked for a waiter to take them to a table.

'Oh, I dunno.' Cassie was too happy to feel like eating. 'Those mince things, I suppose,' she told him, pointing to a plate being carried by a sweating waiter. 'You know, the ones on sticks.'

'You mean kebabs,' said Robert, wrinkling his nose. 'They're made of donkey's innards and old socks. What about to drink?'

'I'll have mint tea, with sugar if they've got it.'

'Jesus, that sounds boring.' Robert smiled. 'I dare say they have wine. Or, if we're lucky, some champagne.'

'Champagne doesn't agree with me.' Cassie blushed, remembering the last time she had drunk champagne. 'You have what you want. I'm on the wagon.'

'You think I'm going to get you plastered, don't you?' Robert reached out to stroke a stray, blonde curl. 'You think

I'm going to get you drunk, and then I'll take you somewhere and seduce you?'

'I don't think anything of the sort.' Still tingling from his touch, Cassie's blush grew hotter and she felt it creeping down her neck. 'You're a perfect gentleman. Frances said so when I told her what had happened in London.'

'I'm a gentleman?' Robert laughed. 'Oh, Cassie, love – don't bank on it!'

Cassie didn't need alcohol to make her want to be seduced by lovely Robert Denham. Since she'd had his postcard, she had thought of very little else, and the other girls had teased her constantly, seeing who could make her blush the most.

The service in the restaurant was ridiculously slow. While they were waiting for their dinner, Robert smoked, drank whisky, and all the while he kept his dark brown eyes on Cassie's face.

They didn't need to talk. They started sentences, but didn't finish them, breaking off to ask each other what they had been saying, laughing and admitting they didn't have a clue.

'Shall we go on somewhere?' he enquired, after they had finally eaten dinner, nibbled some sticky dates and drunk their sweet Egyptian coffee.

'To a club, you mean?' asked Cassie, wondering if a club would let her in with just two stripes, even if she were with an officer. 'I don't think I want to be indoors,' she told him. 'It's a lovely night, so why don't we walk along the shore?'

Robert was so relieved to find that Cassie hadn't changed – that she was still the same sweet, pretty girl with the cheeky grin and the engaging way with her that made his heart beat faster.

Aldershot or Alexandria – he couldn't have cared less where they were, or where they went, provided they could be together. So he paid for dinner, and then they went out into the warm, soft velvet night, which wasn't anything like the nights in deserts, where the temperature could drop to freezing, or a few degrees below.

They strolled along the crescent shoreline dotted with tall palm trees and white-painted houses, some of them very grand. Alex is a city used to lovers, Robert thought, remembering that it was here Antony had fallen for the wily Cleopatra. But Cassie wasn't anything like Cleopatra, who had had two lovers, Julius Caesar and Mark Antony.

Cassie and Stephen …

Stop it now, he told himself, stop spoiling everything.

The moon was up, so it was very bright, reminding him of the winter night in Dorset when he had first met Cassie, and he had decided she was going straight back home to Birmingham.

He shuddered at the thought.

'What's the matter, Rob?' she asked, obviously detecting the tremor which was rippling through him now.

'Nothing,' he said, and held her hand more tightly, as if he was afraid to let her go.

'What are you going to do in Alex?' Cassie asked him as they strolled along.

'Meet up with some of the other fellows from my regiment, have a few drinks, play a few games of billiards, get my hair cut, let a barber shave me properly – and see you when you can get away.'

'I'll be off duty every evening this week.'

'Then we'll see a lot of each other, won't we?' Robert glanced at Cassie's face. 'You're not wearing make-up.'

'No, it just slides off in all this heat.'

'You look much prettier without it, actually.' Robert didn't want to tell her about his dream, but he was relieved to see she looked so natural tonight, not painted like a tart.

Also, she hadn't mentioned Stephen once, and he began to think he had been fretting about nothing. He let go of her hand and put his arm around her shoulders, and then he bent to kiss her on the mouth.

As she kissed him back, he found he wasn't worrying or doubting any more.

The following evening, they went to a different restaurant, and Cassie seemed distracted, not talking much, not eating much, just sitting there and taking sips of lemonade and looking at him now and then, as if she couldn't believe that he was actually there.

'What are you thinking about?' he asked.

'You and me.' She sniffed and looked so sad he thought she might begin to cry. 'When you came to Alex, it was so wonderful to see you. But now I feel – I don't know how I feel – '

'I make you sad?'

'No, of course you don't, but I worry about you all the time, and I want to be with you so much. But I don't want you to think I'm – '

'I don't think you're anything but perfect.' Robert thought, there's no point in pretending I don't understand, when she's sitting there in front of me, and she's blushing like the setting sun, but isn't going to say it for me.

'Come on, let's go,' he said.

'Yes, I suppose I should be getting back.'

'When are you on duty again?'

'At eight tomorrow morning, but – '

'We could walk along the promenade.' Covering her hand with his, he looked into her eyes. 'Or perhaps we could go somewhere private? Somewhere more – ?'

He left the question hanging in the air.

Cassie looked back at him, meeting his gaze.

'You're saying, go to bed.' She felt herself go red again. 'I – well – I must be back by midnight, otherwise the other girls will wonder where I've gone.'

'I'll see to that, my darling Cinderella,' Robert whispered softly. 'I'll deliver you myself.'

'Oh,' said Cassie doubtfully. 'Well, then – yes, all right.'

'All right, she says, as if I've asked her if she wants another cigarette.' Robert took swig of whisky – the waiter had left a bottle on the table, and now he was taking full advantage. 'I'm sorry, Cassie. It seems I've got it wrong.'

'Oh, no, Rob! You've got it right!' Cassie knew her face must be the colour of a robin's breast. She almost wished he wasn't here, looking so irresistible, so lovely. She'd never thought a man could be desirable, for men were huge and hideous, normally. But Robert Denham – he looked almost edible tonight.

He'd soon be going away again. He might be injured, or he might be killed. If she didn't do this, tonight, she knew she would regret it all her life. She refused to listen to the little voice inside her head which said – but if you do, you might regret it, too.

'Oh, Rob!' she wailed. 'I'd love to, want to – I want to more than anything! But – '

'But?' repeated Robert.

'I don't know what people do when – '

'What?'

Cassie's voice sank to a small, embarrassed whisper. 'When they don't want babies. Oh, I know what happens to make a baby. I've known for years and years, and the MO told us all about it when we first joined up.'

She stared down at the tablecloth. 'But I don't know – French letters, all that stuff. The army doesn't issue them to us. I've never even seen one.'

'I know what people do,' said Robert, and an ironic smile

creased his face. 'But, Cass, don't do this if it doesn't seem right.'

'You mean, if I'm too holy?'

'I mean, a first time should be special.' Robert stubbed out his cigarette, and looked round for the waiter. 'We could go somewhere for an hour or two, or I'll walk you back to where you're billeted. You choose.'

'We'll go somewhere,' said Cassie faintly.

'You're quite sure?'

'I'm certain.' Cassie stood up, picked up her shoulder bag, and refused to listen to the voice which was now saying that to use French letters was a sin.

He led her up a narrow alley to a tall, white house with dark blue shutters faded by the sun.

'A hotel?' she asked him.

'You could say that,' he murmured.

'Rob, it's not a brothel?'

'It's a lady's private residence, and she lets out rooms to officers.'

'Oh,' said Cassie frowning, as Robert rang the bell.

Eventually, an old French woman with scarlet nails and lipstick, and wearing a black cocktail dress, opened the door to them. 'Good evening, Madame Croix,' said Robert. 'Do you have a room?'

The woman didn't speak. Instead, she merely shrugged, and then she held out one gnarled hand, sniffing when she saw the money was Egyptian currency, but after counting it she let them in.

He's done this before, thought Cassie sadly. She knew it was unreasonable to hope she was the first. She knew a man who looked like Robert would have had many women. All the soldiers did. She'd seen them queuing up outside the brothels like so many housewives, waiting to buy fish.

But she was disappointed, just the same. She could feel the medals Lily sent her lying between her breasts. She should not be risking her immortal soul for this.

The room was small but very clean, with stiff, white Egyptian cotton sheets on an old gilt and iron bed. The shutters were closed and so the room was cool.

'You had all this planned,' she said.

'I didn't.'

'Yes, you did.'

'Well, all right,' said Robert sheepishly. 'I asked some chaps about the places I could take a girl in Alex, and someone told me this was clean and decent.'

Robert stood back, looked earnestly at Cassie. 'Listen,' he said quietly, 'I don't want to push you into doing anything that you don't want to do. If you like, we'll leave.'

'You've paid your money now.'

'It doesn't matter.'

'I'm sorry, Robert.' Cassie looked up at him. 'I should never have got into this. I shouldn't have led you on. They give us lectures all the time, you know, about what soldiers want, and how it's up to us to stop them getting it.'

'So do you want to leave?'

'No.' Cassie made her mind up. 'I want to go to bed with you.'

'I promise I won't hurt you,' murmured Robert, as he unbuttoned Cassie's dress and kissed her on the temples, and as he stroked her neck.

But Cassie couldn't respond to him. She stood there like a statue, like a woman made of ice.

'What's all this?' he asked, when he found the silver chain and two or three holy medals that Cassie had worn around her neck since she had first left England.

'They're my lucky charms,' said Cassie, shutting out the

sound of Lily Taylor's voice condemning the whole tribe of men, and Father Riley's thoughts on purity.

As they lay together afterwards, Cassie thought it had been just as well that one of them knew what to do. She'd been to lectures, she understood the technicalities, she knew you had to make him wear a thing, she knew that if you went to bed with anyone who was diseased, you'd end up sick yourself …

But she wouldn't have had a clue about the kissing stuff. Or what she was supposed to do to make it nice for him.

It hadn't mattered. He had known, and he'd been kind and patient, he'd told her what was good and what was not, and then he'd made it wonderful.

'But I haven't,' Robert cried, when they were lying comfortably together, and she remarked she didn't mind if he'd had other girls. At least it meant he knew his way around the female body. 'I – listen, Cass! Whatever you might have heard, not everyone – and anyway, there aren't that many opportunities in the Tunisian desert.'

'Then how did you know?' demanded Cassie.

'How did I know what?'

'What would be nice for me?'

'I have friends, they talk about it.' Robert frowned, went red beneath his tan, and Cassie saw she must have got it wrong, that he was not a liar. He hadn't done this before.

'I'm sorry, Rob,' she murmured, going red herself.

'I should think so, too,' said Robert.

'You're a natural genius.' Cassie kissed his frown away.

'You're a cheeky monkey.' But then, to her relief, he smiled again. 'I say, Miss Taylor?'

'Yes, Mr Denham?'

'My brilliant performance must have been some kind of fluke, perhaps? Or shall we say beginner's luck? So, just to make sure we've got it right, perhaps we ought to run through it again?'

'Just so we remember next time, eh?' Cassie smiled and kissed him.

'Precisely,' Robert said.

She didn't *quite* believe him. Somebody who looked like Robert Denham – surely he'd had girls before? Surely he must have practised on many other women before tonight?

But, as Robert kissed her yet again, and as she felt herself begin to glow, she shut her mind to thoughts like that.

Chapter Eleven

'It looks like someone had a lovely time last night,' said Jane MacFarlane, as she and Cassie got ready to leave the villa the next morning.

'Why should you think that?' asked Cassie, yawning.

'You're grinning like an imbecile, and you've got red blotches on your neck.'

Cassie glanced in the little mirror above the kitchen sink. 'Mosquito bites,' she said laconically.

'Mosquitoes, my Aunt Fanny.' Jane MacFarlane laughed. 'You running Annie around again today?'

'Yes, so I'd better shift myself.'

'You'd better dab some powder on as well, to cover up your bites.' Grey eyes sparkling, Jane grinned at Cassie. 'Aye, he's very bonny,' she admitted. 'I'd not mind having a wee crack at him myself. But Annie won't like the thought of nasty soldiers chewing at her girls.'

'He's not a nasty soldier, he's – '

'Jings, Cass, spare us all that soppy nonsense.' Jane took out her own compact, dabbed some powder on the marks on Cassie's neck. 'Aye, that should do it. Off you go.'

Robert stayed in town for four more days. When he couldn't be with Cassie, he met up with other chaps he knew, and they dawdled round the sights of Alex. Or that was what he said they did. They loafed in all the officers' clubs, he added, playing billiards, drinking, smoking, reading magazines.

'As long as you're not loafing with any other women,' Cassie told him, narrowing her eyes at him and trying to make a joke of it, but feeling a sharp nib of jealousy stabbing at her heart.

'Why would I want to be with other women, when I can be with you?'

'You're not with me always.'

'Yes, I am,' said Robert. 'You're always in my heart.'

'Oh, Rob, you say the nicest things!' said Cassie beaming. Then she wondered if she'd cry – and if he meant it. If she'd put her soul in mortal danger for a man who would forget her the moment he left Alexandria.

She couldn't get Father Riley's wise advice out of her head, even though she hadn't taken any of this advice, and knew he'd be appalled and horrified if he knew what she'd done.

Although she couldn't have any leave, Cassie managed to get a few hours off each working day. She and Robert spent another evening at the shuttered house, where time stood still for them, and where nothing mattered outside the stark, white walls.

'What's the matter, Cass?' he asked, after they'd made love and he was lying back against the pillows, playing with her hair – which must have looked a sight, she thought, all messed up and tangled into elf-locks, she'd never get a comb through it again.

'Nothing, Robert.' Cassie forced a smile.

But – as always – guilt was spoiling everything. She wished there was someone she could go and see, someone who would make it all seem right. But of course it wasn't right, and any priest would tell her so.

'Then why do you always look so sad?'

'I'm not sad at all.' Cassie somehow managed to turn the smile into a happy grin. 'I'm never sad when I'm with you.'

She thought he might say something now, something like she made him happy, something like they'd always be together, but he didn't say anything at all. He just shook his head, he smiled a little smile, and he went on messing up her hair.

She was more than happy to walk around the town with him. She wanted to be seen with him, to show him off to all her friends in Alex, to make the point to people like snooty Jane MacFarlane that even though she'd grown up in a little terraced cottage behind a tannery, she could be the girlfriend of a gorgeous man like Robert Denham, a man who could have any girl he pleased.

After he'd gone back to his battalion, she cried herself to sleep night after night. After she'd finished crying, she realised she'd committed at least a dozen mortal sins, pride and lust and covetousness among them.

She found she didn't repent of any of them.

So she was bound for hell.

She didn't care.

'Annie wants to see you,' Sergeant Payne told Cassie. It was three days later, and she was in the motor pool. She was checking over half a dozen new arrivals, jeeps that had come from England and been bounced around a bit, had had some parts worked loose.

'Why, what have I done?' asked Cassie, crawling from underneath a jeep, and pushing a strand of hair out of her eyes.

'God, where would I start?' groaned Sergeant Payne. 'Go on, corporal, go and get yourself spruced up a bit. The major's waiting.'

But I'm allowed to have a boyfriend, Cassie thought, as she washed her hands and face, and as she raked a comb through her fair hair, much blonder nowadays from all the sunshine.

So he's an officer, and I'm an NCO, she thought, as she

made her way across the compound. So what? It's not against the law.

She had a sudden vision of Lily Taylor and Father Riley sitting in the major's office, waiting to tell her off and say she had to come straight home.

'You asked to see me, ma'am?' said Cassie.

She was a little calmer now. This sudden summons from the major couldn't mean anything more worrying than a special mission, perhaps to lead a convoy through the desert, or go and fetch a lorry from Port Said.

'Ah, yes,' said the major, who was writing something in a file, but then looked up and smiled. 'They need you back in Blighty, Corporal Taylor.'

'They what?' demanded Cassie, shocked – for whatever she had really been expecting, it had not been this.

'They what, *ma'am*,' the major said severely. She looked hard at Cassie. 'You've gone very pale. You seem surprised.'

'I – I thought we drivers would all be going to Italy with the army,' stammered Cassie.

'Did you, now?' The major put her pen down on the desk and narrowed her eyes at Cassie. 'A few girls will be going, certainly. They'll need some ATS to drive the lorries and supply trucks, I suppose, and maybe to drive ambulances as well. But they'll be volunteers.'

'I can drive an ambulance, ma'am!' cried Cassie. 'I'd like to volunteer.'

'Cassie, my dear,' the major said, and now her gaze was softening, 'I'm not going to send you off to Italy. It's going to be grim. The Germans and Italians won't exactly welcome Allied troops. Our chaps are going to have to fight their way up that peninsula inch by inch.'

'But, ma'am – '

'I know you must be worried about your boyfriend. But

154

you must think about the army and your country now. You must go back to Blighty, where you're needed. You should be all right on the trip home. The Med's much safer these days, and so is England, too. The Germans aren't still bombing anything and everything in our green and pleasant land – nowadays, they have other fish to fry.'

I'll volunteer to go to Italy anyway, thought Cassie.

But when she did, she was turned down, and told her orders to return to England on the next available troopship stood.

She cursed the major, who had made a pet of her and wished to keep her safe.

She wrote to Robert straight away, to tell him the bad news.

But what if he'd already gone? What if her letter went astray, as so many letters seemed to do? What if they never met again?

But some kind saint or fairy must have heard her offering them anything they wanted, her heart, her life, her soul, if she could just see Robert once again. A week before she had to leave for England, she had a Forces postcard.

'I've got a ride,' he wrote. 'I'll see you Friday.'

Cassie was beside herself with joy. She rearranged her duties, getting Jane to take her place in a convoy of new lorries to be driven to Cairo, while she did all Jane's driving jobs in Alex, ferrying army officers round the city in the big black staff cars.

Everywhere she heard the rumours, mutterings, whispers, guesses and speculations about what would happen next.

Mussolini would be overthrown by his own people.

Italy was going to surrender to the Allies.

Mussolini wasn't finished yet.

The Italian army would fight on.

Germany would pour troops into Italy.

All Italian men would be deported to concentration camps.

The Germans had over-stretched themselves, and they would be leaving Italy to its own devices.

'It's going to be a mess,' said Sergeant Payne.

'I still wish I could go,' said Cassie.

'Taylor, you need your head examined.' Sergeant Payne looked scornful. 'We all know you're in love, and I can't say we blame you – he's a very lovely man. But you don't want to go to Italy. You'd never get to see him, anyway. Unless he got hurt, of course, and ended up in hospital, and even then you'd probably be stationed miles and miles away from him.'

Now Cassie shuddered, for this was her worst nightmare, Robert getting hurt. She wouldn't allow herself to think about him being dead. It was bad enough when somebody she knew was even wounded, when somebody she knew albeit slightly was reported killed. There'd been that girl from Derby, she'd come out a week ago, and on her first convoy through the desert she'd crashed her jeep and died.

'I'm sorry, Cass,' said Sergeant Payne. 'But it will be hell on earth in Italy, with the winter coming on, and the Italians mining all the roads, and the Germans blowing up the bridges, and – '

Cassie stopped listening to Sergeant Payne.

Robert came to the villa to pick Cassie up. He put up with the remarks and innuendoes made by girls who happened to be at home, and then took Cassie out to dinner.

'You're excited, aren't you?' she said bitterly, as they drank their gritty, sickly coffee after they had eaten Cassie couldn't remember what. 'You can't wait to go to Italy.'

'I can't wait to finish this whole tedious business.' Robert took her hand and held it, massaging her fingers one by one. 'We all want to get on with the job and go back home.'

'Some of you won't be going home,' Cassie reminded him. 'I sometimes think of all those men who won't see home again.'

'You mustn't think about it.' Robert looked at Cassie, his dark eyes almost black in the dim light. 'Cassie, shall we go and see Madame Croix? We'll just about have time.'

'Robert, what's that supposed to mean, we'll just about have time? What else do you have to do tonight?'

'Oh, Cassie darling, I wish we had all day, all week, forever!' Robert sighed and kissed her finger tips. 'But I'll need to be back home by midnight, otherwise I'm going to miss my lift.'

So this might be the last time, Cassie thought. I might never see him again, in this world or the next. She refused to listen to her conscience, which was saying, now kiss him goodnight, then say goodbye.

'Yes, let's do that,' she said.

So they went to the tall, white house, where the old French woman let them in, took Robert's money, and then let them find their own way to their room.

Afterwards, they smoked Cassie's cigarettes, and Robert drank some whisky from a flask.

'What's wrong, Cass?' he asked, for Cassie was sitting picking at the sheet and wouldn't look at him.

'I've got my orders, and I'll be on a convoy Tuesday week.'

'Well, the Med is nothing like as dangerous as when you first came out, so that's good news,' said Robert.

'No, it flaming isn't!' Cassie cried. 'I don't want to go back home to England, and in any case I like it here!'

'You'll be more use in England,' Robert told her, pulling her close to him and giving her a hug.

'I'm useful here in Egypt.'

'I'll say you are, my darling.' Robert grinned. 'But we must think of others, not only of ourselves.'

'Oh, shut up, you so-and-so.'

'You mean, shut up, you stupid bugger, don't you, Cass?'

'I'm trying not to talk like that.' Cassie twisted round to look at him. 'Robert, will you miss me?'

'Yes, of course I will, my little bird, I'll miss you more than anything.'

'There'll be birds in Italy, you know.' Cassie looked down at her finger nails, which were begrimed and grubby from working in the motor pool. She couldn't clean them, however hard she tried. 'There'll be lots and lots of pretty birds, with long dark hair and lovely big brown eyes.'

'Maybe there will,' said Robert. 'But I have a preference for little English sparrows.'

'Rob, stay safe.' Cassie looked into Robert's eyes. 'Please don't take unnecessary risks.'

'Risks, she says – and this from somebody who braved the Bay of Biscay and the U-boats in the Med, when she could have stayed in Alsherdot, and ferried bridagiers around?'

'You'll never let me forget that night,' said Cassie. 'I tell you, Robert Denham, I'm never going to drink champagne again.'

'Never, Cassie darling?'

'Never, cross my heart and hope to die.'

'You're going to drink Tizer at our wedding?'

'Our wedding?' Cassie's eyes grew as round as florins. 'Did you say our wedding?'

'Yes, that's what I said.'

'You're asking me to marry you?'

'Cass, you're not usually as slow as this! Of course I'm asking you to marry me.'

'Oh.' Cassie suddenly felt very cold. She pulled the cotton sheet around her body, shivering.

'Well?' demanded Robert

'But blokes like you don't marry girls like me.'

'What's that supposed to mean?'

'You know,' said Cassie, shrugging. 'You're an officer, I'm a – '

'But I thought you loved me?'

'Rob, you *mean* it?'

'Cass, of course I mean it!'

'I'm sorry, Robert.' Cassie took his hand. She stroked the long, tanned fingers which had given her such pleasure and which, like every other part of Robert, she loved with all her heart. 'I'd love to marry you,' she said.

'Then we're engaged?'

'Yes, Robert, we're engaged.'

He looked at Cassie, wondering if all men felt like this when they proposed, as if they'd just done something crazy, as if the ground had opened up beneath them?

Then he thought, but I love Cassie, don't I? She means more than life itself to me? Of course she does!

'We don't have time to buy a ring,' he said. 'But when we meet again, we're going shopping.'

He was relieved to see her smile.

'I'm sorry, I'm going to need to leave,' he added, reaching for his clothes. 'I have to meet the other chaps at midnight.'

'Yes, I know,' she said. 'I must be going, too. I have to take the major to a meeting first thing tomorrow morning, and she'll be so sarcastic if I'm late. Robert, what if – '

Robert put his finger to her lips.

'We'll meet again, I promise you,' he said.

Chapter Twelve

The Germans had been beaten in North Africa, but they'd got it right in Italy, Robert decided grimly. He took the bottle offered by his sergeant, drank some water, and stared down at the dizzying drop below him, glad he had a head for heights.

He'd known the Allies faced a bitter struggle on the European mainland. But, buoyed up by their victories in Africa, he and everyone else had hoped a month or two of fighting, together with bombardment from their heavy guns, would see the Axis armies on the run.

Mussolini was out of office, after all. The new Italian government had welcomed the Americans and British. So why, when the Italians had declared an armistice, were the German armies still in occupation, still holding all the cards?

It was because they'd turned the country into one huge battle zone, with lines of fortresses that stretched from coast to coast, and from these impregnable positions they could fire at leisure at the invading Allies, cutting their soldiers down like standing corn. They were so well dug in and well provisioned that Robert feared it was going to take forever to drive them out of Italy.

'All right, Sergeant Gregory,' he said, standing up and stretching. 'Get the chaps back on their feet again.'

'Yes, sir,' said the sergeant, and he managed a weary grin. 'Onwards and upwards – eh, sir? Up the bloody hill to Bedfordshire, and round the bloody bend?'

'Onwards and upwards, sergeant,' nodded Robert. In spite of aching feet and constant, gnawing hunger, he managed to grin back.

They'd taken a short rest among some boulders, where

Robert had hoped the German snipers who infested these bleak, barren hillsides wouldn't spot them and machine-gun them, peppering them with bullets and splinters of sharp rock. Now the platoon went slogging on along the mountain road towards their next objective.

This was a village that the Germans might still occupy and, if they did, Robert knew they wouldn't give it up without a fight. Or, if the platoon was lucky, the Germans might have gone already, leaving nothing but ruined houses, booby traps and mines.

In my next life, thought Robert, I'll be in the Royal Artillery, not here at the sharp end, in the bloody Infantry. I'll be miles and miles behind the lines, chatting to my mates and polishing my howitzer, firing off a few two-hundred-pounders now and then, and making daisy chains.

He tipped his helmet back a little, wiped his brow with the back of his hand, and felt the rain go streaming down his gas cape. Why did it rain so much in Italy? It must be weeks since they had seen the sun, since they'd felt any warmth upon their backs, and all the time it rained and rained and rained.

In spite of being carried under mackintoshes, rifles rusted, then they wouldn't fire. Men came down with coughs and colds and dysentery, and in the bitter cold of the mountains, their hands and feet swelled up with bright red, purple-blistered chilblains. Some of them could hardly walk, could hardly grip a gun.

Always being hungry didn't help, and they were exhausted, too, for it was well nigh impossible to sleep – it was too cold, too wet, and far too dangerous to drop your guard.

'GHQ won't tolerate any looting,' Robert's CO had told his junior officers before their whole battalion had set out on this mission.

So what are my men supposed to eat, thought Robert.

Their supply lines were so stretched that rations often failed to arrive. Lorries on the narrow mountain roads got mortared or machine-gunned by the Germans on the ridges, were sent spiralling in flames into the deep ravines below.

So, whenever they came across an abandoned farm or homestead, the hungry Allied soldiers helped themselves to any chickens, goats, stored grain or crops the Germans hadn't pinched or burned already.

'I know the men need food, but we must try to keep the borrowing down,' said Robert to his sergeant. 'We can afford to pay.'

'But this Italian money's worthless, sir.' The sergeant shrugged. 'The peasants up here in the mountains, they don't want our money. It's no use to them. They need bread and meat, the same as we do. Sir, these people hate us.'

'We're liberating them!'

'Jerries, Yanks or English, they think we're all the same.' The sergeant shrugged again. 'We're all in the business of smashing up their country, blowing up their houses, and ruining their lives.'

The sergeant stared all round the desolation. 'Our chaps don't like the Italians either, sir. They reckon all the men are cowards, and all the girls are whores. When we were in Naples, you'll remember, fathers and mothers were selling daughters for a plate of pasta. The lads know Italians pinch our rations, then flog them back to us.'

They reached the village and found it was deserted. They camped in a farmer's cellar for the night. The family had been killed, or run away, so there was little left to scrounge or borrow. They found a sack of chestnut flour from which they made some pancakes.

Robert left some Italian money in the ruined kitchen. Looking around, he shook his head. His own home back in

England was certainly very basic, he admitted that, but he hadn't realised that ordinary European people could still live in mediaeval squalor, in houses made of stones all thrown together, with animals in the lower rooms, and people breathing in their stink above.

The next day, they trudged on through the mountains, towards their next objective, another German-occupied or possibly deserted hill top village.

In the past few days, their own battalion had been in several fire fights, taking lots of casualties. Robert's platoon had helped to drive a couple of hundred occupying Germans a little further north. But when they finally occupied a village, almost every house in it would be a burnt-out ruin, thoroughly mined or booby-trapped by the retreating Germans, with donkeys and sometimes oxen lying dead and rotting, some of them half-eaten, perhaps by wolves or bears.

Corporal Kelly swore he'd seen a bear, and some of the more adventurous chaps were keen to bag a bear.

'We'll soon have his coat off, sir,' twenty-year-old Private Blain – a lively, skinny boy from Beaminster – said to Robert, grinning.

'Then we'll turn him into caps and gloves,' continued Private Thornton, Private Blain's best friend and fellow wide-boy. 'We'll flog 'em to the other blokes – or even to Italians.'

'Or send 'em home to girlfriends back in Blighty,' put in Private Blain. 'My girl in Dorchester, she'd like a bearskin hat.'

Robert had a sudden vision of Cassie in a bearskin hat and nothing else, and smiled to himself.

They hadn't had any post for ages, not that he'd expected any, but he wished he knew she was all right, that she was back in England, not still on a troopship tossing in the Bay of Biscay.

'Some Italian back in Naples said bear meat's good to eat.' Private Thornton licked his dry, chapped lips, and Robert heard his stomach growl with hunger.

'You two watch your step,' he said. 'We're here to fight the Germans. So I don't want to write and tell your mothers you got eaten by some Italian bear.'

Then he scratched a sore bit on his neck, wondering if he was getting scurvy, if that was why he itched.

Cassie was back in England, had been there for a month or more, and she was hating it. After Alexandria, she found life in Aldershot so tedious and boring that it made her itch.

But it had been wonderful to see the faces of the other drivers, especially the faces of the nobs, when she had announced that she was going to marry the famous Daisy Denham's younger brother.

Although she didn't actually have a ring – there hadn't been any time to go and buy one, she had added, and the girls accepted that – she had her silver bracelet, and it was much admired.

'Ooh, I say, that's classy,' said a girl from Manchester, whose father was a jeweller. 'It's solid, Cass, not plate. Just feel the weight of it! By heck, it must have cost your bloke a packet.'

'Yes, it *looks* expensive,' sneered Lavinia, one of the toff drivers with whom Cassie had crossed words and swords before, and who had not – unfortunately – been posted somewhere else while Cassie had been in Egypt. 'Well, *quite* expensive, anyway,' she continued. 'It's not the sort of thing most men would feel they had to buy for somebody like you.'

Cassie didn't rise to that. She didn't retort that nobody bought bracelets for Lavinia, who was just an ugly, jealous cow.

She wore the silver bracelet all the time, pushed high up

her forearm and covered by her shirt sleeve. She kept the penny bangle in her army-issue sewing kit, hidden from the other girls, who wouldn't understand why it was precious, for now it was all tarnished, and it looked like what it was, a cheap and tawdry thing.

But Cassie and her fiancé very soon became old news. In the army, the novelty of engagements wore off quickly, for almost every girl in barracks had a husband, boyfriend or fiancé. Motor maintenance, driving jobs and drill filled Cassie's days.

Frances Ashford seemed to be having much more fun in Chester. She was going around with someone very nice, she wrote, but there were complications. So, when they met again, Cassie mustn't be shocked or disapproving.

Cassie wouldn't have dreamed of being shocked or disapproving, not after what she'd done in Alexandria herself. Some days, the guilt and worry were almost overwhelming, and she found she was longing to see Frances, if only to confess, to share the burden, for Frances to say she'd done nothing wrong, that if you were in love it was all right.

But she couldn't imagine what nicely-brought-up Frances Ashford might be up to now.

Perhaps, thought Cassie, she had met a Yank? One of those black soldiers who everybody said had lovely manners, and treated every woman like a lady?

Perhaps she'd dyed her hair? Since the Americans had come, almost all the girls in Cassie's unit had gone blonde – every night, the hut stank of peroxide, and there was a thriving trade in it on the black market nowadays.

She couldn't imagine Frances Ashford blonde.

She wondered if she should put in for a move. If she worked in Birmingham or Chester, she could get to Smethwick to see her granny, and see Frances, too, and find out what she shouldn't be shocked about.

She needed to tell Lily that she was engaged. But she meant to do it face to face, not to spring it on her granny in a letter.

She rehearsed the conversation in her mind.

'Yes, he's single, Granny,' she would say. 'Yes, I'm absolutely sure he's single. I've met all his family, his parents and his brother and his sister, and I know he hasn't got a wife.

'Yes, Granny, he's a nice, clean-living boy, and he's good-looking, too. He's dark and six feet tall, he's really handsome, everybody says so, all the girls turn round to stare at him. He's generous and sensible, as well. You'll love him, Granny – I just know you will.

'Well, no – he hasn't got a trade. No, he's not a Catholic. But I don't suppose he'll mind the children being Catholic.'

What more could Lily want?

A lot of things.

A local man, for starters, someone like a butcher or a baker or a plumber, someone with a shop, a yard, a workbench of his own, a horse and cart.

A Catholic from a decent family, a man whose mother Lily knew to be a good, God-fearing woman, a mother who had raised her children well.

Somebody who went to church on Sundays and at Christmas at the very least, and who would see his own sons did so, too.

Robert didn't fit the bill at all, thought Cassie sadly, and he probably never would.

Cassie had regular driving jobs in London, ferrying top brass around the city. Sometimes, she was in town for several days, and that was quite exciting, seeing so many different people of all nationalities, going to the cinema to see the latest films, or even taking in a show. Occasionally,

Daisy sent her tickets, which made Cassie popular with other ATS.

When Daisy heard that Cassie and her brother were engaged, she wrote to Cassie, inviting her to come and stay at the apartment in Park Lane.

'We must have a drink or two to celebrate,' wrote Daisy. 'If you can get a bit of leave, my sweet, we'll go out on the town.'

Cassie didn't really want to go out on the town, if that meant getting drunk. These days, she was off the booze completely. She was determined to be worthy of Robert and to deserve his love, so she was on the wagon. In fact, she had as good as signed the pledge. But it would be lovely to see Daisy, and she could always stick to lemonade. She wrote to say she'd try to get up soon.

Daisy replied at once, to say if Cassie managed to time her visit right, she'd get a nice surprise.

Then Cassie got another letter from Frances, and she couldn't quite believe her eyes. It's being in the army, she reflected, it changes everybody, no wonder Lady Ashford didn't want to let her join. Well – prim and proper Frances Ashford, who'd have thought it?

'*Mummy and Daddy are going to be so cross,*' continued Frances, when she had confessed she was in love, and felt so happy she was walking on cloud nine, or even ninety-nine.

'*I know it's wrong. I know it's very bad of me, to be seeing someone else's husband, but I can't help myself. They say although we can't help what we feel, we can still make the proper choices. I've decided that's a lot of rot. Where Simon is concerned, I don't have any choice at all. If we can't be together, I shall die.*

'*I do hope I shall see you soon. When do you think you'll get some leave, and when can you come up to Chester? I want you and Simon to be the greatest friends!*'

But all the drivers were kept very busy, and Cassie found she couldn't get any leave. She wanted to see Frances, and of course to meet this paragon who'd made off with her heart.

But it looked as if he'd have to wait.

She managed to arrange a few hours off to fit in with a job in London. She got a lift from Aldershot, and arrived in Piccadilly on a lovely, crisp October morning.

Daisy had said that if she timed it right, she might get a surprise. So she was looking forward to finding out what this surprise might be.

She made her way along the crowded pavements, bought some orange chrysanthemums for Daisy from a vendor with a barrow, and turned right up Park Lane.

When she arrived at Daisy's flat, the butler let her in. He took her flowers and hat and coat, and told her that Miss Denham was soon expected home.

'But Mr Denham is in the morning room,' the butler added, as if it was the most natural, common thing in all the world.

Cassie couldn't believe she'd heard him right. 'M-Mr *Robert* Denham?' she began, as she felt a glow suffuse her face.

'I believe so, miss.'

She couldn't think how Daisy had arranged it. But it was true, and there he was, lost in some kind of daydream, staring out of the window at the traffic in Park Lane.

Cassie just stood and gazed for several seconds, beside herself with joy, happier than she'd ever been in her entire life. 'Rob?' she whispered, scared to break the spell, still hardly daring to believe it.

'Hello, Cass,' said Stephen, turning from his silent contemplation of the traffic far below. 'Sorry, love – wrong twin.'

'Oh – Steve – what a surprise, how nice to see you!' She

couldn't believe she'd just said that, because it wasn't nice at all.

It was as if she had been slapped across the face, and for a second or two she couldn't breathe, she couldn't move, she couldn't do anything at all but stare in disbelief.

But then she battened down her bitter disappointment, and walked across the morning room to kiss him on the cheek. 'Well, Steve,' she managed, 'h-how have you been?'

'Up and down – you know,' said Stephen, shrugging. 'I had a few bad spells in summer. So they changed my medication, and told me to lay off the booze. It seems to help a bit. But without a whisky now and then, my life seems very dull.'

'Dull, my foot!' cried Daisy, who now came bustling in, immaculately dressed in the smart green uniform of the Women's Voluntary Service. 'Hello, my little sparrow,' she said brightly. 'It's very nice to see you, and don't you look pretty? I suppose it must be love! Many congratulations, anyway.'

Daisy kissed her future sister-in-law, and then she smiled archly at her brother. 'Cassie,' she went on, 'you mustn't take any notice of this moaner. I have it on the best authority that he's been seeing some nice girl from Shropshire. They were noticed smooching at the Florida. Then, last Friday evening, he took her to the Ritz. He's also been seen squiring several other lovely women round the town – a rather attractive WAAF, I'm told, and a somewhat saucy-looking Wren, the naughty boy.'

Stephen glowered, but Cassie forced a smile. 'How are you and Ewan?' she asked Daisy.

'We're both fine, my darling, but busy, busy, busy. My goodness, do excuse me!' Daisy yawned behind her hand. 'Poor Ewan's filming almost every morning, we have matinees most afternoons, stage shows every evening save for Sundays – when of course we go to church, ha ha – and fire-watching all night. I get up rather late most mornings, me.'

'How's your mother?'

'She's all right,' said Stephen, who was still looking cross – Cassie supposed with Daisy. 'She – she's very happy for you and Rob.'

'Yes, she's thrilled,' said Daisy. 'You're the blue-eyed girl, mainly because of that sweet dog you gave Mum when you went to Melbury – he's a *huge* success! They're practically inseparable now.'

'I'm so glad that's worked out well,' said Cassie, wishing she could go and have a cry, for she felt so let down and disappointed.

'Now for the surprise.' Daisy winked conspiratorially at Stephen and then she hurried from the room – and for a moment, Cassie thought, she hoped, she prayed, that Daisy had gone to fetch her other brother, after all.

But it was not to be. Daisy came back wearing a big grin and carrying a large, flat cardboard box.

'Go on, Cassie, open it,' she urged.

'But what is it?' Cassie asked, perplexed.

'Oh, come on, my darling, I've a matinee at two o'clock!' Daisy yanked the lid off, rummaged through the layers of tissue paper, and finally took out something which was made of pale blue cloth. 'It's a two-piece costume, tailor-made for you,' she said to Cassie 'Stand up straight. Let's see if it will fit.'

'But where, but how – '

'I got it from the States.' Now Daisy was unbuttoning Cassie's jacket. 'My natural mother lives there, and her husband Nathan works in wholesale. I sent them all your measurements, and this is the result.'

'How did *you* know my measurements?'

'I pinned you into that blue dress, remember? I just

measured it. So – if you haven't been stuffing yourself with stodgy army food, and putting on a lot of weight, it ought to be exactly right.'

Daisy held out the skirt to Cassie. 'Go into my bedroom, there's a love, and put the whole thing on. You'll find some new silk stockings on the bed, and a pair of high-heeled, dark blue shoes beside the wardrobe.'

So Cassie did as she was told.

The two-piece costume fitted like a dream. It was cut to flatter, and so it added artful curves to Cassie's narrow hips and schoolgirl bosom, and showed off her trim waist.

The cloth was soft and finely woven wool. The quality was excellent, and the colour suited Cassie perfectly, flattering her skin tone and bringing out the dark blue periwinkle of her eyes.

When she looked in Daisy's full-length mirror, Cassie saw a lady, all dressed up to go and meet her friends.

'Very nice,' said Daisy, when Cassie went to show them.

'Yes, it really suits you,' added Stephen.

'Thank you,' Cassie said.

But she knew she wasn't half as grateful as she should be. This lovely two-piece costume must have cost a fortune. But she would have given a thousand pretty costumes to see Robert for a minute, for just one split second of being in his arms.

She went and changed again, laying the jacket and skirt on Daisy's bed, and wondering when she'd ever have a chance to wear such things? If she'd ever mix in social circles full of people who went out to do their shopping dressed in clothes like these?

'Steve,' said Cassie, as she rejoined them in the sitting room, 'have you seen Frances recently?'

'No, I'm afraid I haven't, because she's been so busy.'

'Oh?' said Cassie, now wanting to tease somebody, and wanting to pay Stephen back because he wasn't Robert. 'What's she been doing, then?'

'You won't believe it, but she's having an affair.' Stephen suddenly looked like an offended maiden aunt, his mouth pursed up in disapproval. 'She wrote and told me.'

'She wrote and told me, too.' Cassie grinned at Stephen. 'Oh, Steve, your face!' she said. 'You can't be jealous?'

'Of course I'm not, don't be absurd,' retorted Stephen huffily. 'But you must admit it, getting involved with someone like this Simon Helston fellow, or whatever he's called, it's not like Frances.'

'You mean, because he's married?' Cassie shrugged. 'She says he and his wife have lived apart for seven years. Mrs Helston doesn't understand him.'

But it was soon obvious to Cassie that Stephen didn't want to talk about Frances and her lover, and now he changed the subject. 'Daze,' he said, 'have you told Cass about your scheme?'

'What scheme is this?' asked Cassie, wondering what else she might get sprung on her that afternoon.

'Cassie, darling, pop into the kitchen and ask Mrs Jimp to make us all a cup of coffee, then I'll tell you.' Daisy smiled mysteriously. 'In fact, my love, I'd welcome your opinion. I'm hoping to get you and Rob involved, as well as Stephen here – that's if he's interested, of course, and if he isn't buried alive in Shropshire, busy being a country squire.'

'How will you find the money?' Cassie asked, when Daisy had explained.

'I'll ask all my rich theatre friends, of course,' said Daisy airily. 'I've also got some funds put by already, and those will be enough to start us off.'

'But you'll need a regular flow of cash to run this place, to pay the staff to look after the children, to take them out, and all that kind of thing?' Cassie looked at Daisy. 'You'll need cooks and gardeners and cleaners?'

'Yes, of course,' said Daisy. 'I *have* thought of that, and this is what I'm going to do. I'll organise it as a charity, set up some kind of trust, get people to remember it when they make their wills.'

She reached across a table for a large brown envelope. 'I've found this house near Southwold,' she continued. 'It's huge, well-built, Victorian – it's ideal. It has eleven bedrooms, seven bathrooms, a lovely kitchen garden, a paddock for some ponies, great long lawns. There's a cottage for a housekeeper, some stables and some barns. It's close enough to London, but it's still in the countryside. It's near a gorgeous beach.'

'But Daisy, didn't you want to buy the Minster?' Cassie asked, remembering the conversation in the London taxi all those months ago. 'I'd have thought the Minster would be ideal for this?'

'I tried to buy the Minster, but the owner wouldn't sell. Anyway, my sparrow, Southwold might be better.'

'Why?' asked Cassie.

'As I said, it's close to London, and that's quite important, actually.' Daisy looked at Cassie, blue eyes bright. 'These past few months, I've been doing voluntary work in the East End. I've been horrified by the conditions in which some children live. They've got no chance, poor things. Their homes are filthy slums, they never wash, their diet's dreadful, and their parents – the less we say about some of *them*, the better. I was talking to Ewan about it, and he said, why don't we buy a place?'

'You're going to give up acting, are you?' Cassie asked.

'Probably not,' said Daisy, and she smiled candidly. 'Of

course, we won't be able to do anything about it until the war is over. But it's worth doing, don't you think?'

'Yes, it's well worth doing.' Cassie glanced up at the clock. 'Look at the time,' she said. 'I must be going. I have to pick some colonel up at one.'

'You'll come again, and stay?'

'Of course I will.' Cassie kissed Daisy on her powdered cheek. 'I need to go and see my granny some time, but I'll come and see you and Ewan, too.'

'You like the costume, don't you?'

'Yes, I do – it's lovely.' Cassie smiled. 'You're so kind to me, and I'm so grateful, honestly.'

Stephen said he'd walk with Cassie to the army garage where she'd pick up the staff car, so although she really wanted to walk there by herself, she had to let him tag along.

He was still somewhat grumpy. Daisy's gentle teasing about the girl from Shropshire must have touched a nerve, decided Cassie, and this must be why he was so cross.

'Daze and Fraser should have children of their own, and that would keep them occupied,' he muttered, as he and Cassie turned into some mews off Oxford Street.

'Why don't they?' Cassie wondered, not realising she'd said the words out loud.

'I don't know,' said Stephen. 'Perhaps they do want children, but they haven't come along. Or maybe Daisy doesn't want a baby. Maybe she's afraid she'd spoil her figure. She's so ambitious, after all, and so is Fraser. If they had any children of their own, they'd probably be a nuisance. They would get in the way. As Daisy said, she's busy, busy, busy, and she loves to boss us all about. So maybe this is just her latest stunt, organising seaside holidays for kids from slums.'

'I think she's lovely, and what she's doing is marvellous,'

retorted Cassie sharply. 'When I was growing up in Smethwick, living in what you'd no doubt call a slum, I'd have liked a holiday at the seaside.'

'God, I'm sorry, Cassie.' Stephen reddened. 'That was mean of me. It's just – I wasn't thinking.'

'Obviously not.' Cassie shrugged, and quickened her pace along the broken pavement, skirting piles of sandbags as she went. '*You* were born a nob,' she snapped. 'Okay, you didn't have a lot of money. But you grew up in comfort, in a lovely part of England, with a mother and a father who both loved you, and not every kid's as lucky.'

'Cass, I have apologised.'

'Yes, all right,' said Cassie. 'But it's a pity you said it in the first place.'

'I've told you I'm sorry!' Stephen cried, making people turn to stare at them. 'What more do you want – my blood?'

Cassie stopped, looked up at him. She saw his face was flushed, she saw his eyes were glittering, she heard him breathing hard. 'Stephen, are you going to have a turn?' she asked him, putting out a hand to steady him. 'If you need to go and lie down, or sit down somewhere for a moment, we could find – '

'Jesus Christ, you sound just like my mother!' He shook her off and strode off down the pavement, shoving other people aside, and leaving Cassie staring after him.

Cassie saw Frances Ashford three weeks later, when Frances had some leave, and brought her new man down to meet her friend.

Frances and the man were staying at a small hotel in Windsor, within walking distance of the castle – yes, in separate rooms, Frances had insisted in her latest letter – and Cassie managed to get a lift there, meeting them in the hushed and shuttered bar one afternoon.

'Oh, Fran, it's great to see you!' Cassie cried, delighted.

'Hello, Cassie,' Frances whispered blushing, then turning to the man. 'This – this is Simon Helston.'

'Good afternoon, Captain Helston,' Cassie said.

'Simon will be fine, while we're off duty.' Simon Helston smiled, and then he shook Cassie by the hand. 'As you can see, the bar is closed. So would you join us for some tea and scones at the White Lion along the road?'

'That would be lovely,' Cassie said.

Captain Helston was a tall, fair, pleasant-looking man, of about thirty-five or so, guessed Cassie. He was a little lame, she noticed, the result of injuries he'd suffered in North Africa. These meant he wasn't fit for active service any more, and so – as Frances had explained – he did a desk job now, at the barracks where Frances was a driver.

They walked to the White Lion. In the dusty lounge there was a trio of old men who were playing sentimental tunes on squeaky violins and an untuned piano. Elderly, arthritic waitresses were serving tea and solid-looking scones, and on the tables were little pots of watery, artificial cream and runny, blood-red jam.

When Captain Helston gave his order, their waitress beamed at him and blushed – quite obviously, he'd made her day.

Cassie looked around the hotel lounge, and shook her head.

A mere two years ago, she would have thought all this the very height of elegance, of impossible sophistication. But now it just looked down-at-heel and tawdry – dusty, grubby, faded, tired of life.

When Captain Helston said he hoped the ladies would excuse him, but he was in need of nicotine, and it didn't do to smoke where other people were eating, Frances leaned towards Cassie, blushed, and asked her what she thought.

'He's very nice,' said Cassie. 'He's polite – he pulls out chairs for ladies, he doesn't smoke where other people are eating, he doesn't boss the waitresses around. I'd say you've caught yourself a gentleman.'

'But he's old,' said Frances, and she frowned.

'He's not that old,' said Cassie. 'I mean, he's not too old to – well, you know.'

'I don't know, actually,' said Frances primly, as she coloured up again. 'I'm not a tart, whatever it might look like.'

'Fran, I never said you were, don't be so touchy.' Cassie smiled encouragingly at Frances. 'Does he make you happy?'

'Yes, he does.'

'So go on being happy – be happy while you can, that's my advice to you, because we might all die tomorrow. Frances, does he want to marry you?'

'We've sort of talked about it,' Frances said. 'Of course, he hasn't actually proposed, but that's because he *can't* propose to me, at least not yet. If he wants to marry me, he'll need to be divorced.' Frances sighed unhappily. 'Mummy will be furious if I marry someone who's divorced.'

'Oh, Frances, you don't have to please your horrible old mother all your life!' Cassie looked at Frances, shook her arm. 'Go on, live a little, have some fun.'

'It's odd you should say that, Cass, with your mother – '

'My mother was tricked and lied to by a bigamist,' said Cassie. 'It sounds like Captain Helston is playing fair with you.'

Chapter Thirteen

January 1944

When Cassie had a message to say that her commanding officer wanted to see her now, this very minute, she immediately feared the worst.

Robert or Lily Taylor – which, she thought, buttoning up her jacket with shaking hands. Grabbing her hat, she jammed it on her head, and then somehow got herself across the frost-rimed barrack square.

As she walked into her CO's office, she braced herself, determined not to cry. Robert or Lily wouldn't have wanted that.

But Captain Lancing didn't look as if she had bad news. 'At ease, Corporal Taylor,' she began, as Cassie stood there to attention. 'I have a job for you. It's taking a colonel from the Hampshire Regiment back to London. He needs to go right now. We're going to move you, too.'

'Move me, ma'am?' said Cassie frowning, thinking, what – again?

'Yes, so we'll save a lot of time and petrol if you drive this officer in a vehicle that needs to be in London anyway.'

Captain Lancing glanced down at some papers on her desk. 'You'll be based in London from now on. Please don't look so gloomy, Corporal Taylor, it's a damned good posting. You'll drive top brass and various junior officers around, do a little motor maintenance, and general garage duties as and when. You'll be billeted in a house in Chelsea with other ATS. Do you have any questions?'

'I – I don't think so, ma'am,' said Cassie, doing rapid mental calculations – did she have anything at the laundry, had she borrowed anything from any of the girls, did anyone owe her money?

'Good girl,' said Captain Lancing, then she grinned. 'Your friends here in the sticks will be quite jealous. Now there aren't many air raids, and Jerry is too preoccupied in Europe to bother about us, London is the place to be. Lots of Yanks to take you out and spend their money on you, if you're that way inclined.'

'Yes, ma'am,' said Cassie. 'Thank you, ma'am.'

'You'd better get your kit together, then,' said Captain Lancing. 'Colonel Floyd is waiting.'

Yanks, indeed – who wanted Yanks, thought Cassie, as she hurried back to her own quarters. But then she thought, now I'll see Daisy often. I'll see Stephen, too. If there's any news of Rob, I'll hear it straight away.

Fifteen minutes later, she was driving a big black Humber staff car, on her way to London.

Cassie wrote to Robert almost every day, but knew he couldn't be getting all her letters, that some must go astray. So she didn't panic when she didn't hear from him for weeks.

Or she tried not to panic, anyway.

'More success in Italy!' cried a newsboy one March morning, as Cassie walked down the road to the army garage where she was due to spend the day on general motor maintenance.

More success, she thought – about time, too. Robert never grumbled, but she understood from other girls, whose husbands, brothers and boyfriends were in Italy, that the whole campaign was one hard slog, as inch by inch the British and American armies pushed the Germans north.

Whenever they gained any ground, they entered towns and villages to find the houses empty, the people dead or run away, no food, no power, and booby-traps which caused a lot of casualties, however careful everyone tried to be.

The terrain they had to cross was dreadful. They climbed high in the mountains that made the spine of Italy, and they crossed streams and rivers that in winter swelled to raging torrents, their bridges all blown up or swept away.

'*The Germans force the Italians to lay mines. They dig and wire whole districts,*' Robert wrote, when on one blessed day she heard from him. '*Whenever our boys push the Germans out of any villages, you can be sure we Dorsets watch our step!*

'*But it shouldn't be long now, darling Cass. We're all making slow but steady progress and, apart from a few Fascist die-hards, the Italian people are on our side. We're on our way to Rome and, when we get there, the Germans will have to put their hands up, talk or run away. I reckon they'll surrender.*

'*They won't have much choice. They must know they're beaten. If we're lucky, we'll soon see the end of it, and we British chaps can all come home.*'

It was hard to know if Robert meant it about Germany surrendering. Or if he knew this was most unlikely, but was trying to cheer her up. Or get his letters through uncensored – when they got through at all.

Robert meant it, and he was doing his best to make it happen. As the Allied armies slogged their determined way along the spine of Italy, there were plenty of chances to help Jerry make his mind up.

Over the past few months, he and his dependable Sergeant Gregory, together with some of the bravest, brightest lads in his platoon, had volunteered for more than a dozen missions behind the German lines. They'd ambushed enemy convoys as these came round the narrow mountain roads, and sabotaged German transport vehicles taking up supplies.

So far, they hadn't taken any serious casualties, they'd

managed to get their wounded back to base, and Robert dared to hope their luck would last.

'You two don't always have to volunteer,' he said to Blain and Thornton, two best friends who took the most alarming risks with daring and bravado, egging each other on with hoots of glee. 'Sergeant Gregory and I, we could take some other chaps when we go walkies in the hills tomorrow.'

'But, sir – I want to get a medal to send home to me mum,' protested Private Thornton, grinning.

'So do I,' said Private Blain. 'A medal would shut me father up, stop him goin' on about us youngsters knowing nothin', that he's surprised we manage to wipe our arses in the dark. Beggin' your pardon, sir. Go on, sir – be a sport and let us come.'

In late April, Cassie had a letter from Mrs Denham, inviting her to go and spend a day or two in Dorset, if she could get some leave.

'My word, that will be thrilling,' said a driver, and she grinned. 'Visiting your future ma-in-law – you'll have enough of her when you get married.'

'Ooh, you're gonna to get the third degree,' went on another driver, a girl from the East End. 'I remember when I went to meet my Frankie's mum. She'd set up all these tests.'

'What tests?' asked Cassie, laughing.

'She 'ad me in the kitchen makin' rissoles, to see if I could cook. She 'ad me in the wash-'ouse where she was boilin' up great piles of socks, to see if I could mangle.'

'Oh, I can mangle,' Cassie said.

'Yeah, and so can I. But then she didn't like my Cockney accent. She wrote to Frankie, she told 'im it was common, that I should be savin' up for elocution lessons. When I got back to barracks, I wrote a note to Frankie, an' I told 'im it was off.'

'But Mrs Denham's very nice,' said Cassie.

'You wait an' see, my girl. You're gonna take her precious boy away. You mark my words, Cass, nice or nasty, she'll be like a tigress with a cub.'

'Oh,' said Cassie, feeling anxious now.

But she found she didn't need to worry. When she arrived in Dorset, Mrs Denham met her at the station and gave her a big hug.

'Thank you for coming, Cassie,' she began. 'I must say, you're looking very well. London obviously agrees with you.'

'It keeps me busy,' Cassie said. 'But Mrs Denham, how are you?'

'I'm managing.' Rose Denham shrugged. 'It's sometimes rather difficult, you know, since Alex died. But I mustn't grumble. I shall start to cry, and God knows I've done enough of that to last a lifetime.'

Cassie saw Rose Denham's eyes were sad, and guessed she wasn't sleeping much, alone in bed at night. It must be so awful, Cassie thought, to have lost a man she'd loved so much.

When they got back to the bailiff's cottage, Tinker wagged his tail and barked in welcome. Tess and Shirley, Melbury's current land girls, had made some frosted fairy cakes, using hoarded sugar and a couple of precious eggs.

'So, Cassie,' said Rose Denham, as they sat down together in the familiar cottage kitchen with its scrubbed pine table, gleaming pots and pans and dresser full of twinkling china, 'many congratulations.'

'Thank you, Mrs Denham.'

She looked all round to see if Mrs Denham had set up any tests. But she couldn't see any evidence of rissole making, or piles of dirty socks. The only visible socks were those on

Mrs Denham's feet. 'I – er – I hope it wasn't an unpleasant shock for you?'

'A shock?' Rose Denham smiled. 'I don't think so, Cassie. We all knew that Rob was keen on you.'

'But you don't mind him marrying me?'

'Cassie, I'm very happy for you both.' Mrs Denham filled the teapot from the old black kettle on the hob. 'What did your granny say?'

'I haven't told her yet. But I'm going to see her soon, and then I can tell her face to face.' Cassie looked down at her finger nails. 'I don't know how to tell her, actually. You see, Rob's not a Catholic, and I know she'll be upset. I mean, it doesn't matter to me at all, and I'd love Robert, anyway. But Granny – '

'I understand,' said Mrs Denham. 'You're her only grandchild, after all. So she's bound to want the best for you.'

'But she'll have the best for me!' cried Cassie fervently. 'Mrs Denham, don't misunderstand me, I think Robert's perfect! I can't imagine being married to anyone but him.'

'But he's not a Catholic, and I doubt if he'll convert, so I can see it's going to be a problem. Cassie, I think we could dispense with all this Mrs Denham stuff. We're going to be related, so why don't you call me Rose?'

It took a bit of doing, but by the following morning Cassie managed to call Mrs Denham Rose, and not blush as red as one herself. 'So shall you like to be a farmer's wife?' asked Rose, as she and Cassie emptied chicken mash into the buckets to go out and feed the hens.

'I think so,' Cassie said. 'It'll make a change from Brum, of course, and it's very quiet here in Dorset. But it will be much better for our kids, to grow up in a place that isn't full of factories, and smuts, and smog and grime.'

'You won't miss the city?'

'Perhaps I shall – a bit,' admitted Cassie. 'But I like the peace and harmony of the countryside.'

'Oh, it's not all peace and harmony,' Rose said, smiling wryly. 'There's always something going on, some feud or fight or scandal.'

'What sort of thing do you mean?'

'Well, for example – Alex and I had years of trouble with our nearest neighbour. One summer, there was an awful storm, and it caused a cliff fall. Part of our road from Melbury to Charton fell down on to the beach.

'Our neighbour was very awkward about letting us use the road across *his* land, and in the end we had to build another road ourselves, to link us to the one going into Charton. It cost a whole year's profit. It wouldn't have hurt our neighbour to let us use his road for a few years, but he refused.'

'The mean old bugger!' Cassie cried.

'Quite,' said Rose, and laughed. 'Cassie, you're always so direct. I've never met anyone as blunt as you.'

'Sorry, Rose,' said Cassie, blushing red. 'I do try to be more ladylike, I promise you. But sometimes things slip out.'

'Oh, Cassie, don't be sorry! It's quite refreshing, to hear someone speak her mind, and the way you talk is part of you.'

Rose picked up a bucket. She glanced up at the clock. 'I don't know where those girls are, they're very late this morning. Last month, they decided to get lodgings in the village – not that I blame them, Cassie, it must have been very dull for them, sitting here in the evenings with a sad old hen like me. But they're not reliable. Let's go and feed the chickens, and then we'd better start to milk the cows.'

The land girls turned up fifteen minutes later, all apologies. Jumping off their bicycles, they ran into the cowshed, to take over the milking.

So Rose and Cassie did some other jobs around the farm,

then Rose took Cassie for a walk into the village, to buy some flour and salt and coffee beans – there was a rumour that the shop had got some in, and Rose loved good coffee. Cassie breathed in the sweet, fresh air, and thought how much she'd love it here, when Rob came home again.

In the evening, when the cows had all been milked, the stock had all been fed, and the land girls had gone off to meet their friends in Charton, Rose and Cassie sat with mugs of cocoa in companionable silence, and listened to the wireless.

They didn't need to say they were both thinking about Robert, for each could see it in the other's eyes.

'He's very like his father, loyal and honest,' Rose told Cassie. She glanced up from her heap of darning. 'So I'm sure he'll make you a good husband.'

'I'll make him a good wife.' Cassie stitched away, putting the elbows back into a jumper which she recognised as one of Robert's, and pausing every now and then to rumple Tinker's ears. 'At least, I'll do my best.'

'My dear, I'm sure you will.' Rose shook her head. 'You're bound to have some trouble with Steve, you know. He's going to be so jealous.'

'I know the twins are close,' said Cassie. 'But I don't intend to come between them.'

'You might not mean to, but you will.' Rose sighed. 'Stephen has always idolised his brother. Rob's the bigger, stronger, cleverer twin, the one who always led while Stephen followed. You're going to take his place in Robert's heart. Or anyway, Cassie, that's how Steve will see it.'

Cassie didn't need this pointed out.

Nowadays, the formerly friendly, easy-going Stephen was often moody, awkward and bad-tempered, and cross with everyone and everything – even worse than Robert when she'd first met him.

But she still made sure she was especially nice to Stephen. She realised he was damaged, and he needed kindness, especially now Frances had her Simon, and so she didn't hanker after Stephen any more.

She hoped the girl from Shropshire would end up being the one for Steve, the one who'd make him happy – if it was possible for Stephen to be happy?

When she had first met the Denham twins, she'd thought they were the opposite of what they'd actually turned out to be. She knew now that Stephen had a dark and melancholy secret side to him, while Robert was the open, direct, candid, artless one.

Almost everything Robert thought was usually said a moment later. But with Steve she often didn't know what he was thinking, and this made her nervous.

One day, she thought, he might surprise me, and I'm not sure I'm going to like it – whatever it might be.

'How did it go?' demanded Cassie's fellow driver, when Cassie got back home to London. 'Your bloke's old mother – did she get you boiling up the socks?'

'No, of course she didn't,' said Cassie, grinning. 'But she did have a great big pile of mending, and so I darned some jumpers.'

'Get to a decent pub, an' have a sing-song?'

'No, in the evenings we drank cocoa, and listened to the wireless.'

'Bloody hell, that sounds exciting. What else did you do?'

'I fed the chickens, and I milked the cows.'

'God almighty, girl – you're middle-aged already. I tell you, Cassie Taylor, leave's for going out and getting four sheets to the wind, not listening to the wireless, darning jumpers.'

It was so hard for Cassie, all the non-information, the not-knowing. She wished she had a little more of Robert – more letters, a more recent photograph, or even two. Why hadn't they had some done in Alexandria, she wondered, because there were photographic studios everywhere, mostly run by Arabs, Greeks and Lebanese. Why hadn't she thought of that? She'd have liked a book or two of his, a handkerchief, perhaps. She wished she'd pinched his jumper and stuffed it in her kitbag.

But she hadn't liked to ask his mother for any souvenirs. Rose might have thought that Cassie meant she wanted something valuable, and thought she was a gold-digger already, and Cassie dreaded that.

She wore her silver bracelet all the time. She polished her penny bangle too, and it stayed in her sewing kit, wrapped up in a clean white handkerchief, and cherished like the holiest of relics.

She couldn't wear the bangle. Robert had been right, it was made of some cheap alloy trying to look like silver, and had made her skin go green.

But she still treasured it.

In June, she had the news she had been waiting for so long. The Allies marched into Rome. The Germans retreated even further north, so what with that, and the good news from France, people started to hope the war would very soon be won.

The Chelsea billet, where Cassie and the other drivers lived, was a pretty stuccoed Georgian townhouse, high-ceilinged, light and airy. The grey reflections from the river painted patterns on the plaster ceilings, and in summer long French windows opened out on to a little garden, which by now was very overgrown.

One Sunday morning in late August, when Cassie was off duty, and she and some of the other girls were lying or sitting in the garden, reading, writing, knitting, gossiping, she heard the doorbell ring.

Always hoping, always praying Robert would come home, Cassie jumped up eagerly and ran into the house.

'Cass, you have a visitor!' called one of the girls, who was busy making lunchtime sandwiches in the cluttered kitchen, and had been to answer the front door.

It might be Daisy, Cassie told herself.

Daisy had been away on tour with ENSA, but she was expected back this week. Sometimes she dropped into the Chelsea house, always looking like a fashion plate in her lovely hats, her chiffons, satins, tweeds and velvets, high-heeled patent shoes and pale silk stockings, and always bringing presents for the girls – chocolates, cakes or flowers, but God alone knew where she got them.

Or maybe it was Stephen? But she thought Stephen was in Surrey – his CO had a house there, and sometimes Stephen was invited down for the weekend.

So could it, please God, could it be Robert?

It was Frances.

Cassie jammed a smile on to her face. 'Frances, what a nice surprise!' she cried. 'Why didn't you say you were in London? Did you come with Simon? We're all out in the garden, in the sunshine. We've got some beer and cider. Come and have drink with us, and would you like a sandwich?'

'I've already eaten, thank you.' Frances was looking anxious and uncomfortable now. 'Cass,' she said, 'do you have somewhere private where we could go and talk?'

'Oh – er – yes,' said Cassie, suddenly worried about her friend. What had Frances done? Oh, Holy Mother of God, she must be pregnant. Of course, she'd have to leave the army. Simon would do his duty, she was sure. But if Simon didn't, she'd help Frances out. She had some savings –

'Let's go upstairs,' she said. 'Fran, don't look so frightened. We can sort it out.'

Frances followed Cassie into an empty bedroom and sat

down on a bed. 'Mrs Denham wanted me to see you, to talk to you in person,' she began.

'Why, what's wrong in Melbury?'

'She – she's had some absolutely dreadful news,' said Frances. 'She couldn't leave the farm herself, of course, but she didn't want to write to you. She wanted somebody to come down here and tell you, and she didn't want it to be Steve. In fact, she hasn't dared to tell him yet. She wants him to go home.'

'But, Frances, tell me what?' demanded Cassie.

'Robert's missing.'

'Missing,' repeated Cassie, as she tried to take it in.

Then she thought, missing doesn't mean a thing, of course. They mean they don't know where he is, that's all. They're not saying he's been wounded, or he's –

'Cassie,' continued Frances gently. 'I'm afraid it might be worse than missing. Mrs Denham's had a letter from Rob's commanding officer, and he thinks Robert's dead.'

'No, that can't be right,' said Cassie, frowning. 'It's all a big mistake. Frances, think about it, think how clever and courageous – no, Robert can't be dead!'

'Cassie, if you want to have a cry – '

'Why should I want to cry?' Cassie put her shoulders back and forced herself to grin. 'Fran, you're all so gloomy, so bloody pessimistic, you don't have any faith.'

But, later on that evening, when Cassie was alone and trying to sleep, she found faith was very hard to come by, that despair was stronger, and she feared Robert might indeed be dead.

The letter which came the following morning was a cruel mockery of hope.

'We've taken Florence,' Robert wrote. 'It's all moving very nicely now. So I don't think it will be long before we meet again, my darling.'

Yes, thought Cassie wretchedly, but in this world, or the next?

Chapter Fourteen

When one of the drivers in the Chelsea house told their commanding officer what had happened, that Cassie's fiancé had been reported missing and was most likely dead, Cassie was informed she was entitled to some compassionate leave.

But she didn't take it. Robert was just missing, that was all. He wasn't wounded, wasn't dead, and he would turn up again, she knew it.

If he were trapped behind the German lines, she told herself, some Italian family would help him, take him in. Italians weren't all Fascists, and they didn't all side with the Germans.

There were lots of rumours going around about Italian partisans receiving drops of arms and ammunition from American and British planes, then blowing up river bridges, railway lines, and killing German soldiers in ambushes and raids. There were also stories about American and British soldiers going on secret missions behind the German lines, and helping the Italian partisans.

Daisy was optimistic about Robert's chances, too. She was sure he must be holed up somewhere, maybe with Italian partisans, waiting for a chance to get back to the Allied lines.

'But what if he's a prisoner?' Cassie asked, when she and Daisy met for lunch at the Savoy, on a day when Daisy didn't have a matinee, and thus had some free time.

'He'll be treated well, my love, don't worry,' Daisy said, as she ate her ultra-patriotic Woolton pie. 'POWs get food and shelter, and Red Cross parcels, too. So, if Rob's a prisoner, once we find out where he's gone, we'll send him scarves and jumpers, tins of soup and spam, and books and magazines.'

'If Robert *is* a prisoner, he'll escape,' said Cassie, as she toyed with her parsnip, carrot and soggy oatmeal mush that didn't really taste of anything.

'Yes, of course he will,' said Daisy, smiling. 'Yes, my darling – knowing Rob, I'm sure he's working on it now. Come on, love, eat your lunch. Or else you'll waste away, and when Rob comes back he'll be so sad to think you pined.'

So Cassie forced herself to eat, and after she had eaten all her pie, she felt a little better.

'That's my girl,' said Daisy as she signed the bill. 'Let's go and look at gloves and scarves and things. I saw some lovely Fair Isle jumpers in the Army and Navy yesterday. They should have Robert's size. I've got some coupons.'

But although his sister and Cassie were so optimistic, Stephen wouldn't have anything to do with their determination to look for silver linings. Sunk in gloom and misery, he was drinking far too much, and Cassie ached for him. But she didn't dare to try too hard to cheer him up, in case he took it the wrong way.

Nowadays, there was nothing on the wireless to make anybody happy, no comfort for a population that was sick and tired of war. Even though there was occasionally some good news from France, the expected Allied victory had not materialised.

London wasn't the cushy number it had been in spring. Since June, the Germans had been sending over their new flying bombs, and these rained down on London with terrible effect, coming out of nowhere and killing people travelling into work, standing on railway station platforms, walking home from school. The anti-aircraft batteries shot some down, but plenty more got through.

So Cassie was glad to spend a couple of days later that month in the peace and quiet of Melbury, seeing Rose and Tinker.

'We must hope for the best,' said Rose. 'We have to keep our spirits up.'

'You haven't heard any more then, Rose?'

'Not yet, but when I do, you'll be the very first to know.'

Rose looked at Cassie and she smiled encouragingly. 'In spite of what his CO said, I still feel optimistic. Robert will want to live, I know, and that must mean a lot.'

Who are you trying to comfort, Rose, thought Cassie – you or me?

One September evening, when they were both off duty, Stephen suggested going out for dinner at the Ritz. Cassie had never seen inside the Ritz, and she was curious, so she agreed to go.

She thought the place was grubby. The brass all needed polishing, and Lily Taylor would have had a fit. The food was muck. All messed about and titivated, served on great big plates, it was clearly trying to be something it was not.

The meat was raw inside, and Cassie knew you shouldn't eat raw meat – unless your meat was boiled or roasted, you'd certainly get worms – and so she didn't eat it, even though Stephen told her it was meant to be like that. She could have fancied a plate of mince and onions, or a nice pork pie.

She didn't like the way the waiters fawned and sneered and grovelled, all at once. It must be because her escort was an officer, but she was just an NCO.

Afterwards, Stephen wanted to go drinking. Cassie was tired, she'd had a busy week, and she had to drive a truck to Hull the following morning, so she wanted to go home.

But Stephen looked so hangdog when she said she was going back to Chelsea that she agreed to go and have a drink.

'Just one or two,' she told him, 'and then I must go home.'

'Just one or two,' he promised.

The night sky was deep purple, and the moon was up.

Cassie hoped there wouldn't be a raid. She hated it when flying bombs came over, hated waiting for the aftershock, hated seeing flames light up the sky. These days, she hated any kind of fire – even the comfortable red glow from the bailiff's cottage kitchen range, when she went down to Dorset to see Rose.

They walked up Piccadilly and ended up in Soho. They went to a louche club in Wardour Street, packed with army officers and their women. The place was full of smoke and smelled of stale fried food, men's sweat and women's scent.

The women looked like a lot of tarts, thought Cassie. Daisy had taught her how to recognise good quality in clothes, and she could see the frocks these women wore were not the real thing.

Although they all looked confident and flash, their evening gowns were made of rayon, they all wore too much make-up, their hair was badly bleached so that it looked like straw, and their jewels were obviously paste.

Stephen signed Cassie in and ordered drinks.

Stephen was drinking whisky. But Cassie stuck to tonic water, and she made each drink last for an hour, sipping slowly, savouring the pungent, bitter taste.

On a little stage, there was a band, playing the kind of music Cassie liked, and on the dance floor couples swayed and shuffled, cheek to cheek.

She wouldn't have minded dancing, and she liked to dance with Stephen. He was strong and solid, and he always held her nice and tight. But he didn't tip her backwards so she felt off-balance, or tread on her toes, or stick one knee between her legs, like so many other soldiers did.

She smiled at him, one eyebrow raised enquiringly. She nodded at the dancers, hoping he would take the hint.

But Stephen didn't seem to want to dance. In spite of

promising to have just one or two, he was drinking steadily to get drunk, and soon he was getting maudlin, too.

'But Steve, we haven't heard anything for certain,' Cassie told him, when he started on his favourite topic and was fretting about Robert once again. 'So we must go on hoping for the best.'

'I tell you, Robert's dead!' Stephen took another gulp of whisky, and fumbled in his jacket pocket for his cigarettes. 'I'm his twin,' he muttered. 'I would know if he were still alive. I know he's dead.'

'Steve,' said Cassie gently, 'you know we've not had any definite news. So we mustn't write him off just yet.'

'When we were at Dunkirk,' continued Stephen, as if Cassie hadn't spoken, 'when we were both lying on that bloody awful beach, both of us half-conscious, and both of us shot up, I was pretty sure he'd be all right. Then, when we were finally picked up by two different ships, and some boats got torpedoed – Rob's was hit, you know, and lots of chaps on it were killed – I knew he was alive. He knew I was, too. Twins always know these things.'

'But now you think he's dead?'

'Cass, I *know* he's dead!' cried Stephen, banging his glass down on the sticky table and making people turn to stare at him. 'My mother thinks so, too.'

'But that isn't what she said to me,' objected Cassie. 'She said I had to hope for the best, and try to keep my spirits up.'

'Mum doesn't want to admit it, but she knows.' Stephen clicked his fingers at the barman for another whisky. 'Cassie, love, you haven't seen the letter, have you?'

'No, but – '

'Rob's CO explained to Mum that Rob and a few other chaps had gone to sabotage some German guns. The Jerries must have caught them. I reckon Rob's been shot.'

Cassie wished that Stephen would stop talking, and stop drinking, too. Daisy had said he wasn't supposed to drink more than a pint or two of beer, at the very most, and Cassie was sure he shouldn't be drinking spirits.

So, feeling guilty – for, after all, she had let Stephen take her to the club – Cassie peered through the haze of smoke, looking for a waiter, someone she could ask to find a taxi.

But Stephen must have read her mind. He stood up, rocking slightly, downed his drink. 'Let's go on,' he muttered.

'Go on where?' asked Cassie.

'Oh, I don't know, another club or something. Maybe the Embassy. They'll let you in, if you're with me.'

'I don't think so, Steve.'

'Cass, we've done our grieving.' Stephen lurched against the table, nearly sent it flying. 'Let's go and have some fun.'

They climbed the steps up from the club, and then emerged into the moonlit night. Cassie decided she would try to get him to the house in Berkeley Street, where he was billeted.

Or maybe she should take him back to Daisy's place? It wasn't that much further, and Daisy could look after him if he had an attack, which Cassie feared he might. Then he could sleep it off.

Yes, that might be better.

Taking his arm, she steered him west along the broken pavements, heading for Park Lane. She didn't see a single taxi, but she didn't mind walking. When she was off duty, she often walked for miles and miles on these warm summer evenings, with other ATS girls or even by herself.

Now, she knew central London very well, and she loved it, too. Bruised and bashed and battered, it was still a city of wonders, of amazing places which suddenly appeared like magic amidst all the chaos. Palaces, cathedrals, castles, towers and bridges, which had been there for centuries, and after the war would be there still.

They were going down a narrow side street, taking a short cut she had discovered a few weeks ago, when Stephen stopped and grabbed at Cassie's sleeve.

'What's the matter, Steve?' she asked, hoping he wasn't going to have a turn. 'You look very pale. Do you feel sick?'

'No, Cass, I don't feel sick.' But his speech was slurred, he stank of whisky, he was ashen, and she didn't quite believe him.

'Let's get on,' she told him. 'We need to get you home.'

'Just hang on a minute, eh?' He took her by the shoulders and then he pushed her up against a wall, so now she was off balance. He was going to kiss her – more than kiss her, she could feel him hard against her, and she didn't know what to do.

'Stephen, let me go,' she said.

'Oh, Cass, don't go all maidenly on me!' Stephen's dark eyes glittered, and he gripped her harder.

So Cassie kicked him sharply on the shin.

He yelped in pain, but let her go. 'Why did you do that?' he cried, his brown eyes wide with shock. 'Christ Almighty, Cass – that bloody hurt!'

'Listen, Steve,' said Cassie carefully. 'I didn't want to hurt you. You're my friend, and I don't hurt my friends. But, friend or not, you don't have any right to maul me.'

'Jesus, I was only going to kiss you!'

'I don't *want* you to kiss me!' Cassie pulled her jacket straight. 'Stephen, you forget I'm not a lady,' she continued, walking on. 'You do anything like that again, and it'll hurt much more. You understand me?'

'Yes, I understand you.' Stephen shook his head as if to clear it, and suddenly he seemed to sober up. 'I'm sorry, Cass,' he said.

'That's all right, forget it ever happened,' murmured Cassie.

'But I wouldn't have thought that Robert and I were very different?' Stephen fell into step with Cassie, ambling along, matching his walk to her much shorter stride. '*You* can't always tell the difference, can you?' he persisted. 'There was that time at Daze's place, remember? When you thought I was Rob? We're practically identical in looks, you must admit, and we must sound the same.'

'But, Stephen, you're *not* Robert!' Cassie didn't want to hurt him, knew it must be worse for him, because while she was hoping for the best, Stephen had convinced himself that Robert must be dead. But Robert was the one she loved, and she couldn't transfer this love from Robert to his twin.

'I know what it is – I'm not a hero.' Stephen was kicking at the bits of rubble which were lying everywhere. 'Rob was out in Italy, killing Germans. I'm a head-case, stuck behind a desk. Cassie, you're like all the rest of them. You think a man who isn't shooting people is not a man at all.'

'Oh, God, it isn't that!' Cassie would have hugged him, tried to soothe him. But she didn't dare, because he might have thought she'd changed her mind about the kiss.

'What is it, then?' he growled.

'Yes, all right, you're twins,' said Cassie. 'Yes, you look the same. But you're individuals, with different ways of thinking, different ways of talking – everything! Steve, I'm fond of you – you know I am. But I love your brother. What don't you understand?'

'My brother's dead.'

'So you keep saying.'

'Cassie, you can't mean to stay in love with somebody who's dead?'

'I – oh God, I don't know what I mean!' Cassie was aware of Stephen's closeness, and her body was responding, even though her mind was quite determined to keep him at arm's length.

She bit her lower lip, afraid she'd start to cry. 'If you'd been the one in Italy, and he'd been here in London, it would have made no difference,' she insisted. 'Robert would still have been the one I loved. Please, Steve, could we be friends?'

'No more than friends?'

'Yes!' cried Cassie, desperately.

'Oh, all right, then.' Stephen's laugh was bitter. 'Okay, Cassie sweetheart, we'll be friends. I'm sorry I made a pass at you just now. I misinterpreted the signs. I'm rather drunk tonight.'

But, as they made their way towards Park Lane, Cassie was aware of feeling warm, aroused, excited. Stephen hadn't got it wrong. If he hadn't been so drunk, if he hadn't smelled like a distillery, it would have been so easy to be held in Stephen's arms. It would have been so nice to kiss him.

More than kiss him.

In spite of what she'd said to Stephen, he and Robert weren't so very different, and Stephen was a very attractive man.

As the weeks went by and there was still no news of Robert, Cassie started to agree with Stephen – Robert must be dead.

She blamed herself. She was a wicked person. She hadn't been inside a Catholic church for months, for years. She hadn't spoken to the Catholic chaplain. She hadn't answered Father Riley's letters.

But how could she, when she knew he wanted her to tell him she was going to church and to confession, and that she was mindful of everything he'd taught her when she was a little girl, that she was staying pure?

She still went to church parade, of course. She went inside the church. She hadn't travelled so far along the road which led to hell that she was like the atheists, who were obliged to stand out in the rain.

But she went to Church of England services, along with all the other heretics, and so it didn't count. She had been committing fornication, which was a mortal sin. She had allowed herself to feel attracted to her lover's brother. She was a scarlet woman, a corrupter of mankind.

So God had taken Robert, and it served her right.

But, a little later, she began to feel annoyed with God. Then she was cross, then downright livid. She finally decided that if God had taken Robert just to punish Cassie, God wasn't worth believing in, and so she jolly wouldn't, any more.

She took the holy medals from round her neck, and threw the whole lot in the bin. Then, remembering they were made of metal, she fished them out again, and put them in the box for salvage. They could be useful, she decided, made into bits of bombs.

In any case – Lily or Father Riley would very soon be sending her some more.

'But isn't he still seeing some girl from Shropshire?' Frances asked, when Cassie wrote and told her what had happened.

'I don't know,' wrote Cassie. 'I'm worried about Steve. Robert being missing is upsetting him, of course. But he's also fretting because he thinks he's not a hero. He seems to feel that if he'd been in Africa or Italy, killing people, I would want to kiss him.'

'Men are dim,' wrote Frances. 'Simon's very clever at masterminding transport and ordering supplies. But if I've explained just once that I can't sleep with him until he gets divorced from Caroline and marries me, I've explained a hundred thousand times. He seems to think I'll change my mind if he can only get me tight on gin.'

'But don't you want to sleep with him?' wrote Cassie.

'God, yes – more than anything,' wrote Frances. Cassie

could almost hear her wistful sigh. 'But I don't want to have an illegitimate baby. Mummy would be livid. She'd throw me and the baby out into the street. We'd have to beg for bread.'

Chapter Fifteen

Cassie had never quite got round to telling Lily Taylor she was engaged to Robert, and now she was glad. If his twin was right, and Robert was really dead, there would have been no point.

Now, if Lily heard about a missing or a dead fiancé, it would only make her start to cry. Then it would get her going on the wickedness of the world, particularly the wickedness of men, warmongers all – except for Father Riley, naturally, for he could do no wrong.

Lily's most recent letter had been full of awful news. Over the past few weeks the tannery, the railway goods sheds and a whole row of shops had all been bombed. Jerry was trying to hit the Spitfire factory at Castle Bromwich, Lily thought, but that was several miles away.

Their own street was a mess, with broken pavements, fractured water mains, and burnt and twisted cables everywhere. On Lily's side of Redland Street, only Lily's house and Mrs Flynn's next door were still unscathed. Across the way, only nineteen houses out of fifty-odd were still inhabitable.

Poor Mr Mallory at number 27 had had his windows broken and half his roof blown off, but he was refusing to go and live with his daughter in Halesowen. He'd lived in Smethwick all his life, he said, and he'd be dying there.

'The same goes for me, love,' Lily wrote, as Cassie shook and shuddered and worried about her granny being exposed to all this danger, knowing she couldn't do a thing about it, that Lily would never move from Birmingham. 'I couldn't leave your mother all alone, in any case.'

She meant she had to make her weekly visits to the graveyard, to tidy up the gravel and have a little chat with Geraldine, who Lily knew was listening to every word she said.

There was the shrine, as well. She seemed to be convinced that if she kept the shrine as holy and immaculate as she had always kept it, if she got Father Riley round to sprinkle holy water every other month or so, God wouldn't let the Germans bomb her home.

'I hope you go to church and say your prayers,' continued Lily. 'Father Riley tells me London has some lovely churches. There are Catholic missions to servicewomen, too. He's going to write to you and give you some addresses of nice Catholic families in London. He'll write to them as well, telling them to expect to see you soon.'

Cassie pulled a face.

Frances wrote long screeds from Chester, saying how happy she was with darling Simon, and how she hoped that things would all work out, even if it might take several years.

Simon said that Caroline would probably hold out for several mints of money. So if he and Frances ever married, they would be very poor. But Frances wasn't worried. She could always work and earn a living. If her parents didn't like it, that was just too bad.

'I've talked to Mummy and Daddy,' she went on, *'and to my surprise, they don't seem too bothered about me seeing Simon, even though he's married.*

'Of course, my mother said, she'd always thought that nobody would ever want a great, fat lump like me.

'Simon is apparently one of the Cheshire Helstons, and he's related to a baronet. But he didn't tell me. Mummy got a friend to make enquiries. I don't care if Simon is related to this Sir William person, or to Mickey Mouse. But, if it makes my mother happy to believe that one day I might marry into the minor aristocracy, it will make life easier for me.'

Cassie was busy working in the motor pool that morning,

and now she folded up the letters and put them in the pocket of her grease-stained overall.

God, she thought, as she picked up her spanner, poor old Frances, that mother of hers is such a nasty bitch. I'd tell her to go and take a running jump if she were mine.

Yellow, gaunt and scrawny, with a pinched and puckered face that seemed to have no lips or eyebrows, Lady Ashford must be jealous of her daughter's beauty. There was no other reason for her to be so mean. Frances might have been a podgy child but, since she had met Cassie, she had always been attractive, in a statuesque, impressive way.

These days, she looked lovely. Being in the army had given her some much-needed confidence. Drill had made her stand up straight and tall. She was well-covered, yes – but nobody except her evil mother would have said that she was fat. Her skin was like fresh cream, and her dark hair shone in natural waves.

Most men would look at Frances and think she was some sort of heavenly vision.

Robert blinked, opened his eyes, and saw a heavenly vision.

The slender woman who was sitting by the bed, and sewing something white, looked like a Renaissance painting of the Virgin Mary. She was in her late twenties, he supposed. Or maybe early thirties. Older than him, he thought – but beautiful.

She wore a summer dress of pale blue cotton, which flattered her complexion. The fine material looked almost glowing against her soft brown milky-coffee skin. She had dark hair the colour of damsons, carelessly tied back with yellow ribbon. She had a rather long, straight nose, and he could see faint crow's feet at the corners of her eyes.

He couldn't decide if she was real or not, and so he coughed politely, to make her look at him.

She dropped her sewing. She stared straight at him, startled. 'So you're awake at last,' she whispered. 'Please, don't scream or shout,' she added urgently, covering his mouth with her left hand.

'I shan't scream, I promise,' mumbled Robert, who didn't think he could have screamed or shouted, even if he'd tried.

So the woman took her hand away.

Robert tried to move, to lift one hand, to ease the cramp in his right leg. But, to his dismay, he found he couldn't do it. He had no strength at all. He struggled to sit up against his pillows, but he failed, and lay back, gasping.

Then he felt someone help him to sit up, and turned to see a little grey-haired woman dressed in black, who nodded and smiled at him, but didn't speak.

'What am I doing here?' he asked the women. 'Why am I in this bed?'

'We found you on our land,' the younger woman told him. 'There are some German gun emplacements half a mile away. We heard they had been sabotaged. So we've been assuming you and your companions were the ones who'd blown them up.'

The woman looked at Robert with concern. 'At first, we thought you must be dead. You'd lost an awful lot of blood. But then we realised you were just unconscious, and so we brought you here.'

'I think I'm dreaming this,' said Robert, frowning. 'I'm in Italy, aren't I? I don't know much Italian. But I understand what you are saying.'

'I'm speaking to you in English.' The younger woman grimaced. 'I know you British think Italians are a mob of ignorant, stupid peasants. But a few of us can read and write. I went to school in England. My father wanted me to have an English education. He thought it was the best.'

'What is this place?' asked Robert.

'A country house,' the woman told him. 'It's been in my family for many generations. It was a Palladian villa once, and very grand and beautiful. But it's pretty much a ruin now. You British and the Germans have both shelled it, and blown half of it to bits.'

Robert looked round the room, which didn't seem to him at all palatial. More like a peasant's cottage, it was small and whitewashed, with great wooden beams along the ceiling.

The woman saw him looking. 'You're actually in our pigeon loft,' she said. 'In the little room the man who kept the pigeons used to have. But if you think you can hear pigeons cooing, you'll be imagining it. We've long since eaten them.'

Robert blinked again. Looking at the older woman, he saw she was still nodding and smiling amiably at him, and smoothing out the sewing which was lying in her lap. There was a jug of water on the table at her side. 'May I have some water, please?' he asked.

'She doesn't hear,' the younger woman told him. But now she reached across and poured some water from the jug into a glass, and then she helped him drink.

'How long have I been here?' Robert asked.

'A week, ten days – I haven't counted.' The younger woman filled the glass again. 'You've been very ill. You have some shrapnel wounds, and these are healing, but we were very worried because you've been unconscious. Or you were half-awake and talking to yourself.'

'What have I been saying?'

'I couldn't work it out. One day, you were muttering about a penny bangle, you were telling somebody you didn't want to buy one. Or that was what it sounded like to me.' The younger woman shrugged. 'So – we tried to feed you. But you couldn't eat. You just drank water. You've lost a lot of weight.'

Robert looked at his hands and arms, and saw how thin they were, how gaunt and wasted. 'You *are* a real person, aren't you?' he enquired suspiciously. 'I mean, you're not a ghost?'

'Yes, of course I'm real.' The woman touched one of his hands. 'There, do you see? My flesh is warm, not cold.'

'What's your name?' he asked.

'Sofia,' said the woman. 'Do you wish to tell me yours?'

'It's Robert Denham.' Robert felt he owed her that. 'Why didn't you hand me over to the Germans?'

'I don't really know.' Sofia picked up her sewing. 'If they found you here, they'd put us all against the wall. But maybe we Italians want to make some small resistance. To show we can be brave. We know you British soldiers think Italians are all cowards.'

'We don't think that!' cried Robert. 'There were lots of Italian soldiers in North Africa, and some of them put up a damned good fight.'

'My brothers were in the desert,' said Sofia, and she turned her head away.

'What happened to them?' asked Robert.

'They're missing, both of them.' Sofia brushed her hand across her eyes and shrugged again. 'We haven't heard they're prisoners, so I expect they're dead. My own fiancé died at Alamein.'

'I'm sorry.'

'They were your enemies,' said Sofia.

'I'm supposed to be *your* enemy.'

'Oh, we're not Fascists here.' Sofia smiled a bitter smile. 'When the *Duce* fell from power, and we had the armistice, my father gave a party. We hoped our war was over. But then the Germans came.'

Over the course of the next few days, whenever he woke up,

Robert found Sofia or the grey-haired woman sitting quietly by his bed, usually with their heads bent over sewing.

It looked like they were making tablecloths, or sewing sheets, or shirts. But then Sofia told him they were actually sewing shrouds. These days, she added, they used a lot of shrouds, and there would be lots of deaths this winter – food was short, and so was fuel.

At first, they fed him thin, brown soup containing chopped-up vegetables and tiny shreds of meat. But two or three days later, they started bringing plates of macaroni with tomato sauce, and now and then a bit of bread and cheese.

As Robert became more wide-awake and stronger, what had happened started coming back to him.

He and his sergeant and two men had volunteered for what was on the face of it a fairly simple mission behind the German lines. They'd managed to blow up a German gun emplacement on a hilltop north of Florence. They'd almost got back home to their own lines when there'd been a terrible explosion that had blown him off his feet, and he had died.

Or, as it seemed now, he hadn't died.

'Some of our tenants brought you to our house,' Sofia told him. 'You were very lucky that they found you before the Germans did. The Germans would have shot you. But you're still in danger. German officers come to see my father almost every day. They sit and eat his food and drink his wine. Our family goes without.'

'What about my men?' asked Robert.

'I'm afraid they're dead,' Sofia said, and now she shrugged in sympathy. 'We buried them where they died. We had to, because otherwise the Germans would have found them. They would have worked out what you'd done, and then searched all the houses in the district, looking for anybody who'd survived. You were all in British battledress, even though you didn't have any dog tags, badges, anything like that.'

'The CO thought it best, since we were going behind the lines.' Robert rubbed his eyes. He'd gone with his reliable Sergeant Gregory, together with two privates, Blain and Thornton. The privates had been lively, bright, intelligent young lads, and always up for anything. But now they were both dead, and Alan Thornton would never get a medal to send home to his mum.

'I was the officer in charge,' said Robert, suddenly feeling sick with guilt and shame. 'It was my job to get us back alive.'

'It was not your fault,' Sofia told him.

'It must have been, because the Germans saw us!'

'The Germans didn't see you,' said Sofia, quietly. 'It was a mistake. As you were going home, you got hit by a shell that had been fired by your own side.'

'You need a proper bath,' declared Sofia, one October morning. 'I'll try to get some water brought up here, and a small tub.'

Then somebody tapped softly on the door, and Sofia looked around, alarmed. She called out something in Italian, and a male Italian voice replied.

'It's just the doctor,' whispered Robert, who was getting to grips with his Italian and had come to know the doctor's voice.

Sofia left them while the doctor examined Robert. He made encouraging comments in Italian as he listened to his patient's heart, then checked up on his wounds, which were all healing nicely.

'I've been thinking about my family in England,' Robert told Sofia, as he ate his lunch that day, out of bed and sitting in a chair. 'They're going to think I'm dead. I don't know if it's possible to get a message sent?'

'It would be very difficult,' said Sofia, which Robert took to mean impossible. But then she smiled to see him eating with apparent relish. 'This afternoon,' she added, 'I want to get you walking. Did you enjoy your lunch?'

'Yes, thank you very much, it was delicious.'

'I'm only sorry there was so little of it.'

'I had more than enough.' This was an outright lie, but Robert felt very guilty about eating the scarce food Sofia's family could have had instead.

But she encouraged him to eat. 'You're getting stronger every day,' she told him, as she made sure he swallowed every single precious mouthful.

Then, she made him exercise. Sometimes, when there was no moon, she took him down the rickety stairs behind the pigeon loft, and then she got him running around the yard behind the house. 'Soon,' she told him, 'you'll be killing Germans, and the Allies will win the war.'

'I'm going to be a one-man army, am I?'

'Well, not quite,' Sofia said. 'But we can't help you to get back to your unit. It would be far too dangerous for us. So when you're well again, you'll join the partisans.'

Autumn was coming on, the days were cooler, and although the elderly grey-haired woman's fusty black remained unchanged, Sofia's cotton dresses gave way to knitted jumpers, cardigans, and tweed or corduroy skirts.

Robert insisted he was strong enough to leave the villa, to take his chances in the mountains, or to try to get back to his unit.

But Sofia wouldn't hear of it.

'You must wait,' she told him. Then she smiled. 'I can see that patience has never been your virtue, as you English say! You won't be any use to anyone until you're strong again.'

Robert worked very hard at being strong.

'What's happening in the world?' he asked Sofia, as he jogged around his tiny prison, or did press-ups, determined to build his stamina up. 'What's stopping the Americans and British breaking through? I'd have thought we'd have the Germans on the run by now. Sofia, the Allied armies can't be very far away?'

'They're very close to us in terms of miles,' agreed Sofia. 'But it's nearly winter. The Germans are so well dug in the Allies just can't shift them. I think they're going to have to wait for spring.'

One morning in December, Sofia told Robert that later on that day, when it got dark, he would be collected by some friends and taken to the hills, and there he would become a partisan.

'Excellent,' said Robert, who was itching to leave his claustrophobic little jail up in the pigeon loft, which stank of lime and droppings, and to breathe fresh air again.

'But I'll be sorry to leave *you*,' he told Sofia and the silent, grey-haired woman, whose name he'd never learned. 'After all you've done for me. I mean, I'm very grateful. I hope we'll meet again.'

Sofia looked at him and smiled. 'But you're not leaving me,' she said. 'I'm coming with you.'

'You can't do that!' Robert stared at Sofia, horrified. 'Sofia, it will be too dangerous. What if you were found with me? If the Germans caught you helping me?'

'I'll have to take the chance.'

'What about your parents? I've never asked about them, I thought I shouldn't know, but won't they want – '

'My mother died in April of a broken heart, because her sons are dead. Or at any rate, she had convinced herself that they were dead, and she has gone to join them. My father is a tired old man, who has no fight in him. I told him I was leaving, and he gave me his blessing.'

'I think I should meet him.'

'No, you can't do that.' At the mention of her parents, Sofia's soft brown eyes had filled with tears. 'As I said, he's tired. Since my mother died, he struggles to get through the days. He's ill, he's – I don't know the word in English, but I mean he doesn't care. Leave him alone, and let me come with you.'

'Sofia, I still don't think – '

'Robert, I'm leaving anyway,' Sofia told him firmly. 'I'm sick of sewing shrouds. I'm going to be a partisan. If you don't want me to come with you, I'll go by myself.'

Chapter Sixteen

January 1945

Rose Denham couldn't quite believe her eyes, but the letter from the solicitor in Dorchester was clear and to the point.

The owner of Charton Minster, the lovely golden mansion that had once been Rose's home, had died a month ago. She knew he'd died, of course. The elaborate, expensive private funeral had been the gossip of the village. The big surprise was that Sir Michael Easton had left the house to Rose.

But, as she realised straight away, his sole intention was to mock her from the grave, not make her happy. Since he had inherited Charton Minster, back in the 1920s, he'd let it to a succession of bad tenants, each more careless than the last. So now the whole place was a cavernous ruin.

Its last inhabitants, fifty delinquent boys locked up for various crimes from petty theft to arson and attempted murder had – so Mrs Hobson said – destroyed the place inside, just as Sir Michael had no doubt hoped they would.

Rose had no money to repair it, so all she could do was watch her childhood home decay.

Frances had been on leave and staying in Charton when Rose first learned the Minster would soon be hers again, and Frances wrote to Cassie to tell her all about it.

So when Cassie next had leave herself, she wrote to Stephen. If he could get some time off too, she said, they ought to go and see Rose.

'Yes, good plan,' wrote Stephen. 'I haven't seen Mum for months. She wanted me to go back home for Christmas, but I couldn't get any leave, not even a day.'

They travelled down to Dorset on the train. Stephen didn't seem to remember getting drunk and trying to kiss

Cassie. Or perhaps he did, for he was on his best behaviour. He carried Cassie's kitbag, found her a window seat and paid for lunch, treating her like the sister-in-law that she still hoped to be.

'Tinker!' Cassie cried, as they approached the bailiff's cottage, and the chocolate Labrador came hurtling out to greet them, barking and wagging his tail in ecstasy.

Rose came running after him, hugged Cassie and Stephen one after the other, and then she told her dog to just calm down, stop making such an exhibition of himself.

'Steve, look at the size of him!' cried Cassie, as she made a fuss of the dog, who licked her face and hands delightedly. 'Rose, what on earth have you been feeding him?'

'We go out hunting,' Rose replied. 'I shoot the rabbits, he retrieves them, and of course I share the kill with him.'

'I didn't know you could shoot, Rose?'

'I'm a country girl, my dear,' said Rose. 'So I learned to shoot when I was young. It's what people did. Back in 1939, Alex got me polishing up my skills again, in case the Germans came.'

'As long as you're not trapping, Mum,' said Stephen.

'Steve, as if I would,' said Rose. 'I remember when you and your brother used to rescue animals caught in Michael Easton's traps. I'd never trap or snare. It's far too cruel. Well, you two, don't stand there looking vacant – come inside.' She took her visitors into the comfortably cluttered cottage, which smelled invitingly of rabbit pie.

After Stephen and Cassie had eaten supper and washed up, they thought they'd go and look at Rose's house. They could see its lichened roof and chimneys, and some of the leaded windows in its upper storeys, from the lane that led from Charton village to the bailiff's cottage. So now the house belonged to Rose, they both thought they'd like a closer look.

Rose had been emphatic she didn't want to stir up any old hostilities, reminding them the road to Charton Minster was on Easton land. So Stephen told his mother they were going to the pub.

Cassie and he walked down the lane, and then sneaked off across the moonlit fields. Disregarding all the Keep Out, Private Property notices which were nailed up everywhere, they jumped over the stiles, crossed fields, and climbed high boundary walls.

'When Rob and I were kids, we were always trespassing on the old bugger's land,' Stephen said to Cassie as he helped her fight her way through undergrowth, which might once have been a formal garden but which now was merely tangled laurels, brambles, bracken and straggling, dying weeds. 'As Mum was saying, we used to rescue animals caught in Easton's traps. We had a hospital for them in our old stables back at Melbury House.'

At the recollection, Stephen grinned, and suddenly he looked so young and childlike that Cassie could see the children he and Robert must have been – two grubby, black-haired urchins on undercover missions, taking wounded fox cubs and badgers out of traps, then smuggling them back to Melbury.

Finally they made it and stood in front of the old mansion, staring at its dull-eyed, leaded windows from the weed-strewn gravel drive.

'What a dump,' said Stephen.

'I think it's romantic.' Cassie gazed and gazed. 'It's beautiful. It's like the enchanter's castle in a fairy tale.'

'It's a crumbling ruin.' Stephen walked up to the entrance porch, once grand but now decrepit. 'Look at this wood here, Cass,' he said, breaking off a piece of rotting timber streaked with green and orange mould. 'It all needs replacing. The whole building must be riddled with dry rot.'

Stephen tossed the piece of wood away. 'It would cost thousands to repair it. More than the house is worth, I shouldn't wonder. Mum should go and talk to Lady Easton. They could either have a giant bonfire, or they could knock it down and sell the stone for building. Then Mum could flog the land back to the Eastons, if they'll buy it. She doesn't need more stuff to worry about, and all this place would be is one big worry.'

'How do you think she's feeling these days, Steve?' Cassie could see his point about the worry of this rambling great house, but thought it was a pity it might have to be knocked down. 'She must be lost without your father?'

'Yes, she must.' Stephen looked at Cassie. 'Mum was brought up to be stoical, and not to make a fuss. But I can see she's grieving. She still misses him. She always will. Now Robert's missing too, of course, it's hard for all of us.'

'You keep telling me you think he's dead. I hope you haven't shared that with your mother?'

'Of course I haven't, Cass.' Stephen looked apologetic now. 'I'm sorry, Cassie. I should keep my gloomy thoughts and worries to myself. Come on, let's get back.'

'It's the only thing to do.' Rose had not been pleased to hear they'd been to look at the old house. When they told her it was in a terrible condition, she'd merely shrugged and sighed.

'I'll need to go and see Lady Easton,' she continued. 'I'll have to get permission to move the demolition people in.'

'But do you have to knock it down?' asked Cassie.

'I think so,' Rose replied. 'I can't afford to have the place repaired.'

'But it's so lovely,' Cassie said reproachfully.

'I know, my dear, I know.' Rose shook her head. 'Cassie, I was born there, I grew up there. I remember what the house was like when people cared about it.'

'How did you come to lose it?'

'My parents and the Eastons were close friends. The Eastons' eldest son – the one who eventually became Sir Michael – we were friends, as well. In fact, we almost got engaged.'

'But then you married Mr Denham.'

'Yes, and then my father decided to believe I'd broken Michael's heart, and made *him* a laughing-stock, as well. He was so angry that he left the whole estate, the house and land and everything, to Michael.'

'Blimey, what a mean old sod!' cried Cassie. Then, 'I'm sorry, Rose,' she added, reddening. 'That's no way to talk about your father.'

'I've often wished I hadn't been quite so headstrong.' Rose smiled ruefully. 'When I was young, and everything seemed so black and white, I saw my choice as being between the man I loved, and piles of bricks and mortar. If only I'd been kinder to my father, a bit more diplomatic – '

'Oh, Mum, don't cry.' Stephen put his arm around her shoulders. 'It's only an old house.'

'But it was *my* old house. It should be yours. This has been done to mock me. The intention was to give me back my home, then force me to watch it all fall down.'

'There must be some way round it, though,' said Cassie, frowning. 'Why don't we ask Daisy? She might think of something.'

'Yes, she might.' Rose wiped her hand across her eyes. 'She's most resourceful, is our Daisy. Steve, there's some fresh shortbread in the pantry, and shall we have another cup of cocoa, made with milk? The coffee's not worth drinking nowadays.'

Robert and Sofia sat in a mountain hut, drinking acorn coffee from tin cups and eating stale, dry bread which they softened slightly by dunking it into the acrid coffee.

'I still dream of my morning *cappuccino*,' sighed Sofia. 'I dream of fresh, white bread.'

'I dream of eggs and bacon and my mother's home-made sausages.' Robert glanced at his companion, and he sighed as well. 'Sofia, please stop talking about food!'

'I'm sorry,' said Sofia.

'I hate to see you cold and hungry,' added Robert. 'Why don't you go home, while there's still time?'

'No, I've told you half a dozen times, I want to join the partisans!' exclaimed Sofia fiercely. 'So I shall stay with you.'

While he'd been in the pigeon loft, Robert had let his beard grow strong and black, leaving it untrimmed, so now it covered half his face. Although he hadn't had any daylight exercise for months, and so he didn't have a tan, he was naturally olive-skinned, and now he could have passed for an Italian, born and bred.

Like most Italians these days, he was very thin. Sofia had found him clothes so old and tattered that most people would have thought he was a beggar, or a jobbing labourer – the kind of half-wit wanderer who goes from farm to farm, picking up any casual work and sleeping rough in barns.

'You must slouch and shuffle when you walk,' she'd told him, when they'd first set off. 'You must try to look confused and stupid, not arrogant and confident, not like a British army officer. If you have to talk to anybody, you must mumble, and stammering would be good.'

But, even though he was learning the language, and understood much more than he could say, Robert knew he'd never, ever sound like an Italian, however much he mumbled. So he was in almost constant danger of giving himself away.

Or of betrayal.

The German planes flying over Northern Italy dropped bombs, incendiaries, and also leaflets in English and Italian. Those in English told Allied POWs who had escaped after the armistice, and were still on the run, to give themselves up now, then spend the winter in a comfortable prison camp, rather than try to rough it in the mountains. Those in Italian warned that anyone found helping or sheltering Allied POWs would be shot. They also offered cash rewards to anyone giving information leading to arrests.

'There'll be plenty of people who would happily take the money,' said Sofia. 'So don't trust anybody, keep your mouth shut unless you have to speak, and let's hope we don't meet any Fascist bounty-hunters on the road.'

On their journey north into the mountains, hidden under sacks and baskets in the back of an old Fiat truck belonging to a farmer who was a tenant of Sofia's father, and who had dumped them when the road gave out, they'd made some plans.

If they were stopped by any Germans or Fascist militiamen, Sofia would say Robert was her deaf-mute idiot cousin, who had spent the summer and autumn working on her family's farm, and whom she was taking home to his parents in their village up here in the mountains.

Sofia's own papers were in perfect order. The doctor who had treated Robert had forged an identity card for him, so he was Roberto Russo now.

Robert hoped he wouldn't need the card. The doctor had done his best, of course, and Sofia had roughed it up a bit. But, even so, it didn't look convincing.

They had a week or more of wandering, of asking suspicious, anxious peasants who obviously didn't want to talk, of being sent off along steep mountain paths in wrong directions, before they found the partisans – or, as it turned out, before the partisans found them.

Robert had long assumed that unseen eyes were watching them, weighing them up. 'But we must wait for them to come to us,' Sofia told him. 'The people we've met, the farmers who have given us food and let us shelter in their huts and barns, they'll have passed the message on, that we want to join the partisans.'

Sofia was proved right. One day in early January, on a clear, sharp morning after a freezing night, they were going to fetch some water when they met a trio of men with rifles, blocking their path and smoking.

'We've been watching you,' said one.

'We know,' Sofia said.

'Why are you here?'

'We wish to join a *banda*.'

'Who's your gormless friend?'

'A British army officer.' Sofia crossed her fingers – these people might easily be the Fascist militia, after all.

'Yes, he looks like a British army officer – I don't think!' The man who'd spoken grinned. 'Give your bags to him.' He pointed to one of the other men. 'Then put your hands up on your heads, and follow me.'

So, with one man leading them, another herding them and one man carrying their bags, Sofia and Robert stumbled along the track, and then through the wild countryside, hoping they hadn't made a huge mistake.

They finally arrived at a stone house, in a very bad state of repair. It was the kind of summer residence a wealthy Italian family would have used before the war. Well concealed by firs and evergreens, it was a perfect hideout.

As they and their captors reached what was left of a garden, a tall man and some shorter, stocky ones came running from the house. They all carried rifles, and looked as if they'd use them.

'She says he's British,' said the leader of their captors, indicating Robert. 'He looks like a Sicilian village idiot to me.'

'A jolly good afternoon to you, old boy,' the tall man said

to Robert, in a deliberate parody of English. 'Everything tickety-boo back home in good old Blighty, then?'

'No, not particularly,' said Robert, shrugging. 'Please may I put my hands down now?' he added, in stumbling Italian. 'I'd like to scratch my nose.'

The group Robert and Sofia had joined was made up of Italian soldiers who didn't want to end up in German POW camps, and who had wisely hung on to their weapons.

'It was either become a partisan or join the Fascists,' one of them explained to Robert, adding that their main objective was to pin down any German troops who were still occupying the region, while waiting for the Allies to break through and end the war.

'Up here in the mountains, we can look down on them and pick them off,' he added, grinning. 'That's when we have some ammunition, obviously.'

Marcello, their undisputed leader, was older than the others. He said he was a Communist who had been in prison before the war, but had escaped after the armistice.

He was delighted to welcome Robert to the band. A British army officer, skilled in explosives, a trained killer and a seasoned fighting man, he'd always be an asset.

But he wasn't keen to have Sofia in the group, and told her to go home. 'My men will see you safely down the mountains,' he continued, adding that he never liked using women. They were not only unreliable, but if they were captured by the Germans or Militia, women always broke down under torture.

'If you're taken by the Fascists, and handed over to Black Brigade, you'd squeal like a pig,' he told Sofia.

'I would not!' replied Sofia, stung. 'Give me a job to do, and you'll find I can be as brave as any man, and I – '

'You'll never survive a winter in the mountains,' Marcello

interrupted tersely. 'You'll get sick from cold and hunger, and your nerves will trouble you. Go home now, while it's still possible.'

'I will not go home,' replied Sofia. 'The Englishman and I –'

'I need her to translate for me,' said Robert.

'You don't,' Marcello told him. 'You understood what we just said.'

'We came together, and we stay together,' insisted Robert firmly.

Marcello scowled, and muttered something rude about the arrogant British soldier and his bossy, chatterbox *puttana*, which Robert knew meant whore.

'Thank you,' said Sofia, as Marcello stumped away. 'I'll prove to you I'm up to it.'

'You better had, Sofia,' said Robert grimly. 'Otherwise, we'll both be shot – or worse.'

Marcello told them he'd soon be giving them a job to do, reminding them if they got caught, they would be on their own.

'If you're interrogated, and if you betray this group of partisans, other partisans will find you and they'll kill you slowly – that's if the Germans haven't shot you first. So either way,' Marcello said, 'get caught, and you're both dead.'

The job was pinching whatever they could in the way of weapons and ammunition from a shepherd's hut that was currently being used for storage by the Germans, on a road a few miles down the mountain.

They had to kill the sentries, too.

The place had been reconnoitred, said Marcello. Most days, there were just two guards, one a surly-looking veteran, and one a skinny kid, a recent conscript by the look of him.

'No,' said Marcello, 'you can't have any weapons. If you

221

start a firefight, half an hour later this whole mountain will be alive with Germans, and they'll find this house.'

'I won't do this unarmed,' said Robert firmly.

'You can have a knife each, but that's all,' Marcello told him. 'So make sure you kill the Germans, yes?'

'It's a test,' Sofia said in English, and she trembled.

'One we'd better pass,' said Robert. 'I expect you wish you'd gone back home?'

Sofia didn't reply.

Robert and Sofia had soon learned the art of moving silently through any kind of landscape. On the morning of their test, they took some hessian sacks, they scrambled down the narrow mountain paths, and then they wriggled on their stomachs through the undergrowth which had not been cleared since the Germans had arrived, and so was dense with laurel, broom and brambles, making perfect cover.

Italian peasant farmers were fanatical about clearing grass and weeds from the terraces where they grew their crops, because the undergrowth was such a fire risk in the summer. But since the Germans had occupied the country and made life impossible for many of the farmers, had burned some villages and evacuated many others, the weeds grew where they pleased.

At first Sofia and Robert did very well, getting close enough to hear the German sentries talking. Robert signalled to Sofia to move back a little, so they'd be out of earshot.

'I'll go and throw some stones at them or something, to distract them,' said Sofia. 'You get inside and grab whatever you can, and then we'll run away.'

'I don't think that would work,' said Robert. 'We'll end up getting shot. Look, here's what I suggest. You speak some German. So you go a bit further down the hillside, and then get on the road.'

'What do I do next?'

'You walk back up, and when you pass the hut you stop, you smile, you say hello.'

'You must be joking!'

'No, I'm deadly serious.'

'You hope those men will shoot me?'

'I hope those men will want you.'

Then Robert turned Sofia's collar down, straightened the neckline of her grubby blouse, and pushed her long, dark hair back from her brow.

'Bite your lips to make them red,' he added, 'and pinch a little colour into your cheeks. Okay, I think you'll do. So off you go and flirt as if your life depended on it, which of course it might.'

'You will be covering me?'

'Of course I will. Sofia – '

'Yes?'

'Good luck.'

Ten minutes later, Robert saw Sofia come sauntering up the road towards the German sentries, who walked into the road to block her way.

She smiled, and wished them both good morning.

One of the guards was middle-aged, a thick-set, bull-necked corporal. Scowling at Sofia, he asked for her identity card.

She handed it to him.

As he was checking it, Sofia preened and flirted with the other guard, a slight, blond teenaged boy, who giggled, blushed and answered back.

As Robert watched, he wished he had insisted on a firearm. The Germans were both armed with submachine-guns, but he had just a knife.

He was supposed to kill them both. Or, at any rate, he

didn't expect Sofia to kill them, so he'd have to do it. But one was just a child. He really didn't want to kill a child. The older man was doomed, he'd had his life. But it seemed so wicked to kill a child.

Then he thought of what could happen to Sofia in a German prison, or in an interrogation centre run by the Militia, and he shuddered. He didn't dare mess this up.

He watched Sofia talking, flirting, tossing her damson-coloured hair, and finally she took the young blond lad into the hut. The older man stood moodily outside, smoking a cigarette and stamping – waiting for his turn, presumably.

Robert waited for a couple of minutes, and then he made a move. Silent as a snake, he crept up on the guard outside, and then he clapped his hand over his mouth. He jerked the German soldier's head right back, and snapped his neck.

He drew his knife and slid into the hut, hoping it would be light enough to see what he was doing – of course he didn't want to stab Sofia by mistake, and if she was entangled with the boy …

He found her standing by the body of the boy, whose chest was dark with blood and whose blue eyes were open wide.

'You killed him!' he exclaimed, amazed.

'Yes.' Sofia was shaking. 'I didn't want to do it! But I felt I had to kill him, otherwise Marcello – Robert, I feel sick.'

Robert pulled her into his embrace. 'There's going to be more killing,' he whispered, as he held her close and stroked her hair, as he felt her shuddering against him with both cold and dread. 'Perhaps Marcello is right – you should go home.'

'I'm not going home!' Sofia dashed some tears from her eyes. 'But there are bound to be reprisals,' she told Robert, as she looked at the dead boy. 'Two Germans dead – that's probably going to be two dozen or more Italian lives, and if they find our house – '

'If they do, we'll need some weapons, won't we, so we can defend ourselves?'

They took as much as they could carry – guns and bullets, three kinds of grenade and leather belts of ammunition – and slogged back up the mountain, weighted down like donkeys with sacks upon their backs.

'Machine guns!' cried Marcello, when he saw their loot. 'That's excellent, well done!' He glanced up from examining them and grinned. 'Get any ammunition?'

'Of course we got some ammunition,' said Sofia, glowering at him. 'What use would a machine gun be, without some rounds of ammunition?'

'We'll mount one on that sharp bend in the road a hundred metres from the hut, and then we should be able to attack the German convoys as they come up to man their big defences.' Now, Marcello was almost dancing in delight. 'Robert, you can get on with that tomorrow. Get the range right, and we can start to give the bastards hell.'

'I thought you didn't want us starting any firefights,' muttered Robert, but only to himself.

'By the way,' went on Marcello, 'did you get a radio? Did you see any boots? We're running short of boots.'

'No,' said Robert, who had carried almost his own weight of weaponry back up mountain tracks. 'You didn't say you wanted any radios or boots. I'll do my best next time.'

'I'm sure you will.' Marcello grinned again. 'Well done, the pair of you, the black witch and the mountain lion.'

Sofia beamed, kissed Robert on the cheek. 'Yes, well done us,' she said.

'As for reprisals,' said Marcello grimly, while they were having supper, 'there'll always be reprisals when a German soldier dies. If a German has a heart attack while he's having his morning crap, or as he screws some Fascist whore, there'll be reprisals.'

Later, they heard a village in the valley had been burned, and three people shot. Robert felt guilty, and Sofia cried.

Robert wished he could get a message home, but he knew it was too dangerous even to attempt it, and unlike some other groups of partisans, they had no radio.

Marcello used young lads as couriers, and they took his messages down the mountain. But anyone caught carrying a letter written in English would have been interrogated, tortured, and probably put to death. It wasn't worth the risk.

He told himself that Cassie would have faith, that even if she'd been told he had gone missing, or even that he'd died, she would believe he was alive.

What was she doing now, he wondered, as he cleaned a rifle and then reloaded it. He hoped she wasn't as cold as he was on this freezing winter night.

Cassie was sitting in Daisy Denham's warm, luxurious kitchen, busy making plans for Charton Minster.

The more she had considered it, the better it had seemed suited to what Daisy had in mind, and in the end she'd written to Daisy, asking what *she* thought.

A place where undernourished, wan-faced children could spend a week or two enjoying lots of sunshine and fresh air, running along a beach or even learning how to swim – the Minster would be perfect, wouldn't it? As for staff – there must be local women who'd like part time jobs?

'What a clever little sparrow,' Daisy said, as Cassie finished talking, or rather as she paused for breath, because she had a whole lot more to say.

She could help to run the place.

She could do the driving.

She could fetch and carry from the station.

She could organise the laundry. When she'd first left school, she'd worked for a few months for Mr Wong in Smethwick, so she knew how to do it.

'It's not *too* far from London, is it?' she concluded anxiously

'It's quite a distance. But it's nearer Birmingham and all those ghastly places in the Midlands. So we would be able to invite more children from lots of different districts.' Daisy smiled at Cassie. 'It might be ideal.'

'Better than the house in Southwold?'

'Bigger, anyway.' Daisy poured herself some coffee. 'I haven't signed the papers for the house in Southwold yet. It's obvious we would have to spend more money on the Minster. Quite a lot of money, actually. But we wouldn't have to *buy* the Minster, so it shouldn't be a problem – not at first, at any rate.'

'So Rose won't pull it down?'

'I don't think so, Cassie.' Daisy looked at Cassie, blue eyes twinkling. 'Of course there'd be a job for you, that's if you're interested? A job for Robert, too.'

'But Robert's – '

'Robert's coming home, my sparrow.' Daisy tilted Cassie's chin up, looked into her eyes. 'He's coming back to you.'

'I hope you're right.' Cassie wondered if she dared to ask, and then decided yes, she would. 'Daisy?'

'Yes?'

'You're going to be doing such a lot for all these city children. So do you and Ewan – I'm sorry, I don't mean to be inquisitive, and it isn't any of my business, but – '

'Why don't we have some children of our own?' Daisy lit a cigarette, inhaled and looked up at the ceiling. 'There's nothing I'd like better, little sparrow, but it's not to be.

'When Ewan and I got married, we thought we'd start a family at once. We knew a lot of people in the business who had children, and we saw them coping very well. We said we'd have a nanny, and when we went off touring the kids could come along – '

'Daisy, I didn't mean to pry – '

'One miscarriage, then another – rather late this time. So that was quite distressing. Ewan was very upset, poor lamb, for me and for the child. One ectopic pregnancy, I think the doctor called it, and I had to have something removed – I told Mum I'd had appendicitis – and then the doctor said I would be foolish to conceive again. It would probably kill me.'

Daisy's big blue eyes were glittering now, and bright with unshed tears. 'We can't have everything we want in life, my little sparrow, and I know I'm a very lucky woman. I have a gorgeous home. I'm married to a man I love, and I know he loves me. I have a fabulous career. So don't you dare pity me, my sweet. I'm going to be all right.'

As Daisy lit another cigarette, they heard someone come in. A moment later, Ewan walked into the kitchen, dust upon his shoulders and powdering his hair.

'Bombed out,' he began, as Daisy looked at him enquiringly. Then he sat down beside his wife and kissed her cheek and took her hand. 'But it can't have been my turn to die.'

'Oh, my love, what happened?'

'A big incendiary, one left over from a previous raid – something must have triggered it.' Ewan shrugged. 'It seems the show must not always go on. Darling, is there any coffee left?'

'I'll make some,' offered Cassie.

'Thank you, little sparrow.' Daisy smiled, clearly relieved to have her husband home and safe again. 'Why don't we go on chatting about the Minster? Let's tell Ewan all about our plans.'

Robert and Sofia didn't have much time or opportunity for any idle chatting. But sometimes, as they waited to ambush German soldiers coming up the mountain, or as they made their way down to a valley to mine a railway line, there was a chance to talk.

Or for Sofia to start interrogating him.

'You have a girl in England?' she began one evening. She and Robert had been left to guard a pile of arms they'd taken from a patrol the group had ambushed. They'd killed the German soldiers, rolling their bodies down a slope into the dense undergrowth below. The others had gone to fetch some mules to take the stuff back up the mountain to their hideaway.

'Yes,' said Robert shortly. 'I have a fiancée, actually.'

'What's she like?' Sofia asked.

'She's small and blonde and very pretty.'

'Then she'll be a perfect English rose.' Sofia grinned sarcastically. 'Do you have a photograph of this very pretty lady?'

'No, didn't have anything when you found me.' Robert glanced at her and shrugged. 'You don't remember?'

'Yes, I remember now. So, my poor Roberto, you have your pretty lady's picture only in your heart.'

Robert wished Sofia would stop needling him like this, and also wished Marcello and the others would get a bloody move on. It was freezing cold, and he was afraid that any moment a German jeep or two would come careering round the corner, because the recent shooting must have echoed all around the mountainside.

'So which do you like the best of women?' asked Sofia. 'The blondes or reds or darks?'

'The blondes,' said Robert.

'Yet you're so very dark.'

'You're dark yourself,' said Robert. 'We have a saying in English, opposites attract. So do you like blond men?'

'I only like the darks.' Sofia grimaced. 'Blond men, ugh, they look like rats, insipid. Or like Germans. A pretty-pretty English lady can be blonde – that's very nice. But a real man is always dark.'

She walked her fingers up and down his arm.

He moved his arm away.

It was very hard to get explosives. These had to be stolen from the Germans, or collected from the occasional arms drops made by Allied planes. Robert wished and wished he had a radio, so he'd know which way the war was going – were the Allies winning it, or not?

Blowing up river bridges to impede the flow of German troops around the country was Marcello's passion. Robert knew more about explosives than Marcello did, knew how to prepare and fix the charges, and knew how to detonate a bomb.

Whenever they blew up a river bridge, it was a cause for celebration. Even the inevitable reprisals against the poor civilian population couldn't entirely dull the *banda*'s sense of jubilation.

After one particularly successful expedition, as they crept home along the mountain paths, Sofia was singing softly to herself. As the explosives had gone off, and as the bridge they'd targeted had fallen in the water, she had flung her arms round Robert's neck and kissed him on the mouth.

Now, she was linking arms and snuggling close to him. 'My hero,' she said softly, as they trudged along and, as she leaned towards him, she kissed him once again.

'You're a heroine yourself,' said Robert. 'Go on, kiss Marcello and the others. We can't have them getting jealous.'

'I'd sooner kiss a herd of swine,' Sofia said, in English.

On the way home to their mountain hideout, they had bought three chickens from a local farmer, and after they'd all eaten Marcello said he wanted to go down to a village to get some wine.

'Sofia's too tired,' said Robert.

'Of course she's tired, she's just a poor, weak woman,' said Marcello scornfully. 'It's only to be expected. You stay here and look after her, Roberto. We'll bring you back some wine.'

'Roberto won't need wine,' observed Gianni, and made a shunting gesture with his hips.

'Enough of that, Gianni,' snapped Marcello, cuffing him about the head. 'Roberto, I apologise. Come on, lads,' he added, 'we're wasting drinking time.'

'Why did you tell them I was tired?' Sofia demanded angrily, as the men went off.

'I don't want you to waste your strength.' Robert looked at Sofia with concern. 'You're so pale and thin. I know you're doing your best. I know you're not a slacker, but I wish you would go home.'

'You don't like me!' wailed Sofia.

'Of course I like you.' Robert put his arm around her shoulders, pulled her close to him and felt her shuddering against him. 'I like you very much, and I admire you, too.'

'But you don't like to kiss me.' Sofia turned to him and wound her arms around his neck. She kissed him lightly, teasingly at first, as she had done several times before. But then she began to kiss more passionately.

He found himself responding, and Sofia kissed him even harder, rubbed herself against him, murmured soft endearments in his ear, and slid her long, cold fingers through his hair.

'No, Sofia,' he said gently, and took her hands away.

'Robert, why not?' she whispered. 'Listen, I don't want to take you away from your fiancée. I don't want to marry you. When the war is over, I shall marry an Italian. But tonight, we need some loving, both of us. This girl in England, maybe she is comforted by other men herself. She would understand.'

Robert met Sofia's gaze, and saw she looked so lovely in the soft, gold glow of the few oil lamps which were all they had for light. Damson-coloured hair framed her pale oval of a face, and her great dark eyes were bright and luminous with desire.

'Or perhaps you can't?' she added, taunting him. 'Perhaps you're not a man? Roberto *mio*, don't tell me you're afraid?'

'Sofia, I said no.'

Chapter Seventeen

'This year's bound to finish it,' said Stephen, as he and Cassie travelled back up to London after a weekend in Melbury. The train was almost empty, and they had a compartment to themselves. 'Germany has lost the war, and I can't understand why they don't pack it in. The British and the Americans are bombing them to blazes. The Soviets are giving them such a hammering in the east that soon there won't be any German towns or cities left.'

'There won't be much of London left if the Jerries keep on sending over those V2s,' said Cassie with a shudder. 'Bloody awful things. Last week, one of the houses in our street got hit by a V2, and everyone was killed. I reckon Hitler isn't finished yet.'

'Maybe you've got a point,' admitted Stephen, and then he looked at Cassie urgently. 'Cass, why don't you ask to be transferred to somewhere outside London? You'd be much safer then.'

'Oh, don't you worry, Steve, I'll be all right,' Cassie told him wryly. 'Since I joined the army, my granny's sent me dozens of holy medals, all blessed by Father Riley, and they keep me safe. I jangle when I walk.'

'Your granny sounds a game old bird,' said Stephen, and he laughed affectionately. 'I'd like to meet your granny.'

'You will, after the war.'

'Oh, yes – after the war.' Stephen turned to gaze out of the window, watching the darkening landscape rushing by. 'What shall I do, Cass, after the war?'

'What do you mean?'

'The chaps I went to school with – I see them now and then, when they come to London and we meet up for a drink or two. They've all had a high old time. They've been flying Spitfires, sinking U-boats, they've been on Atlantic convoys, they've been serving in the Middle East. But I've been stuck in London, being a colonel's nursemaid, typing lists and ordering supplies.'

'But, Stephen, you were at Dunkirk!' cried Cassie. 'You did your share of fighting. You were wounded – '

'Dunkirk was a shambles.' Stephen turned to Cassie, and she could see the sadness in his eyes. 'It was a defeat. The German army swept us out of Europe like a farmer sweeping straw out of a barn. We all sat on that bloody beach like – well, like sitting ducks. Or like a row of invalids in wheelchairs.'

'But lots of you got home.'

'Yes, we were collected, like children being met at the school gates. Cass, we had no weapons, we had hardly any food, and there was no water fit to drink. We, the well-trained soldiers of mighty British army, we couldn't help ourselves, and people in pleasure cruisers had to come and fetch us home. Oh, Cassie – the humiliation!'

Stephen sighed, then lit a cigarette. 'Cass, when you met my father, he was middle-aged and dying. But in the '14–'18 war, he served in the front line. He was in all the most important battles, and he won the DSO. He ended up a major. All my life I wanted to make my father proud of me. But of course, he knew I was no hero.'

'Steve,' said Cassie gently, 'we don't all get the chance to be heroic. We – '

'I'm nearly twenty-five, and so far I've done nothing with my life. When the war is over, and people talk about it, what they did and where they did it, and I have to tell them I had a cushy job behind a desk, everyone will think I was a shirker and a coward. Somebody who fixed it so he didn't have to fight.'

'No, they won't!' cried Cassie.

'Of course they will.' Stephen stubbed his cigarette out. 'God, I need a drink,' he muttered. 'When we get to Paddington, will you come and have a beer with me?'

'Yes, okay,' said Cassie, thinking, just one beer won't hurt him, and I'd like one, too.

She stared out of the window, wondering how close they were to London. In the all-enveloping blackout, it was very difficult to tell. The long, slow minutes ticked on by.

'Have you seen Frances recently?' asked Stephen, breaking his moody silence.

'Not since she came to London, to tell me about Rob.' Cassie shrugged, then yawned behind her hand. I really ought to go to bed, she thought. I must be up by five tomorrow morning. I have to drive to York. 'But we write, of course.'

'How's she getting on with whatsisname?'

'I think they're hoping to get married, that's if he can get divorced.'

'But he's far too old for her, you know – and he's a cripple, too.' Stephen lit another cigarette. 'I should have nabbed her, when I had the chance. I might drop her a line.'

'Steve, she's very happy with her Simon.' Cassie thought, don't interfere, don't start making up to Frances, don't encourage her to think you love her after all, get her to break off her affair with Simon, change your mind again, and break her heart.

'Simon,' Stephen said sarcastically, and then he pulled a face. 'I think our Frances could do better than a geriatric cripple, Cass – don't you?'

'Leave Fran alone, Steve. Promise me?' Cassie looked at Stephen earnestly. 'What about your girl from Shropshire, how's that working out?'

'She keeps nagging on at me to go to bloody Ludlow to meet her bloody parents.' Stephen scowled. 'Daddy's master of the local hunt and lives for field sports, which I hate – they're pointless and they're boring and they're cruel – while Mummy does the flowers in church, and good works on the side. I don't think they'll be my sort of people.'

'Steve, you never know.'

The train was late, and everything was in total darkness by the time they finally shunted into Paddington. Stephen said to Cassie he'd walk her home to Chelsea, and they could have a drink along the way. He knew a decent pub in Fulham Road.

'It's a long way,' Cassie told him, 'for you to come to Chelsea, and then walk back to Berkeley Street.'

'Oh, that's all right,' said Stephen, as he picked up Cassie's kitbag. 'I don't have anything else to do.'

As they started stumbling through the blackout, he took Cassie's hand. Occasional flurries of sleet were making all the pavements slippery, so she was glad of someone to hold on to in the darkness.

She had enjoyed the past few days in Stephen's company. They'd gone for walks across the winter fields, they'd helped the land girls on the farm, they'd sat together in the snug old pub in Charton, and they'd walked back down the lanes to Melbury in moonlight under dark blue velvet skies. She'd thought, if I had had a brother, I'd have wanted him to be like Steve.

But maybe he would be her brother yet?

Stephen's hand felt comfortable in hers – it was strong and warm, and also solid and reassuring. Perhaps, she thought, if Robert doesn't come back, if Stephen wants to see me?

I do like him, very much. But could I love him, too? Maybe one day I could. He and Rob, they're almost the same person. They look so very similar, and they sound the same.

Stephen's good, he's kind, he's very thoughtful, and I

know he likes me. More than likes me. I could probably help him whenever he gets moody, when he's missing Robert and he's sad. So perhaps, after the war is over –

She gave his hand a friendly squeeze, and when a taxi passed them in the darkness, its headlights yellow slits, she could see a smile on his face. 'All right, Cass?' he asked.

'Yes, fine,' she said. 'But how are you?'

'Oh, I'm okay,' said Stephen, and he shrugged. 'I'm sorry I was going on just now. I get like that sometimes.'

'I think we all do, don't we?' Cassie smiled herself, relieved to hear him sounding like his normal self again.

'I'm looking forward to that beer,' he added.

'So am I.'

The quiet of the night was suddenly shattered by a huge explosion, the roar of engines and a sonic boom that echoed round the empty, silent streets.

'That's a V2,' said Cassie fearfully. 'It must have come down somewhere very close.'

'Yes.' Stephen grasped her hand more tightly. 'Come on, let's go and see.'

'See what?' asked Cassie.

'What's going on, of course.'

'Stephen, I don't want – '

But her hand was firmly clasped in Stephen's, and he began to pull her through the streets.

The rocket had hit a house at the south end of Sussex Place, and it was on fire. But the firemen must have come along within a couple of minutes of the explosion, and several ARP men were also on the scene.

'Stand back, sir,' said a fireman, as Stephen dragged Cassie across the road towards the blazing house, then stood there, mesmerised.

Cassie looked at Stephen anxiously. She saw his eyes were

glazed, that he looked feverish and excited, and that his lips were white. She thought he might be going to have a fit.

She remembered what he'd said the first day she had met him, how his eyes had sparkled when he'd described his own house burning down.

She shuddered, and she held his hand more tightly, as if restraining him.

'Do you know if anyone's inside?' she asked the fireman.

'We think so,' he replied. 'Or, at any rate, there are people living in the attics, and we don't know what's become of them. But we're dealing with it. Please, sir – can you move? You're in the way.' The fireman put one hand on Stephen's sleeve, to push him back.

But, as he did so, Stephen pulled his hand from Cassie's grasp and ducked under the fireman's arm. She didn't realise what was happening until she saw him running towards the burning house.

'Steve!' she shouted, horrified.

She would have followed him. She would have dragged him back by bodily force. But two ARP men held her arms, and hacking at their shins had no effect.

'Steve, come back!' she shrieked, and fought the ARP men, but to no avail.

She wasn't entirely sure what happened next, could never afterwards sort out the whole sequence of events in her own mind. As she gazed in terror, Stephen disappeared inside the house.

Cassie shrieked again, willing him to hear her voice and turn round, come back out.

Then, as the firemen's hoses sprayed the building, the water making rainbows against the orange flames, one wall of the stricken house swayed gently. Then it sort of crumpled, and then came crashing down. Cassie stared and stared, unable to do anything but gaze in terror at the wicked flames.

'Go and see to that one,' she heard a man's voice say, and then a WVS woman turned up out of nowhere, and she wrapped Cassie in a heavy blanket.

'It's all right, my duck,' she soothed. 'You've had a nasty shock. I know it isn't very nice, when you're on your way back home, and you turn a corner, and there's a house on fire. But don't you worry, the men are dealing with it, and everyone's all right.'

'Everyone?' said Cassie, hope leaping in her heart.

'Well,' said the woman, 'the firemen got the family out. But some ARP men were telling us a couple of minutes ago that they saw some lunatic go running into the house. They saw him go right up the stairs, they told us, making for the attics. They don't know where he came from, or what he was trying to do. They haven't found him yet.'

'He isn't mad, he's epileptic!' Cassie wailed.

'Why, do you know him?'

'Yes, he's my – he's my – '

But what could she say, that Stephen was her brother, lover, friend? All those, yet maybe none of them – how could she know? She settled for he's my friend.

'Try not to worry, love,' the WVS woman said. 'They'll get him out, you'll see. But, in the meantime, we ought to get you home.'

The woman led Cassie to a small green van parked a little way along the street, where other WVS women were making tea and sandwiches for the firemen. 'Do you live round here?' the woman asked, as Cassie shook and trembled, and as she tried in vain to hold a mug of scalding tea, which slopped all down her coat.

'N-no,' she stammered. 'But a f-friend of mine lives in Park Lane.' Cassie gave the woman Daisy's number, and then she sat down on the kerb and closed her eyes.

But she could still see wicked, dancing flames, see the

black shape of Stephen running into them, as if he were running into a loved one's arms. She knew she'd always see them, even if she lived to be a hundred.

Daisy came for Cassie in a taxi and took her to the apartment in Park Lane.

'Sit down, Cass,' she said, as they both stumbled – shell-shocked, frightened, disbelieving – into Daisy's sitting room. 'I'll go and make us something hot. Then, when you're ready, you can explain what happened.'

'We were walking back from Paddington,' said Cassie wretchedly. 'We'd been to see your mum for a few days. We'd had a lovely time.' She sipped the coffee which Daisy had laced liberally with brandy. 'Steve was in a funny mood – he was up one moment, down the next. I said I'd go and have a beer with him. I thought I might be able to cheer him up a bit.'

'What happened next?'

'We were just chatting about anything and nothing. I thought he sounded almost back to normal. We heard this big explosion. Then suddenly he was pulling me along. He said we had to go and see the fire.'

'But why would he want to see a fire?' demanded Daisy, frowning. 'He's been here in London since 1942, and he must have seen a thousand fires. Why go and look at this one?'

'I think he found fires interesting, exciting.' Cassie didn't want to talk to Daisy about what Stephen said when they'd first met, about how it would feel to walk in fire. It would have made him sound insane, as if he should have been locked up. 'But anyway, we got there, and this house was burning, and a fireman tried to push us back, but Steve ducked underneath his arm.'

'Then what?'

'He ran into the house.'

'But *why?*' demanded Daisy as Cassie started sobbing. 'I don't blame you, love,' she said quickly, as she came to sit down next to Cassie, as she put her arm around her shoulders and as she held her tight. 'Please, Cassie darling, don't break your heart like this! But I need to ask you why – '

'Daisy, I don't know!' insisted Cassie.

But she did. She knew exactly why. It had been preying on his mind, the fact that he was not a hero. Steve had been determined that he would be a hero, or die in the attempt.

She blamed herself. She had asked that fireman if there was anyone inside the house, and Steve had heard the man reply. 'Do you know if anyone's inside?' she'd asked. Six little words, and they'd condemned him, had sentenced him to death.

She wept and wept for him, more than she'd wept for Robert. She thought the tears would never, ever stop. Steve, she thought, you idiot, you fool! What are we going to tell your mother?

It was such a pointless waste of life.

Robert and Sofia were a team.

Marcello and the others understood it, and let them plan and organise some missions of their own. Marcello was always very pleased to see them coming home with anything they'd stolen from the Germans – guns and hand grenades, supplies they'd filched from German general stores, and on one occasion a whole crate of schnapps.

Robert made sure he and Sofia got their share of schnapps, decanting it into their water bottles and taking it along with him when he and Sofia went off on private raids.

One day, after a raid on a supply store, they lost their way coming back home and were benighted on the mountain.

Freezing cold and hungry, they could not see anything to guide them on an overcast and starless night.

'We passed a shepherd's hut a while ago,' Sofia said, pulling her tattered coat around her body, and hugging herself as she tried to keep warm. 'I think we should go back to it. Otherwise, Marcello and the others are going to find us frozen on the mountain when they come to look for us tomorrow – and that's if we're lucky, if the Germans haven't found us first.'

Robert agreed Sofia was right, so they turned back the way they'd come, hoping they were keeping to the track, which was difficult in the pitch dark. They'd know they'd missed it when they ended up in the ravine a dizzying drop below.

The hut was damp and freezing, but at least it gave them some shelter from the wind. Robert lit a match and saw there was some rubbish in a corner – several cardboard boxes with German lettering all over them, empty packets, paper wrappings, even musty straw.

He wondered if they dared to start a fire?

He lit another match, and with his other hand he began to push the boxes into a small pile. The fire would last ten minutes at the very most, he realised. But for those ten minutes they would have warmth and light.

'No!' Sofia cried, when she understood what he was doing.

'Why?' he demanded crossly.

'You never know who might be watching.'

'You think there's a platoon of German soldiers lurking in the pine trees? Anyway, if any soldiers come, they'll see we're harmless peasants. We'll tell them we're returning from a wedding feast or something, and we've lost our way.'

'Roberto, don't be stupid,' said Sofia scornfully. 'Look at what we're carrying – guns and ammunition we've stolen from the Germans, a sack of flour you pinched from that cook's hut, some tins of sauerkraut, packs of pumpernickel bread. These came from an Italian wedding breakfast? I'll let *you* explain!

'As for pretending to be peasants – you see this coat I'm wearing? I know it's dirty, torn and ragged now, but it came from the smartest shop in Florence – no peasant ever had a coat like this. You stink of high explosive. Your hands are covered with burns and cuts from laying charges and detonating them.'

'So we sit here and freeze to death?' asked Robert, who was now annoyed with her for talking to him in the bossy, patronising way she often did, especially when she thought – or in this case, knew – that she was right.

'We snuggle up for warmth, we eat some pumpernickel bread and drink your schnapps.'

'I must admit I had forgotten about the schnapps.' Robert found his water bottle, shook it. 'It's nearly full,' he said.

They huddled close together, eating bread and drinking schnapps and feeling a delicious warmth flow into them. 'What do you think, Sofia?' asked Robert, as he drank again. 'What's this stuff made of – apples, pears or plums?'

'None of them,' Sofia said, and giggled naughtily. 'This is the best stuff, made of cherries. It was intended for a colonel's table.'

'But it ended up here in our hut.'

'Yes,' said Sofia, and now she snuggled closer, slipping one cold hand inside his shirt. 'Roberto, you're so warm inside your clothes,' she whispered, running her long fingers up and down his chest. 'But me, I'm cold, I'm freezing – feel how cold I am.' She took his hand, pulled it inside her coat and laid it on her beating heart.

Robert could smell Sofia now and, even though she hadn't had a wash for several days, the female muskiness of her was more intoxicating than the most expensive scent.

He could feel the schnapps firing his blood, demanding action, telling him that here was a young woman, a lovely, willing woman, and she wanted him. He kissed her on the mouth, tasting the schnapps, tasting Sofia, and suddenly he wanted, needed more – he knew that he could never have enough.

'I always get my man,' Sofia told him, as they lay together under both their coats upon the musty straw, in a warm, tangled heap of arms and legs.

'You're a determined woman,' Robert said, and offered her the last of what was in his bottle.

She drank and let some dribble down her chin, raising her pale face to his, inviting him to lick it off and laughing when he did. 'As Marcello says, you're a black witch,' he told Sofia. 'You're a sorceress, you're an enchantress. You've put a spell on me.'

But in the morning, when the cold, grey dawn came creeping like a ghost on to the mountain, and Robert woke with a thick head and mother of all hangovers, he found the spell was broken.

Sofia lay beside him, fast asleep, her dark hair matted and her face begrimed, apart from where the runnels of sticky schnapps had washed away a little of the dirt.

He wished he could turn back the clock. Why had he done this stupid, stupid thing? He liked Sofia, he admired Sofia, she had saved his life. She was the bravest, strongest woman he had ever known. But she was not the one he loved.

Sofia stirred and then opened her eyes. 'I know,' she said, as she looked at his face.

'What do mean, you know?'

'You Englishmen, you're good at feeling guilty. You wish we hadn't done those things we did last night. So I suppose you hate me now?'

'I'll never hate you,' Robert said. 'Come on,' he added, pulling on his clothes, then picking up the various bags and sacks they'd dumped when they'd decided they would spend the night in this damp hut. 'We must be getting back. Marcello and the others will think we've run away.'

Rose left the farm and went to London to identify the body.

She was absolutely adamant that Daisy mustn't do it. But afterwards she looked so ill and shocked that Daisy said to Cassie she wished she had insisted, wished she'd told her mother she was a big girl now, and could do this for Steve.

Cassie was afraid that even though she'd privately convinced herself she was to blame for Stephen's death, Rose might say in public that Cassie was a wicked, grasping harlot who had come into her family and caused them all great pain.

But Rose was kind to Cassie. 'Steve always felt that he was second best,' she said, as she and Cassie sat quietly in the cottage the evening after Stephen's funeral, when the other mourners had all gone away. He was buried with his father now, in the local churchyard, underneath an ancient, dripping yew. 'He hero-worshipped Robert,' Rose continued. 'He adored him, literally. When Robert joined the army in 1939, Stephen followed suit – went into the same regiment, applied for a commission, was determined to do everything that Rob could do. But it really bothered him, that Rob was always bigger, brighter, braver – better at everything.'

'I'm so s-sorry, Rose.' Since Stephen's death, Cassie found she couldn't stop crying, found that she was bursting into tears on buses, in the street, while driving officers around, while working in the motor pool. 'I expect you wish I'd never met them. If I'd never come to Melbury – '

'Rob would not have met the girl he loved. Steve had his own demons, which were nothing to do with you.' Rose put her arms round Cassie and hugged her like a mother. 'You mustn't blame yourself.'

But Cassie did.

She knew everybody thought her nerves were shot to bits. Her CO called her in to have a pep-talk, to offer her a transfer, to tell her she could have compassionate leave.

But she didn't want it and, the day after the funeral, she went straight back to London, driving all around a city that was being traumatised by rockets coming over night and day.

She didn't know quite why, but a few days later she realised she didn't feel afraid. She'd used up all her tears, all her compassion, and all her sympathy. Blazing buildings, bombs, explosions, scenes of carnage, screams of people burning, wounded, dying – she could deal with all of it.

She wasn't bothered if the war was lost or won, or just dragged on and on for ever. She couldn't bring herself to care about it any more.

Sofia had been careless.

On a raid with Robert and Marcello and two of the other men, she had tripped and fallen as they ran away from an explosion, and she'd hurt her arm. When they arrived back at their hideout, Robert realised she had broken it.

He managed to set it straight again between two wooden splints, then bind it up with rags. But it was soon obvious Sofia would be no use to anybody for several weeks or more.

Marcello was disgusted, ranting in Italian about it being bad luck to have a woman in a *banda*. He should have sent her home when she and Robert first arrived, he grumbled, and she needn't think she could just lie there, and have the others waiting on her hand and foot. If she didn't work, she didn't eat, and –

'Shut up, Marcello,' Robert said.

'What?'

'I told you to shut up.'

There was a sudden silence. Robert realised everyone was looking straight at him, and also realised he had gone too far. But he couldn't start to back down now, even though he knew the various members of the group could all turn on him, if they pleased.

He wasn't one of them. He wasn't even an Italian. They didn't owe him anything, and he'd just insulted a man they all respected. He waited to feel steel against his throat.

But, after a few moments, when he'd realised they weren't going to kill him, or at any rate not yet, he met Marcello's stare. 'I'll take her home,' he said.

'You won't.' Marcello glared at him. 'You're useful, and I need you here with me.'

'What about Sofia?'

'What about Sofia, Roberto?' Marcello was grinning monkey-like at him. 'What about your whore? If this one dies, Roberto, you can always get another one. Listen, when she came here, she knew about the risks. She knew she wasn't wanted, but she stayed. She hung around like a stray dog. I don't care if she dies like one.'

'I'll take her home,' repeated Robert, scowling at Marcello and wishing he didn't already feel the knife going in his back.

Then, to his astonishment, one of the other men spoke up. 'Let them go,' he said. 'Let Roberto take the woman home, and then come back to us. You will come back, Roberto, won't you?'

The others all joined in – take her home, they said, let the woman go back to her family.

'You're crazy!' cried Marcello. 'You're crazy, all of you!' But he knew he was beaten and backed down. 'All right,' he muttered. 'You can take your *puttana*, but you'll have no arms, no ammunition, and only one day's food. When

247

you've delivered the woman, you come back. If you don't, we'll hunt you down and kill you.'

Robert nodded, but didn't promise anything.

It was the worst of journeys, for the snow was melting and the rivers were all rushing torrents which they somehow had to get across. They were anxious to avoid the Germans, but they still had to steal some food from them.

Always hungry, always tired, Sofia's strength was failing, and Robert found he was hoping he was dreaming, that this was all a nightmare from which he would wake up. He didn't know how he was going to carry on.

But, somehow, they made it.

As they approached the villa – six or maybe seven days later, Robert had lost count – they saw it was a ruin. He wasn't sure quite what he'd been expecting, but it wasn't to see such final, absolute destruction.

The pigeon loft where he had once been hidden was just a blackened shell. The roof tiles lay in broken orange shards upon the paving far below. The villa's walls were pockmarked, burnt and holed by high explosive. The grand, impressive entrance portico was blasted into splintered marble bits.

Robert was so tired today that he understood why many people just gave up, why they lay down and died. If the Germans were still here, he thought he might as well surrender and hope they'd spare Sofia, even if they shot him there and then.

'Get your hands up!' cried a voice.

Robert was so exhausted, so light-headed from starvation and fatigue that he didn't know if he was hearing English, German or Italian, but he raised his hands.

A dozen men in dirty British battledress encircled him, and he saw from their shoulder flashes they were from the

Yorkshire Regiment. As Sofia sank down helpless on the weed-choked gravel, he called out his name and rank and regiment, and he almost laughed to see their faces.

But actual laughter was beyond him.

There were a couple of rooms which must have been inhabitable still, for Robert could see faces at the broken windows. After he'd told his captors that the lady was the owner of the villa, a sergeant agreed to let Sofia go and lie down in one, and helped her limp away.

Robert was taken, still at gunpoint, to the men's CO, interrogated for an hour, and finally he managed to convince the captain he was not a German spy.

'What's happened to the family?' he asked.

'There's only one old man here,' said the captain. 'Oh, and some old witch in black who shuffles round and round the place, wringing her hands and mumbling to herself.'

'I know who you mean,' said Robert. 'She and the other lady saved my life. I hope she's being treated well.'

'She's only some old peasant woman,' the CO said abruptly. 'She looks about a hundred, she's just skin and bone, she isn't going to last into the spring.'

Robert decided that the grey-haired woman was going to last for rather longer than the CO thought. She had Sofia home again, to nurse her back to health. So she could not die yet.

A few days later, he was pleased to see Sofia was looking slightly better. The weather was warming up a little, and one afternoon she let him take her out on to the loggia, where the air was mild and pleasant, and where the weak, late winter sun could kiss her pale, thin face.

'You're going with the army,' she began, before he had a chance to explain he'd come to say goodbye.

'Yes,' he said. 'Sofia, I promise I won't forget you.'

'No?' Sofia shrugged. 'You promised you would go back to Marcello.'

'I didn't promise Marcello anything. In any case, Marcello's war is over, and yours is over, too.' Robert took Sofia's hand. 'You did so well,' he said. 'You were so brave, so daring.'

'But I failed the most important test.'

'What do you mean?'

'I failed to make you love me.' Sofia turned her head aside and wouldn't look at him. 'So now, go with the army,' she told Robert, as she pulled her hand away. 'Go back to your pretty blonde fiancée, and tell her she's a very lucky woman.'

Chapter Eighteen

Cassie got sick of waiting, hoping, praying. She grew tired of being in the army, tired of all the drill and marching, tired of living with a noisy crowd of other women, tired of never being alone.

She spent a quiet weekend with her granny, and realised how much she loved poor Lily – mad, grief-stricken Lily, who longed to be united with her daughter, whose gnarled, arthritic fingers took all day and half the night to polish up the shrine.

Lily's idea of paradise was doubtless something like the three of them – Lily, Cassie and her mother – sitting round the kitchen table with a couple of tins of heavenly Brasso, polishing little statues of the Virgin, while a celestial choir made up of cherubim and seraphim sang the songs of Gracie Fields, Anne Shelton, Vera Lynn.

Cassie had never thought she would miss smoky, smog-stained Smethwick quite so much. But these days she wanted more than anything to be at home again, to see the people she'd known all her life, to hear their voices, to walk down the familiar streets once more – not that many of these streets remained.

The spring came very slowly. January and February of 1945 were cold and dark and sleety. But then the days grew longer, March dragged into April, and April finally seeped into May.

Cassie hardly noticed when the official declaration came, when it was on the wireless that the war in Europe was actually won. She hardly saw the people in the streets, rejoicing, getting drunk and being happy.

Then she had a telephone call from Rose.

'It's wonderful!' cried Rose. 'Cassie, my dear – you won't believe it. I can hardly take it in myself. But I've had a letter from Rob's commanding officer, and Robert didn't die, and now he's back in England! He's been fighting with the partisans in Italy, he's been in the mountains blowing up bridges, and mining railway lines, to stop the Germans – amazing stuff like that.

'He's at a repatriation centre in Hastings at the moment. He'll need to be debriefed, of course, but then he can come home! Cassie, isn't that the most tremendous thing you ever heard?' Rose was crying, laughing, all at once. 'Cass, are you still there?'

'Yes, Rose, I'm here,' said Cassie. 'Yes, I heard you. Yes, it's wonderful,' she added dully, but she couldn't take it in.

'Poor Cassie, you're in shock.' Rose sounded rather strange herself, thought Cassie. 'I'll ring again,' Rose added, 'when I have more news. All right?'

'All right.' Cassie forced herself to speak. 'Look after yourself. Yes, I'll be careful. Bye.'

'Good news, I hope?' asked Captain Bright, who'd summoned Cassie to her office to take the urgent call.

'Yes, the best, ma'am,' Cassie said, but even she could hear her voice was toneless. 'My fiancé is alive.'

'You don't look very happy.'

'I – I suppose I can't believe it.' Cassie stood there feeling numb, the wire from the handset to the base twisted round and round and round her fingers, cutting into them.

'Why don't you have a few hours off?' The captain took the handset back and placed it on the phone. 'Go home to your billet and have a sleep. You've had a shock, albeit a pleasant one. I'll send someone with you, shall I?'

'Thank you, ma'am, but that won't be necessary.' Cassie managed to cover her face before the tears came. 'Give me a minute, ma'am,' she added, mumbling through her fingers, 'and then I'll be all right.'

After feeling frozen for a while, Cassie began to thaw. At first she wouldn't believe it, couldn't believe it. She thought she had imagined the whole thing. What if it was all a big mistake, a huge misunderstanding? What if Rose was wrong? She couldn't trust herself to hope, and then be disappointed.

But then she had a card from Robert, it was postmarked Hastings, and she let herself believe.

She wrote to him at once, a jumbled outpouring of grief, relief and happiness. She said she longed to see him.

She was glad she hadn't had to be the one who broke the awful news about his brother. Rose said she'd do that. 'I'll know what to say,' insisted Rose, and Cassie thought, you don't, but didn't argue.

Robert wrote again to say he'd soon be getting two months' leave. He couldn't wait to see her, he had so much to tell her, and he expected she had plenty to tell him?

'I killed your brother.' Cassie said the words out loud, to an empty bedroom, and then she hung her head.

Cassie and Robert met at Waterloo, their own reunion one of thousands going on as each incoming train disgorged its cargo of returning servicemen.

Some of the men looked awful – sick and yellow, old and ill. But Robert looked absolutely gorgeous, fit and sunburned, if a bit too thin. As he swept her up into his arms and kissed her once, twice, twenty times, Cassie began to cry.

'Come on, Cass – no tears,' said Robert, brushing them or kissing them away.

'Sorry.' Cassie swallowed hard.

'I'd hoped you would be pleased to see me?'

'Rob, of course I'm pleased!' But as she had seen Robert coming towards her down the platform, Cassie had seen Stephen too, a grey ghost hovering behind his twin. These days, she was afraid she'd always see him. 'It's just that I'm – '

'You're what?' asked Robert gently.

Cassie swallowed hard again. 'I'm very, very happy.'

'So am I,' said Robert, and he took Cassie's hand. 'Cass, where shall we go?'

'There won't be anyone at home, they're all on leave,' said Cassie.

'Good, let's go to bed.'

They went straight up to Cassie's bedroom, where light reflected from the river made patterns on the walls, and the muslin curtains fluttered in the summer breeze.

She was so afraid he would have changed, that going through the war in Italy might have made him cynical or cruel. There had been lots of stories going round, about returning servicemen being strangers to their wives and girlfriends, about how men's experiences in battle had changed them for the worse, had even made them violent and spiteful.

But Robert was just as she remembered him in Alexandria – loving, sexy, charming, generous, kind. Somehow, he was also more grown-up, and much more self-assured.

He'd always been self-confident, of course. But now he had a quieter authority about him.

When she'd met him first, he'd shouted and he'd bellowed, and it had taken all her courage to stand up to him. She remembered Frances trembling when he'd yelled at her about the bull.

But now he didn't seem to feel the need to raise his voice to make a point. He'd obviously been doing something which had made him think he had the right to be obeyed.

She hoped he'd talk about it some time soon, would tell her what had happened on those Italian battlefields and in the mountains with the partisans.

'You've got your silver bracelet on,' he said, as he unbuttoned Cassie's cuff.

'Yes, I always wear it.'

'Always?' murmured Robert, smiling as he walked his strong, tanned fingers up her arm. 'Non-religious jewellery, wearing of – against King's Regulations, isn't it?'

'I stuff it up my sleeve, so nobody can see it.' Cassie beamed back up at him. 'I'll always love it, Rob. While you were away, it made me feel I was close to you.'

'What about your penny bangle, then?'

'It's in my sewing kit.'

'I thought you'd lose it.'

'I'll never lose my penny bangle, Rob. It's part of you, it means the world to me!'

Afterwards, they had a doze, Cassie curled up in Robert's arms and warm against his chest.

It would be like this when they were married, she thought happily. If only Stephen hadn't died, it would all have been so wonderful, so absolutely perfect. But she knew she mustn't think of Stephen all the time. She must think of the living, not the dead.

As it was getting dark, Robert went downstairs to make some tea and see if there was anything to eat.

'Madam?' he whispered, as he put the tray down on the night stand. 'Tea is served, and I found some horrible-looking Bourbon biscuits, too.'

'Oh, Robert Denham, you make a lovely butler!' Cassie grinned and kissed him. 'But next time you go downstairs,' she added, 'put some clothes on, or someone coming in might get a shock. There's some sugar hidden behind the packets of dried egg. I dare say you found it?'

'Yes, I did,' said Robert. 'But I left it for the others. You don't need any sugar, Cassie love. You're sweet enough.'

Cassie didn't have any driving duties planned next day. She didn't have any driving duties planned all week, in fact. She was wondering now if everybody had forgotten the ATS existed, if they could all go home.

Robert took her out to lunch at a restaurant in the Strand, and later on they walked in Regent's Park – not that it was a park as such these days, more of a bomb site, rubbish dump for rubble from the Blitz and vegetable patch rolled into one.

'It'll be cleaned up,' said Robert, skirting round a pile of broken masonry almost as high as him. 'You wait and see – in a year from now, we'll all have forgotten about the war.'

Such wishful thinking, said Cassie to herself. But she didn't say anything to Robert, merely reflecting that the war had changed the world forever.

She wondered if he wanted to talk about that awful, dreadful night when Stephen died. She thought perhaps she'd wait and see.

'Shall we go to the cinema this evening?' he suggested. 'We could see that new Gene Kelly film?'

'Yes, that would be nice,' said Cassie, thinking – when's it going to come? When are you going to do your grieving? When are you going to remember you once had a brother?

But she found she couldn't say anything.

They went to see the film, and then they had a drink or two with a couple of American soldiers, who said they were longing to go back home to Texas.

Then they went and called at the apartment in Park Lane,

to see if Daisy was at home. She wasn't, so they walked back slowly to the house in Chelsea, where they went to bed.

After they'd made love, Robert put the light back on, sat up against the pillows. 'I have something to tell you,' he began.

'Have you?' Cassie snuggled up against him, walked her fingers up and down his chest. 'Go on – tell me, then?'

'When I was in Italy, I – I met a girl.'

'What?' Cassie's eyes snapped open and she stared at him. 'W-what do you mean, you met a girl?'

'While I was with partisans, there was this Italian girl, Sofia. She was a partisan as well, and she was a very brave and very clever woman. She and I – '

'You're telling me you slept with this Sofia?'

Cassie willed him to say no, of course he hadn't slept with whatsername – to say he'd been attracted, and they'd had a smooch. She thought she could forgive a smooch or two.

'Yes, I did,' said Robert. 'It was just the once and I was drunk on schnapps. I didn't know if I should tell you. But I think it's better to be honest about this sort of thing.'

'Yes, your mother told me you were honest.' As Cassie's world began to crumble, icicles of misery started stabbing at her heart. She couldn't bear to look at Robert, so she turned to stare out of the window at the black night sky. 'But in my opinion, honesty is sometimes over-rated.'

'You'd prefer it if I lied to you?'

'I'd prefer it if you didn't sleep with other women while you're engaged to me!' Cassie spun back round and glared at him. 'I could have slept with other men!' she cried.

'Yes, Cass, I know,' said Robert calmly. 'Did you, then?'

'No, I bloody didn't, because *I'm* not a tart!' Cassie couldn't understand how Robert could be so relaxed, so cool, so unconcerned. It was as if he'd just confessed to nicking biscuits from a tin, not hurting her in the most awful way. 'But I – '

257

'But what?'

'I wasn't going to tell you this, but since we're being honest – I could have slept with Stephen.'

That made him wince, as if she'd just thrown acid in his face. 'He wanted me, you know,' she said, with vengeful satisfaction. 'Your brother wanted me!'

'So did you?'

Robert's voice now had an edge to it, and part of Cassie thought, don't take this any further, don't deliberately taunt him. Talk about this whole thing sensibly.

But her other self was much too angry to back down.

'Did you, Cassie?' he repeated calmly, dangerously. 'Did you actually go to bed with Steve?'

'No, I didn't, *actually*,' Cassie spat, deliberately taking off his accent. 'But I liked him well enough to sleep with him. *Actually*, I wish I had, because if Steve and I had done the deed, he'd probably still be alive today.'

'Stop it, Cassie.' Robert's voice became a growl, a warning, angry rumble.

But Cassie didn't care. She dug the knife in, twisted it again. She was so upset, so angry that she couldn't help it. 'I loved your brother, Rob,' she said. 'Stephen was so good, so kind to me. When I first arrived in Melbury, he made me feel so welcome. But you were really horrid – surly, rude and mean. I'll always remember what you said that night.'

'What night?'

'The first night I was there.'

'What did I say?'

'You said, "I reckon she's a slum kid, she looks pasty-faced and feeble. I bet you she'll be useless, and bone idle, too."'

'You're imagining things.'

'I'm not, those were your very words!' Cassie glared at him. 'That's what you still think – isn't it, *Mr* Denham?

I'm a slum kid, but you're Mr British Army Officer, kindly condescending to the lower bloody ranks.'

'You know that isn't true.'

'I don't know anything.' Cassie kept her furious blue glare on Robert's face. 'Your mum thinks you're a hero,' she continued angrily. 'Going off to fight in foreign parts, joining the Italian partisans and blowing up bloody bridges – all that stuff.

'But Stephen was the hero. He didn't have your luck, your nerve, your charm, but he stuck at it, trying to do his best. So let me tell you, Robert Denham, Steve was worth a dozen or more of you!'

'I know,' said Robert. 'I loved Stephen, Cass. I really did. I'm missing him like crazy. Somehow, it seems part of me is dead.'

'I don't believe you, Robert. You're too selfish to consider anyone but yourself.'

'I'm sorry,' Robert said.

'What do you mean, you're sorry?'

'I'm sorry for betraying you, for hurting you, and I hope you'll forgive me.'

'Do you, now?'

If he'd begged and pleaded, if he'd cried and grovelled, she would have pitied him – and despised him just a little, too?

Yes, perhaps she would.

But this cool assurance – this patrician arrogance – this British-army-officer routine, this he-hoped-she-would-forgive-him stuff, as if he'd broken something small and valueless by accident, not stabbed her through the heart – it made her want to hurt him, make him bleed.

'It's over, Rob,' she said.

'What?' Robert stared, astonished. 'You're not even trying to understand!'

'Oh, I understand all right!' Cassie glared at him. 'We

were engaged. You went to fight in Italy. You had a bit on the side with some Italian tart. You think I shouldn't mind.'

She yanked the silver bracelet off her wrist and threw it back at him.

'What am I supposed to do with this?' he asked.

'I don't care what you do with it!' she shrieked. 'Lose it, flog it, stick it up your arse, it's all the same to me!'

Then she burst into tears. 'Get out of this house,' she sobbed. 'Go now, and don't come back!'

Robert stared at her and she could see that he was angry now, and for just one moment she was seriously scared.

She shrank against the pillows, ready to defend herself.

But he got out of bed, picked up his clothes and walked into the bathroom. He dressed and left without another word.

Cassie burrowed underneath the bedclothes, welcoming the darkness. She already knew she was a fool, to throw a good man's love away.

But she also knew she couldn't live with Robert Denham, with a man who could forget that she had feelings, too.

She'd only be her stupid mother, all over again.

Robert strode off down the street, which was still full of people, even though it was so late.

He could feel his heart was hammering and his pulse was racing, and knew he'd never come so close to losing it, even in the heat of battle, even when he'd seen his men cut down, and he'd wanted more than anything to kill the bastards who had killed his men.

As Cass had shrieked at him, a naked, howling banshee, he had felt such rage, such fury mixed with grief and guilt and shame, that he didn't know how he had managed to control himself.

As he strode along the pavement, he became aware of people glancing at him nervously. Whenever anybody came towards him, he glared at them so fiercely that they moved out of his way.

He didn't know what to do or where to go, but finally he decided he would find an all-night club, and drink himself into a stupor.

So that was what he did.

Cassie didn't know what to do. She had no driving duties. The capital was full of servicewomen who were surplus to requirements, and on extended leave. They were having a high old time with Yanks, Australians and Canadians, who all seemed to carry bulging wallets stuffed with money, which they were more than happy to spend on British girls.

Some ATS had gone to Paris or Berlin, and the new occupying Allied army was apparently very short of drivers. So Cassie could have gone across the Channel. She could have had her photograph taken as she stood there grinning with other servicewomen by the Eiffel Tower, or walking in the ruins of Berlin.

But she decided not to volunteer. So now she had more leave than she could ever have wanted, and she spent it wandering around the city streets all on her own.

A few days after Cassie had seen Robert, Frances came to London to try to buy some new civilian clothes for when she was demobbed. She was looking forward to hearing all the thrilling details of their grand reunion.

'But not *all* the details, obviously,' she added grinning, when she and Cassie met at Euston station.

But then she looked at Cassie's face, saw the deep circles underneath her eyes, and realised Cassie hadn't slept for days. 'Cass, what's wrong?' she asked.

'It's all off, Frances,' Cassie said abruptly. 'Me and Rob, it's over.'

'Cassie, no!' cried Frances. 'Why?'

'He had it off with some Italian tart.'

'Oh, I see.' Frances sighed and shook her sleek, dark head. 'Cassie,' she said kindly, 'I'm sure that lots and lots of men who have been overseas, they must have – '

'Yes, you're probably right, but that don't mean – '

'Cassie, sweetheart, please don't be so hasty. I know you must be angry and upset. But have you heard what Robert has to say? Have you let him explain?'

'What is there to explain?' demanded Cassie hotly. 'He was engaged to me – he had it off with an Italian woman – end of story. Just because *you're* going with a married man, who doesn't care about his wedding vows! Just because *you've* stolen some other woman's man – '

'Cassie, that's unkind of you.' Frances flushed bright red. 'I only meant – '

'I'm sorry, that was spiteful.' Cassie bit her lip. She hadn't meant to take it out on Frances. 'But could we talk about something else?' she asked.

Frances brightened up again at once. 'We've got a plan,' she said as they walked across the Euston Road. 'Simon and Ewan, Daisy and I, we've met up now and then, and we – '

'When did you and Daisy get so pally?'

Then Cassie thought, so this is how it happens. This is how my world comes tumbling down in a great cloud of dust, how I lose Daisy, Frances, Ewan, Rose – how I lose everything.

'We're not exactly pally, Cass,' said Frances, going pink. 'But we know each other, obviously. Our families live in the same place, and we meet occasionally at parties, weddings, funerals and things.'

'Yes, of course,' said Cassie. 'Silly me.'

'So Daisy wrote to Mrs Denham, asking if she thought I might be interested in her plans for Charton Minster. So then Mrs Denham wrote to me. We've been discussing what we could organise for those poor children. We were thinking – '

Frances chattered on and on, explaining. But Cassie didn't hear a single word that Frances said, and didn't want to hear. What was Rose's house to Cassie now? She would never see it again. She would have nothing more to do with Daisy, who would probably think she was an idiot to let her brother go.

They walked together round the shops with Cassie in a daze, locked deep inside her hopeless misery.

'What do you think of this one?' Frances asked, holding up an orange rayon nightdress edged with mean and tawdry bits of coffee-coloured lace.

'It's lovely,' Cassie said.

'Or is this one prettier?' Frances picked up another rayon nightdress, this time in a violent shade of bluish-purplish-red. 'A bit too scarlet woman, do you think?'

'It's all right,' said Cassie, who couldn't have cared less. 'If it's for your wedding night, you won't be in it long in any case.'

'I'm sorry, Cassie, I'm being very tactless.' Frances looked at Cassie, her brown eyes soft and kind. 'Let's try to find some cardigans instead. Then we'll go and have something to eat, and I must catch my train.'

'All right' said Cassie. 'You can have my coupons, if you like? I don't want anything.'

'Try to eat and sleep, and look after yourself,' said Frances, when she went to catch her train to Chester. 'As for you and Robert – will you think about it, Cass?'

'What's there to think about?'

'You could write to Rob? You could arrange to meet and talk to him?'

'Fran, I can't,' said Cassie wretchedly.

'Oh, Cass, why not?'

'I'm not going to marry a man who'll wipe his feet on me.'

Chapter Nineteen

'Mum, there's nothing wrong,' insisted Robert.

'You can't fool me,' said Rose. 'You're fretting about something, aren't you? When is Cassie coming down to Dorset?'

'I don't know,' said Robert, picking up the *Farming Times* and looking at advertisements for ploughs. 'She's very busy at the moment. There are lots of colonels, brigadiers and generals in London, and she has to drive them all around. Well, not all of them, of course. Mum, stop going on at me.'

'I hope you two haven't had an argument?'

'We need to get the guttering fixed,' said Robert. 'I'll go and see Jack Hobson in the morning and ask if he can do it. If he can't, I'll do the job myself. What are you going to do about the land girls? Do they want to stay on here?'

'Shirley says she might, but Tess is getting married,' Rose replied, and then – to Robert's great relief – his mother started talking about milk yields, the unreliability of the egg man, and the shocking price of cattle feed.

Frances wrote to Cassie, to tell her that the plans for Charton Minster were all going ahead, and everyone in Charton was getting very excited.

'The villagers are very pleased,' wrote Frances. *'It will mean more business for the shops, and instead of being afraid delinquents might escape to rob and murder them as they sleep in their beds, there will be just ordinary children staying at the Minster.*

'Daisy and I are hoping you'll still want to be involved. We haven't said anything to Mrs Denham about you and Robert. But of course we're hoping you and he will patch things up.'

Cassie put the letter in the bin. She didn't care about the plans. She'd never set foot in Charton or in Melbury again. So why did it matter what happened to the Minster?

The other ATS girls in the Chelsea house were going out with American boys, were going to parties, going to dances, getting drunk as skunks, and generally having lots of fun.

But Cassie didn't feel like joining in. When she was not on duty, she lay down on her bed and read her way through piles and piles of movie magazines, given to her by their Yankee boyfriends.

She couldn't go to the cinema itself because she found she couldn't bear the newsreels nowadays. They were full of awful revelations about what had been going on in Germany and Poland, about the camps, the gas chambers, the furnaces, the piles of rotting corpses, and they made her cry.

She couldn't decide what she should do.

She thought she had been desperate to go back home to Smethwick. But now she thought she might stay in the army. She'd probably make sergeant easily – she had the years of service and experience, so she'd be almost certain to get another stripe.

Perhaps she should apply for a commission? She liked the uniforms. Officers had smart, slip-on shoes instead of horrid lace-ups, nicely-tailored skirts and jackets, and they got to wear real nylons, too.

But all her friends were dying to be demobbed, and actually she'd had enough of drill, of marching round a barrack square, of saluting everything that moved, and of obeying orders.

She asked for some demob leave, and she got it. She went back home to Birmingham, back home to Lily, and she tried to get on with her life. She applied for jobs she didn't get, and wondered if she'd be obliged to go back to the laundry after all.

Lily kept going on at her to find herself a man and settle down, to have some children and raise a family.

'There's that nice O'Sullivan boy, he's just come back from Palestine,' said Lily, as they ate their breakfast. 'What about Mrs Flynn's son, Terry?' she demanded, as they ate their dinner. 'You went to school with him.'

Cassie didn't want to think about the nice O'Sullivan boy or Terry Flynn – both of whom had pulled her hair and said she was a bastard while she was at school.

She was missing Rob so much it ached. She hadn't believed that there was such a thing as actual heartache, but now she knew for certain it was all too real.

She polished up her penny bangle, rubbing off the silvering and almost rubbing through the alloy, too. She thought – I'm turning into Lily, treasuring a piece of junk which means more to me than any diamonds, pearls or gold.

She longed and longed to see him, talk to him.

She didn't know what to say.

She started twenty letters.

She screwed them up and put them in the salvage.

She set up imaginary meetings in London and in Dorset. She would get her hair done, she decided, and wear that lovely costume which Daisy's natural mother had sent her from America.

She'd tell him she was sorry for behaving like a hoyden.

Then Rob would smile, and he would take her in his arms, and he would say, don't worry, it's all right. We just had a silly little tiff, as lovers do.

But always, always, always when she'd planned the perfect speech, she'd hear herself again, yelling at Robert, telling him to stick his silver bracelet up his arse.

Then she'd feel sick with guilt and shame.

'Daisy's coming to see the Minster, Rob,' said Rose, holding out the letter to her son. 'She's got a few days off, and says she fancies some fresh air.'

'I thought she was in London, in that new revue?' Robert glanced up from cleaning harness. 'Anyway, there isn't much to see.'

'There's the scaffolding going up to fix the roof,' said Rose. 'She's coming to see us as well, in any case. When will Cassie be able to get down?'

Robert pretended not to hear and went on polishing a bridle which already shone.

Daisy arrived and went to see how things were getting on at Charton Minster. The access road had been a problem – half of it was on the Eastons' land, and Rose knew better than to ask if Lady Easton would allow the Denhams to use her road.

But Daisy didn't believe in having problems.

The day that Rose had signed the paperwork, Daisy had hired a couple of village men with spades and pickaxes and scythes to cut a path straight to the Minster from a public lane.

She'd get it widened and get some men to gravel it later on, she told her mother. She'd also need to see a carpenter about the window frames. Robert hoped his sister would find enough to keep her occupied, and she wouldn't have any time left over to have a go at him.

But Daisy always managed to find time.

'What are you and Cassie going to do?' she asked, as she and her brother sat at the kitchen table one morning after breakfast, while Rose was with her hens. 'Where will you live – in Dorset?'

'We haven't decided yet,' said Robert, getting up to go.

'What about you, Rob – will you be a farmer, or will you do something else?' Daisy got up too and she was at the door before him, with her back against it, so he couldn't leave unless he physically picked her up and moved her to one side.

There was no point changing tack and going into the house. She'd only follow him and pin him up against a wall.

'I know you've had an argument,' said Daisy.

'We've had a disagreement.' Robert shrugged. 'But we can sort it out.'

'When do you intend to do it?' Daisy asked. 'When will you be seeing Cass again?'

'I need to go and meet the vet,' said Robert. 'He's due here any minute. He's always in a hurry, and – '

'Robert!' Daisy glared at him. 'I've written to Cassie twice since you came back to England. I've invited her to lunch with me and Ewan. I've sent her tickets for the premiere of a film I know she'd love to see. But she hasn't replied. What's going on?'

'She might be in Birmingham.'

'She might?' demanded Daisy. 'You mean you don't know?'

Robert merely shrugged again and stared up at a cobweb on the ceiling.

So then of course he got the third degree.

'What are you so scared of, Rob?' his sister asked him, when she'd dragged the story out of him.

'I'm not scared of anything, Daze – and now, if you'll excuse me, I need to get things ready for the vet.'

'When you were in Italy, if you had been caught by German soldiers or the Black Brigade, would you have been tortured?'

'I expect so.'

'Then would they have shot you?'

'Yes, they might.'

'But you weren't afraid?' asked Daisy.

'I suppose I didn't think about it.'

'So why are you afraid to go and see Cassie?'

'Cassie doesn't want to see me, Daze – I told you that.'

'When you told Cassie about Sofia, did you apologise?'

'Of course I did!'

'What did you say?'

'I told her I was sorry, obviously.'

'So that was it?'

'What do you mean?' demanded Robert.

'You didn't say you regretted what you'd done, and wished it hadn't happened? Did you tell Cass you love her and she means the world to you?'

'I –'

'You didn't, did you?' Daisy sighed. 'Go and see her, Rob. Get on a train to Birmingham, if that's where you think she might have gone. Go and say you're sorry properly, tell her that you love her, and everything will be all right again.'

'If I go and grovel like you're suggesting, she'll despise me.'

'I'm not suggesting you should grovel,' Daisy told him patiently. 'All I'm saying is – you should try to find the strength and courage to make up. If you don't, you'll probably regret it all your life.'

'The vet's just come.' Robert moved his sister away from the back door.

'I'm right,' called Daisy, as she followed him across the yard. 'You know I'm right – and Robert?'

'Yes?'

'You'll need to give her something.'

'What do you have in mind?'

'She's got a granny, hasn't she? She's been in Birmingham

for the duration? Maybe Cassie's granny would like a holiday?'

One Thursday morning, as Cassie was helping Lily to clean the little house from top to bottom, she heard somebody knock on the front door.

It would be the rent man, she decided. Or the life insurance man, collecting Lily's weekly sixpence. Or bloody Mrs Flynn, come cadging something yet again.

She thought – oh, let them wait, they can come back some other time. Lily was getting very deaf these days, and so she probably wouldn't hear them. Cassie herself was busy in the shrine, for dusting and polishing all the junk and clutter in the shrine was one of Cassie's daily chores.

Since she and Lily weren't expecting company, Cassie wore an old grey cotton dress which was more than ready for the rag bag, a pair of battered, down-at-heel black shoes, and darned brown socks of which a tinker would have been ashamed.

She had her hair tied up in a red duster, her eyebrows needed plucking, and there wasn't a single scrap of make-up on her face.

Somebody knocked again, much louder this time.

Lily looked up from polishing and frowned. 'There's someone at the door, our Cass,' she said. 'It'll be the rent man. The money's on the shelf behind the Coronation caddy. Go and pay him, duck?'

Cassie picked up the silver coins and went through to the parlour. She opened the front door.

'Hello, Cassie,' Robert said.

She could see all the neighbours' curtains twitching. Some urchins had stopped fighting or playing knucklebones and turned to stare at them. The rent man suddenly came from round the corner, as if this was a play.

'Rob?'

She thought she must be seeing things, that she was in a dream. 'W-what do you want?' she asked him frowning, still not sure if he was real.

'I want to see you, of course,' said Robert. 'I want to meet your granny.'

'I suppose you'd best come in,' she said.

Cassie led Robert through the parlour, past the shrine and into the back kitchen, which looked out on to the brick-paved yard, the mangle and the lavatory – not beautiful green fields.

'Gran, this is Mr Denham,' she told Lily.

'Oh?' Lily was even smaller, bonier and more wizened nowadays, but her blue eyes were bright. 'You're not our usual rent man,' she began suspiciously.

'He's not the rent man, Gran,' said Cassie, raising her voice and bending close to Lily's better ear. 'He's – I worked for his mother in the country, back in '42.'

'You left something behind, then?'

'Yes, I did,' said Cassie, but only to herself.

'Good morning, Mrs Taylor,' Robert said politely, offering his hand.

'Good morning, son.' Lily looked their visitor up and down. When Robert knocked, she had been busy polishing a little metal statue of the Virgin which Cassie's mother won for having the best writing in her class in 1908. Thanks to constant rubbing, the Virgin's gentle face had worn away.

'I won't shake your hand, if you don't mind,' continued Lily. 'My own's all over Brasso. Well,' she said to Cassie, 'don't just stand there, looking like a slice of week-old pudding. Why don't you make the lad a cup of tea?'

'W-will you have a cup of tea?' asked Cassie.

'Thank you, that would be very nice,' said Robert. 'But only if it isn't any trouble.'

'We were just about to have a brew. Go on, son,' said Lily, pointing to the other kitchen chair. 'Sit yourself down there. Cassie, I think we've got a tin of 'vaporated milk.'

'I thought we were keeping that for Sunday?'

'Oh, get it down,' said Lily, 'open it. We don't get visitors from the country every day.'

They drank their milky tea from thick white cups, Lily blowing on hers to cool it down, slurping it through her false teeth, and letting it slop messily in the saucer.

'How have you been?' asked Robert.

'All right, I suppose,' said Cassie, shrugging.

'Do you have a job yet?'

'No, the jobs round here are all for men, unless you're on the game or want to clean the public lavatories. I went for an interview to drive a bus.'

'How did you get on?'

'They laughed at me. They said I was too small to drive a modern double-decker, and anyway they only wanted blokes. They didn't want any women.'

There was an awkward silence. Then Lily got up and said that she was sorry, but she had to pop across the road to Mrs Reed's, because she hadn't paid her club.

'I'll go and pay her later, Granny,' Cassie said. 'Sit down and drink your tea.'

'No, I must go now, while I remember. You stay here and pay the rent.' Lily picked up some coppers from the table, scuttled off, and Cassie heard the front door slam.

Cassie and Robert looked at one another across the kitchen table. Robert seemed to fill the little kitchen, and Cassie wished he wasn't quite so close, and that she couldn't hear him breathing, see the tiny crow's feet at the corners of his eyes, streaked white against his sunburn.

'Cassie,' he began.

'We can't talk here,' said Cassie. 'Mrs Flynn next door,

she'll have seen you come into the house, and she'll have her glass against the wall, and anyway the rent man's due this minute.'

'So when the rent man's been, could we go out?'

'Where did you have in mind?'

'Oh, I don't know,' said Robert lamely. 'Maybe to a park, or something?'

'We're miles from any parks.'

'Then we'll have to entertain the curious Mrs Flynn.' Robert lowered his voice. 'Cassie, I must tell you – '

'What are you doing nowadays, are you still in the army?'

'Yes, but I signed on for the duration, not for twenty years, so they'll be glad to pay me off.' Robert shrugged his shoulders. 'I've had more than enough of killing people, hurting them. I don't want to be responsible for hurting anybody any more.'

'So what will you do now?'

'Well, of course Mum wants me to run the farm. But I'm not very keen. I'd prefer to get a tenant in, and maybe Mum could go and live in Charton.'

'What would you like to do?'

'I want to train to be a teacher,' Robert said. 'I think I would be good at it.'

'Where would you be teaching, then – at Eton?"

'I want to teach in state schools, actually.' Robert shrugged again. 'While I was in the army, I kept meeting men and NCOs who hadn't had the opportunities which I had as a child. But many of them were better, braver, smarter and more honourable than me. Lots of them got killed. Their sons and daughters deserve a decent future, and I'd like to help to see they get one. I'm looking into teacher training courses for ex-servicemen.'

Then Robert smiled a wry, ironic smile. 'I know I'll take some stick for being a nob.'

'Yes, you will,' said Cassie, but she was impressed. 'You said you didn't want to hurt anybody any more. But you'll have to whack the kids, you know, that's if you want them to respect you.'

'We'll see,' said Robert calmly. 'Cassie, I have no excuse for what I did in Italy. But couldn't you forgive me?'

'*Yes, oh yes!*' cried Cassie, but only to herself. '*Robert, I forgave you long ago!*'

'I don't think so,' said the grinning devil who stood at Cassie's side.

'Surely your religion seeks to pardon the repentant sinner?'

'You're not repentant,' sneered the devil.

'Yes, I am,' said Robert. 'I wish it had been different. But I can't change the past.'

'So would you, if you could?'

'I liked Sofia very much,' said Robert candidly. 'I admired her, she was very brave. I hope she'll marry an Italian, have some children, and be happy. But Cassie, she's not you.'

'No, and I bet she's nothing like me.' Cassie sighed and shook her head, glancing round the shabby little kitchen, at the well-scoured pots and pans, at the ancient gas stove with its polished metal taps, at the powdery, white-washed, damp-stained walls.

'My mother married a bigamist, you know,' she said to Robert. 'She died while she was having me, and back through there's her shrine, kept polished up and dusted by my mad old granny. She's still beside herself with grief. You could do much better for yourself.'

'I don't think so, Cass.'

'*Do you love me?*' Cassie asked him, but inside her head. '*If you do, I need to hear you say it!*'

But he didn't.

'Look, Cass,' he continued, 'if you're not working yet, why don't you come and visit us in Dorset? Come and see

Mum and Tinker. Bring your granny. I'm sure she'd like a holiday at the seaside.'

'I dare say she would. My poor old granny – I don't think she's ever seen the sea.'

'You'll come?'

'We'll think about it,' Cassie said.

'Good,' said Robert, standing up. 'I'll get Mum to write to Mrs Taylor.'

'There's still some tea left in the pot,' said Cassie desperately. 'So if you'd like another cup – '

'Thank you, but I must go and get my train.'

Cassie watched him walk off down the road.

It hadn't turned out the way she'd hoped, as she had prayed, as she'd expected. Although she'd willed and willed it, he hadn't tried to kiss her, he hadn't even tried to touch her hand.

Then something caught her eye. She glanced towards the shelf which held the statue of Saint Bernadette, and saw he'd left her silver bracelet there.

She could see her reflection in the little mirror by the statue. She looked ridiculous – no wonder he had smiled.

She pulled the duster off her head. She ran out of the house and after him. 'Robert, stop!' she panted, as the neighbours all came out to stare, and all the street kids scattered. 'Robert, wait a minute!'

He turned and looked at her, he stopped, he patted all his pockets. 'I'm sorry, Cassie,' he said frowning, obviously puzzled. 'Have I forgotten something?'

'You – '

Cassie stood there panting, trying to get her breath back. She had to say the words, she had to tell him that she loved him, that she'd always love him, that she had forgiven him weeks ago.

'I forgot to tell you – '

'What?'

'I love you.' She stood there on the pavement, feeling sick and stupid, staring up at him, listening to the seconds clumping by in hobnailed boots, not daring to draw breath.

'I love you, too,' he said, and Cassie breathed again.

Of course he couldn't, wouldn't kiss her, not in front of all these gawping children and bloody Mrs Flynn. He couldn't hug her, he couldn't hold her tight.

But he could smile his special Robert smile, the one that made her feel she was glowing, that she could walk on water.

'I'll see you in Dorset, then,' she said.

Chapter Twenty

'I've not been on a proper train since 1926,' said Lily, sitting down on the window seat which Cassie had shoved past all the other passengers to get. 'Now, where's my brolly?'

'I've put it on the rack, Gran.'

'Where's me hat?'

'It's on your head.'

'You got the flask and sandwiches?'

'Yes, they're in my bag.'

'Well, isn't all this grand?' Lily Taylor looked all round the second class carriage, eyeing up the window blinds, feeling the quality of the cut moquette, patting the arm rests complacently. 'You say those folks in Dorset paid for this?'

'Yes, Mrs Denham sent the money for the fares.'

'Why would she do that?'

'She's very kind.'

'She's rich?'

'She isn't rich, but she can afford to pay our fares.' Cassie willed her granny to shut up. All the other passengers were staring.

Robert met the train at Charton station, in the little pony trap which Cassie used to drive. He made Lily Taylor comfortable, wrapping her old knees in shawls and blankets.

Their journey on the train had been inland. So now, when Lily saw the sea, she was amazed.

'So this is it,' she said, as Robert reined the pony in so she could stop and stare at the long, curving shingle beach, and at the foam-flecked waves. 'Well, who would have thought it? Look at it, our Cassie. It's so big, so powerful!'

'It's just a lot of water, Gran.' Cassie gave her granny's

hand a gentle squeeze. 'It's very calm today. But you should see it in the winter, when there's been a storm.'

'I'd rather not, if you don't mind,' said Lily, shuddering.

Rose Denham was as kind and welcoming as Cassie had known she'd be. She ushered Lily Taylor into the cottage kitchen, asked about her journey, and poured her several cups of strong, dark tea, appearing not to notice when Lily spilled it on the clean white tablecloth because she was so nervous.

'This way, Granny,' Cassie said, as she helped Lily up the stairs into the bedroom where the twins had slept when she'd first come to Melbury.

'You'll be sleeping in the other bed?' demanded Lily

'Yes, of course I will.'

Looking round the room, Cassie could see it had been freshly painted, that there were new covers on the beds and crisp new curtains at the window. There was a new china bowl and ewer on the marble washstand. There was a pink cake of scented soap, and fluffy, snow-white towels.

Rose had done them proud.

'What about that lad?' asked Lily, who'd been counting doors as they came up the twisting staircase. 'Where's he going to sleep?'

'He'll be in the room along the landing.'

'I hope he doesn't snore.'

'He doesn't, Granny,' Cassie said, then blushed. 'I mean, he didn't when I was living here in 1942.'

Lily Taylor gave her a sharp, old-fashioned look.

At supper, Robert made an obvious effort to make Lily feel relaxed and welcome. Cassie blessed him for it, remembering how she had felt at her first supper in this very kitchen, when he'd glowered and glared and said that she should eat the skin of her potato.

This evening, he was courtesy itself, chatting pleasantly to

Lily, asking if she'd like roast or mashed or both, deliberately not noticing when she slipped her false teeth out and hid them in her handkerchief, then mumbled up her food.

'That Robert lad of yours, he's very nice,' Lily observed, as she and Cassie walked along the cliff path, one warm evening soon after they'd arrived.

'He's not *my* Robert, Granny,' Cassie said.

'Go on, my girl,' said Lily 'I've seen the way he looks at you. If he's not your Robert, then I'm the Queen of Sheba. It's a crying shame he's not a Catholic.'

'If I did get married – I'm not saying I will, but if I did – would it really matter if my husband wasn't Catholic?'

'Well, of course, it wouldn't be what I'd want for you, our Cass,' said Lily gravely. 'But if you brought the children up as Catholics, you'd be doing your duty, and I'm sure Our Lord would understand.'

Lily shrugged her bony little shoulders. 'If your husband loved you as he should, you might persuade him to become a Catholic, too. Father Riley says it's beautiful, how the grace of God can work on even the most obstinate of minds.

'He told me once knew this nice young couple, they lived in Solihull. He was Catholic, but she was a Methodist. Or she was a Baptist. Or something very odd in any case. But she – '

Cassie let her granny ramble on, quoting Father Riley, the fountain of all wisdom. 'There are some steps just here,' she said, a few yards further on. 'Do you want to go down to the beach?'

The land girls had gone home, and Rose had taken on two local boys who had just been demobbed. They lived at home in Charton, so Cassie's fears the cottage might be somewhat overcrowded, and Lily might be overawed and frightened by a mob of strangers, were unrealised.

Lily liked her bedroom, but thought the cottage as a whole could do with a good scrub. There was lots of dust, the skirting boards were scuffed, and the brass could do with polishing.

Cassie could almost see her fingers twitching for her buckets, mops and brooms and dusters. She couldn't help but click her tongue in disapproval every time she walked across the somewhat less than spotless kitchen floor.

After they'd all had supper one evening, Robert asked Cassie and Lily if they'd like to take a stroll.

'I wouldn't, son,' said Lily. 'Now I've got me feet up on the hearth here, and I've got me cup of tea, I'm settled for the evening. But you can take our Cass here for a little skip about.'

'Yes, go on, you two. Off you skip,' smiled Rose. 'Then Mrs Taylor and I can have a little chat. She's promised me she'll show me how to knit.'

'You don't know how to knit, Rose?' Cassie couldn't believe Rose couldn't knit. She might just as well have said she didn't know how to breathe.

'Do you know, I never had to learn.' Then Rose winked at Cassie, and Cassie could have almost sworn she'd seen a little twinkle in her eye. 'But it's a useful skill, and one I feel I should acquire. I might need it one day, don't you think?'

Robert and Cassie walked along the path that wound around the cliffs towards the headland, and then dropped down towards the shingle beach.

'Daisy's project, it's all going ahead,' he said, after they'd been walking for a while in total silence.

'You mean to have your mum's old house patched up, so she can offer holidays to kids from city slums?' Cassie shrugged. 'Yes, we talked about it lots of times.'

'Daisy told me.' Robert held out his hand to help her climb over a stile. 'We'll start with summer holidays,' he continued, 'probably for kids from Birmingham and the East End. When we've got proper heating, though, we're going to use the house all the year round. We'll have adventure holidays, we'll teach the children water sports, we'll take them out canoeing – '

'What will you do for money?'

'Daisy's got her film and theatre friends involved, and I believe her mother in America is going to chip in, too.'

'How do you fit in?' asked Cassie.

'I'll be at college in Dorchester in term-time,' Robert said. 'But at weekends and in school holidays, I'll be here in Charton.'

'You'll be the pied piper, will you?' Cassie laughed at him, but not unkindly. 'I can see you now, Rob, running down the beach, with a load of scruffy kids in tow.'

'I was wondering if you'd like a job here.' Robert crossed his fingers. 'Fran is very keen to be involved. I thought you two could run the place between you.'

'What about her Simon, are they going to get married?'

'I don't know, but Frances says he wants to live in Dorset. He's going to leave the army, and he wants to start a market garden.' Robert turned to Cassie. 'You like Dorset, too.'

'I do.'

'Cassie, are you going to marry me?'

'I – Robert, there's a problem, quite a big one.'

'What?' asked Robert, thinking that if Cassie loved him, there could be no problem which they couldn't solve.

'You're not a Catholic. I'm not insisting you convert, but if we have some children, my granny will expect us to bring them up as Catholics.'

'The children can be Roman Catholics, Buddhists, anything your granny fancies, if you'll marry me.'

'Rob, you really mean it?'

'You asked me that before, in Alexandria.' Robert took

her in his arms and kissed her on the lips. 'Cass, of course I mean it!'

'Then, as I said in Alexandria – I'd love to marry you.'

After Lily had gone back to Smethwick, Robert took Cassie to see inside the empty house.

He opened the front door with an enormous iron key. They went into the musty, dim interior, which smelled of rot and damp. They stood in the vast entrance hall. Then, suddenly, the summer sun poured through the great stained window on the staircase, and patterned everything with blue and gold.

'Be very careful,' Robert warned. 'Daisy's had surveyors in and basically the house is fairly sound, but the woodwork's got a bit of beetle, and some of it will have to be replaced.'

'It all needs redecorating, too,' said Cassie grimly. The hall was painted institutional green up to the dado rails, then sickly cream above. But higher up, in places where the painters couldn't reach, Cassie could see old paper coming loose, and peeling away from damp-stained, mildewed walls.

'It all needs stripping back,' said Robert. 'All this horrible green paint, put straight on top of paper, it's pulling all the paper off the walls. Poor Mum, she'll have a fit when she sees this.'

'Oh, hasn't she been inside yet?' Cassie asked him.

'No,' said Robert. 'I don't think she can bear to come and see the state it's in – at least not yet.'

'But it's still a lovely house.' Cassie gazed all round the hall, taking in the gracious sweep of the great, curving staircase, looking up at the empty space above. 'That bloke who left it to your mother – he was the one who let it get like this?'

'Yes, apparently.' Robert shrugged. 'Well, he did want to marry Mum, but she preferred my father. So this was his revenge.'

'Some people, eh?' said Cassie, and she shook her head. 'Come on then, Rob, let's go upstairs.'

'All right, but watch the floorboards. Some of them might be rotten, and I don't want you to break your ankle, or your neck.'

They walked around the bedrooms, now decrepit, stained and marked with childish scrawls, deliberately vandalised. The wrecks of iron bedsteads stood around like gibbets, casting shadows on the dirty walls.

'We won't have any dormitories or classrooms,' Robert said. He raised a rotting blind to let some noontime sunshine in. 'We won't have echoing dining rooms with lino on the floors, like in some Victorian orphanage.'

'What are you having, then?'

'Daisy wants the Minster to be a home from home. So the children will have proper bedrooms.'

'Rob, you must remember that the kids who'll come here won't be used to gracious living,' Cassie told him. 'They won't have pyjamas, they'll have nits, they'll have awful table manners, and they'll wet their beds.'

'We'll cope, I'm sure,' said Robert. 'You and Frances and a few more women from the village, you'll soon sort them out.'

As they walked downstairs again, Cassie saw the portrait. It was hanging high up on the wall, well out of reach of sticky, dirty or malicious fingers.

It was of a woman in Elizabethan dress, her starched white ruff discoloured by mildew, her complexion dimmed by dust and grime. But the likeness was remarkable.

'Look, Rob – it's your mother!' Cassie turned to Robert. 'Rose, when she was young.'

'Yes, it looks a bit like Mum,' said Robert. 'But although she's getting on a bit, she's not that old! I think it must be an ancestor.'

'Fancy having ancestors,' said Cassie.

'Everyone has ancestors,' said Robert.

'You know what I mean.' Cassie smiled at Robert 'I'm so glad your mother's got her house back.'

'So am I.' Robert gazed round the desolation. 'But it's going to be a long, hard slog, to put it straight again.'

'You're used to long, hard slogs.'

'I am.' Robert looked at Cassie, suddenly grave. 'Cass, I'll work day and night to get this whole thing up and running, to make it a success.'

'We'll do it together, Robert,' Cassie told him firmly. 'I love your mum, you know. If I could have a mother, I'd have one like Rose.'

Cassie had been afraid he'd dig his heels in, but Robert didn't argue when she said they ought to marry in St Saviour's church in Birmingham.

Lily Taylor moaned and fretted, muttered it was going to be an awful hole and corner job, which of course it always was when one of the couple wasn't Catholic.

She grumbled, sighed and added she was praying nightly for Robert to receive the gift of grace. She'd got a little booklet she was going to send to him, and she'd got some cards –

'You leave Rob alone,' said Cassie sternly.

'Father Riley said to me, if Robert wants instruction – '

'Robert's capable of asking for it, in his own good time.' Cassie gave her grandmother a hug. 'You mustn't worry, Granny – everything will be all right.'

Lily didn't comment. But she'd got that look upon her face, the one she'd had when she had first decided Cassie should become a land girl.

Cassie braced herself for months or even years of slow attrition, as Lily and Father Riley did their best to talk her husband round.

Epilogue

Robert was right, it was a long, hard slog.

But it was worth it, for the Minster proved to be the perfect place for Daisy's vision to become reality.

Cassie and Frances worked together to create the perfect holiday home for city children from all over the country. They never stopped. Once they'd got the heating sorted out, the Minster welcomed children and their teachers all year round.

'You mustn't work so hard,' said Robert, looking up from his marking one cold evening. 'You should be resting nowadays, sitting with your feet up, knitting shawls.'

'Cassie doesn't know how to rest,' smiled Rose.

'I'm not overdoing it, I promise,' Cassie told them. 'If I have any problems – if I feel tired or ill – I'll have a holiday from the Minster and rest up.'

The baby was a dark-haired, dark-eyed girl, who was hardly visible amidst the lace and shawls and frills in which Lily insisted baby girls should all be wrapped when they were christened.

Maybe it was just as well the child was such a bundle, Cassie thought. The church was freezing, so she was glad of Daisy's present of a fur-lined coat, under which she wore her smart blue costume.

'You look lovely, darling,' Daisy said, in the ringing tones which filled whole auditoria with ease. 'It didn't take you long to get your figure back, I see.'

Cassie glanced at Lily, who was screwing up her face.

Daisy didn't look anything like an actress. She was wearing classic, smart dark clothes and wasn't painted up.

But Lily was clearly thinking that this woman did not know how to behave inside a Catholic church.

'Come on, Granny, please don't look so gloomy,' whispered Cassie, as Lily leaned on her walking stick and held on tight to Robert, whose soul she still hoped one day to save, and whom she'd come to love. 'This is a special day for all of us.'

'You're right, our Cass.' Lily Taylor nodded, and she smiled with satisfaction as Father Riley christened Lily Rose.

About the Author

Margaret James was born and brought up in Hereford. She studied English at London University, and has written many short stories, articles and serials for magazines. She is the author of fifteen published novels.

Margaret is a long-standing contributor to *Writing Magazine* for which she writes the Fiction Focus column and an author interview for each issue. She's also a creative writing tutor for the London School of Journalism.

An active member of the Romantic Novelists' Association, she contributed to the 50th anniversary anthology *Loves Me, Loves Me Not*. Margaret's short story is *The Service of My Lady*.

For more information on Margaret visit:
www.margaretjames.com
www.twitter.com/majanovelist

More Choc Lit

From Margaret James

The Silver Locket

Winner of CataNetwork Reviewers' Choice Award for Single Titles 2010

If life is cheap, how much is love worth?

It's 1914 and young Rose Courtenay has a decision to make. Please her wealthy parents by marrying the man of their choice – or play her part in the war effort?

The chance to escape proves irresistible and Rose becomes a nurse. Working in France, she meets Lieutenant Alex Denham, a dark figure from her past. He's the last man in the world she'd get involved with – especially now he's married.

But in wartime nothing is as it seems. Alex's marriage is a sham and Rose is the only woman he's ever wanted. As he recovers from his wounds, he sets out to win her trust. His gift of a silver locket is a far cry from the luxuries she's left behind.

What value will she put on his love?

First novel in the trilogy

The Golden Chain

Can first love last forever?

1931 is the year that changes everything for Daisy Denham. Her family has not long swapped life in India for Dorset, England when she uncovers an old secret.

At the same time, she meets Ewan Fraser – a handsome dreamer who wants nothing more than to entertain the world and for Daisy to play his leading lady.

Ewan offers love and a chance to escape with a touring theatre company. As they grow closer, he gives her a golden chain and Daisy gives him a promise – that she will always keep him in her heart.

But life on tour is not as they'd hoped. Ewan is tempted away by his career and Daisy is dazzled by the older, charismatic figure of Jesse Trent. She breaks Ewan's heart and sets off for a life in London with Jesse.

Only time will tell whether some promises are easier to make than keep ...

Second novel in the trilogy

Visit www.choc-lit.com for more details including the first two chapters and reviews, or simply scan barcode using your mobile phone QR reader.

Why not try something else from the Choc Lit selection?
Here's a sample:

Trade Winds
Christina Courtenay

Short-listed for the Romantic Novelists'
Association's Pure Passion Award for
Best Historical Fiction 2011

Marriage of convenience – or a love for life?

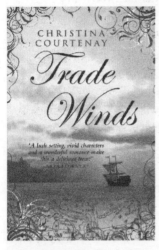

It's 1732 in Gothenburg, Sweden, and strong-willed Jess van Sandt knows only too well that it's a man's world. She believes she's being swindled out of her inheritance by her stepfather – and she's determined to stop it.

When help appears in the unlikely form of handsome Scotsman Killian Kinross, himself disinherited by his grandfather, Jess finds herself both intrigued and infuriated by him. In an attempt to recover her fortune, she proposes a marriage of convenience. Then Killian is offered the chance of a lifetime with the Swedish East India Company's Expedition and he's determined that nothing will stand in his way, not even his new bride.

He sets sail on a daring voyage to the Far East, believing he's put his feelings and past behind him. But the journey doesn't quite work out as he expects …

Visit www.choc-lit.com for more details including the first two chapters and reviews, or simply scan barcode using your mobile phone QR reader.

Highland Storms
Christina Courtenay

Who can you trust?

Betrayed by his brother and his childhood love, Brice Kinross needs a fresh start. So he welcomes the opportunity to leave Sweden for the Scottish Highlands to take over the family estate.

But there's trouble afoot at Rosyth in 1754 and Brice finds himself unwelcome. The estate's in ruin and money is disappearing. He discovers an ally in Marsaili Buchanan, the beautiful redheaded housekeeper, but can he trust her?

Marsaili is determined to build a good life. She works hard at being a housekeeper and harder still at avoiding men who want to take advantage of her. But she's irresistibly drawn to the new clan chief, even though he's made it plain he doesn't want to be shackled to anyone.

And the young laird has more than romance on his mind. His investigations are stirring up an enemy. Someone who will stop at nothing to get what he wants – including Marsaili – even if that means destroying Brice's life forever …

Sequel to Trade Winds

Visit www.choc-lit.com for more details including the first two chapters and reviews, or simply scan barcode using your mobile phone QR reader.

The Scarlet Kimono
Christina Courtenay

*Winner of The Big Red Reads
Historical Fiction Award 2011*

**Abducted by a Samurai
warlord in 17th-century
Japan – what happens when
fear turns to love?**

England, 1611, and young
Hannah Marston envies her
brother's adventurous life. But
when she stows away on his
merchant ship, her powers
of endurance are stretched to their limit. Then they reach
Japan and all her suffering seems worthwhile – until she is
abducted by Taro Kumashiro's warriors.

In the far north of the country, warlord Kumashiro is
waiting to see the girl who he has been warned about by a
seer. When at last they meet, it's a clash of cultures and wills,
but they're also fighting an instant attraction to each other.

With her brother desperate to find her and the jealous
Lady Reiko equally desperate to kill her, Hannah faces the
greatest adventure of her life. And Kumashiro has to choose
between love and honour ...

Visit www.choc-lit.com for more details
including the first two chapters and
reviews, or simply scan barcode using
your mobile phone QR reader.

Love & Freedom
Sue Moorcroft

*Winner of the Festival of Romance
Best Romantic Read Award 2011*

New start, new love.

That's what Honor Sontag
needs after her life falls apart,
leaving her reputation in
tatters and her head all over
the place. So she flees her
native America and heads for
Brighton, England.

Honor's hoping for a much-deserved break and the chance
to find the mother who abandoned her as a baby. What she
gets is an entanglement with a mysterious male whose family
seems to have a finger in every pot in town.

Martyn Mayfair has sworn off women with strings attached,
but is irresistibly drawn to Honor, the American who keeps
popping up in his life. All he wants is an uncomplicated
relationship built on honesty, but Honor's past threatens to
undermine everything. Then secrets about her mother start
to spill out ...

Honor has to make an agonising choice. Will she live
up to her dutiful name and please others? Or will she
choose freedom?

Visit www.choc-lit.com for more details
including the first two chapters and
reviews, or simply scan barcode using
your mobile phone QR reader.

The UnTied Kingdom
Kate Johnson

The portal to an alternate world was the start of all her troubles – or was it?

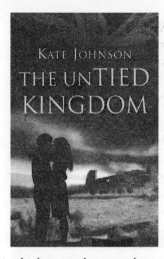

When Eve Carpenter lands with a splash in the Thames, it's not the London or England she's used to. No one has a telephone or knows what a computer is. England's a third-world country and Princess Di is still alive. But worst of all, everyone thinks Eve's a spy.

Including Major Harker who has his own problems. His sworn enemy is looking for a promotion. The General wants him to undertake some ridiculous mission to capture a computer, which Harker vaguely envisions running wild somewhere in Yorkshire. Turns out the best person to help him is Eve.

She claims to be a popstar. Harker doesn't know what a popstar is, although he suspects it's a fancy foreign word for 'spy'. Eve knows all about computers, and electricity. Eve is dangerous. There's every possibility she's mad.

And Harker is falling in love with her.

Visit www.choc-lit.com for more details including the first two chapters and reviews, or simply scan barcode using your mobile phone QR reader.

Please don't stop the music
Jane Lovering

How much can you hide?

Jemima Hutton is determined to build a successful new life and keep her past a dark secret. Trouble is, her jewellery business looks set to fail – until enigmatic Ben Davies offers to stock her handmade belt buckles in his guitar shop and things start looking up, on all fronts.

But Ben has secrets too. When Jemima finds out he used to be the front man of hugely successful Indie rock band Willow Down, she wants to know more. Why did he desert the band on their US tour? Why is he now a semi-recluse?

And the curiosity is mutual – which means that her own secret is no longer safe …

Visit www.choc-lit.com for more details including the first two chapters and reviews, or simply scan barcode using your mobile phone QR reader.

'Refreshing, funny and romantic, it's like a breath of fresh sea air with a cast of terrific characters.' KATE HARRISON

Turning the Tide
Christine Stovell

**All's fair in love and war?
Depends on who's making
the rules.**

Harry Watling has spent the
past five years keeping her
father's boat yard afloat,
despite its dying clientele.
Now all she wants to do is
enjoy the peace and quiet of
her sleepy backwater.

So when property developer Matthew Corrigan wants
to turn the boat yard into an upmarket housing complex for
his exotic new restaurant, it's like declaring war.

And the odds seem to be stacked in Matthew's favour.
He's got the colourful locals on board, his hard-to-please
girlfriend is warming to the idea and he has the means to
force Harry's hand. Meanwhile, Harry has to fight not just
his plans but also her feelings for the man himself.

Then a family secret from the past creates heartbreak for
Harry, and neither of them is prepared for what happens
next ...

Visit www.choc-lit.com for more details
including the first two chapters and
reviews, or simply scan barcode using
your mobile phone QR reader.

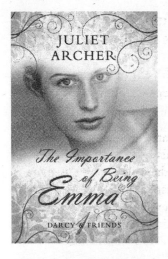

The Importance of Being Emma

Juliet Archer

Winner of *The Big Red Reads Fiction* Award 2011

A modern retelling of Jane Austen's *Emma*.

Mark Knightley – handsome, clever, rich – is used to women falling at his feet. Except Emma Woodhouse, who's like part of the family – and the furniture. When their relationship changes dramatically, is it an ending or a new beginning?

Emma's grown into a stunningly attractive young woman, full of ideas for modernising her family business. Then Mark gets involved and the sparks begin to fly. It's just like the old days, except that now he's seeing her through totally new eyes.

While Mark struggles to keep his feelings in check, Emma remains immune to the Knightley charm. She's never forgotten that embarrassing moment when he discovered her teenage crush on him. He's still pouring scorn on all her projects, especially her beautifully orchestrated campaign to find Mr Right for her ditzy PA. And finally, when the mysterious Flynn Churchill – the man of her dreams – turns up, how could she have eyes for anyone else? …

Visit www.choc-lit.com for more details including the first two chapters and reviews, or simply scan barcode using your mobile phone QR reader.

Introducing Choc Lit

We're an independent publisher creating
a delicious selection of fiction.
Where heroes are like chocolate – irresistible!
Quality stories with a romance at the heart.

Choc Lit novels are selected by genuine readers like yourself.
We only publish stories our Choc Lit Tasting Panel want to
see in print. Our reviews and awards speak for themselves.

Come and support our authors and join them in our
Author's Corner, read their interviews and see their latest
events, reviews and gossip.

Visit: www.choc-lit.com for more details.

Available in paperback and as ebooks from most stores.

We'd also love to hear how you enjoyed *The Penny Bangle*.
Just visit www.choc-lit.com and give your feedback.
Describe Robert in terms of chocolate and you could win a
Choc Lit novel in our Flavour of the Month competition.

Follow us on twitter: www.twitter.com/
ChocLituk, or simply scan barcode using
your mobile phone QR reader.